PERMANENT MAKEUP

PERMANENT MAKEUP

TERRA ZIPORYN

PALTA BOOKS

2014 Palta Books Trade Paperback Edition

Permanent Makeup is a work of fiction. Names, characters, places, and incidents either are the product of the author's imagination or are used fictitiously, and any resemblance to any actual persons, living or dead, events, or locales is entirely coincidental.

Published in the United States by Palta Books, Jeffersonville, VT.
www.paltabooks.com

Publisher's Cataloging-in-Publication Data
(Provided by Quality Books, Inc.)

Ziporyn, Terra Diane, 1958-
      Permanent makeup / Terra Ziporyn. -- 2014 Palta Books
      trade paperback edition.
        pages cm
        LCCN 2013923291
        ISBN 978-0-9913137-0-9 (pbk.)
        ISBN 978-0-9913137-1-6 (ebk)

      1. Mothers and daughters--Fiction. 2. Family
      violence--Fiction. 3. Domestic fiction.
      4. Psychological fiction. I. Title.

PS3626.I66P47 2014   813'.6
                QBI14-600004

Printed in the United States of America

*To the mother and daughters in my life,
Charlotte Ziporyn, Pallas Snider, and
Sage Snider*

OTHER NOVELS BY TERRA ZIPORYN

TIME'S FOOL

THE BLISS OF SOLITUDE

DO NOT GO GENTLE

ACKNOWLEDGEMENTS

So many people deserve credit not only for making *Permanent Makeup* a better novel, but for making me a better writer. Even the most wildly imaginative fiction is inspired by or based on real human beings, and many people whose paths have crossed mine in the course of my life have influenced my writing, inspired characters, or taught me lessons—both consciously and, undoubtedly, unconsciously—that underpin my stories. I would be remiss, however, if I didn't single out a few specific people who were invaluable as I wrote and rewrote *Permanent Makeup.* First and foremost are the members of my writing critique group: Sonia Linebaugh, Gary McCann, Caleb Griffin, and Marcia Aguiniga. Judy Frank's incisive and encouraging critique of an earlier version of the novel was both generous and incisive. Mark Willen, M.L. Doyle, Sally Whitney, Jill Morrow, and the other Late Last Night Book bloggers also gave me courage to push through to publication. Thanks also go to Lyn Horan, Bonnie Gollup, Marilyn Sandler, Jerry Weinberg, and Cheryl Plum for believing in me and feeding me with their faith over the years. Above all, I give my eternal gratitude to Jim, Pallas, Sage, and Solon, without whom I never would have had the heart to keep writing, or, really, to do much of anything.

Beauty is truth, truth beauty.
That is all ye know on Earth,
And all ye need to know.
                    —John Keats

Let nature breathe around you like a
lovely idyl, where far from artifice and its
wanderings you may always find yourself
again, where you may go to draw fresh
courage, a new confidence, to resume
your course, and kindle again in your
heart the flame of the ideal, so readily
extinguished amidst the tempests of life.
                    —Friedrich Schiller

With Apologies to John Donne and Alfred, Lord Tennyson

Time be not proud
There is no call for tears, idle tears
The days that are no more never were

PROLOGUE

To: MargaretLAX@earthlink.com
From: Mama & Zeenie
Subject: Us (and you)
Attached: Permanent Makeup

Dearest Margaret,

I'm writing this with Zeenie, not an easy task.

I'm one opinionated broad. Sue me.

She's charming as well, right? But still terrified of computers, so, as you have probably already figured out from the bold, I'm typing for her.

It would have been considerably simpler to write you a note by hand, Margaret. Your mother insisted on using this contraption. I wrote you a lovely letter, which your mother said you'd never read.

What I told her was that you can't read cursive. No one your age can read cursive.

I find that hard to believe. And appalling.

Actually, I told her it would have been easier to text than email you. But this is where I'm challenged, too, so we compromised. I'm just hoping you still open yours—I was reading that kids your age consider email passé.

What I did insist upon was a proper dating and formatting of this "letter." There are some things a person is too old to change.

Anyway, Margaret, I know this must be confusing. What is attached will be easier. It was written by both of us—no confusing italics and bold faces. Of course, it's not easy writing with another person under any circumstances. We've gone back and forth more times than I can tell you revising things, questioning things, moving things, all that.

However, we are both now pleased with what we're sending you. We both stand by every word.

Let me get to the point. We miss you, Margaret, and we love you. We've told you that scads of times before, but, of course, it hasn't helped. You left home, just as I left home at 17, and Zeenie did before me. For a while we assumed it was a break. Now, though, with summer gone and school rolling around again, we know you're not coming back.

Do you see a pattern? Perhaps not. When you're 17 you think you are a pioneer, that you are clear-eyed in a way that no one before you could have been, that you are the first person in the human race to have the answers and will go out to fix the world that your mum and gran and all their loony chums have messed up so royally. Truly, though, do you think you have come upon some kind of original answer, some better solution?

Margaret, you've called me a hypocrite. Zeenie too. You think Zeenie and I pander to stereotypes that you, and only you, reject and transcend. We "make you sick" with our lies and our cover-ups. You, in contrast, are the only pure soul on earth. Only you are honest. Only you are free. We've heard you on that. Many times.

All I can tell you is, although we didn't choose the path you have chosen precisely, we weren't all that different from you. And, yes, both of us can see you now about to delete this email, disgusted that, once again, we are lecturing. So we'll stop with that now. It does no good, I suppose, to remind you that we, too, were once 17 as well.

Someday, Margaret, you will no longer be 17. It's hard to grasp that, of course, but please try to appreciate that what you feel about "now" today probably isn't what you will feel about it

later. Everything that happens is forever, or could be. So be careful.

You are probably plugging your ears by now, sick of the lecturing. Truth be told, it's damn hard for me not to lecture, Margaret. I'm a trained social worker—I'm "holier than thou" by training. Frankly, it's a habit that's hard to break. As for Zeenie, well, she's the first to say she's just an old "buttinski."

That's true, my dear. I am the first to admit it.

And, for heaven's sake, even if all that weren't the case, we're your ma and grandma. We're naturally inclined to lecture you, whatever our other qualities and training might happen to be.

So, you see, we came up with a better plan. No more lectures, however tempting the urge. Instead, we decided to tell you a story, a story of our lives and how we got to this point—the point you see as so absurd and hypocritical and all those other things you've called it.

This is for you, Margaret. We put it together out of love for you.

All our love,

Mama and Zeenie

CHAPTER ONE

She was not a night person, but she had no choice: she had no one else to do it for her. At well past midnight she started the Toyota, squinted through the fog and the rutted, narrow streets of Annapolis, and, with great relief, parked directly in front of the shop. Skirting two suspicious figures who were undoubtedly dealing drugs or transacting some equally sordid business, she hurried toward Inner Beauty Skin Care and let herself in, bolting the door behind her and noting that she must have the locks changed first thing in the morning so that Carole could no longer use her key.

The little bitch had quit two weeks ago with a Monday morning phone call: "Hello, Maxine, Carole here. Listen, I won't be coming in today because I'm starting a new job. Bye now." No notice, no apologies, not even a "good luck finding someone new." Just up and left her like that, left her with a full schedule of clients, the first one due to arrive two hours after the call, and no one to greet them or answer the phone or set up the equipment, not to mention hire and train a new girl.

That was all bad enough, absolutely classless (though quite characteristic of Carole), but the horrid woman still had the key, and Maxine suspected she was breaking in at night, doing God-knew-what (Taking back her collection of coffee mugs and mascara? Pilfering moisturizers and toners? Soliciting some *tsotsi* on the corner for extra cash? Who knew with that woman?). All Maxine could tell was that someone had been coming into the salon at night because several mornings this week she had found lights on that she remembered turning off before leaving work, the toilet cover up when she always left it down, and yesterday, chillingly, a dirty coffee cup in the sink.

There was no one in the reception area. The appointment book on the desk was still open to September and the magazines splayed just as she had arranged them before going home yesterday, yet another duty recently tossed onto her already congested agenda. She peeked into the kitchen, and this time saw nothing amiss—no stray dishes, no spills, no open cabinets. The hall light was off, the bathroom light as well. She headed down the hall toward the work rooms, a bit tentatively but unflinchingly, a gnawing terror in her stomach quelled by the recurring conviction that she not only had to do this but that every step would turn trepidation into reality, the latter (however dreadful) inevitably more tolerable than the former. She reminded herself that Carole was no match for her. If she had been, she would have resigned respectfully, but clearly she had been terrified of the consequences—easier to do the ugly act all over the phone. In any case, Carole wouldn't dare fight back now if she were caught breaking and entering, and Maxine would merely call the police before that pea-brain could think of a paltry excuse. Maxine reminded herself of all this, and yet her heart continued to pound.

All was still in the electrolysis room, and in the makeup room as well. Still, Maxine sensed something awry. It was almost a sense of a quickening, the way you feel a house come alive in the night, breathing and groaning, perhaps due to squirrels in the walls, the wind against a window, the settling of a floorboard. And yet it was more than that: she could sense that someone, not a rodent but a thinking, calculating human being, was physically present. Carole had to be in the supply room. There was no other place left. This was the only room in the salon that was perennially chaotic, even when Maxine had a halfway decently trained receptionist to help keep things tamed. No wonder Carole was tempted. She was undoubtedly coming in here for needles for her no-good husband, a man Maxine suspected had a serious heroin problem (Carole, too, for that matter, though she dressed like she lived in Beverly Hills, was a tramp through and through—you can have a girl take out the trash, as Maxine had always said, but you just can't take the trash out of the girl).

Trying to ignore her racing heart, Maxine grabbed an umbrella from the coat tree. She swallowed, raised the umbrella in front of her, and entered the room. She flipped on the light switch and called, "Carole—this is preposterous! Come out now. You can't get away with this!"

Her eyes searched the room, littered with half-empty cardboard boxes (boxes that Carole would normally have taken to the recycling bin had she still been employed) and countertops strewn with plastic-wrapped packages of syringes and cotton balls, sterilized needles, inks, and lotions. Were the boxes exactly where they had been last night? She couldn't recall. It was possible that the two stacked nearest the closet had actually been side by side yesterday. Her memory wasn't what it once was, and, really, she should have written this down to be sure. In any case, there was no one in the room now.

And yet—she sensed the life. The room almost seemed to breathe in unison with a human being's real breathing, and suddenly Maxine knew: the closet. Still holding the umbrella in front of her, she made her way through the boxes toward the closet door, repeating "Come on now, Carole. There's no use in you hiding because you're dead meat now. Out!"

She felt absurd uttering such threats, keenly aware that she was a distinctly flabby and slightly arthritic "gentle-lady" who had never used physical violence on anyone. At the same time, finding that she had enough pluck to utter these threats and, just possibly, enough wrath toward Carole to implement them, impressed and invigorated her.

Taking another deep breath, she pulled open the door like she was taking off a Band-aid. Between two rather large RAD boxes she saw a down comforter, completely covering what had to be a human body. What an absolute dunderhead, she thought. Either that or she's shot herself straight out of the stratosphere on something.

"That does it, Carole. I'm calling the police and reporting you for breaking and entering."

As she turned to do so, however, a head popped up from under the comforter, a woman's head of long, layered, gleaming chestnut hair that most distinctly did not belong to Carole.

Maxine stepped back, the umbrella immediately useless. "Oh my God!"

"Please. Please," said the woman, whose face was puffy and purplish, and not at all the clear-complexioned visage that the polished hairstyle had suggested. "Please don't call the police."

"I most certainly will."

Maxine hurried to the reception desk and grabbed the

phone, cursing her arthritic fingers that instinctively, almost miraculously, wove hair-thin needles into and under her clients' skin but struggled with every other mundane task. She had managed to push the "9" and the "1" of "9-1-1" when the woman from the closet snatched the phone from her hands and slammed it back into the receiver.

"Please. Call Dodie."

Maxine stepped back. She could now see that this woman, slender in her mid-thirties, almost statuesque but stoop-shouldered, had a black eye, several long scratches and bandages on her pockmarked cheeks, and a puffy upper lip—as if someone had beaten her soundly. "Dodie? My Dodie? What on earth . . . ?"

"Call Dodie. She'll explain."

CHAPTER TWO

The idea of hiding Shelley in Maxine's salon had come to Dodie in a moment of inspiration. No one at Safe Port knew about it. In fact, had they known she might well have been fired. Taking justice, or caregiving, into one's own hands was simply not standard protocol. In fact, it was downright unprofessional, and she had been working at Safe Port long enough to know this. Nonetheless, Dodie had felt almost from the start that Shelley was a special case and one for whom ordinary procedures were not going to work. This was because Rocco Herkimer was no ordinary man. He was no more brutal than the rest of them, but he had connections that led him to pull up to Safe Port one sunny fall morning and park his pristine white Jaguar right out front, motor running, ominously looming in a way she had never seen before.

Shelley had known this visitation was coming. And when Dodie, bringing her a morning cup of tea entered the living room, she, too, knew why Shelley sat on the couch with her face wrapped in draperies, peering through the window. "That's his car," Shelley whispered. "Dammit."

Dodie went to join Shelley on the couch and peeked out behind her. "Are you sure? Can you see his face?" But Dodie knew that it had to be Rocco. He was just the kind of guy who would know how to track a woman's shelter and would show up to make a mockery of it. Besides, the car had House of Delegates plates.

"What kind of moron is he? He's going to be front-page news."

"He's the kind of moron who thinks he's God," said Shelley. "He can talk his way out of anything. And he knows it."

Rocco, Shelley had explained to Dodie when the taxi from the hospital had first delivered her there the week before, was not only the kind of person who never questioned his own righteousness. He was also the kind of person who never gave up. His victory in the last election was testament to that spirit. He had run for various seats in three prior contests, in three different counties, and lost time and time again, often by huge and embarrassing margins. Every election had been a vast drain on his resources, time, money, and connections, but never a drain on his confidence or determination.

"Well, you have to give the guy credit, I suppose. Determination is usually considered a virtue," Dodie had told her.

"Yes, but it's all about his ego, not about some kind of noble cause." Shelly, who, Dodie had already discovered, was often as sharp as a tack despite her despondency, went on to explain that until last year she had been the woman behind the man (though rarely publically). After each loss she had watched over him, and, often, helped him make a new life for himself, moving to new towns, changing careers, coming up with various creative and progressively improbable money-making schemes, schmoozing with the latest and eternally regenerating group of mover-shaker wannabees, and, repeatedly, had helped him put his feet back into the ring once more. This cycle had gone on for years.

"There's no stopping Rocco," Shelley had said. "And, depressingly, I now see that that is one of the main reasons I'm so drawn to him, sap that I am. Sick, isn't it? He has this kind of astonishing, almost superhuman, invincibility. Even in the face of what you'd objectively call defeat, enormous public defeat. I can't resist it."

Shelley added that although she was now officially out of the picture, she also grudgingly gave Rocco some credit for fighting on: through a brilliant set of Machiavellian machinations (which, she noted, were largely at her expense), he had successfully completed his first year serving the citizens of Maryland in their House of Delegates, and was, on paper, a fine upstanding citizen, husband to sweet Lily, the daughter of longstanding U.S. Representative Gilhoun's first cousin, and a tobacco farm heiress. What he did to and with Shelley on the side was old news, or not news, until she had made it news. That had been her undoing.

"He's going to kill me."

"I'm calling the police then."

Shelley was shaking, and Dodie even thought she saw hives on Shelley's upper lip.

"They can be here in two minutes," Dodie assured her.

"So what? They'll make him leave. And he'll be back tomorrow."

"You have a peace order, don't you? This is a clear violation."

"Big deal....He knows where I am. Don't you see? It's over. I'm gonna die."

Dodie sighed. She had heard this kind of cynicism before, and the rational side of her knew there was considerable truth to it. Despite all the progress they had made in the past decade, the official protections, the societal recognition, the sheltering infrastructure, the reality was that most of the women who passed through here remained in grave danger, at least once they left—which all of them did after a fairly short period of time. At best, the shelter system could offer temporary reprieve, much the same reprieve that the restraining orders provided. Worse, in the end, the reprieve often resulted in still more—and often more serious—danger, once the woman tried to return to normal life and had to face the abuser to whom she had now drawn public attention. Often the restraining orders themselves were worthless as well, and everyone pretty much knew that. But it was the culture to assure clients, and Dodie felt she had no choice but to call the police and have the threatening man removed from the property. She dialed while Shelley, shaking and heaving, collapsed into a heap on the couch.

Shelley, it turned out, was right. Rocco had driven off as soon as he spotted the squad car through his rear-view mirror. He was too smart to risk being exposed again, and quick enough to ease around the corner before anyone could spot his distinctive plates. But that evening Dodie got a call at home from the night staff telling her they had an emergency: Shelley was "an absolute basket case," at the window constantly, unwilling to eat or sleep, convinced that Rocco would return, probably in the middle of the night. Could Dodie possibly come in and calm her down? Of course she could. Did she ever say no? She was a professional, after all, and that meant she didn't live by a time clock. Not that Dodie wasn't royally pissed. Going to Safe Port after hours would mean yet another night away from the kids, another night when the boys would be up past midnight, Lawrence's homework would get stalled, and Thomas wouldn't practice the piano. Margaret, it was true, would get all her homework and practicing done no matter what and get into bed at a respectable hour, but she would also roll her eyes and say, "Don't worry, Mom. I can handle them," which, Dodie well knew, meant that she resented having always to be the grown-up at the tender age of 14 while Dad tinkered in the greenhouse and Mom was busy saving everyone except herself. However, Dodie knew she had to go: Shelley actually had good reason to worry. In fact, given that Rocco clearly knew the whereabouts of Safe Port, Shelley's very presence there put the entire operation in danger.

As it turned out, going into work was a good decision. She spent two hours talking to Shelley, angling the topic away from Rocco and instead drawing her out about the miscarriage, letting her muse, meander, and cry. Dodie could immediately see that this was a huge need for Shelley, not surprising, since the miscarriage had virtually been overlooked in the wake of all the relocations and other trauma—the fractured ribs, broken nose, and ruptured spleen, most obviously. Though the baby had been unplanned, and perhaps even unwanted (that point was moot now), it had essentially been beaten out of Shelley, and she clearly needed someone with whom to talk. Dodie wished she could have referred Shelley to a pregnancy loss support group, something that would have been available had the Medical Center been willing to keep her rather than sending her to Safe Port so soon. But the reality was that— except for the intractable vaginal bleeding, which was now under control—the physical damage was relatively minor, and she was on the mend. What Shelley did need in these first days at the shelter was considerable time and tending when it came to her emotional damage, and so Dodie nodded patiently and sympathetically as Shelley tried to reconcile her utter dislike of children and motherhood with her overwhelming feelings of emptiness and grief, as though this lost, impromptu child justified her entire existence and had been washed away, along with all hope.

Eventually Dodie had managed to persuade Shelley to go to bed, promising to watch at the window until midnight when, she told Shelley, she really had to return home to her family. She had peeked into the bedroom at 11 and had been pleased to find Shelley sound asleep, softly snorting and swallowing. She chatted with the night assistant Linda for a while, checking the window sporadically, and left Safe Port just before midnight, realizing with some resentment that she would inevitably be returning home to a sink full of new (she had already done dinner's) dishes, children demanding homework help despite the hour, and a husband who probably wanted her attentions and affections as well.

As she turned into the dark street from Safe Port's walkway, she nursed her misery, something she hated doing but just couldn't help, especially when she left work this late. In fact, feeling sorry for herself was something she found herself doing more and more, whatever the hour. Even when she woke at dawn and felt infused with promise and potential, her enthusiasm quickly drained after walking into a day scheduled tight with obligation, invariably complicated as it was by burned-out bulbs, clogged drains, and flooded basements, as well as the moods, misunderstandings, and equally ennervating intrusions that ended the day too soon and too incompletely. As she turned she mused that her life had essentially become one of replacing lightbulbs, patching holes, ordering objects, and generally overseeing the upkeep of material things, which, sadly, had come to include the human beings she tended. Here she was, she often thought, turning into bed for the night, and feeling as though nothing, really, had happened since she woke up that morning except for her ceaseless and ultimately futile hobby of fighting entropy, replacing and reordering objects that inevitably slipped out of wherever she wanted them to be. Time not on task was consumed in an endless battle to move objects back and forth from one place to the next, whether it was women, children, or books, toys and papers that had to be brought from downstairs to upstairs and vice versa, to be carried, purchased, lugged in from the car, stowed, shelved, cooked, washed, sorted, filed, and, often, soon enough, tossed. Whatever repetitive or ephemeral task she completed in it, again and again each day always turned out to be over before she could blink.

As she approached her car, a burly man in a pressed white shirt and tie appeared out of the shadows. "Excuse me." he said. "Hello? Can we talk?"

Averting her gaze, she quickened her step. "Idiot," she thought about herself. "If anyone should know better than to walk down the street alone at this time, it's me. Who do I think I am?" She groped the bottom of her purse for her cars keys, wishing she had remembered to walk with them claw-like between her fingers, but she felt the man approach her before she could reach the door.

"Hello?" he repeated. "I'd like to speak with you."

She tried to get the keys into the lock, still looking only at the car, and at that point he grabbed her by the arm. Her instinctive twisting and yanking did nothing except compel him to reel her in. Tucked into his chest, embraced by him actually, all impulses to pull away stopped in her brain. Nearly asphyxiated by the cloying odor of his aftershave, she felt like a lioness stunned by a hunter.

"Relax, okay? There's no reason to be scared. I just want to talk to you."

The voice was sweet, affectionate even, but it was most definitely the no-nonsense voice of Rocco Herkimer she had heard on the radio ads. She recognized his face from the paper, too. He looked more clean-shaven in his publicity photos, but the squarish, commanding jaw and busy eyebrows were obviously his. He seemed to have come out of nowhere. The white Jaguar was nowhere to be seen. She began shaking, not so much scared by him as she was ashamed of her foolishness for failing to follow protocol and putting herself in this position. Tears starting falling as she remembered her family.

"Please let me go," she managed to say. "I've got kids waiting for me at home."

He grabbed her tighter and maneuvered her against the side of her car, still embracing her. His voice was calm, even suave, as if he were trying to seduce her. "Of course. Of course you do. I just want to talk to you for a minute."

As he relaxed his grip slightly, she resumed struggling. He tightened his hold and pinned her shoulders against the car window. With one hand holding her in place, he put the other over her mouth.

"Hey, doll, you have to relax. Just listen a minute, and I'll let you go." He took his hand tentatively off her mouth and looked at her with the captivated eyes of a lover, rekindling in her a long repressed memory of nausea mixed with desire. "Are you going to listen?"

"I've got to go home to my children. Let me go."

"Just listen for two minutes." He kept her mouth uncovered but held her tightly by the arm.

"Are you listening?"

She nodded, glaring at him, releasing a tear at the realization that however smart or savvy she was, whatever good she tried to do in the world, it meant nothing next to his pure physical size and strength. She was a prisoner of her body, and he was a beneficiary of his. That was the stinking world in a nutshell. All she could think was that when, if, he ever let her go, she would do everything in her power to keep Shelley safe from him.

"Let go of me. I've got to get home to my kids."

"I'm not holding you," he said, as calm as if he were her beloved father or teacher. "You're just listening to me, right?"

"Please let go of me. You're hurting me."

"We're just having a conversation."

"A one-way conversation....Please let go of me!"

"Look, I just want you to hear the other side of the story, okay? Nothing wrong with that. It's just that I need to talk to you about a lady in your...in your place there. You know her? Shelley? Shelley Slavin? A mouthy broad with long brown hair? Thirty something?"

"I can't name names."

"You know her, though, right? She's new, must've come in the past few days."

"Just let me go. Please."

"That's a little shelter you got there, can't fit too many in it. You must know her, right?"

"How on earth did you get the address?"

"It's about Shelley Slavin—well, you need to know she isn't right in the head. I'm not blaming her. She's had it rough, poor kid. I guess I made a mistake trying to be nice to her."

What was he talking about? This was a man who had beaten Shelley for years—Dodie had seen the court records, the hospital reports—and then, after dumping her for another more politically expedient woman, come back to knock her up, only to then beat the baby out of her. Now he was stalking her in the face of a peace order. Dodie hardly thought that Shelley could be delusional. But all she said was, "I see."

"Of course you do. And of course now that you do you're going to help set the record straight, right? It's only professional, after all."

"I really need to go now."

He tightened grip on her arm and smiled faintly. "I'm almost finished. I just want to make sure we understand each other. You see, as I said, I made the mistake of being nice to her a couple of times. She's worked for me now and then, and I guess she wished things were different than they were. But, you know, the lady keeps getting hooked up with these lowlifes and can't face it. I guess she likes to fantasize there's something between us—kind of raises her up, you know? But I don't have anything to do with it, you see what I'm saying?"

"You're saying you had nothing to do with Shelley's problems."

"That's what I'm saying. And that's what you're going to call and tell the reporters tomorrow, right? Because I know you want to go home to your children."

"Yes, I do. Could you please let me go now?" Clearly there was no point in challenging a man like Rocco.

He released her arm and pulled a folded sheet of paper from his pocket. "Here are the media contacts who tried calling me today about this thing. You just call each one of them, explain who you work for, and let them know she's delusional. Make sense? He was looking straight into her eyes, nodding with what appeared to be genuine warmth. "I just want to make sure we understand each other."

"I think we understand each other just fine."

"Good." He gave her the paper. "So...just to clarify—

now that you know the truth—that you, or your group, won't have any trouble telling the papers that she's mentally ill, right? I had nothing to do with any beatings, any babies, none of that stuff. You get that, right?"

"I get that."

He held her arm as though he was merely helping her into the car, and watched as she drove off.

CHAPTER THREE

The Monday before Maxine discovered Shelley sleeping in the closet of her supply room, Dodie entered the salon at precisely 8:30 a.m. She found Shelley huddled in a corner, looking as bruised and battered as she had the night before and wearing the same crumpled slacks and sweater that she had worn when Dodie had left her there Friday night. Shelley rocked back and forth like a strait-jacketed inmate with her legs tucked up to her chest and her arms around them.

"Oh my God. You scared me," Shelley said.

"Sorry. I told you I'd be back early. Ready to go?"

"Go?"

"You can't stay here all day. My mother will be in by 10 or so."

"Where am I supposed to go? I can't go home. You know that."

"Of course not."

"And I can't go back to your shelter either."

"I know that, too. But I've arranged for you to spend weekdays at a private home, one of the smaller shelters in our network. You can't stay there overnight—these places usually only have a bed or two, and they're booked—but you can spend the day there, or a few days, until we figure out what to do....You can sleep here. I just can't have you here when the salon opens."

"What we should do is talk to the press. And get in front of a judge....Of course, that's not going to happen. It can't. He'd kill me first."

Dodie hadn't mentioned her encounter with Rocco to Shelley, not wanting to traumatize her further. But she assured her that no one was calling the press for anything. "The only thing we're going to do is get you well again, and to keep you safe until that happens. You can stay here at night until we figure out a better plan."

Dodie needed a better plan soon. As perfect as the salon was for stowing Shelley, she had no intention of telling Maxine. She could get away with that for perhaps a week at most. Maxine always left the shop promptly at five and rarely, if ever, arrived in the mornings before ten (she insisted on keeping "civilized" hours, or something as close as she could get to civility in America, a place she considered little short of savage). However, Maxine was also exceptionally perceptive about her environment, one might even say paranoid, and after a few days she would undoubtedly notice something awry. Dodie was also acutely aware that her role in this scheme was far too onerous to maintain for more than a few days. In addition to feeling uncomfortable taking Shelley's salvation into her own hands—highly unprofessional, she kept imagining her colleagues telling her—she also knew it was only a matter of time before Rocco Herkimer sniffed out even these more obscure daily havens. Still, Shelley needed time to get her strength back so that she could figure out some way to move forward, possibly by leaving town, although right now she was adamant about staying. Annapolis was a small place, and so was Anne Arundel County, but without too much upheaval Shelley, who had an accounting degree and plenty of office experience, could probably find herself a job in Baltimore or Washington and stay out of Rocco's path, at least if she chose to do so. Quite often, the women Dodie worked with left the shelters to go right back into the line of fire. Shelley showed all signs of doing exactly the same, at least once the sheer terror that still engulfed her, and showed its signs on her ravaged body, transformed itself, as it almost always did, into self-loathing and misplaced sympathy for the perpetrator.

Shelley clearly could not sleep in Maxine's salon forever, but for now it seemed like the only choice in terms of everyone's safety. It was the only place in town Dodie knew that Rocco Herkimer, or, for that matter, the vast majority of males, would never set foot. Her midnight confrontation with him had already convinced her that Shelley could never go back to Safe Port, or to any part of the shelter network. She had to disappear. A shelter ceased "sheltering" if the abuser could find it, and Dodie suspected that Rocco had contacts to help him find just about any official or semi-official shelter in the county. Then, too, Shelley was in no shape right now to travel or set things up for herself anywhere else. She was ambulatory at this point, and could manage to shower and dress herself, but mobility was slow and painful, her wounds still needed frequent tending and dressing, and emotionally she was as skittish as a toddler. And so, the night after her confrontation with Rocco, Dodie had brought Shelley and her measly suitcase—filled with a few changes of underwear, several miscellaneous blouses and sweaters, and a cosmetic bag—to the salon and fixed up a bed for her in the supply room closet.

She saw no reason to involve Maxine in any of this. Dodie had always had access to the salon, primarily because Maxine worried that she might someday be incapacitated, and over the years Dodie had readily checked the heat, retrieved a phone number, or covered the desk as needed. She knew Maxine wouldn't have minded her coming in without telling her. To be fair, in fact, Maxine would probably have understood if Dodie had explained the whole sad story to her. However, explaining such things to Maxine took far more forbearance than Dodie felt she had.

That morning Dodie was running on less than five hours sleep. This was hardly unusual. Sleep deprivation had myriad effects on people—mood swings, depression, sexual dysfunction, weight gain, stimulant abuse, and thoughts of suicide, among them—but on her the result was an unshakeable apathy, particularly with respect to her job, and to the task at hand. When she had first started social work, every mission of this nature had filled her with a palpable rush, almost a full-body pulsation and exhilarating sensation of doing right and righting wrongs. Fueling her even more was her conviction that her career was a conscious rebellion, even a cleansing, from her mother's way of life, which she had grown up despising as willfully frivolous, a wasteful devotion of human talent (something she believed her mother had to a much greater extent than she herself did) to superficial, self-indulgent, and, in some cases, sordid causes. She, in contrast, had chosen to take on some of the world's most insidious evils, directly providing help and support to people suffering from genuine, life-threatening, and soul-wrenching problems. For the past couple of years at least, however, she found herself going through the motions, saying all the right things day after day, things she had been trained to say and had said so many times. She did this partly out of habit, but primarily out of an abiding sense, carried with her from earliest memories, that if she had to answer to someone at the end of her life she would want to say she had done the right thing.

Where this conviction had come from eluded her. She had been raised without religious dogma, her mother's Judaism essentially amounting to a unspoken mantle of self-righteous superiority mixed with paranoia, coupled with a few token behaviors such as lighting the Shabbat candles as her own mother had before her, cooking noodle kugel and brisket on the holidays, and dredging up occasional Yiddishisms from her unconscious. And yet somehow Dodie had developed this sense of ultimate reward that kept her doing just about everything she did every day: it was a vague conviction that there would ultimately be some prize, some sort of trophy or at least recognition for doing things right, as if life were a history class or a contest. She supposed it was her own secular version, perhaps biologically driven, of the heavenly reward so many people hoped to receive for whatever suffering they were enduring at the moment. No matter how often she reminded herself of the absurdity of this expectation, it seemed to drive her behavior a good part of the time.

It was only this irrational desire to be the good person, to live the right life, that had compelled her to unwrap herself from the sheets even earlier that morning and head directly to the phone. It was this same irrational desire that had made her spend the pre-dawn hours (before any child had risen for school) calling various contacts around town until she found a shelter or safe house to lodge Shelley for the day. And it was this same irrational desire that had gotten her to shower, dress, hurry the kids through breakfast, pack the lunches, watch them climb onto their various and staggered-schedule buses, and then head directly for the salon early enough to avoid Maxine and evacuate Shelley before the two of them had to encounter each other.

But even as Dodie had gone through these motions, she had couldn't help thinking that she had chosen an abysmal career, one that focused on the ugliest aspects of human character, and, even worse, aspects that couldn't ever be repaired, given human nature. In all the years she had worked in women's shelters, Dodie couldn't even begin to count the number of damaged souls she had met, or begin to remember the coercion, pain, cruelty, drug abuse, alcoholism, eating disorders, cutting, knives, strangulation, sodomy, brutality, accusations, demoralization, put-downs, terror-mongering, paranoia, slaps, punches, chainsaws, car chases, rapes, shovings, blowtorchings, chainsawings, and all the other endless, complex webs of dysfunction and myriad forms of degradation that the most ordinary human beings inflicted on one another, and on themselves. Human beings were brutal beasts—in fact, they were worse than beasts because of their pretenses to being otherwise—and in her job she had heard it all and all its consequences. It was part of her daily life. Intellectually she knew that Shelley's story was extraordinarily moving, and potentially important to the well-being of many women, especially when you considered the nature of the perpetrator; at this point, however, it was just another job to her.

"I feel like a child," said Shelley, as she emerged from the bathroom, the night's unruly tufts of hair still sticking up at odd angles as if she hadn't even bothered to look in the mirror. "What a fucking mess I've made of my life."

"You?" Dodie picked up Shelley's suitcase and tried to shepherd her toward the door of the salon. "You didn't make the mess." She could see that tomorrow she'd have to come early and supervise wound care. As they approached the car, she saw that two of the bandages on Shelley's cheeks were hanging by a thread, and one was saturated with dried blood and yellow pus.

"I have the absolute worse judgment in men...."

"You and everyone else."

"Everyone else is not hiding in a skin care salon. Everyone else is not afraid to walk out on the streets."

Dodie opened the passenger door for Shelley and helped her in. The woman still had trouble moving and contorted her face as she tried to shift herself into a relatively normal position. Dodie helped bring Shelley's right leg into the car and settled the foot onto the floor mat.

"Stop blaming yourself. Stop blaming the victim."

"I'm not. I'm just saying I don't think I've ever had what you'd call a normal, healthy relationship." Shelley blinked repeatedly, but this only forced the pool of tears over the hump of her lower lids. The tears spread like rivulets over each cheek.

"I know a little something about this, you know, and one thing I'm sure of is that you didn't invite the abuse. No woman does."

Shelley wiped her nose on her forearm, and the crying subsided. "I stuck with the asshole. I knew damn well what he was. It's not like he hadn't done stuff like this before....I shouldn't have provoked him."

"How did you provoke him? By asking him to rape you or beat you?"

Shelley shook her head.

"Let me tell you something, Shelley." Dodie instinctively eyed the rear-view mirrors and then briefly moved her head to check for Shelley's attention, as she often did with her children. "No matter what, it's not your fault. A woman doesn't invite abuse. And it's not her job to dress or act a certain way to prevent it either."

"No. Of course not."

"Golda Meir said it best. You know her, right? The former prime minister of Israel?"

"Of course."

"She was outraged when Israeli legislators proposed a curfew on women to lower the incidence of rape. That made no sense to her. The *men* are attacking women, she said. So if there has to be a curfew on anyone, it should be on them."

Shelley nodded, and this time closed off her nose by pinching the nostrils shut and inhaling. "That's good to hear. I mean, I agree, basically. But the thing is, it's not like a rape or assault or something on the street, with a stranger. I keep coming back for more. For years. At some point, I should know better. At some point I should learn something."

"People aren't very good at learning. You know that, right?"

"I suppose. But I'm especially bad at it. Seriously bad...."

Dodie shook her head. These conversations, which she had with her clients almost daily, often made her hate being a woman. Despite her cheerleading demeanor, she found herself increasingly skeptical of the notion that any woman could change. Florence, Safe Port's director, often waxed poetic about how each and every female, however free of overt, legally admissible abuse, was coerced by social expectation into an inevitable trap of dependent desperation. This, Florence said, include all of them, even her staff, the spewers of sanctioned wisdom and self-proclaimed saviors. Dodie hated stooping to such thoughts, and tried to dismiss them as self-indulgent cynicism, but occasionally when she walked into the chaos of her house physically and emotionally exhausted after a long work day, she succumbed. And now, too, envisioning Shelley's strained face, hearing the ingrained, wooden hopelessness in her voice, she felt herself filled again with this sense of her own naïveté.

"Let's just get to this shelter place already," said Shelley, her tone slightly more animated. "If they have a spare couch, I'm going right there."

"It will just be a few more minutes. Try to relax."

"I woke up twenty times last night sleeping on that floor—it was so bad I almost wanted to go back to the hospital where they wake you up every few hours. Even a little couch, a love seat. Anything upholstered....Actually, this car is a step up." She leaned her head back against the headrest. "Definitely a step up."

"Don't worry. This is only temporary. But safety comes before sleep. Sorry about that, but it's the reality."

Shelley didn't hear her, however, as she was already unconscious, her neck cambered upward and her head, snorting and sucking air through snot-sodden sinuses, wedged between the headrest and the glass.

CHAPTER FOUR

Maxine did exactly what Shelley suggested doing the night she discovered her hidden in the supply closet: she called Dodie, who confirmed Shelley's story and promised to come in right away.

"Well. There we have it," said Maxine, hanging up the phone. "She says you can stay. So."

"I'm so sorry. I didn't mean to trespass or anything. I...I just didn't have anywhere else to go."

"*Ag*, don't you worry now, sweetpea. If my daughter thought you needed to be here, I'm sure you did....But what a mess you are! Of course, I'm almost as bad—haven't taken a brush to my hair since this morning....Would you like coffee? I could certainly use some."

"That would be wonderful."

"Why don't you have a wash then? You'll feel better."

Maxine steered Shelley, stunned from sleep and shame, into the bathroom. Grateful for a moment of solitude, she went to brew a pot in the kitchen, noting that she would have to have Dodie call and cancel her appointments as soon as the sun rose, or at the least the first one or two. She certainly wouldn't be up to facing anyone's face after a night like this. That was a shame, too, because, on top of all the Carole troubles, her revenue was not what it had been. All those charlatans in town doing laser surgery, and she included the well-papered MDs in the lot, were stealing her clientele right and left, promising instant, one-shot miracles. Unsightly hair gone, wrinkles erased, scars eradicated, all in a single (expensive) burst of near-infrared light, or so these rascals promised. The reality was that miracles could happen, but only with a lot of time and effort. And laser surgery, Maxine contended, was far from a miracle. Not only did it not work, but it often left women permanently disfigured and scarred, considerably worse than they had begun. And yet here she was hemorrhaging electrolysis and scar camouflage clients to these laser wizards, and the cosmeceutical business along with them, since even the most highbrow dermatologist was hawking somebody's product line. These days the dermatologists were even selling RAD products, featuring them in glass cases in their waiting rooms and distributing glossy flyers and pamphlets about them to patients.

"These nincompoops have no clue that their laser beams destroy the epidermis, absolutely and permanently. Even the ones that know clearly don't care." It was a rare client who didn't hear Maxine chant this mantra at least once per visit. As she labored on their faces, backs, or limbs, often devoting an hour to a square centimeter or so of skin, she would explain that by the time the victims noticed a problem, the dermatologist or other laser-wielding sorcerer had taken the money and run. "But does the word ever get out? No. Because people, Americans in particular, are gluttons for the quick, easy fix, the miracle cure, the magic bullet. Absolute rubbish!"

If Maxine knew one true thing it was what her mother had always told her while combing out her tangles: it hurt to be beautiful.

When Maxine had first started pushing permanent

makeup as the mainstay of her business, she had been convinced it would be the answer to her prayers. Not only did it fall completely outside the medical doctor's bag of tricks, but giving someone a new brow line or reddening lips was often a simple but lucrative matter of one or two appointments. Ideally, of course, the permanent makeup clients would also come back for touch-ups, but that didn't matter much in terms of bottom line. What mattered was that she had finally found something that appealed to American superficiality as well as their insatiable need to reinvent themselves, something that no one else did, and something at which she was particularly skilled. She had always had a touch with a needle, a skill required for both permanent makeup and other skin care arts, which was why she was the only person in town who could perform genuine electrolysis. She could distinctly feel the hair root through the needle, inserting it at just the right angle and for just the right length of time, and she had the patience and dedication to do this over and over again, usually for months or even years, until the follicle was entirely dead and the client entirely satisfied, both hair- and scar-free. But most Americans didn't have the patience for this kind of hands-on, meticulous care. They wanted miracles. And this was where using the needle for permanent makeup should have done the trick.

It did do the trick, at least superficially. Her days were largely filled with a parade of aging Junior Leaguers and decrepit beauty queens, many of whom drove themselves long distances, some from as far as Virginia or Delaware, for the advertised makeup. Meanwhile, she continued to perform minimal skin care services, including electrolysis, peels, and iontophoresis, on a surprisingly large number of unmarrieds and menopausals for various body parts depending on age and lifestyle. Most of her clients gushed about having a place to confide their most embarrassing and unspeakable problems at last, and to know not only that nothing was too hideous to perturb Maxine, who saw everything as a solvable clinical issue, but that all secrets, beauty and otherwise, were safe with her. Although she had an infuriating share of no-shows and impossible crackpots who, perennially unhappy, never returned for follow-ups, she easily filled their places with a never-ending supply of desperate women seeking refuge. Not counting coffee breaks and lunch, she saw clients nearly back-to-back from 10-5 on Mondays through Thursdays, and packed solid until 2 on Fridays, when she closed up early.

Still, the bills were winning the battle. She had raised her rates several times, predictably losing a few clients in the wake, but the cost of new equipment and travel and rent and insurance continued to overwhelm her. She had to place a weekly advertisement in the local paper and each month in the city magazine, like any other self-respecting, self-improvement service in town. She had to keep up with the exorbitant rent on the salon, located as it was on a relatively quiet and tidy block. And because she conducted herself with the utmost professionalism, she also had to attend continuing education meetings twice a year, keep up her certifications, follow OSHA regulations and CDC guidelines, use FDA-approved products, and keep abreast of the latest in sterilization techniques and blood-borne pathogens. She often marveled at how it had seemed easier to support herself, two babies, and even her lug of a husband back in Capetown when she was running a simple skin care and electrolysis operation. Perhaps it wasn't possible anymore to be a sole proprietor, at least one with ethics and standards of the sort she had, or with the insurance that killed you here in this lawsuit-happy country. She simply didn't know.

"She cannot stay here," Maxine told Dodie, almost before she had crossed the threshold. "That's the bottom line."

"Of course, Zeenie....Do I smell coffee?"

"Help yourself. Don't you think you first owe me the slightest explanation? It was only your word that has kept me from calling the authorities."

Dodie filled the mug Maxine kept on the rack for her, having forgotten momentarily her vow never to drink salon coffee without first checking the refrigerator for half-and-half, a provision she supplied for herself whenever she remembered to stop by the salon on her runs home from the supermarket. Maxine's intractable frugality (and, in Dodie's opinion, helplessness) meant that, when the half-and-half was out, she was obliged to drink her coffee black or endure chalky remains of half-dissolved Cremora. Coffee with half-and-half, or even better, real cream, was one of the few luxuries Dodie allowed herself, and was frequently the only incentive she had these days to pull herself out of bed. This was going to be a black coffee morning, however, and she probably should have realized that when she got the 2 a.m. phone call

"All right now," said Dodie, exiting the kitchen and greeting Shelley, who was just emerging from the bathroom, looking considerably more pale and bleary-eyed, if slightly less bruised, than she had the night before. "Let's all sit down and talk."

"By all means," said Maxine. She settled herself into the receptionist's chair behind the desk in the anteroom. "Please, sit down, the both of you."

Dodie encouraged Shelley to nestle into one of the two

upholstered Victorian Grandfather chairs and then perched herself on the edge of the borderline ratty satin loveseat. Maxine surveyed them both from behind the desk like a schoolteacher.

"Well, now," said Maxine. "I'm waiting."

Maxine wanted the whole story, no holds barred. And so Dodie explained.

"All that is very sad, very sad indeed," said Maxine. "And, Dodie, dearie lamb, naturally, I would do anything for you, anything. If you are at risk, in any way—I want you out of this. You hear me?"

"I am just doing my job, Zeenie."

"Your job does not involve taking clients out of shelters and putting your own physical person on the line. I'm rather sure of that."

"My job is to serve the needs of my clients."

"No matter. I want you out of this."

"I'm sure you do. So do I. But the point right now is that Shelley here—you see her, sitting here? Shelley can't go out in public. That's the problem. She simply can't go out."

Maxine ran her tongue over her lips and looked Shelley over as if she were judging a gourd at a county fair. "So what are you saying, Dodie? She has to stay here? That's out of the question!"

"I wasn't suggesting anything of the sort....This was a...temporary solution. Until we figure out what to do."

"We? Apparently you haven't gone over this month's numbers with me yet, eh, dearie lamb?"

"I don't follow you. Last I checked you had back-to-back clients just about every day."

"My dear, it is now nearly dawn," Maxine told Dodie. "I have clients scheduled this morning, and, of course, with our delightful Carole gone, I can see that I myself will have to prepare the rooms for them. That means that in the next two or three hours you and this lady....I'm sorry, dear, I seem to have forgotten your name."

"It's Shelley," Shelley mumbled. "Shelley Slavin."

"Shelley. Like the poet?"

"Ha! My mother would have liked to think that. But it's more like a nickname for Michelle. Shelley. I'm sorry to drag you into this."

"Please, don't apologize. My point was simply that you, Dodie, and you, Shelley, Michelle, or whatever it is, are going to have to come up with some kind of answer in the next two or three hours. I can't have a person loitering on my property, lurking in the back rooms, or whatever it is you think she would do while I worked....It's a matter of privacy for the clients, if nothing else."

"Of course not," said Dodie. "I was planning to take Shelley over to a shelter where they have room for her during the day. It's just that nights there are a problem."

"What's to keep Mr. Brutality from finding her at this new shelter, may I ask?"

"Not much. But it's a private home, not an official shelter. And not Safe Port, which is listed on websites and known to the authorities, should anyone ask."

"What? You always assured me that the location was private. You're telling me those buggers can look you up on the Internet?"

"Well, no, of course not, not the address. But the name Safe Port and what we do, yes, of course you can. The private home isn't listed anywhere, though. So it will probably take him longer to track her down if I can place her."

"If it's private, why can't you just ask the people to let her sleep on a couch, or a sleeping bag, or whatnot?...Surely

the accommodations must be superior to my supply closet."
Maxine nodded at Shelley. "That's true, isn't it?"

"I can't do that, Zeenie," said Dodie. "The family isn't
willing to take in any more than they already have."

"As I said, she can't stay here. That's the problem. She'll
be recognized. And, Dodie, please, before you go I'm going
to need you to cancel my 10 o'clock—actually, anyone
booked before 11."

"The problem, as I said, is that she can't go out in
public....Anyway, I'll take her out with me today, and you
won't have to worry about her embarrassing you in any way.
In fact, you can just pretend she isn't here. We'll figure this
out soon enough. I promise."

"Soon isn't good enough, Dodie."

"Zeenie, what you have to understand is that we've got
to get Shelley away from here, from this area, which isn't
easy to do for anyone—just pick up your whole life and
move away at the snap of a finger! That's not so easy, you
know."

"I've certainly done it, dearie lamb. Picked up and
moved my whole life to be with you, as a point in fact."

"That's not the same thing, and you know it."

"I gave up everything, Dodie. My whole world, my
beloved country, and what did I have here? No one.
Nothing. Except you, of course."

"No one was staying in South Africa at that point,
Zeenie, and....Oh, forget it."

"It's you who forgets, Dodie. And never understood."
Her daughter's blind loyalty to her new country, and her
inability to acknowledge how difficult it had been to leave
South Africa, frustrated and infuriated Maxine. Equally
infuriating were Dodie's assertions of the moral superiority
of both the United States and, by extension, herself.

"What is it about this situation that you can't grasp, Zeenie? Whatever you say, this kind of thing can't be resolved overnight. And especially someone like Shelley who is still recuperating. Psychology aside, she's not physically capable of going off on her own right now. And, whatever her physical state, she just can't go out in public here. She's just too recognizable a target in a place like Annapolis."

"I cannot have her here."

"Perhaps more to the point from your perspective, Zeenie—as long as Rocco thinks Shelley's around, I'm a potential target, too."

"Well. That is a point. Yes, a good point." Maxine opened a drawer and rummaged through it, finally pulling out a pair of reading glasses. She took a tissue from the top of the desk and methodically wiped both lenses, holding them up to the light, and then rubbing out a few residual spots. Glasses in hand, she walked over to Shelley, staring down on her intently, silently, for at least a minute.

"What are you doing?" Dodie asked.

Shelley shifted uncomfortably.

"Hush," said Maxine, putting on the glasses. She softly ran her fingers over Shelley's cheeks, tracing the scars on her forehead, circling the newer bruises, brushing her fingers over the swollen lips, and then lifting the chin to inspect the neck.

"You have burn scars here."

"Yes."

"From him?"

"Yes....Not this time. Those are old."

"The other scars as well?"

"Yes."

Shelley's cheeks, once again dampening with tears, slipped from Maxine's hands. She backed up and continued to stare. "What did he do? Apply a hot poker to your face?"

"Essentially. Cigar, actually. Just once...or twice."

"All right. Look," Maxine said at last, taking the second armchair for herself. "It's Friday, and I'm only here until 2 today. So you can come back then and have the place for the weekend. But after that, Dodie, I'm telling you—she has to go."

"Fine. That's no problem. We'll find a solution, even if it ends up being the cot in Randall's greenhouse....C'mon, Shelley. Get ready so that we can get going. Obviously I have many phone calls to make before the day ends."

"I'm so sorry, I really am," Shelley said to Maxine as she limped past her and headed toward the bathroom. "I'm so, so sorry."

Maxine lowered herself in the armchair and watched Shelley navigate the hall by holding out her hands to the walls and scrutinizing each step as if it were a dank, low-lit cavern. Dodie took the reading glasses from Maxine's hand, folded them neatly, and put them back in the desk drawer. She returned to Maxine and bent over her chair so that their heads nearly touched. The bathroom door clicked closed. "And by the way, what you said before was a lie," Dodie whispered, or, rather, hissed. "You did not leave Capetown because of me. You left because of Dr. Alvarez."

CHAPTER FIVE

For as long as she lived, Maxine marveled at her ability to get herself to that seminar in Johannesburg, a seminar that, unquestionably, changed the course of her life. She was never able to fathom what exactly had given her the strength and determination to persist in her arguments with Toad, who sustained his view that she was only doing this to complicate his existence. And, to be fair, her arguments in the beginning were rather weak. Antioxidants per se meant nothing to her back then, and, on the surface, this particular seminar was just one of many opportunities that often came her way.

It helped that the seminar was at the esteemed Alvarez Institute, led by Dr. Ruf "Vitamin A" Alvarez himself, a fact that made it inherently more credible and desirable than the standard continuing education courses she occasionally attended in Capetown. Further, the materials, touting the sea change in skin care promised by this new scientific understanding, naturally made her think that this seminar would boost her status in the trade. Even so, her absolute conviction that she needed to travel up to Johannesburg to attend this particular seminar—and her ability to maintain the stamina to defend her right to attend it—must have come from some premonition that this decision would change her life. Either that, she later thought, or her desperation to move up and on had reached a boiling point.

Whatever the explanation, she had instinctively known that she had to attend the Alvarez seminar and thus had to devote two entire weeks, manipulative wiles in full gear, to get three days off—and the money to fund them. As far as work was concerned, she was her own boss, so, theoretically, there was little challenge on this front. In fact, the dreaded world of "work" was to her a respite, a refuge from normal life, a time when everything, however annoying or tedious, was predictable and controllable. Home, in contrast, was a moving target, filled with the recurring toil of cooking, dishes, cleaning, and laundry, and, worse, with the unpredictability of moods, whims, and demands of human beings who weren't paying her. And the worst of these moods, whims, and demands were Toad's, not the baby's. The baby, Dennis, was demanding and irrational, of course, an exhausting whirlwind of need and ego that tired her physically with lifting and hauling and supervising and sanitizing and fueling, but, still, he had a cockeyed grin and an exaltation in the mundane that regularly melted her heart. On top of that, the baby got better every day, and, whatever the momentary challenges may have been—waking at 3 a.m., projectile vomiting, teething, raging, whining, whatever—they were replaced by new, different, but equally ephemeral challenges in short time.

Toad's challenges, on the other hand, never changed, and his grins were not only rare and calculated but had long ago ceased to delight her. His overarching goal in life, or so it had starting seeming to her almost as soon as they had returned home from their honeymoon, was to take her hard-earned independence and transform it into servitude. If she was not earning a living for the three of them, she was waiting hand and foot on him, ostensibly in gratitude for his (official) renunciation of freedom. And here she could never be adequate, no matter how hard she tried. The roast was never cooked to the desired tenderness. The beer she bought was the wrong brand. The house was a bloody pigsty—didn't she know how to dust? The telly was fuzzy—and that, somehow, was her fault, as she must have hit some dial while ineptly dusting. The baby cried too loudly, or too often, or too inexpediently. And despite all the nights Toad spent out "with the boys" or all the days he spent lying on his back in the front room while she worked, she could never go out with her girlfriends without a major altercation.

Maxine therefore fully expected that getting Toad to agree to the seminar idea would be a herculean battle. Not only would she have to scrape together the travel and tuition expenses from her stash (which normally became Toad's beer money, on the many occasions he was running short), but she had to cajole him to care for Dennis for a full three days and two nights. This included feeding, walking, supervising, and, yes, even nappy changing, all of which Maxine considered minor inconveniences for a man who left the house for employment at most two days per week. Screaming and crying did no good with him. This she knew from bitter experience. Nor did logical argument. All of these tactics had to be deployed first off, but it was necessary for him to say no for several days, and to swagger around like a little czar afterward. However, this was how it had to start, despite her fury at having to justify herself to a slug with nothing better to do with his days than lie on the sofa, a place he had pretty much been planted since his family put the chain on the market and started eyeing Australia. Eventually, she knew, he would internalize the arguments and present the idea as if it had been his own, but she needed to plant the seeds and live with the wrath for at least a few days while the idea germinated in his head. As long as he felt he was in control, she could do just about anything.

And so she began with the provocation: "It is not a waste of money. It's an investment."

"An investment in a vacation for yourself to J-burg, is what it is...an escape from your maternal duties is what."

"You can handle Dennis for a few days, for goodness sake. And it's hardly a vacation." That was a concept with which he should be familiar, she thought, wishing she could say it out loud. Really, the man's whole life was a vacation. "It's education. Essential education....Don't you see how this is going to make us, Toddie? Dr. Rufus Alvarez says antioxidants will change skin care practice forever, fundamentally, and he's right. He's already a pioneer in topical vitamins, you know—way ahead of his time."

"Whoop de doo."

"Do you know you can charge for these kinds of treatments? I could give up the whole hair business and all that mess and simply concentrate on skin care—imagine that!"

She knew that he would never even try to imagine, or to understand, since, despite his dependence on it, he considered her entire livelihood, or anything to do with cosmetology, to be a joke. He spent an entire evening after that first interchange ranting at her about extravagance, and wondering how, after her complaints about business falling off a bit, she planned to pay for this excursion. She softly countered that she had put some extra pennies away every week to save up for her continuing education and, besides, she'd be staying with her parents, not only saving costs but dispensing with that obligation as well. He responded that he wouldn't be able to care for Dennis while he was working, and, gagging her impulse to retort that this was hardly an issue, she observed that if he did have to do some deliveries, well, then, Dennis could certainly ride along.

The tactics ultimately succeeded, as expected. After several weeks of recalcitrance on his part, and ego stoking and temper control on Maxine's, he began to speak as though the seminar was, in fact, his idea. Maxine was elated, of course: as if freedom from housekeeping, husband-tending, and childcare weren't compensation enough, the chance to study with Dr. Rufus Alvarez was clearly a once-in-a-lifetime opportunity. But she also knew there would be an enormous price to pay for this concession upon her return, not the least of which would be a lifetime of reverence, praise, and gratitude because the man had chosen to behave like an adult for a few days. Even worse, she realized that the very predictability of this victory stoked her growing revulsion for her husband, a feeling that had been flaring in her almost since the beginning of their marriage, kindled partly by his utter contempt for good, honest labor, but primarily by his contempt for and exploitation of her own respect for them.

"Truth is beauty."

These were the words written on the blackboard when Maxine first entered the classroom, and, indeed, they were the first words uttered by Dr. Rufus Alvarez when he began to address the students. From the moment she saw him, she knew that "Dr. Ruf," as his students called him, was, indeed, the embodiment of truth and beauty both. She also knew, implicitly, that embodying these qualities made him the most trustworthy man on the planet. He had all the outer trappings of stereotypical masculine perfection as she (and the romance novels) saw it: thick, glossy hair the color of strong espresso, a classic aquiline nose, an imposing chin notched with a sweetening cleft, and just enough weathering on his cheeks to give him the attractive authority of middle-aged masculinity without a hint of impending infirmity. He was over six feet tall, trim as a teenager, and that first day, as in all the photographs she had seen of him over the years, attired in an expertly-tailored suit adorned with a radiant tie. Most of all, though, he had intense dark-chocolate eyes accentuated by arched, uplifted brows, and these eyes locked into hers whenever he spoke with his impeccable prep-schooled accent, his gaze assuring rapt attention to whatever she said or did. He was, in short, impossible not to trust—and, indeed, impossible not to want.

In class, however, she kept such thoughts to herself. There was so much to learn, and Dr. Ruf had so much passion for the subject that it was impossible not to want to absorb every bit of it. In three days he promised the class that they would learn not only how to analyze complexion according to the latest scientific understanding of skin type and aging, but appropriately prescribe the best products and care regime for every individual client. The class would also learn about the developing science of antioxidants—vitamins A, C, E, and beta carotene—and the coming revolution in topical aesthetic science that they promised. They would even cover general business and marketing needs for a single-proprietor shop like hers.

Maxine had always had a good head for science, and it paid off here. She lapped up the knowledge and was the first to have her hand up nearly all the time. Lectures ran from 9-12 every morning, followed, after lunch, by three more hours of supervised clinical work on each other, all under Dr. Ruf's supervision. The man was a marvelous lecturer, walking up and down the aisles every morning and looking each of his students in the eye as he talked, ensuring that each and every one of them understood his premises. He was mesmerizing, this man, not only a skilled plastic surgeon with a thriving two-city practice, but also a published and pioneering research scientist and caring dermatologist who ran his own world-class skin care clinics. He was also someone with an eye not just for beauty but also for talent, and he almost immediately spotted Maxine's aptitude and enthusiasm for the subject.

"Soybean, aloe, horse chestnut, pomegranate, date, grape seed, teas—you will hear about all sorts of rubbish being implanted in skin care products to inhibit or reverse skin aging, or so it is claimed," he said. "Chamomile, comfrey, curcumin, allantoin...plastic, for all I know— desperate people have tried just about everything. However, there is only one real solution to skin damage because there is only one real cause of it. Does anyone know what that might be?"

Maxine was the first to raise her hand. "Sunlight," she said. "Sunlight destroys the skin."

Dr. Ruf nodded sagely, and approached Maxine's desk, looking down on her approvingly. "Correct. The sun is our greatest enemy, although, of course, it is also our salvation—we need the sun to live, and the skin needs it, too, as a source of vitamin D. That's the dilemma—how to live with the sun and its life-giving properties, and yet also how to prevent its damage." He reached his hand toward Maxine's face, nearly touching it. "Beautiful young skin like you see on this young lady—so vulnerable, yet so needy. Protecting this is our holy grail."

Maxine turned her face toward her desk and started scribbling madly, for once wishing she wore makeup to camouflage the flush she felt across her cheeks. He removed his hand, but kept smiling down on her as she scribbled. At last, receiving no response, he returned to the front of the classroom and addressed the class.

"What is important to grasp here—the key fact you must take home with you if you remember nothing else from this seminar—is that photoaging is at core a vitamin deficiency disease. It is caused immediately by exposure to light—light, which, in turn, contains free radicals that destroy our natural, protective vitamins. The chief amongst these is Vitamin A.

"This is why," he continued, "the antioxidant vitamins are the only ones that really matter. Write that down, now, because you will need to remember this for the rest of your careers. The antioxidants are key. Especially vitamin A and its derivatives. Now—pencils ready? I want you to note the two main functions these vitamins have in the body. Ready? Good." Maxine's pencil was still scribbling. She was good at note-taking, and, further, needed to distract herself from dwelling on Dr. Ruf's fingertips and how they had seemed to touch her without even meeting her skin.

"The first function of the antioxidant vitamins is protecting cells from oxidative damage," Dr. Ruf proclaimed. "The second is exerting a hormone-like effect and directly commanding the DNA in the skin cells, activating the transcription of specific genes. The result is a whole cascade of events, with which I won't bore you, but which are absolutely critical to structural changes in the skin, structural changes that improve the skin's appearance and actually undo photodamage. These genes, once activated, set a whole series of reactions in motion that help, even rejuvenate, the skin—increasing firmness, bleaching out hyperpigmented spots, smoothing surfaces, and even reducing wrinkles."

Maxine wrote all this down as well.

"Class—you must eradicate this myth from your minds forever as well. Skin aging is not inevitable. It is not our fate, not if we intervene. No, the reality is that photoaging is a wasting disease, a preventable one, due to free radicals from sunlight. This damage, as I said, starts a whole cascade of events—among them deficiencies in key hormones, vitamins, and other micronutrients, and the depletion of other essential factors. But, thanks to the miracle of modern science, we are not helpless here. Not at all. We can replenish these light-sensitive vitamins topically—and that is our power, indeed our duty, as aestheticians. *Your* duty."

Dr. Ruf sat down at his desk in the front of the room and beamed at the class. "Any questions?"

The class, even Maxine this time, was silent.

"I see I have overwhelmed you....Let us just review then. Why is Vitamin A critical?... Come now, class, I've given you all the answers already. Again—why is Vitamin A so critical? Young lady with the lovely silver necklace? This is not a trick question." He gestured to a woman in the front row that Maxine immediately pegged as a blonde bimbo—no more than 22, she wagered.

"It helps with the DNA in the cells."

"Absolutely right. It helps regulate DNA in every cell of the body. Vitamin A is essential for activating enzyme systems and keeping keratinocytes and fibroblasts healthy and happy. So—what on earth is the problem then?"

No one answered.

"Really now, class. It's simple. The problem is that exposure to light destroys our natural vitamin A. Without this vitamin in the skin, the cells cannot truly be healthy."

Dr. Ruf stood again and reseated himself on the front of his desk. He crossed his legs and looked right at the dippy blonde in the front row. "We have another enormous problem, however—getting those vitamins in through our horny outer skin layer. This is called—write this down now—the cutaneous permeability barrier. It is located in the stratum corneum interstices and mediated by the lamellar bilayers. Look at the Figure 1 on the handouts. Do you see? Do you all have that down?"

The other ladies looked perplexed. It didn't bother Maxine in the least. She loved these terms. She knew that they all had meanings, and could, if necessary, be looked up in a dictionary at home even if she didn't understand them now. They were terms well worth learning, too, because she knew from experience that when she quoted them back to clients, they looked at her in awe.

"It may all sound like scientific mumbo jumbo to you, but it has enormous meaning for you as clinicians. Why? I'll tell you why. Because this barrier means that you can slather on an expensive cream until kingdom come, but unless the cream penetrates this layer, you are wasting your hard-earned cash—or your clients' hard-earned cash, as the case may be," he continued. "And so you have two goals. Can anyone tell me what they are?"

The silence stunned her—no wonder cosmetologists had a bad name. No longer able to restrain herself, Maxine raised her hand and waved it madly to divert Dr. Ruf's eyes from the first row. At last he saw her and nodded. "Yes, my dear, lovely skinned girl with all the answers. Would you be so kind as to tell the class our two goals are in combating photoaging?"

"I'll do my best," she said. "The first goal is to get the right substance into the product. An antioxidant, to be more precise."

"Correct," he said. "Vitamin A, Vitamin C, Vitamin E,

and beta carotene—these are our armamentarium. The rest of the rot, to paraphrase the late—very late—Dr. Oliver Wendell Holmes, Senior, could be sunk to the bottom of the sea, which would be all the better for mankind, and all the worse for the fishes....And, what, my dear, is the second goal?"

"*Ag*, as you were saying, even the best product does no good at all if it can't penetrate the horny layer of the skin. So penetration—that's the other goal."

Dr. Ruf paused, and nodded at her admiringly, a dimple materializing in his cheek as he smiled. "Marvelous, marvelous, first rate. What, my dear, did you say your name was?"

"Maxine. Maxine Van Vecten."

"Very good, Mrs. Van Vechten. Very good, indeed. And, Mrs. Van Vechten—please see me after class, luv, if you don't mind."

He had insisted that they go out for coffee, something he did every day after his classes or consultations. Coming originally from South America, he said, he had never been able to get the bean out of his blood. He began each morning with a strong black cup and kept himself running throughout the day on pure-grade caffeine, despite the fact that in his view the South Africans hadn't a clue as to how to brew a decent cup. He did know one place near the training center with an accommodating waitress who did her best to ensure him something remotely potable. And there, over an entire pot of coffee, Maxine had apparently continued to impress him with her natural aptitude and mental quickness. He had an eye for these things, he assured her, and he saw that she had the potential for greatness in this field. He was never wrong on this kind of thing. Strictly professional, he told her about the ancient but as yet untapped world of micropigmentation—both an art and a science, like all aesthetics, and one for which he was seeking new practitioners. He said that she could expect to have a glorious future in the field, assuming she turned out to be as good with her hands as with her mind.

Perhaps she should have been wary when Dr. Ruf offered her private instruction during this very first coffee. After all, wariness, particularly toward men, was her normal stance. Over the years she had battled off her share of shady males, ranging from (literal) snake-oil salesmen, sleazy Indian servicemen, nasty lowlifes looking for shelter, and irate but lubriciously appeasable landlords. Her father had taught her early on how to take care of herself, and from her earliest girlhood she remembered him telling her to assume the worst. Thus, she was almost instinctively on guard. And yet, with Dr. Ruf, she felt no need for her standard armor. It came down to trust, she supposed, the truly extraordinary confidence and ease with which he instantly filled anyone he encountered. Where all else in her life, however much she personally aimed at simple decency, felt half-baked, jerry-rigged, adulterated, or, frankly, sham, Dr. Ruf was clearly the real thing. He was well-educated (English boarding schools, rumor had it), professional, polished, poised, and self-possessed. He was Grade AAA, like nothing she ever encountered. In his presence, she was brought into a different, safer world, one of intellect, truth, respect, and honor, and thus one in which she could fling off her normal defenses against human vulgarity.

Besides, even given the slight possibility that he could have wanted something more, and, remembering his fingers near her cheek, even given her discomfort with her own, half-conscious, wish for something more, how, in all seriousness could she have refused such an offer from such a man? He was offering to take her on as his private student, showing her the intricacies and potential of micropigmentation, which, Vitamin A notwithstanding, promised to lift the field of aesthetics (Dr. Ruf's preferred term for her profession) to unprecedented heights. Private instruction was by far the best way to learn the techniques, and, given all the other demands on his time, he only made this offer to that rare diamond in the rough who crossed his path. She assured herself that merely singling her out for private instruction was by no means a salacious act: it could well have been as much a testament to her potential as a practitioner as to her personal attractiveness.

Maxine thus never thought twice about the offer, nor did she question why this virtual stranger and, indeed, teacher, flirted with her and touched her, even on that very first day. Not only did it seem natural to him, and sweet, but she understood the whole business essentially to be a pleasant charade, a lovely pretense, rife with suggestion but assumed by all to be obligation-free. Rufus Alvarez was by nature the gentleman, by nature the flatterer, in fact, and thus Maxine could easily dismiss his behavior as "just his way" rather than something directed specifically towards herself. Throughout the course of this first day, she had observed him holding doors open for many of his female students, laying a fatherly hand on their shoulders, helping them reach glassware high overhead, and gratuitously complimenting them on bags or shoes or earrings, and she had already accepted such gestures as his natural, and characteristic, chivalry. A refreshing change, actually, in this colorless age of women's liberation.

The offer of instruction seemed equally innocuous, and perfectly understandable. She had heard from colleagues long before that Dr. Ruf occasionally mentored promising students. Why shouldn't she be one of them? She was hardly a batty-eyed child but a mature woman with over a decade of experience to her credit, including experience running her own salon. It seemed completely plausible to her that her aptitude had been obvious in class and equally plausible that a man with Rufus Alvarez's instincts and vision would identify her upfront. And so, when he asked her to consider private instruction, she had not the slightest trepidation. She knew, just as she knew when she signed up for the seminar, that this was part of the plan.

They had lunch together after the next day's class, and agreed to meet that evening in his outpatient clinic, where he would show her some early results of his micropigmentation work. Dr. Ruf showed her slides, prepared for a professional meeting, of women with dull, lifeless lips outlined and colored permanently into full, bursting blossoms; wispy lashes thickened and darkened to fringe beaming eyes; missing and awkwardly penciled brows transformed into natural-looking, eye-defining lines; and even an old facial scar retoned to match the surrounding skin imperceptibly. This was all work that Dr. Ruf had done there in Johannesburg on his own patients, willing volunteers, and it was permanent. They could wake up in the morning looking as beautiful as they had the night before, he exclaimed to Maxine. They could save hundreds of hours a year applying (or removing!) makeup—what a boon for the day's busy, working woman—and hundreds, thousands of dollars in expensive cosmetic products. There was no need to reapply lipstick or liner every few hours, he said, and no smearing or smudging ever, which was a huge leap forward for any woman who needed to be neat and professional throughout the day, as well as for the athlete or, when you thought about it, any woman on the go. The older and infirm, those with shaky hands or failing eyesight, could count on a perfectly outlined eye and expertly colored lip with absolutely no effort or concern, as could the woman allergic to traditional cosmetic products. Natural looking permanent makeup was a revolutionary idea, Dr. Ruf told her, one that would change women's lives far more than any political movement. It promised to give women, historically slaves to beauty, the time, money, and freedom to do more with their lives than ever before, and promised to give them the self-confidence to do so. All that was involved was a few hours at his clinic and, perhaps, a touch-up every two to five years.

"No one is doing this yet," he explained, shutting off the projector. "At least not in the world of legitimate medicine or aesthetics. If you take this on, add it to your practice, you will become a trendsetter, a pioneer. And quite a well-compensated one at that."

"I can see the appeal. But why—why is no one doing it if it's so wonderful?"

"That's a very good question. And I'll give you a good answer." He blew upward to keep a boyish shag of hair from grazing his right eye, and grinned at her. "No one is doing it—at least in legitimate medical circles—because they haven't yet discovered it, my darling. The reality, though, is that it's being done all the time, and has been done for centuries, thousands of years, really. Micropigmentation, you see, is merely a glorified word for tattooing. We wouldn't call it that to the patients, at least not initially, but that is essentially what it is."

"Tattooing?"

"Think about it. Inserting permanent dyes under the skin, that's all. Ecclesiastes had it right: truly, there is nothing new under the sun."

"The sun," she said, laughing. "Our old friend."

He didn't laugh but approached her and took her hand. "So," he said at last. "When will I see you again?"

"To train, you mean?" She didn't know why she said this. Clearly this was what he meant, or what he meant to be taken as his meaning. Yet it actually made her a bit weak-kneed, sappily senseless over it all, a state she hadn't been in since her teenage years, and she suddenly felt awkward, even embarrassed. Perhaps this was the opportunity to put a stop to things. But, then, perhaps she was just imagining, flattering herself. The man undoubtedly had a wife and children. What was he—well over forty, perhaps even fifty years old? Certainly this was all business. She had to put a stop to it.

"I don't know," she said. "I can't see how I can come up here again. Getting Todd—my husband—to watch the baby for three days has put me into seven years of indentured servitude, I'm afraid."

"You can't learn these techniques by osmosis, you know. Nor can you learn them in three days. Surely he has to understand that. If you are to be my apprentice—and, darling, you need to apprentice if you are to be any good at this—you're going to have to come back once a month for at least a year or two. We can't even *begin* to talk about full lip color, not to mention camouflage or skin repigmentation, before you've mastered the basics. And then, of course, working on a live subject is essential. You can't possibly anticipate the problems you'll encounter until you've spent considerable time working with living, breathing clients."

So it was indeed all business. That was good. But it wasn't good because she couldn't possibly come up to Johannesburg like that. "That's a problem. I wish it weren't a problem, but it honestly is. Aside from the money to come up here, I simply don't have that kind of freedom."

"I see. Well, then, what about Capetown? You live in Capetown, don't you?"

"Yes. I do." She wondered how he knew. Her accent? Or had he looked up her registration records? Perhaps he merely took a keen interest in every student. In any case, the fact that he knew, rather than disturbing her, filled her with joy. And, suddenly, she didn't care. She was going to do it, train with the great Dr. Ruf and absorb whatever he had for her to absorb. There was no need to think things through any further because only a fool would turn down such a chance.

"Well, then, we don't have a problem at all. I'm down there a week a month, doing surgeries at my clinic, checking in on the laboratory, that sort of thing. I can fit you in, I think."

"Still. It seems like a huge amount of time. So many meetings."

He put his fingers gently on her cheek, suggesting to her how cherished every one of those meetings was going to be. "Consider how much training you'd want someone to have who was going to be working on your face. Naturally you'd want them to be properly trained, wouldn't you?"

"Naturally."

"Super then. Call my secretary in Capetown when you get home, will you? She'll set you up for next month."

CHAPTER SIX

Whatever happened that first fateful day in Capetown, and forever after, she attributed to the skirt. People often said you should never underestimate the power of appearance, which was true enough, but what they perhaps didn't realize was that most of this power was over oneself. It wasn't the specific skirt—she actually didn't remember whether it was the white with the pink roses or the ruffled turquoise broomstick she had loved in those days—but rather the very act of wearing a skirt of any sort that changed everything. Back then she nearly always wore a dress or skirt in a professional context or whenever anything mattered, but she had worn trousers in Johannesburg, perhaps because, as a "student," she felt more casual and less on display. That day, however, she had closed the shop two hours early, a prerogative she had as sole proprietor, and gone straight to Dr. Ruf's on the outskirts of Capetown. Thus she was dressed in her more typical garb.

The skirt helped her from the beginning. Within a minute of the call from his receptionist, Dr. Ruf came out into the reception room to greet her personally, and she felt his eyes on her all the way down the hall, the way she always felt, or, perhaps more precisely, imagined she felt, random male eyes upon her whenever she walked in a skirt. There was something about the lack of constriction, the breeze up her legs and the awareness of the space between them, that freed not only her posture and gait—she flounced, almost, her rear end waggling slightly under the loose fabric—but also heightened her sensory awareness of both herself and her impact on others. Something about a skirt made her acutely aware of her body and its desirability, and she sensed herself emanating something distinctly feminine and attractive as she moved through space. She had this sense even when she felt heavy or pimply, dirty or sweaty, and inevitably, whenever she had this sense, she also noticed that anonymous men suddenly spoke to her, smiled at her, and were kinder to her than average strangers. Dr. Ruf was always kind—that was his nature—but today in the skirt she felt particularly at ease with his kindness, more natural, less self-conscious. As a result, it all flowed.

He began by giving her a brief tour through his Capetown quarters, and she quickly discovered that the layout played a role in freeing her as well. Eventually the facilities here would expand into a world-class day spa and research institute, but back in the '70s, when Maxine trained there, it was still a modest operation, comprising a sprawling and spanking new building on the outskirts of town, set on several acres of open land, with various unused offices and a dozen or so busy scientists working to develop new vitamin A products that would someday comprise the RAD line of cosmeceuticals. Unintimidating, the complex also felt like a place in which she could let down her guard. Like everything else Dr. Rufus Alvarez did, the Capetown clinic was gleamingly immaculate and tastefully appointed throughout, leaving clients and visitors with a sense that they had been lifted above the ugly fray—the same sense she herself always felt just in being with Rufus Alvarez.

"It's exactly like a spa, a retreat! Gorgeous!," she

exclaimed to him as they passed through the clinic wing.

"We do our best. Women often hesitate to have work done, not because they don't desire it, crave it even, but rather because they realize that going home afterwards is so bloody dreadful. Days, weeks of bandages, swelling, infection risk, and, consequently, ghastly turtlenecks, scarves, hiding, lying—you know the sequence very well. So it didn't take much for me to ask myself—why put my patients through all that? Better that I swallow a little upfront expense, and give them a chance to stay here at a lovely respite from life. Here they can relax, indulge, and get first-rate medical attention until they're ready to reemerge as swans. They can tell everyone back home they're off to a spa. And, quite honestly, they are."

"Marvelous....But surely it costs?"

"Everything costs, Maxine. Beauty costs."

"Well, yes, of course."

"Everything worth having costs, my darling."

Apparently not everyone agreed, however, or could afford to agree, because, "inevitably," he told her, several of the suites were vacant. The problem seemed to be lack of caregivers more than lack of interest—he was thinking of taking on more day staff to meet consumer demand, although he would need more clinicians as well as menial workers to offer the kind of service he demanded. Someday he would expand the clinic to take advantage of the space, but for now there was no end of work for everyone on staff. In fact, many of them were putting in ten hour days. The frantic sounds of typing from a front office confirmed his point, and, without knocking, he took Maxine inside. A well-preserved older woman with upswept hair that could have been either pure white or platinum blond sat behind the typewriter. She lowered her spectacles and smiled at them.

"Maxine, meet my business manager, also known as the woman who introduced me to the world, Lila Alvarez. Mummy, meet my latest protégée—Maxine Van Vecten."

Maxine extended her hand, but Lila Alvarez never stopped typing. "Pleased to meet you, luvvie. Welcome, welcome, welcome, and sorry for my distractedness at the moment. We really must have tea sometime."

"Why, yes, wonderful," mumbled Maxine. "I would enjoy that....How wonderful for you both that you work together."

"Mummy is indeed the brains behind this operation. I might be a whiz with my eye and my hands, but the record-keeping is quite beyond me. Thank goodness she has a mind for numbers."

"Yes, that's a whole other world," said Maxine. "And how nice to be...to have someone you can trust do the books for you. I can't tell you what I would give to have someone like that so I could concentrate on the work. Actually, I have a mother with a mind for books as well, but she gives it all to my father's business, I'm afraid."

"Mummy keeps a tight ship. She designed the entire business section of my training courses as well. I know my limitations, and that happens to be one of them."

Lila kept typing away. "I do apologize," she said. "But I really must get these invoices in the mail by five o'clock."

"Of course, Mummy dear. We're so sorry to disturb you. I'm going to continue giving Zeenie a tour, so we'll leave you be." He put his arm around Maxine's shoulders and led her toward the door.

"Rufulito," Lila called after them, typing the space bar repeatedly. "*Por favor, no te olvides de* Mrs. Cohen's write-up. *Y también*—the receipts for the syringes delivered today. You can bring them here before we leave for *la comida esta noche*."

"Not a problem, Commander."

"*Seis en punto agudo, mi hijo, porque* Lenore will have our roast *fuera del horno a las siete*. Please don't lose track of the time, *mi hijo. Por favor.*"

Lila Alvarez was a shrewd woman. After her son had closed the door behind him, she dialed Lenore and told her to hold the roast and to plan on a simple fry-up for her lone supper that evening.

Dr. Ruf meanwhile continued his magisterial tour of the grounds, introducing Maxine to several of the kindly and kempt staff, and, after giving her a brief overview of his lesson plans for the next few weeks, he led her back to the quietest wing, the one with the vacant suites. These lovely and private retreats, while arguably wasteful from a purely business perspective, served both of them exceedingly well in those early days. Occasionally they'd work first in Dr. Ruf's office, or work on a patient in the clinic, but they'd almost inevitably end up deciding that work could better be accomplished in one of these isolated alcoves. Moreover, because Maxine was, indeed, a natural, and mastered everything quickly, as the months passed, there was considerably less working—and considerably more retreating.

The retreating part was sublime. Nothing in her life before or since had approached the thrill that came from being the object of this great man's devotion, or from having the power to drive and control such a man and to divert his attention from his work to you. How utterly different this was from her increasingly dreaded, degrading encounters with Toad, the only other man she had ever known so intimately, Toad and his reptilian sliminess. At first she hadn't known any better with him, or any differently, and for the first year or so satisfaction of curiosity itself was enough to give her a degree of pleasure. More recently, however, and certainly since Dennis had arrived, relations with Toad had become more what she imagined a "bad trip" would be in the drug culture: a hint of ecstasy, perhaps, a few tingles and taunts mechanically stimulated, but anything hinting of sustained pleasure quickly tainted by vivid visions, sometimes palpable, of snakes and lizards, eels, serpents, and oozing frogs descending upon her, crawling about her skin, and repeatedly, unrelentingly inflicting their slimy selves against, upon, and inside her. There was no delicacy or sublimity here; even a kiss was an oblivious thrust of rapacious serpent breaking through her tightened lips, licking her stilled tongue, scraping its scum against her teeth, joyless, loveless, predatory, venomous even, deadening any vague hint of pleasure in her and filling her with a nearly irresistible impulse to bite down and sever the creature forever.

Rufus Alvarez was a different matter entirely. "Ah, lips juicier, and more luscious, than cherry plums," he had pronounced to her early on, simply leaning over her and reverently, respectfully, and, seemingly guilelessly, studying the contours of her face with his index finger. Dr. Ruf never failed to find some striking, utterly convincing, and seemingly personal way to extol the loveliness of her idiosyncrasies, whether her particular skin tone, hair color, fingers, or even aroma and taste. His attentive words, gaze, and touch all made it abundantly clear that she was the essence of womanhood and of beauty.

"You're roundabout thirty, isn't that so?," he had said to her, early on. "The perfect age in a woman, in my opinion. Young girls, with their baby fat and vapidity, don't even begin to approach this exquisite beauty, when form and substance become one, potential becomes actuality. Only at maturity do you see a face like this—cheekbones at last defined, a countenance made irresistible and mysterious with its vague hint of sorrow."

No one, and certainly not Toad, had ever spoken to her this way. She did not know how to reply, nor did she have the vocabulary to counter or challenge him. Still, the enigmatic smile he produced in her seemed only to add to her appeal.

The only occasional spoiler was her recurring doubt that Rufus Alvarez wanted her the same way she wanted him. This was a man so unapproachably perfect that, in spite of his beautiful and sometimes inscrutable words, she sometimes found it hard to fathom what he saw in her. His painful attractiveness of face, body, and soul were troubling enough, but the real concern was her unremitting sense that he lived on some enchanted plain that she could never approach. This sense easily morphed into uncomfortable insecurity that undermined her ability to abandon herself to him thoroughly, a feat that she believed required not only a suspension of disbelief in general but more specifically an absolute acceptance that some other creature authentically desired you as much as you desired him. Dr. Ruf was as brilliant as they come, naturally quick about everything (nothing escaped his attention—her new scarf, the distinct line separating the Indian from the Atlantic Ocean, the subtle shift from submission to surliness in George, his colored driver) and impeccably educated, too, frequently spouting off quotations from poets and philosophers the way Toad spouted off football scores. Of course, he had his medical training as well, and kept himself up-to-date in the literature, not narrowly like so many prunish scientists did, but across the board in skin care, dermatology as a whole, and even internal medicine. His office had framed copies of the papers he had published in the top journals, too, read by practicing dermatologists throughout the world. Here he was with her, a woman without a university degree, certification in cosmetology, yes, but hardly of his league. Dr. Ruf had read everything, been everywhere, knew how to eat foods whose names she couldn't even pronounce, choose a wine with aplomb, dress in silk ties that cost more than her weekly income, and walk in such a way that you'd think waters parted before him on the streets. The only way she knew how to respond to his worldliness was to keep her mouth shut a good part of the time, an uncharacteristic behavior but the only tactic guaranteed to keep her from revealing her utter ignorance.

After a while she began to understand that Rufus Alvarez, however godlike, got something from her as well. Uneducated and unworldly she may have been, but he was clever and perhaps old enough to appreciate a disciple. He fronted the money when she wanted to convert her hair salon into a skin care clinic, and wordlessly, non-judgmentally accepted her paltry repayments month after month, year after year. An hour back home or at work was also enough to remind her that she had herself a prince, or perhaps it was a knight in shining armor, someone so many cuts above the other men she knew that she did him a disservice casting aspersions on his motives and character. Everything suggested that he was as pure in his devotion to her as in his obvious devotion to his work. It wasn't like he was cheating on a spouse (she couldn't say as much for herself). The man lived and had always lived with his mother, for crying out loud, a sweet old lady, long ago divorced, who clearly devoted her life to her adored son.

Furthermore, the clandestine nature of their relationship

was her doing, not his. That they met only once a month was a reflection first of her married status, and, later, after she had purged Toad from her life, of the realities of being a single working mum with two school-aged children. She was not about to bring a man into her bed with young Dennis and Dodie still at home, and she wasn't about to go off gallivanting into the night while the children still needed goodnight kisses.

Then, too, she understood that she was warm and loving, fresh and kind in her own way, a way that some of the more hardened women in his circles couldn't ever be. And there was a side of the man that, although publicly brilliant and outspoken, was privately shy and withdrawn, painfully so. This side included the middle-aged man who lived with his mother, who had never married or formally committed to a woman, and who poured himself into work rather than relationships. To this side of Rufus Alvarez she understood herself to be a source of pure and easy joy, someone who gave love without making demands, or so she saw it.

She also recognized, whenever self-doubt crept upon her, that Dr. Ruf, like all men, craved young flesh and variety, and although she was hardly a spring chicken (and a mum to boot) he was, after all, 12 years her senior. She did not find this particular thought comforting, but she reminded herself that he genuinely seemed to desire her specifically, and on a regular and long-term basis. Besides, she often thought to herself, "No one has ever adored me like this before—except perhaps my mother, in those few months before I opened my mouth."

CHAPTER SEVEN

"Follow the rules, Dodie. She can't stay here."

Randall wasn't even looking at her. He was siphoning water from their backyard rain barrel into several spray bottles lined up along his workbench, trying to start the flow by erratically twisting and lifting the tubing that ran into the yard through the wall.

"That's why the shelter system was set up." He shook the tubing harder and batted it with his fingertip until at last a weak but steady stream began flowing into a bottle.

"I don't think you understand," she said. "We need to discuss this. Now."

"Dodie, everything's going to freeze soon. You know I have to get the water inside while I can."

"This very second?"

Of all Randall's greenhouse rituals and indulgences, Dodie hated the rainwater collection the most. She understood that rainwater was probably more effective, or, as he put it, less "stressful" for the plants than chemical-laden tap water, at least in theory, but it was beyond her how this particular liquid could possibly be preferable given that it had travelled through the notoriously polluted Annapolis atmosphere, traversed their sap-laden yard, and then festered outside for days, sometimes weeks, in a splintery, mildewed container. Randall insisted that all the organic debris, including the dust and pollen that collected in the water as it passed through the air, was natural, and thus good for his orchids. She suggested that standing water in the backyard only bred mosquitoes. In fact, his obliviousness to the West Nile virus endemic infuriated her. If he didn't care about the community, didn't he at least care about her, or the children? Or himself?

Officially, the man was in charge of the health and wellness of human beings, a public spokesperson for the school system, but for years the only health and wellness that had concerned him was that of his orchids. Orchids were so much more compliant than children, she supposed, and there were no administrators and politicians involved trying to raise their test scores to save public face.

Randall had built the greenhouse himself about the time that Margaret was born. Dodie had opposed it from the start. Flowers should not be cultivated—their beauty was innate. If she was ever to devote herself to some sort of gardening project, or put her time into anything other than people, it would be wildflowers. She would scatter the seeds all over the lawn and let them do what they would. To cultivate and cull beauty outside of nature, as he did, blinded you to the beauty that was already around you, in the trees, in the bay, in the rivers, even in the faces. All this fuss of his was a waste of time, and futile to boot, since to her mind the natural beauty of the world around them could never be matched.

Even wildflowers required free time for a bit of planning and tilling, however, and giving up free time was something Dodie regarded as her penance for having a job, children, house, and husband. Thus, she had settled for a row of calla lilies along the front walkway. These were officially cultivated flowers (though often considered a weed back in

South Africa), and thus not quite to her tastes, but still, they were wild in aspect and required very little care once in the ground.

Meanwhile, Randall built the greenhouse for himself, and, as the years passed became increasingly obsessed by it, to the point where she teased him about getting a port-a-potty so that he'd never have to leave his domain, which pretty much met every other conceivable need. At first glance it seemed like little more than an add-on greenhouse, accessible from the kitchen via what had once served as their back door and filled, as one might expect, with rows of potted plants, orchids in various stages of bloom, watering cans, and pans of charcoal, fir bark chips, and sphagnum moss. But over the years it had grown into a full-fledged chemistry laboratory as well, replete with test tubes, a microscope, gel plates, pH testing strips, magnifying glasses, and distilled water, as well as a library with monographs, photographs, and a computer; a kitchen with an old refrigerator and cookplate; and a garbage dump where fluorescent light boxes and discarded plastic bags that once held fertilizer and gravel sat for months before being hauled to the street.

The only compelling reasons Randall had to return to the original house were to sleep and use the bathroom. He did appear for occasional parental and marital tasks, but she often suspected this was more out of a sense of duty than desire. Even the sleeping bit was optional ever since Randall had put a cot in the greenhouse for the nights he had to time irrigations or move plants in from the cold at dawn. It was on this very cot that she now hoped to settle Shelley, given that Maxine's time clock was ticking, and they had still found no better place for her to be.

"Well, hello, my fierce-faced beauty," Randall said,

approaching his prized lavender *Recchara*, his water bottles now filled to satisfaction. He fingered the flower's showy, flared labellum. "I see you are hungry again."

Randall poured some of his newly collected rainwater around the roots and then, after checking the soil, sprinkled a bit more, followed by a few sprays of fertilizer. His devotion to the flowers panged Dodie, not in small part because he tended to regard them as his harem, and, worse, because she understood this regard: she had always viewed orchids as a strikingly immodest, even obscene, species, flashing as they did their private parts to the world and being widely praised and acclaimed for doing so. However, the display of this particular bloom leaned more to the comical than the alluring, with a labellum that looked more than anything like a clown with a make-shift beard pasted to its chin.

"Randall, did you hear me?"

"Of course I did. And my answer is no. At some point you have to draw the line between home and work."

"All I'm asking is that she stay here a week or two—until she recovers enough to fight her own case."

Dodie had tried to explain to Randall that shuttling Shelley back and forth between a safe house and the salon wasn't working, but apparently he was incapable of hearing her. How much of a sacrifice would it be to house a desperate woman with nowhere else to go?

"Don't you understand? I've got enough on my head right now."

"This wouldn't be on your head, Randall. I'd do the heavy lifting. You wouldn't have to do anything, or change anything—even the sheets!"

He stopped spraying and turned to her, his face purpling.

"The state's breathing down our necks. *My* neck. The last thing I need is a battered stowaway—with Rocco Herkimer on her case."

"The state? I thought this was a county thing."

Randall's face was engorged, the way it always got when he was overheated. She could see coils of sweat worming down the sides of his neck, collecting under the band at the top of his t-shirt. Potting and puttering under fluorescent lights was his latter-day equivalent of boyhood lacrosse escapades. Although he worked up a good sweat from it, indoor gardening in middle age yielded far less corporeal benefit than had running down fields and clubbing classmates at age 17. Whatever flesh had once comprised his massive chest and shoulders had shifted up around his neck and down around his gut—though, at 6'2", the overall bulk suggested strength from a distance, particularly when he neatly packed his gut inside an oversize sports jacket. Much like men who comb over their balding pates see virile Elvis-like waves when they look in the mirror, so Randall assumed his youthful athleticism when he strode the halls of county schools.

"It *is* a county thing," Randall told her. "But according to that *Sun* reporter, and a bunch of butt-in-ski parents, the county is violating state code. Obviously MSDE can't sanction us doing something illegal."

"Illegal?"

"In a manner of speaking, yes. *Slightly* illegal."

"Slightly illegal? Is that like being 'a little bit pregnant'?"

"COMAR regulations state that all students in grades K-8 must be provided with PE instruction every year. And we don't do that in this county. We haven't since 1973."

"So it *is* illegal. I don't see any ambiguity there."

"The kids can take PE if they choose. So it's kind of

ambiguous."

"That's not what 'must' means, Randall. If they '*must* be provided with instruction,' then there's no ambiguity whatsoever."

"I know that."

Dodie pulled a stool up to one of the benches and put her head in her hands. The flicker of the fluorescent lights often gave her a headache, although this time she wasn't sure if the problem was the lights or Randall himself. What drove her out of her skull with him was his absolute inability to be outraged. Whereas her *modus vivendi* was to find heinous offenses everywhere, and rage against them, his was generally to acknowledge them and go on with his life. He hadn't always been like this. He had once been a passionate crusader for the sound mind in the sound body, the "vigorous" life, he had called it. He had once even spearheaded a lunch hour walkathon, recruiting otherwise slothful preadolescents into encircling the school's athletic field for about 15 minutes a day and distributing tokens every time they "passed go," tokens that could be traded in for Frisbees, bracelets, markers, water bottles, headphones, gift certificates, software, and even, for one overachiever, a camcorder.

The program was so successful that it spread countywide, written up in both the *Sun* and *Capital* as a breakthrough means of giving couch potato preteens something more productive to do after lunch than shame and skewer their peers. Soon after Randall's promotion to assistant principal, however, his crusading spirit began dissipating, and it was gone completely by the time he started working at the central office.

These days, the only "vigor" that seemed to matter to him was hybrid vigor. The thrill of re-blooming one of his *oncidia* or *dendrobia* had long ago replaced the thrill he once got from stuffing the ball or blocking a pass, and what seemed to drive him was not so much the beauty of his flowers but rather the power that came from creating that beauty, specifically from creating new hybrid varieties with even bigger, brighter, and more abundant blooms. Whenever she thought about this she felt a raging, but, thus far, unexpressed, desire to shake him silly.

Randall attributed this change to maturity and experience. Things were more complicated than he had once thought, he often explained to her. Change took time, change inconvenienced people, and change had to be managed skillfully. Dodie understood all this, but she still didn't understand how he had lost the gut-level recognition that change had to happen, even if the fight had to be quieter and well-finessed.

That fight had been beaten out of Randall years ago, leaving Dodie to deplore what she thought of as Randall's "insufferable thinness." Despite his obvious physical girth, he lacked the low-burning flame that drove even the most seasoned realists to continue a crusade and, worse, showed no signs of the courage and subversiveness that had brought them together. These were qualities that they had shared, and, in fact, that had made working at Central Middle School even slightly endurable. They had both been very young (he in his early twenties, she not out of her teens, and interning), rebels and free-thinkers in spirit, but forced by public school pretension, insecurity, and insularity to operate under the assumption that anything a child said or did was inherently misguided, conniving, and/or destructive. Instinctively identifying more with the students than the administration, they found in each other partners in crime, thumbing their noses at rules, though rarely detectably. The first time they had kissed had been in the ball closet of Randall's gym. They had both known all the while that this was an abomination for which the children themselves were vigorously policed. They had also both known this flagrant act could itself have led to immediate termination. She still remembered the many times they had to suppress their amusement when Randall ceremoniously hauled one child or another into her office to report some far less heinous offense. As their relationship developed, the ball closet became the venue for a variety of more consequential transgressions, ones that were never quite as intoxicating once they had moved to his more civilized bedroom.

That Randall had died years ago, or, at least, grown up. She thought of Wendy at the very end of *Peter Pan*, the book she had just finished reading to the boys. Wendy, now married with a child of her own, was far too old and practical to go flying off to Neverland to do Peter's "spring cleaning." Randall, similarly, no longer lived to subvert stupidity, battle oppression, or fix the world, but rather to tend his own garden, both literally and figuratively. "Dodie is saving the world for the both of us," he often said to friends. "You can't do that through the public schools, contrary to popular belief."

Perhaps she should have seen this coming when he was promoted into administration, but until recently she had been too ensnared by her own routine to notice, much less care. He had, indeed, become "the man," and had forgotten what it was like to be the little guy. He now had the respect he never had in the classroom, he had a pension coming, and he had just enough taste of power to shut off his own perspective and redirect his energies toward the fulfillment of his employer's dreams. Worse, he brought this new persona home with him each night. When he walked through the door, it was more like the return of her father than her lover—all the fun came to an abrupt halt. On the rare moments Dodie bothered to think about this situation, she hated herself for allowing it to continue. But she did nothing. She supposed she had never left him largely because she was too stubborn. Or was it too unambitious?

She reminded herself that Randall didn't beat her, nor expect much of her. He didn't demand clean dishes, or even home-cooked meals for that matter, and he respected her work. He didn't demean her, insult her, force her into doing anything she didn't want to do or be anything she didn't want to be. That was abuse, coercion, the kind of thing that got her clients into shelters. And yet she sometimes couldn't help but feel that Randall coerced her anyway, coerced her into keeping the house in at least a modicum of order, coerced her into providing meals (even microwaved ones) for the family, coerced her into keeping track of who had homework or lessons or Hebrew School or soccer practice, who had a dentist's appointment, and who had taken Zyrtec or needed a new prescription for albuterol. She felt especially coerced because Randall didn't know or even care about any of these things, just assumed she'd take care of, or care about, them while he went on and cared only about his seedlings.

She was not self-pitying about it. She knew full well that she had it better than Shelley, or any of the sheltered women. She knew she had it good, in fact, so far as modern married lives go. She even believed that Randall loved her, or loved having her there for him, and that he loved that she did all the things she did. And yet she felt no more capable of extricating herself from the coercion inherent in all relationships between men and women than did Shelley or any of her clients.

The love, even the lack of overt abuse, was not enough to free her. Would anything be enough? Perhaps the problem wasn't that men coerced women into lives they didn't want, she thought, or that men, even the most well-meaning of them, robbed women of their freedom and autonomy. Perhaps the problem was the women themselves. Could it be that even the freest of women, of which she considered herself to be an example, robbed themselves of their own liberty? Could it be that men, ultimately, had little or nothing to do with it? It was a depressing idea, one she would have to mull over when she had more time—as if she would ever have more time!

Randall did still seem to enjoy talking to, or, rather, at her, but unless they were solving a practical problem, their conversations tended to be one-sided disquisitions in which she silently listened to him denigrate co-workers, belabor the persnickety Royal Horticultural Society, or ramble about the "prigs" on the hybridizer's forum and their insane "drive for yellow" in their blooms.

He could froth for hours about the exquisite pink labellum of his Showy Lady Slipper or complain bitterly about the sexual deceptiveness of the *Orphrys,* which doomed his dream of hybridizing his Dancing Dolls with his Mirrors of Venus. On her part, however, she had nothing much to say to him, and even less desire to say it, unless they were dissecting a child's behavior or negotiating a new carpet color. When the kids were grown and the house complete, Dodie feared there would be nothing left to say at all.

She had a taste of this nothingness when Margaret, Lawrence, and William spent a week with Randall's parents the past summer. Night after night she had returned to a bleakly neat house, set to work on a meal, and, an hour later, found herself sitting across from Randall riddled by a sad, sinking emptiness, almost to the point of weeping. Willful effort allowed her to respond amicably about the day, parse the nutritional value of the food, and rue the vastness of that month's electricity bill, but all through dinner she had a recurring awareness that nothing was ever to be hoped for again. She flashed back on meals almost identical to this one with Randall before the children were born, meals at which she had cooked the same chicken Florentine for two and luxuriated in having the empty time to savor a whole bottle of wine with it, but back then she had felt buoyed by the unconscious anticipation of surprise, change, children, challenge.

Now everything anticipated had become history, and she no longer saw Randall as a source of all that was fresh and wondrous. How was it, she asked herself, that the moment you stopped being young you started being old? She saw nothing ahead but more long pointless dinners with the same pointless and contrived conversation, punctuated by the unspoken visions of decline, loneliness, and, eventually, unfathomable and unconquerable pain.

She looked up from the workbench to see Randall painstakingly scooping perlite into empty shoeboxes. "Randall. I'm just talking about a few days here. A week or two at most."

He stopped scooping. "Dodie, look. It's always you who has to put herself on the line. Let someone else take her— let your mother take her for God's sake. The last thing I need right now is to stir up more water."

"You won't be stirring. As I said...."

"My job is already on the line. Scapegoating is the school board's number one hobby, and I'm the goat staring right into their headlights."

"Interesting way of putting it."

"Whatever....If you don't care about me, Dodie, think of the mortgage, the car payments, the kids—think of yourself!"

"If you just explain the situation to them...." The words slipped out spontaneously, but she stopped herself. He was right. There was little recourse for logic and evidence in a system where dead or dying idealism and courage were endemic. So many board members had begun as militants or rebels, no less so than Randall or herself, fighting for new gyms or asbestos removal or textbooks. Just like Randall, however, once elevated to positions of authority and spoon-fed carefully honed, partisan information from the friendly educrats trying to protect their positions, they inevitably became lobotomized defenders of the status quo.

"You've got to stop thinking you're a kid with no responsibilities," he told her. "Grow up."

"I'm trying to, Randall. I'm trying to put my own needs aside and help someone. I *thought* that *was* what it meant to be grown up."

"Dodie. Please. Rocco Herkimer's been good to the schools. He just got the council to fund two new Astroturf fields and shook extra facilities funds out of the state."

She watched Randall methodically fill each of the shoeboxes with bulbs he had dried under the lights at back of his workbench.

"Are those my calla lilies, Randall?"

"Yes, it was time to take them in before the frost hit. I dug them up this afternoon—it's not easy. I never know where you've buried them."

"Well...thank you."

"I'm not even sure it's really necessary to take them in, Dodie, what with global warming. But I'm not willing to take a chance."

She stood behind him and watched as he inspected each bulb and placed it carefully into the bag. He did this every fall for her, dug up the bulbs and stored them until he could replant them in the spring. She would have let them die outside, not out of spite but out of negligence. She lowered her head and let it rest on his shoulder.

"I'll put them in the garage for you," he said. "It's too humid in here for them."

"Thank you."

She went to get a sponge and pushed the dirt that the bulbs had left on the workbench into her hand. He smiled at her, and she smiled back, thinking that perhaps he was right after all. Maybe she was a perpetual adolescent. Something just hadn't shut off in her that seemed to have shut off in everyone else. Life would be considerably easier if she could just go through the motions and fulfill her daily duties without worrying so much about whether things were right or just, logical or important. Perhaps she was too quick to blame him when it was she who refused to move forward— or, really, when it was simply the time in their lives when such things were to be expected. As Peter Pan had observed in that cold, heartless way of youth, they were both simply "too grown up to fly." It was probably unrealistic, after all, to expect to be in love past the age of 20 or 25. Being in love took a sort of credibility and blankness that rubbed off after a couple of decades. She knew far too much about life today to believe that anyone else, or anything she could create with anyone else, was all that amazing or fresh or new. Perhaps she could feel something, at least a fleeting reawakening with a new person, routine, or approach, or even feel something with the idea of wooing or being wooed, but she doubted she'd ever again feel anything approximating that sustaining, breathless, magical whoosh that propelled her through every moment in those first months with Randall.

Besides, there was no time. When she was younger, she had no one but herself to think of. Neither of them had anyone but themselves. The open, limitless future was an aphrodisiac, and back then it had felt like nothing ever was or had been or would be, except themselves and some enchanted little space—his bedroom, her couch, a secluded cove off the bay, or even the fetid floor of the ball closet. As long as they were together, they were invincible explorers, the very first two to wander this strange, lush, wonderful world that they created whenever they touched. They could still create a world, but it was a world shrunken by a huge order of magnitude, finite, ordinary, even desolate, and the process of creation often a joyless inconvenience, at its worst a duty and its best a briefly pleasurable call of nature.

She wrung the sponge out in the sink. Randall had finished bagging the calla lilies and was staring at the ceiling fan.

"This thing is blowing too fast."

"Just shut it off for a while. It's freezing in here."

"It's not for our comfort, Dodie...." He unfolded a stepstool and placed it under the fan. "I can never remember how that little string works."

"I'll see you later, Randall."

"Where are you going?"

She realized that she didn't know. And then it came to her: "I'm going to the salon. To check on Shelley. Just make sure the boys get to bed by nine."

"Okay. Fine." He proceeded up the stepladder to fiddle with the string.

She took the shoeboxes of calla lilies off the workbench.

"I'll bring these out to the garage on my way."

Just being out of the house made her feel lighter, freer. Her headache was gone, and once again she knew what she was doing. She stopped at Boston Market and picked up enough food to last Shelley several nights. She decided that she'd call some of the shelters on the Eastern Shore and in Baltimore County first thing in the morning—maybe they could move Shelley out of the county temporarily until she had more time to heal. This still might not be possible for a few days, but, with a plan in place, or even in the works, she couldn't imagine Maxine not being amenable. Maxine, unlike Randall, liked adventure, as long as she was allowed her due share of kvetching along the way. At least Dodie hoped so, since, clearly, Randall was not going to budge. She would discuss possibilities with Shelley tonight, and then, perhaps, she could stop by Maxine's condo on her way home. It would be harder for Maxine to say no in person.

Dodie was shocked, however, when she walked into the salon to find Maxine herself, sitting behind the receptionist's desk and presiding over a bottle of chardonnay. Shelley was sitting on the loveseat, sipping a glass of wine herself and looking considerably more animated than Dodie had ever seen her.

"Why, hello there, my sweet," said Maxine. "Come join us."

"Maxine. What are you doing here on a Sunday night?"

"I forgot my address book—so forgetful these days, you know? I wanted to phone up Dennis this evening and couldn't find my numbers. I don't suppose I could offer you a glass?"

Dodie remained just inside the door and shook her head. The dizziness of wine was yet another part of her life she had packed up forever. She supposed something must truly be wrong with her, but she had recently realized that she simply didn't enjoy the taste or the effect of alcohol, never had. In the past year or so, she found it left her heart pounding and ears ringing to boot and had decided to give it up entirely. Her primary reason for drinking at that point in life was for nothing more than social peace, which seemed a fairly stupid reason to drink, but once she had quit it was astounding to discover how much peace drinking had indeed brought her, and how much distress and discomfort she averted in others by just quietly accepting and sipping and pretending to enjoy the implied dissipation. No wonder teenagers continued to drink. The human being clearly had some kind of need to put itself in an altered, giddy state—alcohol, hallucinogens, or similar substances had a vital place in virtually every known civilization—but, for whatever reason, she failed to share this need with the rest of the species. Was she more highly evolved, or sadly blocked from accessing the full range of human experience?

"You don't know Dennis's number by heart? Your own son?"

"You know my memory, sugar plum. Besides, your friend Shelley and I have just had a delightful little talk. Come join us—we'll tell you all about it."

CHAPTER EIGHT

It had mainly been Utzi the Iceman's idea. Incredible, Maxine had mused, considering the old rover's uselessness, but every so often he showed signs of the solid common sense and intelligence that he typically tried so hard to hide. She generally regarded the man as a dope, albeit an amicable one, when it came to practical matters, but she was pleased to report to Dodie and Shelley that he had come up with the basic arrangement on his own, the business aspects of it and all. "I have to give the old boy credit," she told them. "It's a good idea."

They had been out on their Friday night date, a week after Maxine had first discovered Shelley hidden in her supply closet. Maxine had left the office at two o'clock promptly but instead of beginning with the usual hot soak, had indulged herself in a good long nap—to compensate for her sleeplessness earlier that week, from which she had never recovered. At five she checked with the Iceman to make sure he had made reservations at Yellowfin. He had orders to make their weekly restaurant reservations no later than Wednesday night, Annapolis restaurants being impossibly busy on so many weekends of the year, particularly in the fall, but seven times out of ten he forgot to do so without her friendly reminders. Besides, she had to get him revved up for the evening, as, now and then, he lost track of time. "This drives me bonkers, as you might imagine. I ask very little of him. Clearly, the little I ask pushes him beyond his miniscule limits."

What Maxine didn't tell Shelley and Dodie was that, in spite of all her complaining, she was basically content with their arrangement because the Iceman was good company and, in all fairness, he asked very little of her either. On their standing Friday night date, they went to one of several favorite restaurants, with dinner usually involving fresh seafood or steaks and a good bottle of wine. She didn't remember how the deal had evolved, but both of them understood that each week, usually on Monday or Tuesday, she picked the restaurant and let him know that he was to reserve a table no later than Wednesday. At the restaurant, he paid, and, if he limited his alcohol intake enough to drive, he could accompany her home and stay the night. His track record here was about fifty-fifty, but this was fine with her: she had limited interest in intimacy with old grizzly sots, and going through the motions with dignity these days took so much effort. Now and then she found him to be sweet and amusing, enough to stoke up some vestigial desire, and occasionally, she had to admit, even enjoyed both his company and his body. But these occasions were increasingly rare.

That night, however, he had been on target. Perhaps it had been his old military influences that inspired him to rise to a crisis, but when Maxine had explained the Shelley situation to him, he had an almost immediate answer: "Make lemonade out of lemons, Zeenie."

"What precisely do you mean, sir?"

"What I mean is that you've got it made. This lady clearly needs your help. And you need hers. So work out an arrangement." He went on to explain that Maxine had the ability to transform Shelley into anything she imagined, and certainly someone unrecognizable to Rocco Herkimer and his legions. At the same time, Shelley apparently had the ability to answer phones and file papers (an ability that he assumed anyone breathing had), and since she needed to loaf around the salon anyway, she might as well be put to work.

"Shelley is your new Carole, my dear. That's all. If she doesn't work out, you can always chuck her. But for now, fix her up, and let her fix you up as well." He downed his second glass of Johnny Walker in a swallow and held the empty vessel up to her.

He was so cocky she felt like splashing her chardonnay into his face. However, she raised her glass to his and let him clink it triumphantly. She did not relish the idea of doing major and uncompensated work on Shelley—and it would take considerable time and materials to do the kind of job required—but the idea of having someone there on Monday to take over Carole's duties made her giddy. For the first time in two weeks she felt that ephemeral ease that sometimes filled her when a creditor inexplicably decided that she was, after all, in the right, or when a particularly obnoxious client abruptly stopped making appointments. A sudden, unexpected solution—it almost made her feel blessed. She felt so good, in fact, that she thought she might even let the Iceman come home with her tonight, however much he drank, and even if he wasn't willing to rewire her torchier as she had been asking him to do all month.

Dodie liked the idea from the start, if only because it *was* an idea. The idea of taking Shelley back to Safe Port was unthinkable, and yet Florence, Safe Port's executive director, had all but ordered her to do so last Wednesday, as soon as Shelley Slavin's whereabouts came to her attention. Florence had called Dodie into her office first thing that morning and talked to her in a way she had never done before—as a teacher to a student, or a parent to child, rather than one colleague to another. Taking a client into her own hands, outside the system, was not only questionable ethically but quite obviously dangerous. In fact, Florence had hinted to Dodie that her job was on the line for this. It was simply not procedure for staff to make these kinds of decisions unilaterally. Dodie had explained, although she knew it wasn't completely true, that it was Shelley herself who had insisted on leaving Safe Port, since it was obvious that Rocco had tracked her down there. Given the immediate threat, Dodie had decided that an emergency unilateral decision was warranted.

She also told Florence, quite truthfully this time, that the evening before, upon leaving for dinner, she had almost thought Rocco Herkimer had returned. As she walked down Safe Port's front walkway toward the street, she had heard a rustle in the bushes and then a sound like the whine of a digital camera. She had hurried to her car, which, this time, she had managed to park only several houses down the street from the shelter. She didn't look back until she was in the driver's seat with the doors locked. But when she drove around the block and waited at the light on the corner, she had seen the white Jaguar in her rear view mirror.

"Do you really think it was him?" asked Florence.

"That car's pretty distinctive. I didn't see the plates, but there aren't that many white Jaguars around."

Florence sniffed and shook her head. "C'mon. How dumb can he be?"

"What? We're talking serious personality disorder here, Florence. He believes he's above the law, right? You know the type."

"We can get a restraining order against him, a peace order, for you, too, Dodie. If he's stalking you, I mean."

"I can't pin anything on him this time. Maybe I just imagined the camera thing. I'm a little on edge these days."

"Well, given your position, and the people involved—I'm not surprised. I just don't understand why you didn't come to me about this." She batted her left thumb repeatedly against the edge of her desk, the way she always did when she was about to reprimand someone. "Don't ever do that again. You know that's not how we work."

Dodie nodded, and Florence brought the thumb to a stop by clenching it inside her fist.

"In any case, you will not be leaving here again without an escort. I'll talk to security. We should probably implement that policy for everyone, come to think of it."

"Florence, I'm concerned about the sanctity of Safe Port altogether. If he knows the location—it's only a matter of time."

"There I disagree with you. Even if he knows, which I guess he does, plenty of shelters are public. Some even have websites with names, contact information. You might even argue we're unnecessarily cautious here."

"They have better funding, better security."

"Yes....We'd have to shut down, move anyway, if the address got out."

"I don't think he's going to broadcast it. Not right now anyway. The last thing Delegate Herkimer wants is his name associated with a battered woman's shelter—assuming he's sane, which, as I was saying, may be a mistaken assumption."

"No kidding. He's stalking us in a Jaguar, Dodie. Anyway, at the very least I'm getting that escort system going right now."

Florence had had no better luck than Dodie finding a place for Shelley. The shelter network was crammed to the gills, and even if someone had a bed, no one wanted to take on a medical case like Shelley, who still needed a fair amount of skilled nursing care. Dodie thus decided to tell Florence that Shelley was "all taken care of," implying that she had found a friend or relative to care for her until she recovered. She knew that if she had told her the truth that Florence would have ordered her, probably tearfully, to send Shelley home, or, at best, to social services, which would be useless, as usual. Florence was a warm person, decent and even destructively sentimental at heart, but, Dodie also knew that—like Randall, and like everyone who rose to positions of power—Florence was slavishly devoted to rules and that all her actions stemmed from the terror that she would lose her fiefdom from violating them. Dodie admired and respected Florence in almost every way, but she also knew that she would never again grasp that the end sometimes justified the means.

"I think Utzi's idea is fabulous!" said Dodie to Maxine and Shelley as soon as they described it to her. "Brilliant! Where will she sleep, though? She can't keep using your waiting room as a boudoir."

"That air mattress I use with your children," said Maxine. "That was the best gift you ever gave me. Ingenious! It takes 30 seconds with an air pump."

"I hate to be so much in the way," said Shelley.

"You'll set the mattress up each night in the supply room and put it away before I arrive. It won't be a bother at all then. The bathroom is all set—just clean up after yourself, which would be part of your job anyway. Now, Dodie, why don't you run along to my place and get the things so she can sleep more comfortably. Bring a pillow and linens. Sheets, pillowcase, blanket, towels, face cloths, and so forth. And more bandages, whatever salve you're using, and ibuprofen. We have everything else here. Go on, now! She must get her rest because I have scads of work for her tomorrow. Carole has left us with a mess of unpaid bills—bedlam! And we'll have to call and reschedule quite a few clients to make this work. *Ag*...get on with you now. Is there a reason you're both staring at the walls?"

Dodie squeezed Shelley's hand. Then she smiled for what she thought must have been the first time in weeks, and the three of them set themselves to work.

CHAPTER NINE

Maxine could not abide an unfixed face. And clearly Shelley needed some fixing. Maxine realized that the kind of transformation required couldn't be achieved overnight, but she could make major inroads if she devoted weekends and occasional evenings to Shelley. She would have to use almost every cosmetologic skill she had, even those she hadn't practiced in years, from cutting and dying the hair, to removing the broken capillaries, to needling the scars and lines, to, of course, applying a heavy dose of permanent makeup. Completing the latter project would take considerably more time, and it couldn't begin until the latest wounds had healed. Still, she suspected that the superficial changes in the first month alone would be enough to convince Shelley to stay on long enough to master the receptionist's job, as well as, she hoped, to stay on indefinitely, since training new receptionists topped Maxine's list of bugaboos. Shelley, she promised, would not only be beautiful, but, more importantly in this particular case, unrecognizable.

Shelley's end of the deal was this: She would start out working in the supply room with the label "temp" if anyone asked, sorting boxes and then, as soon as possible, move on to filing the bills that Carole had left undone for so many months, taking messages, setting and rescheduling appointments, and explaining basic operations of the salon to potential and new clients calling for information. Once she felt stronger, she would also be expected to clean the bathroom and kitchen, as long as she kept out of the way while doing so—that was not the sort of activity one wanted the clients to notice. Coming to the salon was supposed to be an oasis, not an unpleasant reminder of duties neglected back home. Shelley was also, of course, to tidy up her own droppings and tracks from the start, no matter how she felt. It was essential that no one who entered the salon during office hours would suspect it housed an overnight guest or, perhaps worse, served as a hospital ward. Maxine agreed that under this plan Shelley could stay in the salon, day or night, until Dodie figured out what to do with her. She wasn't respectable enough for the clients to see, at least not yet, but Maxine felt she could take care of that particular obstacle within a few weeks. She planned to bring in donuts or muffins every morning, the two of them would order in lunch (as Maxine generally did anyway), and Dodie would stock the refrigerator with Lean Cuisines so that Shelley could microwave her dinner once Maxine had left. Dodie also brought over a stack of old paperbacks from the shelter that Shelley devoured with considerably more appetite than the food.

"Funny thing. I used to be in the makeup biz, too. Sort of, I mean. I didn't personally do the makeup," Shelley told Maxine, when the two of them were alone together for Shelley's first "consultation." Maxine had stayed on after hours to do this—it had been a fully booked day—but both of them were anxious to get started. And for Maxine there was no getting started without an initial consultation.

"What do you mean, dear? I thought you were in politics or whatnot."

"Rocco, my boyfriend, my...well, whatever he is. Was. He was...is...you know, in politics. But, he before got elected he...." She looked over her shoulder, presumably out of habit. "Well, maybe you've heard of 'Mr. Prepay to Lay.' You may have heard of him. On the news?"

"Can't say I have."

"It's a long story. Another county, maybe before you were here. But, anyway, that was Rocco, my infamous ex."

"What on earth does that mean: 'Prepay to Lay'? It sounds obscene."

"Not obscene, but definitely illegal. He ran a funeral home—among other things. Or I thought he did, anyway. That's what I meant about the makeup. Kind of a joke."

"I see."

"I did the accounting, and front office stuff. Not the makeup. Ugh. Fortunately, he didn't make me deal with the bodies." She looked over her shoulder again. "But there was some face fixing going on there, of course. Permanently, too, if you get my drift.

"I suppose." Several years ago Maxine had met a woman at a seminar who worked at a local morgue, applying makeup to corpses to mollify the bereaved. She had been astounded at the stories this woman told about the heroic efforts Americans demanded to combat the inevitable decay of the flesh, not only by pumping the body full of formaldehyde to stave off bacteria and suggest natural turgidity but by painting the faces and stuffing, gluing, pinning, and propping eyelids and lips to create preternatural vitality. "Now move your head like this, sweetpea," she told Shelley. "There you go. Now I can look at that eye better. My goodness, that's quite a bruising he gave you. It's still engorged."

"Actually there wasn't that much makeup. Or business

for that matter. Weird, huh? Death is usually a fail-safe business plan."

"There I'm with you."

"But, of course, now I understand why." Shelley went on to explain that Rocco hadn't been in the death business as much as in the embezzlement business. But she hadn't known that at the time, nor had she known that she had apparently been in the embezzlement business as well. Maxine marveled at the girl's willingness to spill the beans to a near-stranger, especially given all she had been through, but she quickly pegged Shelley as one of those chatterbox types desperately trying out every new acquaintance as a possible source of free psychological counsel. She had many such women as clients, and sometimes she wondered if this desperate need to share personal dilemmas was tied to the similarly desperate unhappiness, insecurity, and even, ultimately, loneliness that led them to seek her services. However, in Shelley's case, Maxine also recognized a keen intelligence and seasoned cynicism lurking under the skin of subservient insecurity and desperation, and she found herself curious to see how long it would take to surface.

"How long will it take? Fixing me up?"

"Oh, my dear, that I can't say. We'll start at the beginning and see what we must do. The hair—well, we can take care of that tonight. That's the easy part, of course. What color would you like to be?"

"I'd like to be what I am. Of course."

"Of course? Not many women say *that*, you know. I've met very few who don't loathe whatever it is they are. The blondes want to be dark, and the brunettes ginger. The gingers want to go fawn and have the freckles removed while you're at it. The naturally curly long for sleek and smooth, while the sleek and smooth yearn for body and wave. No one wants to be themselves. The grass is always greener." She handed Shelley the color cards. "What would you like?"

"I've never really thought about it. I like highlights, the shine they give my hair. I get those every six weeks. Without fail. Except lately, of course. Otherwise I have the hair of a mouse, really. But color? I don't know. It seems drastic. It wouldn't be me."

"Dearheart, I believe the situation you're in calls for drastic. Don't you? This is your chance to be the woman you've always dreamed of being. Why not go blonde? You're young enough to get away with it!...Hell, *I'm* young enough to get away with it. Or so my gentleman friend says."

"I'm not a blonde type."

"How do you know? Try it!"

"How about just a gentler brown maybe? I'm not that daring."

"It's your choice dear, and I must say that staying dark will certainly make the face easier—it's harder to go lighter, which we might want to do with your skin if you choose blonde. But you look through these pictures, and pick out whatever you like. There's no need to decide tonight if you're not ready. We can take care of the hair anytime. Now then, let's think about the face." Maxine ran her fingertips over Shelley's cheeks, lifted her chin and twisted her neck, and pushed back the bangs. She breathed deeply and slowly, palpating the scars on the forehead, the cheeks, and under the chin, and then scrutinized them with a handheld magnifying glass. "Yes," she said at last. "This will do. I can see you had your hands full as a teenager, didn't you? With the spots, I mean."

"Oh, God. I still get acne. Whoever said it was for

teenagers lived in la-la land."

"Oh, my dear, I've seen women in their fifties still battling spots. Those hormones still plague us for decades they do, and they have all sorts of new tricks. But, truly, it's worse in the younger years. You've got the battle scars to prove it—not to mention the ones your friend added."

Shelley winced. "At least I keep the foundation people in business."

"Not to worry. This is a perfect palate for some fabulous permanent makeup. Yes, indeed. We'll fill in the brows nicely—dark will work on you, so we can go ahead with the darker hair, if you choose. What happened here, incidentally? Many women your age have lost their brows by overplucking, but you've got one much fuller than the other."

"Cigarette."

"Cig...I see." Maxine kept Shelley's bangs uplifted with her left hand and massaged the scar on the forehead with her right. Shelley was, under all the scars, a natural beauty, blessed with high cheekbones, full lips, and a nose just misshapen enough to lend intrigue. Maxine imagined that she was the type of woman with the time and money that allowed her to clean up, or, rather, cover up, her scars quite well. She also had a smashing figure that you only found on women her age who had bypassed childbearing, and that undoubtedly helped draw eyes away from any blemishes that makeup couldn't fully cover.

"Ah, well, we'll have the brow and this area back for you soon enough. I do beautiful work with hypochromics. Have you glanced at the book yet? My portfolio out front? You need to check the one with the scar work. Many befores and afters, mind you, some where you can barely make out the marks even when you're searching for them. No one would see these things at a glance."

"I'll take a look."

"I've had client after client who would not go out in public without scarves, thick makeup, hair all over the place like yours, to cover things. Some of the women I've worked on have had scars on their bellies from childbirth, stretch marks and so forth, mind you, and they wouldn't wear bikinis. Or short sleeves if they had marks on the arms, as so many do after accidents and burns and so forth. And every one of them—it's a wonderful thing—after the work they could live normal lives again, wear whatever they liked, enjoy the beach, show off their arms without the least concern."

Maxine tugged the skin on Shelley's forehead upward and then to each side. "Ah well, don't fret about this one. It's small, not too deep either. You have no idea how much worse it can be. One lovely lady last winter came in here saying she wanted so much to wear a sleeveless gown to her daughter's wedding. She had toned arms from exercise you wouldn't believe on a woman of her age." Maxine patted Shelley's bangs back into place and sat back on her stool, pumping some sanitizer from a bottle on her cart and rubbing it into her hands. "That was quite a case. She told me later she was 62, and from her face you might have put her at 40 or 45. But from those arms, my God—you would have sworn she was twenty-five. At most. Twenty-five. But it was a pity she couldn't show them off, kept them covered always with shawls and jumpers and the like, because she had the most ghastly marks from an accident on her upper arm, near the shoulder, dreadful purple lines and zags. Even with makeup she worried constantly that she'd sweat or wear it off and offend someone. You should see her now! She wore a gorgeous turquoise gown to that wedding, exquisite, and sleeveless, naturally, custom designed for her. They had the ceremony down at the Chesapeake Bay Foundation, the beach, a glorious spot for weddings if the weather favors you, and she looked younger than the bride. The picture's in the portfolio, so you must be sure you take a peek. I told her she absolutely must send me a picture for my book, the transformation was so stunning."

Maxine listened to the familiar words and phrases tumbling from her mouth. She realized that she no longer had to dredge up facts and figures or concoct explanations; rather, they rose from within her mechanically, triggered by a question or a gesture on the part of a client and delivered in impeccably packaged tomes that required no conscious effort. She found herself reflecting on her words in counterpoint with the sentences that spewed from her mouth and realized that half the time she wasn't even processing, or understanding, what she was saying. She also found herself conscious of something she generally forced herself to forget: one of the reasons she talked so much, and sold her treatments so commandingly and so effectively, was that she had long ago stopped being a believer.

It wasn't as though she was a charlatan. She adamantly believed that the machines and lotions and powders did what they promised to do, precisely what they promised to do, in fact. If there was a wrinkle, it would be reduced. If there was a discoloration, it would be recolored. If there was a growth, it would be removed. But what she had realized long ago—but would never admit to her clients, for it would be suicide—was that while she could make change and alter individual components, she had no ability to restore a woman's essential attractiveness.

She had first realized this one crystal blue afternoon, the kind she had never since seen outside of South Africa, shortly after Dodie had left for America. She and Dr. Ruf had both escaped from work early and driven out to Llandundno Beach, a whimsical and essentially nostalgic venture for them both at this late point in their relationship. Although they had once retreated to this and other secluded, enchanting spots regularly, and desperately, their meetings in the past decade had tended to be more often at cafes or even the reception area of her salon, public meetings all about banter and business, even if that business was between long-time and still affectionate friends. That day, though, her newfound solitude, combined with the irresistible perfection of the day, led him to suggest Llandundno on a whim.

Perhaps out of habit they found themselves huddled together in a shaded cove they both knew intimately, watching the waves break and waiting for sunset while nibbling the triple cream brie he had packed in a cooler and enjoying one of his precious bottles of Bonarda. At one point he had set down his glass on a rock and taken her face in his hands, gazing at her in a way he hadn't for at least a decade with what could only be called reverence. He had ordained her "fully ripe," the essence of mature feminine perfection, utterly serious. She had heard it from him so many times before, but in the past there had been some thread of credibility in it. This time she laughed and called him a liar, reminding him of his inability to keep his eyes from the young bikini-clad figures they had passed on their way to the cove. He returned her laugh, admitting that young girls were beautiful no matter what rot they did to themselves, but assuring her that maturity in women, as in a good wine, or cheese, had its own inimitable charm. Eventually she had succumbed as she still always did to him, glistening and melting into his arms, but, at the same time, she found herself filled with a new and profoundly disheartening realization: for all Dr. Ruf's clinics and products, all his hopeful claims and amazing interventions, the truth was that beauty was not skin deep at all, but, indeed, inside, innate, and, for that reason, also ephemeral and unmanipulatable. Neither she nor even the brilliant, kindly Dr. Ruf had any power over it, once it was gone. Furthermore, Dr. Ruf's contention that all young women were beautiful no matter what they did to themselves had a debilitating corollary: all old women were repulsive.

She would never convey such thoughts to her clients, and would defend to the death a woman's right to improve the moment (so much of what mattered was in the mind anyway), but for many years after that she stopped applying her tricks or wiles to herself, and generally found it made no difference. The less she did, in fact, the better she looked. If she wore the lipstick to sell it to her clients, she found she looked worse—brash, unmatched, desperate. If she piled on foundation and colored her lids, she found she looked unapproachably precious and matronly. She soon realized that the less one did to young skin, the more attractive one was. Dodie was a case in point, even today. Now in her thirties, mother to three children, she still looked like Lady Godiva with her long, silky hair and pure, untouched glowing skin. You couldn't make her look bad, unless you tried to make her look good, really. With older women, it was just the opposite. Eventually, of course, Maxine worked on herself anyway, because it was simply human nature to try (vainly) to derail itself. She tried to mask her failings, superficially, with blond dye and hair straightening, and all sorts of makeup, lotions, creams, and powders. She stood before the mirror squinting and grunting, taking whole evenings to zap the hairs on her chin with the electrode (no one else in this town knew what they were doing when it came to electrolysis) or needling the skin above her upper lip. Despite these efforts, it was still excruciating to look in the mirror each morning if she didn't try to delude herself, and often she'd step back in horror, wondering who exactly it was she was seeing. Eventually, if she forced herself to look long enough, she could persuade herself that what she saw was reasonably attractive, if not even remotely close to the person she saw herself as being in her mind. But whatever she tried, and whatever she objectively accomplished, she knew—and, really, everyone could see— that she was still old, still emitting age. And whatever color her hair or however smooth her skin, she was still going to die.

"It must be so fantastic to be able to improve someone's life overnight."

"I suppose. But, really, Shelley, you must stop using terms like 'overnight.' This is not overnight. It is scientific and painstaking, step by step. Time is a key part of the process. You must understand that. And, as I said, we can't get to the face quite yet, not until you fully heal. But, meanwhile, now that I've seen the lay of the land, we can plan. So. You ready to hear my thoughts?"

"I'm not going anywhere."

"I still want you to think about blonde, seriously. It will be a more dramatic change. Eyeliner, clearly, and you'll not only be unrecognizable—you'll be ten, maybe twenty years younger! And we can do whole face, the lips, outlined and reddened, after a bit of multipannic collagen actuation, MCA, to plump things up, you know, fill in those cracks. I even think you're a candidate for a little blush application, if you'd like. We'll see how it goes, what you need, when we get that far."

95

"Wow. Basically an overhaul, huh? Wow."

"Wow, indeed, dearheart. But now, you see, in your circumstances, we have to aim high, don't we? Blush is much more involved than the eyeliner, you see, much more demanding a technique than lips in fact, but I'm one of the few in this country who can do it for you. You've come to the right place, my pet, I'll tell you. I'll give you the works. Why not? Yes, indeed, my luv, the works!"

"Whatever you think."

"What I think is that we must camouflage the scars, right off the bat—that's easy, with a little needling first to get everything smoothed out, and to induce the collagen and melanin pigment while we're at it. And get those nasty telangectiomas cleared from around the nose area, with a bit of electrolysis. That works so much better than lasers and will clean you up in no time at all."

"I've heard that hurts. Electrolysis, I mean."

"Just momentarily, for a lifetime of beauty. You'll find it nothing compared to what you've been through, my dear....But that's down the line. Just now I think we should start with the RAD machine to smooth things out as well. You have some nasty acne scars—they'll be gone in a cinch."

"That sounds good."

"And more importantly, of course, the treatment will allow the cosmeceutical products to better penetrate the skin. So they'll work faster."

"Huh?"

"You know, dear, some people smear and slather their faces with the most expensive and exotic of creams—to no avail. They are throwing away their money. Because, as you may recall from school, your skin is protected with an essentially impervious waterproof outer layer. You see?"

Maxine pointed to colored clinical diagram displayed on her wall. "Nothing is going to get through *that*. But, you see, with the RAD machine, an ingenious invention by the brilliant physician, Dr. Rufus Alvarez, the vitamin A that these products contain, the miracle vitamin A, truly, can slip in through the opened pores. And—*voilà*—they can do their work and restore your natural beauty to you."

"Does it hurt?"

The fear in Shelley's voice was almost childlike, Maxine thought, and she took that as a sign of progress. Dodie often told Maxine that she sounded like an infomercial, but Dodie didn't understand just how much clients craved authority, or how that authority was essential to her work. Her recitations were essential parts of building trust, and the more she tossed off facts and figures, the more her clients would entrust her with their precious skin, as much, she often thought, as a young child trusts a mother putting iodine on a wound.

"That's a matter of opinion. It tingles a bit, that's all, unless you're a squeamish type of gal. Which clearly you're not....Let me tell you something, sweetpea. Women waste more money on vitamin A than there is tea in China, but with me it's going to bring your skin back to life. That's correct. My approach will genuinely revive your skin. You see, what these other women don't understand is that prolonged use of those creams will eventually dry their skin. It will even strip off that protective layer—the 'horny layer' it's called—like a paint stripper. These ninnies put on these expensive creams, and they're essentially rubbing their faces with an electrical sander. I'm quite serious. A sander. And then you're genuinely in trouble—open to sun damage, any damage, and these women are paying through the nose for it to boot!

Shelley looked up at Maxine and drummed her fingertips onto her cheekbone.

"Don't look at me like that. And keep your fingers from your face. I assure you that I'm one of the few operators in your country—yes, one of the very few—with the experience and the training to do this for you. Some of these are very advanced techniques. Paramedical techniques, to be precise. Mainly used in burn victims and other accident victims when restoring natural appearance is critical. But you wouldn't know it from the number of clowns out there who pretend they know what they are doing. *Ag shame*, I feel so for the women here—a country with no uniform standards for the industry. None! It's up to them, the consumers, to make a wise decision, and they just don't have the background....They have no idea what they're up against. No idea at all!" She examined Shelley's face again with the magnifying mirror. "Yes...A perfect palate, ultimately....And we might as well get rid of the dark hairs on your upper lip while we're at it. Why not?"

"Vibrisae." Shelley tried to smile and rolled her eyes.

"Say what?"

"Vibrisae. Mammalian whiskers. I've been getting those waxed for years, but nothing works....I guess it's just inherited."

Maxine nearly dropped the magnifying glass, then carefully laid it on the stainless steel cart behind her. "Inherited my *tuchus*! You put them on yourself....Are you aware there is nothing more horrendous to a face than waxing?"

"You're joking."

"Oh, my....You and so many other women, all doing assault and battery on their faces. Let me tell you. There is nothing worse you can do for a hair than to yank it out—all you do is stimulate regrowth, and regrowth of thicker and darker hair. When you wax, you do all the yanking at once, *en masse*. You're creating a monster out of your face."

"Wonderful."

"Not to worry my dear. A little electrolysis on your lip, and you'll have nothing but downy baby fuzz once again....We'll work this all out, you'll see."

"Let's just do it. It's not like I have anything better to do."

"Ah, but, you see, we are not going to rush this. I'll write up a complete plan for you, and then you'll see how it's a step-by-step process, and a long one at that....Creating a face is like roasting a brisket—the key is taking your time. And, of course, a person undergoing a major life trauma is generally a very poor candidate for any kind of work. You, of course, being a prime example of a poor candidate. The hair, as I said, I can do any time. Tonight is probably not the best time, now that I think of it, first because you're not confident about the shade, and, also, because, to be honest, I'm about to keel over, if you want the truth. Hair coloring is the least of our problems, however. We can do it whenever you've selected a shade. But the other work cannot be rushed. We are going to proceed, of course, but we are going to do it safely and correctly. And effectively....Slowly, carefully—that is the only way to succeed. The only way I will proceed."

"I'm trapped here then. For God knows how long."

"My dear, as I said, it is not wise to alter one's physical appearance, while undergoing major stress in life. It's best to wait until the issues causing the trauma are resolved—would you like to do that?"

"That will be when hell freezes over."

"Well then, there you go. Have a bit of faith in me, will

you?"

The phone rang from the waiting room. "Not again. Will they ever let up?"

"Do you want me to get it?"

"We're working. The machine will get it."

Maxine almost never broke from a procedure, or even a consultation, to dash for the phone. Not only was it irresponsible, but she didn't move that fast anymore. Anything could wait. People rarely called in the evenings, except to break appointments for the next day when they were too ashamed to tell anyone in person, but she listened anyway for a voice, just in case. You could always hear the waiting room dialogue from the makeup room loud and clear, although no matter how many times she had told that to Carole, the woman had insisted on conducting private conversations with her family, girlfriends, and dentist while Maxine was working with clients. Countless times she had had to stop her work to reprimand her, but Carole had never been one to take instruction.

"Zeenie? Are you there? Pick up if you're there." It was Dodie's voice, loud and clear from the machine.

"Oh, rot. Excuse me." Dodie was Maxine's one exception to the "anything can wait" rule. Maxine hoisted herself up from the stool, smoothed down her skirt, and headed into the waiting room.

"Yes, dearie lamb. Are you still on the line?"

"Oh, hello, Zeenie. I thought you might be there....Can I please speak to Shelley?"

"She's currently indisposed. We're having a consult."

"She can't come to the phone?"

"No."

"Okay. Well. Then you tell her this, okay? Tell her that I just got a call from Rocco Herkimer. Here. At home."

"Oh my."

"You heard me. He somehow got my number—which, I assume, means he also knows my name and address. God knows how he tracked me down, but he knows I have something to do with Shelley, and he's obviously still on her case."

"Now what on God's earth could he want with the woman at this point? She's safe and out of the way."

Shelley came into the waiting room. "What's going on? Rocco?"

"Hush, dear, Dodie's trying to explain....Dodie, you must call the police at once."

"Why? He hasn't done anything...much."

"What do you mean? The man is stalking you."

Shelley began pounding both fists together, like a mortar and pestle. "Please let me talk to her." She beat harder and faster.

Maxine shook her head. "*Ag*, stop that, for crying out loud." She handed Shelley the phone, shaking her head with disgust. "Really now."

"Dodie?" said Shelley. "When did he call? What did he say?"

"He must have found my number somehow. I thought maybe he was lurking outside Safe Port last week—took my picture, I think. I thought I heard a camera when I was leaving one night, maybe, I'm not sure. Anyway, he seems to have somehow gotten his minions to figure out who I was. I don't know. Whatever....Anyway, he was calling to see if I had done what he asked. You know. Or maybe you don't. He wanted me to call the *Capital* and other reporters to tell them you were a nut case."

"He what? When? He talked to you? You didn't do that, did you?"

"Of course not. I don't see why he's so worried about them anyway, when you aren't making a case of this."

"He's worried because they already wrote that he had a pregnant girlfriend....I didn't tell them that, you know. They found out, somehow. Someone's on a witch hunt for him."

"It's not really a witch hunt when the person is, in fact, a witch, so to speak....Anyway, he called me. So. It is what it is."

"Oh God. Did you tell him that you'd call?"

"I told him nothing. I hung up on him."

Maxine took the phone from Shelley. "Dodie. Please. You must call the police. You're not safe if that man knows who you are. He knows where you work. And where you live, it seems. You must call for protection....You know that better than I do."

"He doesn't definitely know where I live. Just my phone number. I mean, I suppose he could track it, but....Anyway, I'm calling Florence Friedburg about it. She'll handle it. I just wanted you to know."

"You wanted to scare the bloody *kishkes* out of me is what."

"He's a lunatic," said Shelley. "Tell her to call for a restraining order."

"Did you hear that? Shelley agrees with me....What does Randall say?"

"I haven't told Randall. And I don't intend to."

"Did he threaten you?"

"No, he did not. And that's part of the reason I won't call for protection. I don't have grounds for protection. Yes, he accosted me that one time outside Safe Port, but I don't have any witnesses. And he didn't really hurt me. Just scared me. He did touch me—he shouldn't have touched me—but he's too connected to let that get him down. Now he's just called me and asked me a question. Yes, he asked it in what I would call a threatening, insinuating tone. But his literal words were nothing. If anything, he was polite. Overly polite."

"Well then....So. What did you tell him?"

"I told him nothing. As I just told Shelley. I hung up on him. And called you right away. I wanted Shelley to know he means business. But I have no intention of calling the press, obviously. I'm not going to do that for him or play his game. And I'm not asking for protection. I'm fine. I just thought both of you would want to know about it, that's all."

CHAPTER TEN

Utzi the Iceman (aka Otto Shapiro) had largely named himself, although Maxine had played a role in the "Utzi" part. He had explained the origin of his moniker on their first meeting as they gingerly pushed dry chicken onto the edges of their paper plates and tried making it palatable by mixing it with noodle kugel. They were tabled together by pure chance at the Temple's bi-annual Tot Shabbat, so his explanation was sporadically disrupted by several young grandchildren climbing under and around the table as well by the futile parental admonitions.

Maxine had a limited tolerance for youngsters (even when they included her own descendants) and even less of a taste for potluck meals on paper plates. Nothing, however, would stop her from supporting Dodie's decision to involve herself and her children in the Jewish community. Despite her earlier protestations, even outright rejection of her heritage, and despite the complete disinterest of Dodie's *goyishe* husband (who was off at some soccer practice with their middle child and regularly boasted about the children's "hybrid vigor"), Dodie appeared to have had a change of heart now that her three children were growing up. She had even gone beyond the token associations with the religion with which she had been raised and had joined this jolly and service-oriented temple, one in which people tacitly tolerated the pretense of an omnipotent creator and occasionally even deigned to sing praises to some unsexed "sovereign" in return for inclusion in a community that packed bag lunches for the homeless, funded kid-friendly Purim and Tu B'Shvat festivities, and organized bus trips to D.C. to protest Israeli-Arab policy. The Tot Shabbat was yet another of these perks, a way to get out of cooking a family dinner, chat with neighbors who otherwise never left their minivans, and let the kiddos expend energy on what would otherwise be another debilitating Friday night at home. Maxine was more than delighted to witness her Dodie and the grandchildren's immersion in this world, particularly given the alternatives in the modern American city.

Utzi had come with his daughter Joan and her family mainly for the free food, which, otherwise in his case, would have been microwaved fish sticks or frozen macaroni and beef. He was explaining that, as a retired fellow, he had time not only to enjoy his grandchildren, but also to fritter away the days with impracticable, even unlikely, schemes. His current project involved researching and writing a book on the middle-aged, Neolithic man found frozen with his broken arrows and fur wrappings in a South Tyrolean glacier. Certainly Maxine had read about the Iceman in the papers in the early 90s? She had not, generally restricting herself to local and South African news, which, at that particular time, were the same thing, and more than enough for any one person to absorb. Unfazed, this Otto Shapiro, with the obliviousness to the interest or comprehension of his listener that she associated with men and children, explained that the mummified corpse had been lying in the ice largely untouched by time since about 3300 B.C. Scientists called him Similaun Man, or Man from Hauslabjoch, but the popular press had taken to calling him

"Ötzi" (pronounced "Utzi" or "Ootsie"), or, more commonly, "Ötzi the Iceman," after the Oetzal Ridge, from the environs of which he had been extricated. Otto Shapiro said that he himself had been known as the "Iceman" since his Navy days, and thus had felt an immediate connection to the hapless "freeze dried" fellow who not only shared his nickname, but also, apparently, his arthritis, his digestive troubles, and his taste for climbing.

"And, of course, the man was a macho brute, a mountain man. Much like myself."

Surely he was joking, thought Maxine. This rotund, twinkly-eyed codger emanating Old Spice was as far from brutish as she could imagine. Everything about him—from the white bristle-brush mustache to the combed-back hair edging the gleaming pate to the blotchy red complexion to the oversized hornrims—suggested a life pushing papers, not hunting buffalo. He had even bothered to dress for this children's dinner in a navy blue blazer and to garnish himself in a blue crab-patterned tie with an American flag pin. She supposed that his ample girth, jowls, and thin compressed lips gave him a vague air of command, or at least of intransigence, which might help explain the "Iceman" business. He seemed to be retired Navy, too, something she regarded as a form of brutality, albeit a civilized one.

"You don't seem all that brutish to me, Utzi Iceman. Given the savage activity under our feet, in fact, I'd say you're a model of civility."

"Point well taken. Although it's Ötzi *the* Iceman, to be precise."

"I notice that you cut your chicken expertly with that knife and fork, for example. You've even placed a napkin on your lap, always a good sign in a man—or iceman, I suppose."

"Come, on, Zeenie," Dodie pulled at her elbow. "You lead the *birkat* for us."

"I don't know it."

"There's nothing to know." Dodie handed her a notecard bearing the transliterated blessing. "We all sing it together. Just stand and lead. It's the prayer they do after meals."

"That's a man's job."

"Not anymore."

"You've already had me light the candles, dear. That's a woman's job....Why don't we give this nice Utzi Iceman here a turn, eh?" She turned to him. "You'd like a job, wouldn't you?"

"We'll do it together."

Reluctantly accepting his hand, Maxine shrugged and rose as he pulled back her chair. "I'll need my glasses if I'm to read this." She looked at Dodie. "In my handbag, sweetpea."

A heavyset matron with an auburn pageboy and makeup so thick you could see it from their table stood at the front of the hall holding a hand-held mike to her lips. She tapped the mike with her forefinger to test it. It clearly worked quite well. You could hear her take in a deep breath of air and smack her lips together. Before Maxine could even get the chain of her glasses adjusted around her neck, the woman and many of the families in the room began chanting the blessing with gusto, just as Dodie had promised. Maxine stood silent, mouthing the words, although Utzi the Iceman, to her great surprise, seemed to know what he was doing.

"Baruch atah Adonai, Eloheinu Melech haolam, hazan et haolam kulo b'tuvo, b'chein b'chesed uv'rachamim. Hu notein lechem l'chol basar ki l'olam chasdo. Uv'tuvo hagadol tamid lo chasar lanu, v'al yechsar lanu, mazon l'olam va-ed, baavur sh'mo hagadol. Ki hu El zan um'farneis lakol umeitov lakol, umeichin mazon l'chol b'riyotav asher bara. Baruch atah Adonai, hazan et hakol."

Mouthing transliterated Hebrew, she inevitably found herself several syllables off, either getting ahead of the crowd, or lagging behind. Three consecutive words ran together, and then, without warning, the chanters would pause in the midst of a single word or prolong a random syllable. She remembered how confused she had felt as a child in services, convinced that the transliteraters were punishing her for not knowing how to read the actual Hebrew letters. She was certain there must have been something buried in the Hebrew that told everyone else what to do, something they were withholding from her. Often lines would repeat without warning, or everyone else would seem to know when to run words together and when to pick up or slow the pace. Even in the *kaddish*, the sacred prayer for the dead, she would inevitably find herself tripping over her tongue at some point along the way, no matter how many times she had heard it or tried to chant it with the congregation, and no matter how determined she was to get it right because she was thinking of her grandparents and her mother's sister Bella whom she had never met because of Hitler.

By the second line, Maxine merely pretended to speak.

"I can't remember a word," she told him. "But I do know that is not the whole thing."

"The whole thing goes on all night. This is a reform congregation—they pick and choose."

"The English I can read," she said. And together with the others she read, with distinct articulation, "Blessed is our God, Sovereign of the universe, who sustains the entire world with goodness, kindness and mercy. God gives food to all creatures, for God's mercy is everlasting."

She looked at the children, who had been pulled up from under the table and were standing alongside their parents. Utzi the Iceman's young grandchildren Chelsea and Alexander elbowed each other, while their parents towered over them, oblivious, or pretending to be. Dodie at least had had the presence of mind to separate her two, Maxine observed, with little William firmly held in place by the shoulder. Margaret, who at ten was mortified to find herself at this preschool gala, looked up at Maxine and rolled her eyes.

"Through God's abundant goodness we have not lacked sustenance, and may we not lack sustenance forever, for the sake of God's great name. God sustains all, does good to all, and provides food for all the creatures whom God has created. Blessed is our God, who provides food for all."

"They should stick to the Hebrew." The Iceman held Maxine's chair out for her. "Often it's better not to know what you're saying."

"What, you don't believe that God is good?" asked Maxine.

"I'm 70 years old, honey. You don't want to know what I believe."

Maxine shook her head and sat down. The others reseated themselves as well, although little Alexander escaped to join some impromptu hide-and-seek game that seemed to have generated spontaneously around the edges of the hall during the final words of the blessing.

"Looks like they have a whole gang here," said Dodie. "Too bad Lawrence is missing out."

"Just as well," said Maxine. Perhaps young Alexander would have stayed put had her grandson Lawrence, his Sunday School classmate, been present. More likely, though,

Lawrence by this point would have been running wild with the other boys. "I don't think I've heard that blessing or lit the *shabbas* candles in 30 years. Maybe 40. Maybe never." She looked at Utzi the Iceman. "Did it seem right to you, with the whole lot of us yammering together?"

"The gobbledegook I can do without. The candles I like, though. There's a warm feeling to see a woman setting up like that. I still remember my mother lighting the candles every Friday night. She kept at it into her nineties, week after week. Even when she could barely stand."

"She was a lucky woman then. My fingers are cursed, I'm afraid. When you can't even manage a match, you know you're in trouble."

"You know, Zeenie," said Dodie, "it never ceases to amaze me how you manage to do the work you do, so intricate, with your hands. You don't seem to have the slightest problems there."

"It's habit. Ingrained, I suppose. Thank God that hasn't been taken from me. But in matches I have met my match!"

"I can light a match, Zeenie," said William, Dodie's youngest, who was four at the time.

"You'll do no such thing, William. Matches are for grown-ups."

"Mum lets Margaret light the candles at home."

"Once!" said Margaret. "Not when I was four. And Lawrence isn't allowed either."

"You're still a kid, and she let you!" William argued.

"That's very silly of your mother then," said Maxine. "You are four years old, William, and you are not to light— or touch—matches!"

Utzi the Iceman leaned in toward William, and, eyes narrowed, told him to listen to his grandma. William, chastened, ran off to join Alexander and the other older boys.

"So, Dodie tells me you came here from South Africa," Joan said to Maxine. "You were there through the worst of it."

"It was her choice," said Dodie. "We were here years before that, but she stuck it out to the end. Or almost....And she keeps going back for more."

"Well, of course," said Joan. "All transitions are tough, however welcome."

Maxine held up her hand while she tried to grind a mouthful of chicken into something she could coerce down her throat. The truth was, she had struggled very little. South Africa had become ancient history for her the moment her mother had died. Once that last connection had been severed, she had no longer been able to think of a single legitimate reason to stay in a place she loved, but one in which she understood she no longer fit. Life there had by that time reverted to a state of nature, with too many people, too few things, and, as a result, random, horrifying violence a part of daily life. Perhaps it would someday be cleaned up, but at the time that seemed unimaginable: everything seemed to be going backwards, what with the rampant disease, poverty, organized crime, extreme unemployment, carjackings, home intruders and murders, and record-high levels of rape. To be fair, she had never entirely felt that South Africa was fully her country anyway, in part because her parents, though both loyal and upstanding citizens, seemed to regard it as a temporary refuge, or even guesthouse, their real home, even if they never availed themselves of it, being Eretz Israel.

"Family is everything, you see. I had so very little of it, and they were all here in the states. A whole new generation was growing up without my even knowing them. Dennis, my son, brought his two out a couple of times from Connecticut, but that's hardly the kind of relationship you want to have with your grandchildren. Honestly, they were little more than photographs to me, not full human beings. And, Dodie here, well since Dodie refused to set foot in South Africa ever again, I hadn't even met my beautiful granddaughter, who was over two by the time I transplanted myself." She blew a kiss to Margaret across the table. "*Ag*, it was a good decision, and it had to be. South Africa has become a developing nation. There's no place for whites there anymore."

"Leaving was the easy part for Mum," said Dodie. "It's staying away that she finds so difficult."

Maxine folded her napkin and placed in on her plate. "My daughter and I have different views on this. Politics aside, South Africa is a beautiful country, and I miss it dearly." She turned to Dodie. "This makes me loony tunes, doesn't it now?"

"Oh, please, Zeenie. That's about as far from the truth as you could be. It *is* a beautiful country. Just a deeply troubled one, that's all."

"Trouble trouble everywhere," said Utzi. "And not a drop to drink."

"That's correct, sir." Maxine turned to look at him. "Trouble everywhere, and not just there. You have to put politics aside here, too. You just don't see it. You carry on endlessly about South Africa, but, as I've said, you remain utterly blind to your own racism. And I don't just mean your Ku Klux Klanners and skinheads. It's your unconscious racism which, to my mind, is the worst kind possible."

"Really, Zeenie," said Dodie. "That is a tad extreme."

"It's not extreme in the least. Every day you see people denied jobs, loans, houses, and school spots, and it's clearly got something to do with their skin color or sex or sexual orientation. Even if it isn't said, it's clear."

"That's true," said Joan. "We simply claim they lack this or that qualification, don't we? Disgusting."

"It's more than that. Minorities here are made to feel that any time they get anything it is because of Affirmative Action and not because they genuinely deserve it, or because they are genuinely the best qualified, or even just plain qualified."

"But still, that's qualitatively different than what went on in South Africa," said Dodie. "I'm not making excuses for what we do here, not defending it, of course. But it's simply not comparable to an entire culture systematizing racism."

"No. It's not comparable. It's worse. The problem here is not treating people badly because of race. It's continuing to think that race means anything at all. You just can't—won't—see this, will you?"

"We just disagree. That's okay, Zeenie....Anyway, one thing we do agree about is that America isn't perfect. No argument there."

"Ah, well, I think that calls for a toast, eh?" said Utzi the Iceman. "Hear hear!" He raised his glass. William shoved the remains of his cookie across the table as though it were a hockey puck.

"All right then," said Dodie. "I suppose that's a sign to stop this enlightening conversation. Lovely as it's been."

Dodie and the other parents began gathering up the paper plates while Margaret showed Chelsea how to sculpt bowls and flowers out of the melting candle wax. Maxine added William's half-eaten cookie to her plate before Dodie collected it.

"The little boy's got his grandma's hair, I see."

"He comes by his honestly—a blond '*shiksa*' for a father," Maxine said. "You would not want to see *me* in my honest state."

"That's for me to decide, dear. To me, you are a vision of loveliness."

"To me, you need to get your prescription checked. But thank you kindly. As I said, you are clearly a gentleman, Iceman or not."

"A gentleman who has had a long day, I'm afraid." He clenched his right shoulder and grimaced. "Would you be so good as to pass that dreadful Mogen David?"

"I doubt that's going to help you much."

"Don't let the sugar fool you. The alcohol content is still sufficient for my purposes."

"Unfortunately, the taste is not."

"That is also a matter of opinion. Little Chelsea here thinks it's scrumptious, don't you dear?"

Chelsea wasn't listening, as Margaret was showing her how to reattach the head that had just rolled off her wax witch by holding it next to the candle flame and using the melted wax as glue. Utzi downed his wine in a single gulp. "Don't be misled. The joints hurt as much as ever, however much of this stuff—or any stuff—I imbibe. But I find that with a little bit of alcohol, I just don't care quite as much."

"I don't think that would work for me." Maxine's arthritis was mainly in the fingers, and slowed her ability to do the little things she needed to do during the day—open bottles, replace needles, set timers, and so forth. Knock on wood, her knees only ached moderately when she climbed stairs, and her shoulders felt just vaguely stiff when she woke. These were minor annoyances. Only her fingers caused her serious pain, and no amount of alcohol was going to help with that—clearly she couldn't work in an intoxicated state. Fortunately, though, what Dodie had said was true: once she started working a needle on someone's face, her hands danced dexterously, and painlessly. Years of practice and habit were apparently as effective as alcohol in blinding her fingers to incapacitation.

"Ötzi the Iceman, you know, was another victim of this dreadful affliction," Utzi said, pouring himself yet another glass of wine. "But he, apparently, was making some effort to get help. He seems to have undergone some early form of acupuncture. Or so some experts have speculated. He had tattoos all over his body. And many of them correspond exactly to certain known acupuncture points."

"I thought acupuncture began in China. Are they sure?"

"I couldn't tell you. All I know for certain is that this Iceman is doomed to have random strangers look him over and invent his history for millennia. Apparently, you can't escape or hide forever—even if you spend your time hiking alone in the Alps."

"I suppose dead men actually *can* tell tales, can't they?"

"Exactly. He can tell the scientists so much about his life, and what killed him, even. The scientists can tell, or guess, from the pathology reports—x-rays, body scans, and whatnot. They can see if joints are worn away and whether or not the wear and tear is likely to be from injury or time or the unearthing process itself."

"So—that's how they know about the arthritis, I suppose."

"Seems plausible enough, doesn't it? The guy was in his mid-forties, maybe even 50s, which was damn old in those days. As for the acupuncture, though, yeah, it's all pure speculation. Pretty dubious at that. But obviously the tattoos were there for something. He had 57 of them."

"He must have paid a pretty penny."

"Six straight lines, about half a foot long each, on his back, plus a cross inside one of his knees. And then parallel lines all over his back, legs, and ankles."

"Sounds more like witchcraft to me."

He poured another half inch of Mogen David into his glass after she declined his offer to fill hers. "Anything's possible. It must have worked at least a little, given his line of work."

"Perhaps he was just decorating himself for the ladies."

"I doubt it. The tattoos were pretty ghastly—though, who knows what women liked back then, eh?"

"Women like them now, too, in some parts of West Africa anyway. So do the men. They like scars as well, for that matter. You know that ghastly scarification they do in those countries? You don't even get your beauty there until you're scarred. The most beautiful person in the village is the one with the most scars."

"Well, there you have it. I still have a lot to learn. Actually, though, that's one of my missions—to find out a bit more about tattooing, and what the Iceman was doing with them. If they were arthritis treatments, well then, I guess the docs may be grabbing up some of the tattooing business from the lowlifes and addicts."

"That's quite a bigoted statement, especially from someone who seems so well-read."

"What do you know about tattooing, my dear?"

"Quite a lot, actually. It's my life. My livelihood."

"Eh? I thought you said you did some kind of makeup."

"*Permanent* makeup. How do you think the 'permanent' part fits in? We inject dyes under the skin to produce desired aesthetic effects—eyebrows, lines, lip color, camouflage. The dyes, the technique—it's all tattooing, really. Of course, we tiptoe about the term with certain clients, at the start.

Can you imagine Mrs. Chase Smith-Howe's reaction if she knew she was having her eyebrows and lips tattooed?"

"You must show me sometime," Utzi the Iceman said. "I would be remiss in my research if I missed out this chance to learn tattooing hands-on."

"I can't promise you hands-on," she said. "That takes years of training. But I would be delighted to give you a tour, if you like."

"A tour, eh? Well, that sounds like a much more pleasant form of research than squirreling away at the library. It would be my duty to take you up on the offer now, wouldn't it?"

"Next Friday night then," said Maxine. "Stop by at 4 if you can. I'll be finishing up the last client, and I can show you the works."

"Excellent. And then, if you would be so kind, we could share a Shabbat dinner once again. Only this time I promise you something more palatable than rubber chicken."

CHAPTER ELEVEN

Utzi the Iceman hadn't even had the decency to call when he stood her up on that first date. This didn't bother her. It didn't particularly interest her either, as she quickly decided that any sense of violated obligation was her own foolishness. Obviously he had been doing nothing more at that first Tot Shabbat than making polite conversation. What choice had the man had? She had been even more foolish to expect friendship, much less romance, at this stage of the game. Even if her hair was blond and her creases carefully submerged below layers of expensive and alluring cover-up, she was still rotting inside. If anything, the makeup and the hairdo gave her away, announcing through their very impeccability that she had something to hide. She fooled no one, and certainly not a man who had been sitting ten inches from her face all evening. So on that Friday afternoon when he failed to show for the arranged tour, Maxine simply picked up Chinese take-out and went home for a long soak and a night of cable.

Two weeks later, however, a deluxe gift basket was delivered to her salon filled with more gleaming Macintosh apples, Vermont cheddar, snack crackers, mixed nuts, and chocolate truffles than she could eat in a year. There was also a bottle of Dom Perignon with a small white card taped to it: "Forgive me. I'm rotten to the core. But if you're willing to forgive one bad 'apple' (night), let's reschedule at your convenience. I'll call you and hope you answer, and forgive, me.—Otto (the Iceman)."

Maxine put the basket out in the waiting room for her clients but took the card home to tape to her bedroom mirror alongside miniature school portraits of her grandchildren, a fan Dr. Ruf had once brought her from Buenos Aires, and several reminders about dentist and mammogram appointments. The Dom Perignon, which turned out to be just one of many such treasures the Iceman had reserved, they used to toast his redemption on their first Friday night out.

As she eventually came to understand, he had not called her because he had been incapacitated by one of his intermittent depressions. He had been plagued by these episodes for most of his adult life. While he conceded that, at times he may have been overly sensitive, or self-indulgent, he generally considered his moods to be justifiable reactions to genuinely sad and traumatic events. In fact, he prided himself on his ability to be jovial and upbeat the vast majority of time when, objectively, he should have been perpetually demoralized. For his entire life, he explained in dribs and drabs, he had not ever done anything he had set out to do. He had never had the career he wanted, the women he wanted, the home he wanted, the adventures he wanted, or the fame and glory he wanted. Even when he reshaped his childhood dreams to fit present realities, whittling grandiosity into sensible, human-sized projects, he never seemed to be able to make things happen the way he had planned. His scheme to lose 50 pounds somehow turned into gaining 15, and his hopes to open a deli somehow turned into a day in bankruptcy court. His desire to provide supportive guidance to his children somehow turned into general neglect, punctuated by misplaced but well-directed barbs about their vulnerabilities, particularly those he secretly shared. His promise to be a devoted, loving husband somehow turned into acrimonious, prolonged divorce proceedings that left him with little but bitterness for family life, and for people in general, as well as the conviction that he was fated to a life of loneliness, and that, worse, he deserved this fate.

The biggest disappointment in his life was the omnipresence of the Naval Academy. The ubiquity of this institution in Annapolis, in fact, was the primordial reason that even trivial circumstance could so easily ignite his low-burning ember of despondency. As a boy, he had always wanted, even expected, to be there someday, not so much as a warrior, but as a scholar. His heart had always been in the books, and his vision of where books led was within the formidable walls of this institution that he walked past every day and whose intimidating denizens seemed nothing short of gods. The Naval Academy was the first place he ever saw people scrubbed and controlled and smart and in command. It was a place he could aspire to, a place where, someday, if he worked hard enough in school, he could go and become godlike himself. Even better, there was no tuition, which he believed would appeal to his family with little money for fancy education.

As he approached college age, however, he learned that nothing comes free. The years of service he would have to pledge to the Academy in exchange for four years of education were the least of it. Even the life he would have to risk in exchange for it was trivial. The price he could not pay, no matter how willing he might have been, was the leisure time required to get the grades, train the body, and donate the service hours required of successful applicants.

Since the age of seven he had been working as the delivery boy for his father's liquor store—an activity which had earned him the nickname "Iceman" at the Academy, where he regularly delivered large quantities of ice to serve the institution's voracious needs. By the age of 13 he was stocking shelves and doing inventory after school as well, working a grueling schedule, even on weekends, that only allowed him an hour a night for homework. His high school grades were passable but hardly stellar, and the sports and community service that would have propelled him into the Academy never came to be. He went to the University of Maryland, which back then let in just about anyone, to study accounting and then returned to manage, and, eventually, own, the family shop. Thus, despite his longstanding aspirations, he found himself serving the needs of the neighboring Academy and its more fortunate community for most of his life, but, as the son of struggling Jewish immigrants should have expected, never being one of the anointed.

It was this low-lying disappointment, and the constant reminder of its source, that left the Iceman vulnerable to mood swings. It took very little to push him over the edge—a vision of his ex-wife with her new husband, another national chain replacing a local business on Main Street, a chiding from his doctor about his dangerously high triglycerides—but after a week or two of wallowing, he'd see the sunbeams grazing the surface of the Bay, one of the donut brigade would call him with a new joke, or his daughter would insist he come for dinner, and he pushed away the despair that once again seemed pointlessly self-indulgent, not to mention a waste of precious time. Then he'd display his usual affable and optimistic persona until another slight or minor offense crossed his path.

The most recent source of his mood swings had been the Iceman project, which, oddly enough, seemed equally capable of pushing him both up and down. As he pondered this man's ancient existence and modern reemergence, he often found himself vacillating between two polar reactions—both "how can you *not* think everything you do matters?" and "how can you even *pretend* that you matter?" On the one hand, here was a man who had been a nobody, just another primitive guy chopping down trees and hunting wild game to survive, pouring every ounce of his energy into where to get the next meal, and yet 5,000 years later everyone knew about him, loved him, claimed him as their long-lost ancestor, speculated on the most minute details of his life—what he wore, what he ate, how he lived, what he did each day and on the day that he died, even what he thought, and felt. On the other hand, Ötzi the Iceman, for all his notoriety, was a man frozen in the ice for millennia, and that very fact alone screamed out that none of this stuff had made the slightest bit of difference. Yes, plenty of people today asked the questions, but did the answers matter? Did this man's choices or problems or triumphs mean anything at all? Certainly the answer would have to be no, had the man's body not been discovered thousands of years later, a fate that nobody else could realistically expect.

"What this Iceman project reminds me," he told Maxine, halfway through that first (of many subsequent) bottles of Dom Perignon, "is that each of our lives are made up of hundreds, thousands of little details. Some are what you would call picayune." He relished the last word, enunciating each syllable like an opera singer might. "You know—what tie is appropriate, what carpet color matches the sofa, what brand of soap should I buy. Other details are huge, monumental—should I marry this woman, should I buy this house, should I go back to school. But it doesn't matter. Picayune, or monumental, none of them matter in the slightest. Not in the long run. However vital the question may seem right now, in five thousand years we'll all be dead."

He had painstakingly obtained a corner table at a quiet BYOB café downtown and, both delighted by the effort and solaced by the champagne, she let him go on.

"When the heart stops, so does meaning."

"Well, that's certainly a cheery way of looking at things, I must say."

"That's what I'm saying. Working with this material reminds me incessantly that from a longterm perspective all persons, all decisions, all matters, are alike, alike in utter insignificance."

"That's not what they say in the *shul*."

"The rabbis, of course, disagree, and to some extent they're right. Even if our personal achievements turn out to be illusory, our actions still matter and the way we treat others can genuinely change the world. Our good deeds leave their marks, even after we die. But it's damn hard to hold on to that kind of thinking when you consider Ötzi the Iceman."

"I suppose."

"Look, this theoretical chain of events your actions could spark might outlast you for a generation, maybe two, maybe more if they wrote books about you," the Iceman continued. "Maybe. But you know what? However much I console myself with such thoughts, or try to remember to use them to guide my actions, I can't help feeling that the way Ötzi the Iceman had treated his wife or children or neighbors 5,000 years ago is completely irrelevant today."

"Ah. So this is why you locked yourself in a cave and

stood me up? You're now free to do anything to anyone because none of it matters?"

"You misunderstand. These are my little musings, that's all, just part of the project and, when I think too much or drink too little, just part of life."

What had put him under, he explained, had not been any vague philosophical meandering but rather the discovery of a book on Ötzi the Iceman by a lady journalist a day or so after he and Maxine had met. Although for nearly a decade he had planned to write a book, *the* book on Ötzi, the mere existence of a book in and of itself hadn't fazed him. Over the years, there had been others, or rumors that others might be in the works, but until now none of them had ever concerned him much. Even the works of the scientists could usually be dismissed as those of vain publicity hounds. But this particular book was another story: erudite, thorough, published by a reputable university press, and widely regarded as definitive. He knew he had run into a wall as soon as he scanned the back cover and read the introduction. The author had done everything he had been planning to do, and she did it all so well, so reasonably, so thoroughly. She also had more authority and connections than he did. The best he could hope to accomplish now was an update of this excellent book, and she would undoubtedly be doing that herself.

His spirits revived considerably, however, after a talk with Nelson Rose, a retired Naval Academy history professor who was part of his Monday morning donut brigade. This was the one part of his life he would not miss, no matter how hard it was for him to drag himself out otherwise. Originally impromptu, this group of five graying Annapolitans, all of whom had known each other in one way or another over a lifetime, had coalesced when they noticed each other coming into the Dunkin' Donuts for coffee week after week. Nowadays, having nowhere else to go most of the time, they spent a good two hours every Monday resolving various national and local dilemmas, recounting war stories, and offering words of wisdom to the young mothers and lone working women who passed within earshot of their table—"My wife used to give ours a nuki," "I'd keep that little guy off the powdered sugar if I were you," or "*New York Times*, eh? Let this geezer here tell you a thing or two about the way this country really works, my dear." Unlike their younger, more guarded selves, the club also shared tales of current exploits and challenges, whether medical woes, family sagas, or, as in the current case, Utzi's frustrations with the Iceman project, which, given his recent experience with the disheartening book, he was on the verge of abandoning. The donut brigade members were like his brothers. Not only did he feel he could be himself with them, but they were inherent parts of his life, the only part he couldn't conceive of avoiding very long even when in the depths of despair.

Nelson, who had been encouraging him on the Iceman project from the start, had stressed that his goal as an author shouldn't be to be first, but rather to be best. "That's the way academics think," he said. "Hundreds of people have written about the Civil War. But that shouldn't stop a scholar from pursuing the subject. Not only can a new voice build on what has come before, and amplify it with newer, better information, but he can provide an entirely fresh perspective....You have to learn to think like a scholar, not a businessman, when it comes to this writing thing."

"You don't understand," Utzi the Iceman had objected. "There's nothing left for me to say. Every little detail about the find, the dig, the man's life, the process of analyzing the clothes, the tools, what was in his gut, how they preserved the body—even the backbiting between the scientists and press and politicians—it's all there for everyone to see."

"You'll be surprised when you actually start to write," Nelson assured him. "Then you'll see how much of you comes out, even if you're starting with the same material. You'll discover you have your own personal twist on the topic."

This was true. He did not think like the others, never had. In fact, the more he had thought about it as the week went on, the more he had realized that all the things that kept nagging at him as he read and pondered, all the things he had dismissed as distractions, were, in fact, signs of his calling. What drove him particularly crazy was the way all the scientists kept assuming that poor Ötzi was somehow iconic, representative of his age. The media were just as bad. They constantly made inane assumptions that stopped him from reading, made him question their judgment, but, until now, he had always assumed that he must have been missing something. What did he know? He had a bachelor's degree in accounting, not a doctorate in archeology.

Nelson's words, however, had convinced him: these scientists, and the journalists who worshipped them, were mindless, brashly jumping from the particular to the universal at every opportunity. If Ötzi bore a wooden dagger or a copperheaded spear, they assumed they were seeing some transitional man between the old and the new stone age, merely because otherwise they would have seen bronze tools. If one of the seams of his clothing seemed inexpertly mended with twisted grass, they assumed he must have been temporarily strapped while up in the mountains for the season because otherwise he clearly would have stitched it with twisted animal hair. If Ötzi wore leather clothes, they were baffled—wasn't there weaving done at the time?

Wasn't it simply possible that Ötzi just felt like trying something new, or doing something different? Wasn't it simply possible that Ötzi lived his own way? Certainly he, Otto Shapiro, could have carried an old stone dagger up an Alp himself, even today in the 21st century, had he so chosen. He could have donned leather wrappings and stuffed his shoes with grasses to keep his feet dry, or tried stitching a seam with grass just because it was there on hand. He could have done this for the challenge, for some kind of bizarre party or rite, or just because he wanted to live a different way or try something new. If he had been caught up in a freak ice storm or pinned to a glacier for the next five thousand years while doing whatever it was he chose to do, would scientists have thawed him out and assumed that in 2010 all people carried stone daggers and wore leather hides, or that he must have been up in the mountains herding his sheep because that was the only reason anyone in that time—to their knowledge—would have gone into the mountains? Or would they just have thought that one man, for whatever reason that one man may have had, was out in such garb on that day and met with bad luck? How dare those so-called experts assume that a single human being somehow told them the story of a whole culture? How dare they assume that their happenstance find was anything more than one man, or laden this man with the burden of speaking for his entire clan, his entire time period, and explaining that world to future generations?

He was tired of all this. Those people might have been "experts," but they were just as susceptible to human fallibility as anyone else, grasping at straws to make a case that wasn't there to be made. Many had a tendency to jump to absurd conclusions based on the meagerest of evidence, perhaps because they knew how well the media lapped up this kind of thing.

No, to him Ötzi the Iceman was just one human being, who did things because he chose to do them, out of convenience and idiosyncratic whim. He had the ill fortune of leaving a trail, and for that he was destined to be misunderstood not for the mere five or six or eight decades of his life like most human beings, but, rather, for millennia. The gullibility of these people (except perhaps Hans Seidler, the University of Vienna anthropologist, who after a number of years of equally dubious behavior seemed to "get it" and realized this was just one man, not an entire culture) was exemplified in the Piltdown man fiasco, which you would think would have taught these folks something about damping down unwarranted and overly convenient conclusions. But apparently history had taught them nothing. A bunch of ambitious scientists desperate to establish reputations or rack up honors or prize money would always, he supposed, use the smallest shreds of evidence to build elaborate explanations, forgetting, whenever convenient, the time-honored scientific principles of sample size and repeatability. Perhaps it was time for them to acknowledge, as any normal person with common sense already knew, that archeology was simply not a science, and let it go at that.

Perhaps he, Otto Shapiro, could write the story of Ötzi from this perspective. The man was not representative of his age. He wasn't a precious clue to life in the Neolithic, or a turning point in modern archeology. He was a single person, a unique individual who had walked the earth back in 3300 B.C., and no one would ever know just who he was and what he thought. Otto Shapiro, a sympathizer who happened to have been born 5,000 years later, could therefore feel free to make up the details of that man's life by coming up with something plausible for them, but he also realized that never would he, or anyone, ever truly understand what went on in the life, or the mind, of another man, whether that man lived 5,000 years before him or lived today.

For the first time, he felt free, like the giant weight that had been keeping him from writing anything had been lifted. Because he now saw that there was no real science here, no absolute conclusions, or rights that he could get wrong, he was free to unshackle his imagination. Obviously some other people had already taken this route. In fact, fantasies about Ötzi the Iceman were everywhere. One man he read about had built a home and lived like Ötzi for five years, taking a break every night to write up his experiences for Science Wonder Productions and putting himself on display all day for a paying public. Another woman, Marie Mosely of Dorset Avenue, Bournemouth, after being told by the scientists that she was Ötzi's closest living relative, concluded that he must have been a good Irishman on a trip east who met with ill-fortune; she wondered if she needed to insist that he be given a good, decent burial. Even the Norwegian anthropologist Torstein Sjövold had apparently been unable to resist several trips to the Hauslabjoch to relive the Iceman's experiences. The lovely thing about fantasies was that no one could claim or judge his. No matter how many others had indulged theirs, his would be uniquely his own, neither right nor wrong, and utterly original.

"They're often completely off-base," he told Maxine at the point in their first dinner when the champagne had been just about depleted. "You have just as much of a chance of being right as they do. That's power."

"It's like being a detective, really. One adventure, one unsolved mystery, after another."

"Only instead of watching Sherlock Holmes, it's you doing the thinking."

"Exactly! I can't tell you how exhilarating it feels when you realize that these so-called experts were no better at it than you. They do all kinds of crazy guesswork. And the more I research, the more I read, the more I can see how they're often just winging it. It's power. I can't put it any other way."

That power was something most ordinary people never got to feel, he explained. Through his forays into research, his attempts to solve a mystery and figure something out that no one had ever figured out before, he felt he mattered. "That's what's incredible," he said. "That's what lets me work."

"I can see that." And she could. As annoying and demanding as many of her clients could be—and, increasingly, seemed to be—she had always enjoyed the feeling that she could lift their spirits or even change their lives. When she had been younger, she had been driven by an almost missionary-like zeal, and even today felt a small sense of relief from this burden every time she explained the life cycle of facial hair to a chronic plucker or dissuaded a silly young girl from wasting her money on skin products at the dimestore. She also knew the thrill of power when, with her own hands, she was able to disguise a glaring keloid, vanquish telltale capillaries from a nose, or transform clogged pores, milia, and comedones into glowing fresh skin. However, the idea of sitting in a library all day and ordering up articles sounded dreadful, and about as far from "power" or influence on the world as she could imagine. She had always been a "hands on" sort of person.

"I wouldn't have the patience."

"Of course you would. Certainly it takes patience to remove little hairs from a woman's upper lip, one by one—doesn't it?

"*Ag*, of course. But it's routine. I don't have to think all the way through, figure things out along the way."

He reached across the table to stroke the top of her hand, but she reached for her glass instead.

"When I think about Ötzi, all my problems go away," he told her. "I think about him—a middle-aged guy, some irritable bowel problems, pain in the hip and leg from arthritis, wondering where his next ibix meal is going to come from, herding a bunch a sheep up an alp, getting into fights with a bunch of ruffians. I think about that and realize—after 5,000 years that's what a human life amounts to."

He was almost breathless.

"That's all we know, that's all it was. All he was...."

"I suppose."

"So then I think—what do all these ridiculous headaches and squabbles and aches and pains of mine matter? In 5,000 years it will all just be a matter of scientific curiosity, and probably not even that. It all amounts to nothing, so just relax."

"Well. That's depressing, isn't it? I suppose that's what brought you so low."

"Just the opposite. Many things depress me, but the Iceman is not one of them. Reading about him, thinking, guessing, writing about him—all of those things are nothing but exhilarating. When I think about his life, what he did, where it led him—and what it all means now—I feel free.

Free to enjoy myself in any way I choose."

She found herself smiling, nodding, and then, to her surprise, even wishing she had let him stroke her hand. Whatever it was he was saying, his passion seemed genuine, even endearing in its incongruous innocence. The man was getting on in years, but then so was she, and at this point clean clothes and brushed teeth were about as much as one could hope for in the physical realm. Even his stockiness didn't faze her, as it only suggested that he might not notice hers, and, besides, she had never gone for those whippet-like men, so trim, dapper, and impeccable that they made her feel self-conscious and inadequate.

Nowadays it was easier to be with someone like the Iceman. In fact, his very smushiness marked him as a victim of his appetites, something she had always considered a promising sign in a potential lover. Dr. Ruf, of course, had been the exception. He had been as streamlined and sleek as they come, and that had hardly diminished his ardor, but back in those days she had been fairly streamlined and sleek herself and thus not the least bit threatened by beauty in a man. Now this blustering codger, with his ill-fitting tortoise-shell glasses, silly mustache, and even his tough, bulldoggish face, felt much more comfortable, and comforting. She liked the way he put her at ease. Besides, he seemed sincerely interested in her, solicitous about her arthritis, intrigued by her tales of South Africa, and even seemingly fascinated by the pre-dinner tour of the salon, and the intricacies of micropigments, biocompatible fillers, and needle assemblies. He was an educated man and also knew a lot about the world, especially parts of it that she didn't know but needed to know, such as food, wine, business, the Naval Academy, and Annapolis. Then, too, he knew a lot about Ötzi the Iceman, something she most definitely did not need to know about but found fascinating in a baffling sort of way. How anyone could even think to write a book, much less know the first thing about how to do so, also fascinated, and impressed her.

She fingered the base of the champagne glass, sliding her thumb and index finger around the slippery glass base. When he reached across the table and placed his hand around the top of hers, she let it stay this time, smiling back at him like a teenage girl.

CHAPTER TWELVE

Maxine brought the old Polaroid about half a meter from Shelley's face, as far as she could without distorting the close-up. "Please hold still—just like that, yes....I don't know what I'm going to do once the film goes. I'm afraid they no longer make it these days. Honestly, I don't know what I'm going to do." She rested her elbows against the bulge of her belly to steady her hands and snapped the shot. "Just a second more now. Be still....Good thing I had Dodie ransack the Internet. I do believe she bought up every last piece of Polaroid film in the world for me!"

The precious paper containing the emergent picture started clicking out of the camera's bottom. Maxine watched it, instinctively holding her breath as though she were having a mammogram.

"You could go digital, you know," said Shelley. "It's even faster than Polaroid, and you don't need to keep buying film. You don't need film at all."

"Oh, dear, no. That's computer voodoo—too advanced for my pea brain....No, I'll stick with this warhorse, so long as the film holds out. I'm far too old a dog—dam, I suppose, would be the correct term—to learn new tricks. When the film goes, you see, that's my sign....It's getting to be time, anyway. Honestly it is....You do not want to have arthritis in your fingers, believe you me. The knees are bad enough, the shoulders, first thing in the morning...but the fingers. Awk! Oh, my dear, what you don't know—just thank God for your youth. But, *kenahora*, at least my hands still work, eh? Maybe they just can't forget what they've been doing so long. They shake, you know, when I hold a cup of coffee—GP says it is 'essential tremor,' whatever that means—but when I've got those tools in my hands, they're as steady as a surgeon's, and hardly any pain....I suppose it's ingrained. Habit—one advantage of being an 'old dam,' then, though, eh?"

Maxine detached the photograph, still largely a series of gray blobs, and waved it slowly through the air. "Magic, I always say! As soon as it dries, we'll have our 'before' picture.'"

Shelley grimaced as the incoherent blotches materialized into an image of her face. "Scarface."

"You know, dear, you're healing up nicely, as well as can be expected anyway. But you really cannot transform yourself overnight, even with all my tricks...." Maxine clipped the photograph to Shelley's file. "You must also realize that you cannot possibly see what's truly there. Or, rather, what others see of you."

"I wish. But—let's be honest. It's pretty hideous."

Maxine shook her head. "Rubbish. You've noticed, I'm sure, how we women always see the flaws in ourselves far more than others do. Sometimes that's all we can see, in fact—the flaws."

"I suppose."

"We only remember the negative. If someone absolutely adored your dinner party and raved about the roast and the salad and the pudding and so forth, if she went on and on about your brilliant decor and exquisite hostess gown, but then put a bit of salt on her potatoes—or even failed to comment on the potatoes altogether—well, what do you do? You know perfectly well what you do because you're a normal female. You don't *kvell* over the compliments. Oh no. Instead you—all of us—we obsess on the failed potatoes, perhaps never serving that particular recipe again, perhaps never even inviting that particular friend for supper again."

Shelley laughed. "That's true. That's so pathetic."

"That's reality. We are humiliated, shamed, devastated beyond comprehension by a single criticism, however mild, however many compliments accompanied it. Am I right? Or back in school—isn't it sad how you only remember the one comment about forgetting to use a pencil on the equations but can't remember the praise for getting the problems correct? That's the female mind for you—or the mind of most insecure human beings, which, in my experience, is most of us females. And when it comes to our bodies, we're the worst. I can't speak for the fellows, but I know it's true with me, and for every gal I've ever met. That's why 90% of my clients are women—they run in here because that one flaw, perhaps one that no one else has ever noticed, drives them to despair. All women see is a single new spot, and they're phoning up the surgeon. Am I right? All we can see is our flat chest or large bum or that single hair on the chin. And when we see it, it overwhelms us, becomes the entire universe. It is vanity, my dear, pure vanity. We blow the slightest imperfection out of proportion. We just can't see the whole picture, not with ourselves."

"Well, we want to improve ourselves, I suppose. But I don't think it's vanity. Not really. What's vain is dwelling on our assets. Or pretending we're perfect."

"It's vanity. Believe me—it's my business, vanity is. We

women make ourselves miserable—miserable!—over the tiniest of flaws. And that is vanity. But whatever you label it, the point is that we miss the big picture. That's why we can't see what others see, or the way they see. That's why you always see your flaws more than others do. You have a single spot on your chin, and that's all your eye sees in the mirror. It becomes enormous, overshadowing the beauty of your eyes or the glow of your skin. You cannot judge yourself, believe me. A man has a big pot belly hanging over his belt and thinks he's a Hercules. He has a bald spot, combs the bloody thing over, and thinks he's Adonis. A woman gains a pound the day after a dinner party, and the next day she's close to suicidal. Am I right?...My point is simply that what seems insufferably hideous to you is barely noticeable to others, who, in most cases, are too absorbed with their own issues to pay all that much mind to yours."

"Okay, well, I suppose you're right. But the thing is, that mark—it's not just a spot with me. It can't be."

"I know it seems that way. And, of course, you think about how you got it, and there's more to it than just a blemish on the face. But you must understand, or try to understand, that it's simply not. It's not everything. Please. That dreadful man has done a number on your face. Nature hasn't helped with the pockmarks, of course, but you wouldn't believe what I've seen in my day. Burn victims— whole sides of faces with no color at all. Vitiligo—the same thing. Huge white patches over the forehead and the chin. Cherry angiomas bleeding beet red across the cheek. What you have is nothing—nothing!—compared to what those women go through every day. I've seen the walking wounded here, truly. Hair as dark and thick as a man's beard growing from chins and cheeks, sagging and lopsided lips, rosacea that would send anyone into a closet, hairy moles crossing the lipline, warty noses, and oozing spots and cysts so inflamed there's no skin left. You have no idea. I've had more than my share of skin butchered by tweezings and peels and lasers and waxings, endless butchering, not to mention the botched brow, line, and lip jobs by fluffheads I've had to undo. Oh, my dear, I don't even know where to begin, the carnage I've seen on the human face. Natural and induced in the name of beauty both."

"I just know I can't stand looking in the mirror."

"That will change, don't you fret. Just think, too—once we have you fixed up, you can get this hair off your face as well...." Maxine put on her reading glasses, scooted her stool forward, and pushed up the wild wisps of hair that obscured Shelley's forehead. "You'll be able to show the world your full lovely face, which is, you know, a perfect oval when you can see the whole thing." Maxine picked up a clipboard on which she had already collected her notes about Shelley and unclipped a piece of paper on which she had scribbled a timetable. "Take a look, dear. I want you to see the whole concept before we begin. I spent hours coming up with this last night. Oh, my dear, together with your new hair color and style, and your new wardrobe—you're going to become an entirely different person. What do you think?...Eyeliner, brows, lipliner, lips, scar camouflaging, blush. You see? The works. The liner, eyes, we'll do that first after the hair, and you'll see immediate change. It will make your lashes seem considerably fuller, longer. I almost always do lash enhancement with the liner. You will be amazed at the difference....I thought a beauty mark on your cheekbone might be lovely, too, and, of course, much fuller, but lighter, brows. We'll pop in some colored contact lenses, too, at the end."

"This is so much...."

"Of course, we might consider dyeing the lashes blond instead, perhaps go blue with the eye color as well. Have you always wanted to be a blue-eyed blonde? It can happen, you know! You won't see that on the timetable here. We'll slip in the work while we're waiting for healing...And then some needling of those scars, the burns and acne both, yes, before we do the camouflage, I think....The needling always makes the skin healthier, smoother, and then the micropigmentation works even better....Yes, indeed....A package worth thousands of dollars, I might add."

"That I can believe."

"All pro bono, as they say in the legal world!"

Shelley looked at the paper more carefully, nipping and tugging her upper lip with her lower teeth. "But we won't be done for a year, a year and a half, according to this....I can't wait that long!"

"Really, dear, you can. You can't *not* wait that long, in fact."

"But—what about my . . ."

"What about your what? What other plans do you have, pray tell?..And for shame, let loose of that lip, will you? I won't be able to do a thing for you if you keep tearing yourself apart like a cud-chewing cow." Shelley looked blank as Maxine retrieved the paper from her and tucked it into the file. "Please consider reality, luv. You can't go out on the street, you haven't a home or a job, as I understand it. Isn't that so? Here you have both. In the meantime, we'll fix you up safely and beautifully, so that, when we're done, you can walk about town, anywhere, without fear of harm. Isn't that the goal?"

Maxine began riffling through the papers on the clipboard. From what Dodie had told her, Delegate Herkimer paid for her condo, which was under his name, and justified his largess by using Shelley to work on his political ventures, employment that was clearly no longer required. Perhaps Shelley didn't fully realize what damaged goods she was, damaged not just because of Rocco's recent inflictions but because her apparently passive, even reactive, approach to life in general made her the kind of lost soul that men like Rocco preyed upon. Perhaps no one had ever told her so, or helped her find her way, but there was no better time than now for someone to do so. Maxine believed that the first part of reformation always began with a little pain, physical or otherwise.

"Now where in heaven is that bloody form? It's supposed to be right on top here."

"But how can it take so long? We're doing the hair tomorrow, right? That should take a few hours, tops."

"Hair is dead cells, an entirely different animal than the living, breathing skin. You understand? When it comes to your eyes and lips, cheeks and so forth, we can't play games. We don't get another chance, and I won't take the quick and easy way."

"I understand that."

"Haste makes waste, as they say. Too many of these operators today do the full face in a single session or two. They are nothing short of sloppy. Proper application is slow. You must understand that. Properly done, each section takes at least an hour, maybe two. Plus by going in stages we can see if you have any unexpected reactions—dreadfully important. I've seen a woman whose entire face blew up like a tomato after one of these marathon application sessions. She had to go home and out on the streets like that, and then bury herself for weeks until it all came down again. We can't have that...."

Maxine clipped a paper onto the top of the clipboard

and picked up a pen. "Now, if you don't mind, I need to complete and have you sign this form, to make sure we've covered all bases. I've got your name here, address, well, we can just put here, I suppose....Age?"

"Thirty-four."

"Is that so? You and Dodie are the same age then. Imagine!"

"She had a much better mother."

"That, my dear, I doubt. Very much."

"Believe me, no matter what you did to Dodie, no one can compare to Jaclyn."

"Your mother, I assume. This Jaclyn?"

"Actually, she was born Doris Wartofsky. But you're not supposed to know that."

"She changed her name?"

"She was in the 'arts.' Or so she claimed. And Doris Wartofsky just didn't sound right for that. She reviewed plays and movies for the local paper. Ballets sometimes, too. I don't think she got paid, but she was very into that."

"Was she now?"

"Later, when I was in high school—I think—she also had this talk show on our local cable station. She brought in a different guest every week—you know, people like the ballet mistress, the conductor of the Bloomfield Hills orchestra, some poet..."

"Bloomfield Hills. My, that sounds utterly lovely now, doesn't it?"

"*They* think so. It's not Detroit at any rate."

"I see."

"Don't let the name mislead you. Think crass, n*ouveau riche*—it's that type of place. Everyone full of themselves, and so ignorant. I couldn't wait to leave."

"Don't you have family back there?"

"No one worth seeing...."

"Just a moment, dear." Maxine unclipped a paper and then reclipped it to the top of the board. "Ah, here we go. So—you were telling me about your mother then. She had her own show, eh?"

"Yeah. On cable, if you count that. She would wear these dashiki thingies and chain smoke and gush a lot about how brilliant her guests were and how hard their lives were as artists and such....Meanwhile, I was home with Roger."

Maxine smiled and waved the clipboard toward Shelley. "So then, now you must sign this. Are we clear on everything?"

Shelley rested the clipboard in her lap and rolled the pen between the fingers of her right hand. "I feel like I'm signing my life away."

"Shelley, dear, I cannot emphasize enough that the quick and easy way is dangerous. Here, and everywhere else in life. I will absolutely only do one area at a time—too much trauma to the face will interfere with the healing process. Tomorrow we do the hair, but we must still give you a few more weeks to get back your strength—because, mark my words, you want to be in the best health possible before we begin micropigmentation. Good health facilitates optimum skin recovery. Are you with me?"

"Yes."

"Good. When you're ready, we start with the eyeliner, to reshape the look of the eyes. But that will only be the beginning. You'll take a few days, maybe a week, to heal. We don't want to traumatize the skin. Four weeks, maybe six later, we do a follow-up. The color almost never takes perfectly the first time, so I fill in the blanks at that point. You must recover again, at least four weeks. Then we can move on, perhaps to the brows. That's another two months....

"Two months."

"Shelley, listen now, you must be clear on this: We've got so much to cover—brows, lip liner, the lips themselves—which need even more recovery time, usually eight weeks for most people. You must leave two months, sometimes more, for each of these. Maybe—depending on what's healing—I'll try working on the capillaries in between. We'll see. And the R.A. machine to get some vitamin A into those little pocks as well, while we're at it. We can do that rather soon, perhaps after the eyes are done, certainly before the blush and the larger scars. And, then, it might also be possible to do M.C.A. while we're waiting to work on those nasty scars on your neck for you, and the one on your forehead—it will be like you've never had them."

"M.C.A. Now I'm completely lost."

"Multitrepannic collagen actuation. I explained it before, I'm sure. Perhaps I used the lay term—skin needling."

"Oh. Right."

"M.C.A. is the technical term. It gets the collagen going. And the melanin. It's brilliant, astounding, developed by medical doctors, dermatologists. It stimulates new collagen deposits without damaging the epidermis. The needle only penetrates the outer layer, the stratum corneum, creating a tiny hole, a micro wound if you will, but one that will easily heal, you see? Like a puncture, a pinprick. But it damages the underlying dermis just enough to induce the release of growth factors that will then stimulate new collagen. Collagen, you may know, is a vital, essential protein, a fibrous protein. It's what connects and supports the skin. Together with elastin it's what gives your skin firmness, flexibility, everything we want in skin, what we lose as we age. So we attempt to restore it, restore the collagen, to any kind of damaged skin—that's the dream of every skin care specialist, no matter what technique she's using. Stimulating collagen."

"I see."

"And, you know, needling is so beautiful, so perfect, because it often also happens to restimulate melanin production. So the scars color up a bit as well. A bonus, truly. I don't think they expected this in the beginning, but it turned out to be yet another benefit of the procedure. So. You see that's why I suspect a bit of needling will reduce some of your larger marks, making the camouflage, the micropigmentation, even more successful."

"Makes sense I guess."

"Of course it makes sense. Now stop dilly dallying and sign the form. It's not like you have all that many other options now, is it?"

"There I'll agree with you." Shelley lifted the consent form from her lap, signed it, and thrust the clipboard towards Maxine. "Here then."

"It's just a pity that the dermatologists are all so sold on that horrid laser business these days. So costly, and so ineffective. It even leaves people scarred, but—what can I say? They've been sold a bill of goods, and so have American women. Anyway, don't you worry. The M.C.A. coupled with the micropigmentation is all you need for those scars. You'll see soon enough. Even the forehead area....You do understand that scar work is very advanced, not something you dash off in an afternoon?"

"I understand that. Yes." Shelley began chewing on her lip again.

"My dear, Shelley. My dear. You need to think of it like painting a wall. You can't get by without primer, without several coats, not if you want a proper job. You will see with the liner, for example, that it's going to look quite sharp the first night—too sharp, probably, glaring, obvious. But then it's going to start flaking off as you begin healing. And fading. That takes another week or two. You must not scratch or pick at it during this time. But I'll tell you more about that when we're finished. You'll see then that we need a 'second coat.' Some clients may even need a third, though I doubt that will be necessary. That's why clients must return to have additional color applied, usually after a month or so...."

Maxine unclipped the signed consent form and other papers from the clipboard and tucked them back into Shelley's folder.

"So there's your year—easily, you see? But, you know, also, you'll be able to leave here, free to walk about and so forth, before we're entirely done. We'll see. And then you'll be free to do as you please, live wherever you choose...."

"But...but what will I do here? For a year? A year!"

"Surely you haven't forgotten already? You'll be working for me, of course....In fact, this is far more than enough talk now, isn't it? Come. Let's go across the hall, and I'll show you the filing system. I expect we'll see Dodie here in a bit as well. She promised to pop by later to introduce you to the appointment book. Carole, naturally, managed to double book several touch-ups for this coming week, and I'm hoping you can get that straightened out. I have no patience with the book, you see, the lines are too close for my eyes— but a competent receptionist such as yourself should be able to set things straight lickety split."

CHAPTER THIRTEEN

"**B**londe! I still can't believe it!" Shelley extended the hand-mirror an arm's length above her head to scrutinize herself from the top down. Earlier that evening Maxine had chopped her layers so short that she was left with a close-cropped, nearly boyish cut with just a few stray curls dangling like scissored ribbon at the nape of her neck. Now they had finished turning her honey blond, a shade Maxine said worked particularly well with darker skin tones.

"I still can't believe it's me."

"It is astounding how a hairstyle can transform you, isn't it?"

"I'm in shock. All my life I've been afraid to do anything more than a few highlights—and look at me!"

"I'll bet you're sorry you never did it before, eh?"

"The only thing is, now I have to look at that scar all the time. Not that I don't have plenty others to look at already."

"Oh, pish. I actually forgot you had that dreadful thing. That's the truth. I completely forgot about it until I pulled back your bangs. Don't fret—I'll leave a few stray hairs over it when I blow you dry, and, of course, tomorrow you can temporarily cover it with makeup. I'll give you something that will nourish your skin at the same time—don't let me forget....Just wait until we cover all the scars, my dear, permanently cover them, I mean, and brighten your face and permanently reshape the brows and lips. Just wait until we get at those veins around the nose as well—that alone will take off twenty years, in an afternoon!"

"Great. Twenty years would make me about 14."

"Don't boast."

"I'm not boasting. I'm thinking 'zit city.'"

"Hmph. I'm sorry, but—minus the spots—who wouldn't want to have the skin of a young girl? Most of us would kill for it."

Shelley looked in the hand-mirror again for perhaps the fiftieth time that night. "I'm not sure how much is the cut and how much the color. Both, I suppose."

"Well now, we wanted maximum transformation, didn't we?"

"I don't look like myself anymore. I don't even feel like myself."

"Of course you're yourself. Only better. Every change we make will only make you more like you. Or more like the 'you' that you are inside, you see? The 'you' that you *should* be."

"I don't know. It's a drastic change, really, to walk around like this. Blonde."

"Pish. You just need to live with it a bit, not here in the salon, of course, but in your real clothes, in your real life, and you'll see what I mean. You're simply now able to be what you've always been."

"What real life?"

"The life you'll have when this is done. Time does pass, dear. You're old enough to know that."

"It's just that, I don't know, it doesn't feel right somehow."

"Please. You're not used to yourself, that's all, the same way no one can quite recognize themselves the day after any haircut. That startled feeling you get when you catch yourself in the mirror goes away very quickly....I first went blonde at 25, mind you, and that was more years ago than I care to remember. But I can tell you—I never thought twice about it....Normally, of course, our plan as aestheticians, whether we're speaking hair color or makeup or anything, honestly, is to make a person look better, not different. We want to enhance, not change, the natural beauty. In most cases. But here we are going to do both!"

"That's good to hear. But I'm not so sure how much natural beauty I have for you to work with."

"Hmmph. You will be pleased, Shelley. Believe me, when I'm done, I can't say if you'll feel like you, as you say, but I assure you that you won't *look* like you. And that is the whole idea, now, isn't it? . . ."

"When I was a little kid, I used to think that if I had been blonde, I would have been entirely different person."

"Hmmph."

"No, I mean, if I had been blonde, I would have thought I was pretty, I would have acted like a pretty girl, not a smart one. I wouldn't have *had* to be smart. Or nice. I wouldn't have *had* to try. People just would have liked me for being me."

"Oh dear."

"It's true."

"*Ag.* I doubt that very much....Now where on earth is that hair dryer?" Maxine rummaged through the supply cabinet above the sink. "Honestly, that woman Carole was a piece of work. She had a way of putting everything different places every day. Makes you wonder what—if anything— went on in that mangled, muddied brain. What a bloody mess!...Your next project, Shelley, no question, is getting these cabinets in order. Even before you finish up the supply room. First thing tomorrow...."

"I can't believe going blonde didn't change the way people reacted to you. At least a little."

"Well, naturally it did. Every change in your look will change the way you feel about yourself, conduct yourself, and thus the way others react to you. Naturally it changed reactions. But reactions are not you."

Shelley stroked her hair again. "Maybe. But I really feel different. I don't mean feel differently *about* myself. I mean feel like I am actually a different person. Completely, like I don't know myself. It's a bit terrifying, to tell you the truth. I don't know what I'm going to do, or say—or think."

"Well. That's astonishing. Seriously, from my own experience...well, I'd hardly say going blonde made me stupid or vicious or anything like that. I remained myself, you know. Stupid and vicious by nature, whatever my color!" She stared at Shelley until she saw a trace of a smile. "I will grant you one thing, however: you might have been able to become a new person so far as the boys were concerned. Males, for the most part, are dopes. I've never met one who could detect a dye job. Possibly that fellow wouldn't recognize you right now."

"He wouldn't. But he wouldn't be the only one. Really, I barely recognize myself."

"You know, I remember once it took my Utzi a good three weeks before he noticed I had gone a shade lighter. Golden blonde to near platinum, mind you, and he didn't see a thing for three weeks. Three weeks! And even then I had to prompt him. 'Did you notice anything different?' I asked him. 'Uh, yes,' said Mr. Magoo. "Actually, I *was* thinking you perhaps did something. What is it now? You changed your glasses, er, is that it?' Shelley, my love, I'm telling you the truth—for the life of him, he couldn't discern what I had done, daft old mutton-brain. He could barely see a difference."

"Unbelievable."

"Completely believable. In fact, as I said, that's the male sex for you. They don't notice a change that you want them to notice, and they are often just as easily clueless to those you don't want them to see."

"Most of them, I suppose."

"Of course you suppose. I've never in my life met a man who could tell a bleach job. The blokes think every blonde they see—even the most brazen bleach-heads, the hideous home jobs without the slightest shading who look like they dumped a bucket of oil paint over their heads—these clueless fellows think every one of these girls was born looking like a Swedish model. Oh yes—even girls they saw as black as coal the week before. They're like dogs with a bitch in heat—their brains stop working altogether. Hah! Yes, you may fool him for all I know. You may indeed. But, as I say, you must change for everyone, not just him. Because, eventually, even if no one tips him off, which most likely someone will, especially if he's got them looking, well, eventually he'll catch on to wherever you are, once you're out there in the world again—it may just take him a bit, you see?"

"Maybe. But it will also be much easier to avoid him this way."

"Mark my words. You cannot count on the hair alone. No, ma'am....The idea here is that we make sure that no one can recognize you. No one. And I assure you that some people aren't so gullible. You may think you are unrecognizable, and, perhaps you are to some extent, to some people, particularly those of the male persuasion, but not to everyone. And not forever, not completely...."

"I don't know. It's a real transformation. You said so yourself."

"*Ag*, Shelley. You are a person who cannot afford to take chances. *Any* chances....We must get to a point where you feel you are unrecognizable—to anyone, not just him."

Shelley pulled back as Maxine brought the dryer toward her head. "You really didn't feel the slightest bit odd the first time you colored your hair? I got palpitations just from putting in the highlights that first time. It felt—unnatural. Wrong."

"It's perfectly natural."

"It almost felt evil."

"Oh, please. You sound like Dodie when you talk that way. I don't know what it is with you young people, but it's like you think you're purer than everyone else or something. Anything that's not what you deem 'natural' is horrible, disgusting to you. Pish. What is 'natural' anyway? Getting old and ugly at age 25? Living with wiry hair and spots when there's something you can do to fix yourself? Let me tell you, Shelley, it is natural to fix yourself. That is what human beings do. Natural human beings."

"I don't think putting artificial chemicals in your hair, not living with what you were born with, is exactly natural."

"Of course it is." Maxine switched on the dryer and held it above Shelley's head, fluffing what remained of her hair with her fingers as she ran the air over it. "It's the most natural thing of all."

"There is such thing as growing old gracefully, you know."

"I doubt that very much." Despite her youthful adherence to Dr. Ruf's maxims, Maxine was now inclined to regard the aging process more as a matter of sticking one's head in the sand. There were certainly cultures that venerated the elderly, but she doubted that it felt any better to be old and wizened in them. Even if you put the aches and pains aside—no one could possibly enjoy those—was it genuinely possible to admire, even celebrate, one's skin creases and thinning gray hair? Some white hair was beautiful, and, then too, some people with darker skins, many of whom she could remember from home, never wrinkled and almost seemed to glow with age. Essie, Dr. Ruf's kitchen woman who could tell firsthand stories about Prime Minister Hertzog and the ascendance of Afrikaans, never looked a day over 35, and Maxine herself could still recall marveling at the throngs of middle-aged nannies waiting on bus lines whose taut, glistening arms and foreheads looked as creaseless and resilient as wet seal skin. The sun, though, as Dr. Ruf so frequently emphasized, put an end to aging with grace, at least in those susceptible to it, which was most everyone. "Nature is the model of perfection," he would say over and over, and yet now, thoroughly free of his influence, she questioned whether that was true once you got past that first bloom, or whether he himself had ever tried to reconcile that philosophy with his harangues against the sun. What she didn't question was that his various tricks and tactics could delay the process, at least for a while.

"Your sentiments about what natural means are common in the young, when nature is often kind," Maxine told Shelley, "but wait another decade or so, my dear, and see what you have to say about the beauty of nature....The human being has fought nature from earliest times. That *is* our nature, when you come to think of it—our nature is to fight nature....Oh, dear girl, you are so misguided. Because whether you think something is natural or not, it's not necessarily good, now is it?"

"I suppose not."

"You suppose correctly. You're a very silly thing to think what is natural is beautiful. Perhaps in a baby, a young girl—but after that, we, well, most of us, need to enhance or improve nature. There is nothing at all wrong—or unnatural—with that, no more than there's anything wrong or unnatural with a doctor fixing a broken bone or giving you an aspirin for a headache. Natural, or what you call natural, anyway, does not necessarily mean good. And certainly not attractive now, does it?"

"Certainly not."

Maxine was convinced that Shelley's professed self-loathing would subside as their work together continued. "Inside, my dear, we are all beautiful. I have never denied that, not ever. All of us—and yes, even you, whatever you say. But whatever we can do to bring out that inner beauty, the real us, we should be doing. That is what we humans do, have always done, if you know a bit of history. My goodness, our ancestors were tattooing their bodies back in the Ice Age now, weren't they? Utzi the Iceman, my gentleman friend, you remember, loves to tell that story, but I'll spare you...Anyway, at the first gray hair or wrinkle, most of you younger gals change your 'natural is beautiful' tune, but...in my day, we understood that beauty takes a bit of effort. You make such a big thing of it, when it's what women—all people, really—have been doing since time began."

"I suppose you're right."

"Of course I'm right. And in my case I learned the lesson quite young. I had no choice. Gingers fade early, you see."

"Twenty-five is young. I mean to go gray...."

"It's not exactly gray. More what you might call sandy, and then, eventually, white. The sheen goes off. Something about the pheomelanin, I think it is. It's all part of the aging process, just as some men start balding in their twenties, or a few unlucky ones, in their late teens."

"Wow."

"I'm afraid it's a curse of the gingers, early fading. As I said, it may have to do with the pheomelanin, the pigment that gives the hair its redness. Or perhaps it's lack of the eumelanins. No one fully understands, even now. Guesswork. Loss of eumelanin grays you, and, of course, we gingers never had much of it to begin with. "

"So going from red to blonde didn't feel odd to you?"

"I was so young, pet, so young. I can't keep the details from that far back, but can tell you with certainty that I don't remember feeling anything except delighted....As a girl, my color was brilliant, and I kept it long—as long as Dodie's. 'Flaming tresses,' was what a gentleman friend used to say. But, of course, as a ginger, mine all went to sand by the time I was her age. I loved my long hair in my younger days, too, but then I began looking like a hag, you see, the way most of us do if we don't go short by middle age. Long hair does that to most of us older gals, isn't that so? It pulls down our faces, emphasizes the lines, not something any of us want. In my day, you'd cut by 25, 30 at the latest, although your generation seems to push it to 40, even 50, or beyond, especially if they've treated their skin properly. But it gets us all in the end...." She switched off the dryer. "There now, are you a new person, or what?"

Shelley stroked the wispy curls at the back of her neck.

"You know what they say, don't you? The older you get, the shorter and lighter you go. Dodie, well, somehow she's kept her glow, God love her...She was never one to follow the crowd."

"She's stunning."

"At heart she's a natural girl. A hippie you might say. Born twenty years too late, of course, but most definitely a hippie at heart. And she has good skin, you see, so it works for her. I suppose. I've offered to brighten her a bit when she seemed a bit off. But she'll have none of it, and to look at her—I think she's right....There is nothing more beautiful than natural simplicity. Dr. Rufus Alvarez, who puts all these beauty products together, always used to quote some poet on that. When you have lost the 'happiness of nature,' he'd say, 'let its perfection be a model to your heart.' That is so true. Isn't it? We just try the best we can to return ourselves to what we were, once it is no longer in our reach...."

"Well, anyway, I really like what you've done. I just have to get used to the new me, that's all."

"Ah, Shelley, you are on the road back to beauty. You must simply take my word for it. I wish the road weren't as long as it is, but you will find it worth the journey, trust me." Maxine began coiling the cord around the body of the dryer. "Now get up and get yourself ready for bed. Use that satin case I gave you over the pillow—it will keep you from mussing the styling overnight, you understand? And do sleep well. I have loads of reorganizing for you tomorrow, both here and in the supply room. You should have time for both. Now that your hair is done you're ready to do receptionist work too, greet and book the clients and so forth, at least if you keep the cover-up on the bruises. And then, in another week or two if those bruises are down enough, we'll do a mock-up on your face. Assuming you get enough accomplished. Then you'll truly see what you will become."

CHAPTER FOURTEEN

"I see you have a new girl," said Eleanor Norris, a perennial client who squeezed visits for her seemingly infinite dissatisfactions between chiropractic and massage therapy sessions. Mammoth-boned and similarly proportioned, she overwhelmed the tiny makeup room the way large dogs overwhelm a coffee table and yet gracefully cruised the remaining space to hang her Prada bag on the door hook. "You'll be relieved to know I remembered to turn off my phone this time."

"Thank you, dearest. Bloody distraction those things are, and God knows what they do to the equipment, all those invisible rays hovering ....Please, have a seat, and we'll get started."

Maxine scrubbed her hands for the second time that morning with warm water and soap. She scrubbed for a good two minutes, counting the seconds to herself the way she had been trained. It was appalling how many of the younger ones didn't know, much less practice, the simplest hygiene, and even more appalling how the clients didn't care, and would often run to the cheapest ninny for work, never putting two and two together to equate cheap with short-cuts, lack of cleanliness, and, most specifically, inadequate training. In this regard Maxine was indeed, as she so often claimed, an "old dam," and she had no intention of abandoning sensible habits, however costly. The worst part was all this washing and scrubbing turned her own hands raw and chapped, especially as the air dried in the fall. She would have to do a treatment tonight herself.

Maxine began working plastic surgical gloves onto her hands, adjusting every finger with slow, downward tugs. "Bugger that Carole. I'm still living with fallout from her scatterbrains. Can you believe—she ordered larges yet again." She pushed the excess latex down toward her fingertips. "No matter what, everything bunches at the tips....I do apologize."

Eleanor smoothed the back of her tennis skirt and settled herself into the make-up chair.

"I can't work this way, not with this kind of precision work," Maxine continued. "They make these gloves for a man's hand, you see. I get the surgical ones. You must have the right size. Especially for delicate work."

"Naturally."

"You have no idea what I had to put up with. The simplest things—and you'd think a person who had only to order these once or twice a year could get it right, wouldn't you? Well, you see, now with this new girl, things will be improved."

"I trust they will."

"If she can get her nose out of a book, that is. The girl goes through them like candy, those tiny print paperbacks that ruin your eyes....Presumably she'll know the difference between medium and large anyhow—won't you now, Michelle?"

Shelley, who they had decided to call by her given, but never used, name "Michelle" in front of the clients, replied from the front room. "Did you need something, Maxine?"

"I was just saying to Eleanor here that now that you're

with us we're going to be much better organized."

Shelley appeared in the doorway of the makeup room. "I'll try my best."

"I'm sure you'll do splendidly," said Eleanor. "And I see you're a reader. Wonderful!"

"The truth is, Michelle does get a bit dotty over her books. But I must give credit where credit is due. She did a masterful job cleaning up my files and keeps the waiting area spit spot....Michelle, dear, while you're here—could you please help me set these glasses? Just pull them up over the mask. It's hard to do with these bloody clown gloves on my hands."

"I saw you were reading Turow," said Eleanor. "Are you enjoying it?"

"It's okay. Not my genre of choice, but beggars can't be choosers."

"He's a fascinating man. My brother and sister-in-law live down the street from him. Out in Chicago."

Shelley gently lifted Maxine's reading glasses, which hung from a chain around her neck, and placed them properly on her face.

"Fine, dear....Very well, thank you....All done then."

Both Maxine and Eleanor were silent until they heard Shelley settle herself behind the front desk.

"Seems like a nice gal. Bright."

Maxine held her rubbery hands up in front of her face and laced her fingers together to tighten the fingertips. "Oh, yes. She has a degree in accounting, even studied marine biology, I'm told – not that it does her much good. Believe me, though, I'd have taken in Betty Boop if she'd shown up at my door. Anything after that Carole....Now, what are we doing for you today?"

"Just a check-up on the eyeliner and brows."

"Any problems?"

"No—actually they look pretty good to me. Do you think the left brow will still fade some though? It seems darker than the right to me. A little bit."

Eleanor, sitting stiffly with her exposed thighs stuck to the plastic chair, inspected her chewed nails while Maxine scrutinized her face with a magnifying glass. Eleanor's skin was in surprisingly good shape for a person who spent half the year sailing on the Chesapeake Bay inhaling martinis. Clearly six months of needling, not to mention the hydrating oil capsules, were helping. "You're making good progress. You'll still lose a little color, I think. When did we do this? Last week?"

"Last Tuesday. It's just the left looks darker than the right."

"Let's give it a bit more time then. It's not unusual for one side to finalize faster than the other. Another week, I'd say, and then it's likely the color will balance out. If you're still unhappy, call me, and I'll touch you up. Meanwhile— why don't you let me use the machine to work some crystal mask into that scar tissue, eh? Around the eyes? With you coming in so often now, you're going to see some real progress with that, and now with the color—it's going to be stunning, absolutely stunning. You'll need to keep applying the hydrating oil, of course, and the retinol."

"That's fine....I booked half an hour, so that should work for us both. Oh, and I'll need some more of that exfoliating gel you carry. I forgot to take it last time...Is that poster new? Gorgeous."

"Utzi finally blew up my prints from my last trip to South Africa—years it took him, but, by golly, he finally managed to finish. That's Table Mountain, Capetown, floating right there on the sea. Takes my breath away every time I see it."

"Stunning. It really is stunning. Although, you know, it's also...hard to grasp, isn't it, that there's such beauty in a country like that. When were you last there?"

"It's been over three years. I'm saving my pennies, mind you, to go back. I want to take Utzi. He's never been."

"Wouldn't that be nice!"

"He'll never understand until he's seen it. No one can understand until they've seen it."

"Honestly, Maxine, I sometimes wonder how you bore it. South Africa. My word!..I suppose it's family that keeps calling you back."

"I have no family there anymore. Not to speak of."

"Well, home is home," said Eleanor. "But, still, you know, it must be painful, going back. The history. The violence, I mean. Of course, maybe we hear wrong...."

"Truly, it's the most beautiful country in the world....I miss it."

"That picture certainly makes it seem beautiful. Unworldly even."

"You have not seen the earth until you've stood on Table Mountain in Capetown and seen the Atlantic Ocean greeting the Indian."

"Breathtaking, I suppose."

"Breathtaking....Hold still now while I place the electrodes, will you?"

"Oooh—that always stings."

"Well, that's the sign we're getting some penetration. Be glad."

Eleanor flinched and swallowed. "But still, you know, how horrid to have that beauty mixed with all the ugliness. Socially, I mean."

"Yes."

"Horrid."

"Really, though, dear one, you make it out worse than it was," Maxine sighed. She felt the speech rising up in her and knew that she would have to let it out, despite her better judgment. "Today, yes, it is horrid. I'll give you that. Violent. Corrupt. Impossible really. But when I was growing up...."

"All the pass laws."

"You know, dear, America is horribly racist as well. In fact, in some ways I'd say it is worse here than in South Africa. Far worse."

"Worse?"

"Yes. Because here they pretend they are not racist. That makes the racism even worse."

"I certainly don't pretend. I'm not sure I understand."

"No. You Americans never do. Because, you see, people who are in the majority group can rarely see themselves clearly. That's just the point. In South Africa—awful as it was—at least we saw it. We admitted it. It was wrong, terribly wrong, but it was honest." She pressed the electrode slightly harder into Eleanor's temple. Eleanor shifted in her seat and winced as her thighs unstuck themselves from the plastic.

"I'm sorry, but...we don't segregate people by race here. Or discriminate."

"But we do, luv. We do. *Ag shame*, my grandchildren just had to check a box on a school form to confirm whether they were white or Hispanic or African or whatnot. If that's not racism, what is?"

"But they don't have separate bathrooms or sit in the back of the bus....I mean, we used to do that, I know. And I suppose in some parts of the South, in this very county, in fact....Why, just on the news last night that handsome Delegate Herkimer was talking about helping our public schools with that civil rights agreement—you know, that vow they made to bring those underprivileged children up to the same standards as everyone else by 2014? It does seem like a bit of a fantasy, I'll admit, but at least we try."

Maxine bit her lip. She often thought that the worst part about living in the United States was being made to feel guilty, evil even, for having lived for so many years in that godforsaken, accursed land. She did not feel guilty. There was no question that many of the practices in South Africa had been shameful and revolting, but, goodness, so were many practices here. People's inability to see their own foibles never ceased to amaze her, although she knew very well that logic and evidence were pointless with people who had already made up their minds. Bafflingly, these were often the most highly educated, kind-hearted people you could imagine, but they had a sort of blind belief in right-and-wrong, good-and-evil, and inexorable progress that made them impervious. If she started rattling off the incriminating statistics to her many clients who couldn't resist throwing in snide remarks about South Africa on occasion, they would remind her that this country now had a black president. Yes, there had been problems, the United States had a shameful history, but progress had been considerable. My goodness, hadn't they just read things were improving? Test scores were going up with the No Child Left Behind and Race to the Top business, people were addressing health disparities, and so forth, and certainly things like this took time. They went on and on then about Abraham Lincoln and the Constitution and the Civil Rights Movement. It was enough to make her want to muzzle them.

It wasn't just her clients either. Explaining the concept of insidious racism to Utzi was like explaining the concept of electromagnetism to a wildebeest. Even Dodie, who should have been able to understand, was constitutionally unable to acknowledge anything positive about South Africa whatsoever. But Maxine saw it clearly, daily, everywhere, became acutely conscious of it whenever someone made an ignorant, self-righteous crack about her beloved and beleaguered country.

"I'm sorry to say it, but life here is different if you have dark skin," Maxine told Eleanor, pushing the electrode into the skin just a tad more firmly than she knew would be comfortable. "You must know that, deep down. Am I right, Michelle?...Michelle, do you hear me?"

"Yes, I hear you. " Shelley came into the room. "I think you're right on the mark, Maxine. The political talk about equity and justice and closing achievement gaps is a bunch of…it's just talk. Sound bites….But it's pure b.s., if you look at how we act. What always gets me is the news. Crime reports. They always tell you if the suspect is black or Hispanic. Right? Same thing with those neighborhood flyers they put up on telephone poles. But if the suspect is white, race isn't mentioned."

"Well, of course," said Maxine, wondering if Shelley's astonishing sympathy was genuine or sycophantic. "To be a black male in this country is to live a nightmare….Here, Michelle, bring me some fresh wipes, will you? Just two or three will do for now. Almost done now, Eleanor."

"Ah, I'm actually a bit sad to hear that. Interesting conversation we're having."

"It's more than interesting, I'm afraid….If you ask me, the things you Americans do to fight racism actually create more of it. I'm quite serious. Racism is despised here, on paper, in speeches. But here you can never escape your race. Never."

"I suppose. But at least here everyone is equal under the law."

"Equal but separate." Maxine tucked the electrodes back into their slots on the machine. "I say this as a Jew. My parents fled Europe to escape the Nazis, you see. So I feel I have a right to speak my mind on racism...."

"Well, of course you do. In this country anyway.... You know, I agree with you completely that we're far from perfect in this country. But, seriously—are you seriously saying things are worse here than under *apartheid*?"

"Think about it. In 'separate but equal' at least everyone got something, even if we all knew it wasn't quite in the same way, place, or time. But at least they admitted that the coloreds and blacks were missing out and made some effort to compensate them for that and give them a parallel existence. Here they admit nothing. So most people who don't fit the majority suffer in silence."

"I see what you're saying, I suppose, but—I just don't think that's the same thing as telling someone they can't come into a restaurant because of the color of their skin."

"It's not the same thing. It's worse. Because it's hidden—don't you see? You Americans are deluding yourselves if you think you aren't racist. You confuse what ought to be for what is. The result is unacknowledged discrimination, the worst kind. Because something that is not acknowledged cannot be addressed....There now. You're all done. Just relax a few minutes here and let the mask penetrate further."

CHAPTER FIFTEEN

Shelley knew that this time something was going to have to change. Really change.

She had thought this before, but never with conviction. No matter how many times the need loomed before her, no matter how uncomfortable she felt or how humiliated, misunderstood, or damaged, in the end he had always managed to convince her that his very being depended on her love. When he couldn't get away with putting the blame for his behavior on her lack of love for him—which was certainly his first impulse—he inevitably took the blame upon himself and swore that he was the one who would change. He booked a trip to Cancun or bought her an emerald bracelet or promised to stop drinking so much. He got down on his knees and apologized, begged her for forgiveness with those teary, baby boy eyes, and professed his eternal love. He had good excuses for everything, and ultimately, they were all about Shelley and her well-being: whatever he did, however cruel or selfish or even crazy it might have seemed at the time, he did it either to help her become a better person, one deserving of his love, or else to help acquire the money or prestige or power that a woman like her deserved to have in her man. When he talked like this, which he did frequently, nothing else seemed to matter, or even to have happened.

Even the time he had last beaten her after she expressed her hurt and confusion about his marriage to Cyndi, he had somehow managed to come out the good guy. She had first heard about this marriage by reading the announcement in the newspaper, and his reaction to her questioning and complaints had been to pull her across the living room by the hair and head-butt her into a corner, after which he proceeded to box her into the wall, yammering about minding her own business until she slumped to the floor, barely conscious. But even after that particular beating, as he sat solicitously at her side in the emergency room with both of them pretending that she had been mugged, he assured her that this marriage had all been done for her. He swore to her that he didn't love Cyndi in the slightest and was just using her to get ahead. In fact, he considered Cyndi to be an annoying, spoiled airhead who drove him "bonkers" most of the time. Shelley, he vowed, was his true love, the only one he could talk to, the only one who really understood him and with whom he could be his true self—couldn't she see that? And, in fact, he had come back to Shelley many times since, often with flowers and jewelry, even more often with ardor, and frequently with long rueful speeches about the cruelty of life, which kept him from her and kept him enchained to a ditzy, delicate princess like Cyndi.

Every time he returned, though, it was increasingly difficult to believe him, and now, from a distance, Shelley realized how manipulated she had been. The longer she spent in hiding, without any contact from Rocco, the more the answer seemed obvious.

Looking back on it, too, she could see that Rocco's reaction to the news of her pregnancy had been inevitable. Had she let him argue his case, of course, he would have claimed to have been in a particularly bad mood that day because of the *Capital* article. And, indeed, his mood had been justified. After more than a decade, some reporter had dredged up the story about the funeral home scandal—describing, with classic journalistic *schadenfreude*, how Rocco Herkimer, respected member of the Maryland House of Delegates, had been convicted of bank fraud during the 1990's back in Bowie, scamming sick and elderly customers out of over half a million dollars.

To be fair, Shelley hadn't read the paper that day. If she had, she would probably have been more delicate with him. Even at that point she saw Rocco not as a bad guy, but, like everyone else, a well-meaning guy who sometimes made mistakes, or had bad judgment. Furthermore, this business had been a long time ago, and, whatever you thought of Rocco or his judgment, it was pretty low of the paper to drum it up when he had things going for him at last. What really worried Shelley, too, although she didn't say it to Rocco, was that the paper was eventually going to drag her into this at well. She had been named way back then as an accessory to the crime, and Rocco, never one to put blame on himself, had even publicly accused her of masterminding the whole thing out of jealousy. He had been a respected businessman, a budding public figure, and she, college education notwithstanding, a mere secretary living in a studio apartment supported by her boyfriend. Resentful of his success, she had been portrayed as having finagled a way to skim money off the top of his business—she had, after all, been the one signing the checks and writing the letters.

Fortunately, there had been absolutely no evidence supporting these claims, and the attorney had done a fairly good job keeping Rocco quiet during the trial. It was obvious to everyone except Rocco, too, that she was largely innocent. How could she not have been? She may have been naïve, but she was not a criminal. She was simply doing what Rocco had told her to do, and he was her boss. It wasn't like she was all that sophisticated about business, being just out of school and hardly a whiz-bang accountant.

While she may have had no idea how the funeral business worked, Rocco clearly had, and so she never had a reason to question things. In fact, for the first couple years, there was nothing to question. Rocco, although the owner of the home in name, generally let Frank or Maurice run things, since they had been working with Rocco's Uncle Remo for years and knew more than Rocco did anyway. In the early years, Rocco put more of his energies into schmoozing with his buddies from the Chamber of Commerce, building a marketing strategy, and, when these tactics started boring him, becoming a local politico, spending countless hours becoming a presence at the Elephant Club and, ultimately, campaigning for county council. When he lost the election, he spent considerably more time at work, but, even this had seemed like a positive development, given that Frank and Maurice didn't have Remo's charisma and were losing considerable business to the better-connected competitors. To Shelley, and to Frank and Maurice as well, it seemed that nothing but good could come from Rocco turning his creativity and charisma into the business rather than the campaign trail, a seemingly hopeless enterprise for a relative newcomer in an intransigently Democratic community where successful politicians tended to be flush with money and long-term connections. Rocco's warm and reassuring television commercials ("Rest Easy about your Eternal Rest") evoked a regular stream of inquiries from frugal and well-meaning seniors who wanted to save their children from funeral expenses. It was hard for them, or for anyone really, to resist the reassuring promises coming from this well-spoken, well-pressed, picture-perfect man. By putting down a deposit—usually a few thousand dollars, sometimes more—they could "rest easy" knowing that, after extracting a small service fee that could usually be paid from the accumulated interest, Rocco would handle everything. He would safeguard their money and hold it in trust for them. As a result, they could have the funeral of their dreams, or at least the funeral that they themselves could afford, and their children and loved ones would have one less thing to worry about in that difficult time to come. Rocco was at his charming best, joking that his nickname was "Mr. Pre-Pay to Lay." He'd ask Shelley to serve prospective clients endless rounds of coffee and tea if they hesitated to take out their checkbooks, or even run out for bagels and donuts when it became a particularly hard sell. Aside from the morbid humor between Shelley and Rocco privately (they jokingly called him "Mr. Pre-Pay to Decay"), nothing seemed particularly amiss.

After they had won over ten or twenty customers, Rocco got down to business. Every few weeks or so, he would tell Shelley to write a check to "cash" from one of the accounts and sign the customer's name. Sometimes he'd also ask Frank or Maurice to do the same thing. At first Shelley had questioned this—how could it be legal to sign someone else's name on a check? However, he had calmly explained to her that this was part of the deal: clearly he couldn't invest the money for the client, if he didn't have access to the account, could he? And clearly he couldn't ask the client to do this kind of thing when part of his "service" was handling their investments for them. These explanations seemed plausible enough, although as the requests to write these checks—and, later, letters authorizing the closing of many of the accounts altogether and paying them out to Rocco, Shelley, or the funeral home—Shelley began to feel increasingly uncomfortable. At that point, however, her questions and hesitancy were met with utter scorn, and sometimes threats, by Rocco. This was her job. This was his business. If she didn't like it, she could leave.

What Shelley and the other employees didn't know was that Rocco was cashing these checks or depositing them into his personal and business bank accounts. Meanwhile, he was also dipping into the considerable pool of prepaid funeral funds from bank accounts established by his Uncle Remo before he had sold Rocco the home. Over two years, Rocco ultimately closed over a hundred customer bank accounts by forging and causing to be forged their signatures on letters to the bank purporting to authorize the closing of the prepaid funeral expense accounts. As a result, the bank closed the accounts and issued checks payable to the customers. Rocco simply had Shelley endorse the bank checks using the customers' name and deposited the proceeds in bank accounts he controlled.

Most of the customers were too old, ill, or naïve to ask questions, but, eventually, some began to ask why they weren't getting the bank statements they had been promised. When Shelley couldn't handle these calls, she passed them on to Rocco, who easily assured most of them that part of his service was managing these funds for a small fee he would collect at their eventual deaths—why should they be bothered when there were so many more important things to think about in life? Apparently he didn't assure all of these customers, however, because after a couple of years, the State Board of Morticians had received enough complaints to initiate an investigation. At that point Rocco asked Shelley to take files home and told the Board that all prepaid funeral expense account monies in the bank accounts had been reinvested in life insurance products. The Board—convinced that the reinvestments had actually been in Rocco's considerable gambling and business expenses, loan payments on a spanking new condo and a high-end sports car, and various lavish hotels, restaurants, gifts, and vacations— suspended his license for defrauding clients by closing their accounts and cashing in on the proceeds without authorization. Rocco faced a maximum sentence of 30 years in prison for bank, mail, and wire fraud, and the home itself faced a maximum fine of $1 million. Rocco hired an attorney from a high-priced D.C. firm. Largely because this attorney was able to argue that much of the fraud was attributable to Shelley's incompetence rather than Rocco's cunning, the sentence was ultimately reduced to a hefty fine, as well as repayment of losses to surviving victims.

Rocco sold his condo, used the proceeds (as well as Shelley's salary) to pay the fines, and, nearly penniless, moved with Shelley to western Maryland where, for several years, they no longer lived the high life. At the time Shelley had thought that neither of them would have lives of any sort, high or low, again. Even if they were both fortunate enough to escape years in prison, after all the public humiliation she was convinced that they would at the very least have to hide in some obscure town for the rest of their lives. Just a few years out of school, she still hadn't accepted the "this too shall pass" philosophy, so often urged upon her by Mrs. Simpson, her beloved next-door neighbor back in Bloomfield Hills. Mrs. Simpson had often intoned this and other sage advice, on many occasions when teenage Shelley found herself sipping hot chocolate in the Simpson kitchen. Back then, such attitudes had seemed impossibly sugar-coated to Shelley, who was then at an age when time passed slowly and every wound seemed monumental and mortal. Shelley was well into her thirties before she understood that Mrs. Simpson had been right. Everything, anything—however horrifying, even apocalyptic it might have seemed at the time—eventually receded into the homogenizing trench of memory. Perhaps these memories surfaced now and then enough to provoke a shudder, even a tear, but eventually and inevitably they morphed into just another evanescent anecdote, its particular poignancy lost in a muddy quagmire of other once poignant anecdotes. Eventually, after several moves and career changes, neither Rocco nor Shelley would think much about those years, and when they did, it was almost as though they were talking about long-dead and not particularly beloved relatives, not their own past lives.

Rocco hadn't seen things that way that afternoon he appeared in her apartment waving the *Capital* article over his head, however. He had been steamed ever since he had seen the article, and he was threatening to sue this reporter for libel. "Who cares what happened 10 years ago?" he said. "I paid the fine, and it's over. Don't they have any real news to report?"

"No one reads the 'Crapital.'" Shelley assured him that anything in that paper, if it was noticed at all, would be forgotten within a week—wasn't it always? She also assured him that the public had even shorter memories than the individuals they knew personally, and some new scandal would inevitably come along tomorrow to distract them. As long as Rocco talked the talk, and continued to show up at their spaghetti dinners and groundbreaking ceremonies, fought to let his constituents keep their handguns and horde their tax dollars, they wouldn't care that he had exercised poor judgment back in his younger days. Repentant sinners were often even glorified—that was the story of America, after all, the story of humankind, for that matter. The fact that he was human and had screwed up, that just made him more like them. Certainly a regular guy with egg on his face was preferable to a holier-than-thou egghead. Certainly the pundits and politicians would merely conclude that Rocco understood his public and that Rocco was one of them. And so the public would certainly forgive him, or, perhaps, not even believe that any of this garbage was true, just the product of his enemies, the sick, crazy-liberal gossips who had nothing better to do with their time than lash out at a man trying to get the government off their backs.

Rocco went into the kitchen and began staring into the pantry. "Where's my Chex mix?"

"There should be some on the third shelf, right."

"Obviously there 'should be some on the third shelf, right.'" He used the high-pitched, mocking voice that made her cringe. "That's where you're supposed to keep it. But there isn't any."

"I guess we're out. I'm a day late on the grocery store, Rocco. I had a doctor's appointment this morning."

He pulled himself out of the pantry and spun toward her. "What?"

"An appointment. With Dr. Allison."

"That chick doctor?"

"OB/Gyn. Yes."

"You didn't let a guy look up your snatch, did you? Because I've told you a thousand times, Shelley...."

"Yes, I know. No male doctors. Dr. Allison is a woman."

"Well. Yeah."

He fished out a package of double-stuffed Oreos from

the pantry and ripped it open with his teeth, sending two cookies spinning across the floor. Then he sat himself at the breakfast nook. "You're supposed to have Chex mix for me, Shelley. Always."

She retrieved the stray cookies, dumped them into the sink, and brought Rocco a plate. "Would you like some coffee? Milk?"

"Don't get lovey dovey on me, Shelley. You should have told me you had that appointment."

"I'll get the groceries tonight if you want. I'm sorry."

"It's not the groceries—you're just supposed to tell me. You know that....Why didn't you return my calls?"

"You called at 10, Rocco. And 11. I just got home and saw the messages, but you said you'd be over here at 1."

"I beeped you twice, too. Why didn't you answer?"

"I told you. I was at the doctor. They don't allow electronic devices."

Rocco slammed his fists on the table, so much that the plate bounced into the air, sending more cookies onto the floor.

"Goddamn it, Shelley, when I beep you or call you, you got to respond. What if something happened to you? How am I supposed to know you're okay if you don't respond?"

"I'm okay....But, Rocco, please, I've got to tell you something. Something good. I think."

"Pick up the goddamn cookies."

Once again, she got down on her hands and knees and retrieved the cookies, which were about to be crunched under Rocco's left foot. Then she sat down at the table and took his hand. "Rocco. Dr. Allison says I'm pregnant."

In spite of everything (including her common sense, in hindsight), she had genuinely expected Rocco to be overjoyed. Rocco had always loved kids, and, supposedly, he also loved her. Sure, they weren't married. And, sure, he was now officially married, for strictly political reasons, to Cyndi. But he had never been constrained by traditional mores. He had never said one word condemning Shelley's several friends from Goucher who were raising kids untraditionally—one raising a daughter on her own (the father had refused to marry her), another recently divorced with a toddler, and a third who had a two-year-old son with her lesbian lover (they had reputedly used artificial insemination). He may not have broadcast these kind of situations to his constituents—that would have been political suicide—and they didn't exactly socialize with these unconventional families (they didn't exactly socialize with anyone, for that matter), but he never impugned their morals or called them names. He had plenty of buddies himself with kids out of wedlock and stepchildren and so forth.

Shelley also assumed she could have and raise this kid without Cyndi, or the rest of the world, knowing that Rocco was the dad. Money wasn't the problem, nor was time. The pregnancy hadn't been planned, and she had never really envisioned herself as a mother, but as the weeks had passed and her period never come, as the suspicions of a pregnancy began to crystallize, she found herself imagining life with a baby, and a child, more and more, and liking what she imagined. She felt alone with Rocco, despite his love. He loved her, but his career came first. And now that his career was public, and he was married to Cyndi, she saw that he would never live for her. But a child of theirs would be hers to love and shape. And perhaps a child would even help Rocco cultivate the more tender, loving sides of his nature, sides she knew he had but, because of his macho upbringing, often had so much trouble expressing. In fact, the macho side should have been proud to have sired a child, a proof of his virility. He frequently talked about how beautiful and brilliant their children would be, or would have been, had they been able to have them. At heart, she saw him as a traditionalist. All this led her to assume he would be overjoyed to be told she was carrying his child, and that he would trust her not to reveal that to the world.

That was what she had thought, but she had been 180 degrees off kilter.

It didn't help that the phone rang right after she told him the news. He snatched it up, put his ear to the receiver, and, almost immediately, slammed it back down. "Goddamn it," he said to himself. "Don't you ever call her again, you hear me?"

"That was rude. Who was it?"

"You know damn well who it was. Your boyfriend."

"Rocco...."

"How do I know he isn't the father? Huh? How do I know?"

Shelley went to the phone and pressed the called ID button. "Rocco—it was Comcast calling. Comcast."

"Isn't 'no men callers' on your list, Shelley? Isn't that one of the rules?"

"Comcast is not a 'man caller.'"

"How can I know that, Shelley? He calls you when I'm not around, he comes over here to work on your television....How the hell am I supposed to know what you do with him, huh? Are you trying to kill me?"

"Rocco, that's ridiculous, I...."

"Goddamn it, Shelley, I thought you loved me."

And that was it. Once he started thinking she didn't love him, it was like something got unplugged in his brain. That was how it always started. Like someone overcome by epileptic fit, or possessed by a golem, Rocco, feeling unloved, exploded, striking, pushing, shoving, speaking in what seemed like Satanic tongues. This fit would continue, unresponsive to all external stimuli, until his raw rage and atavistic aggression had reduced her to an unresponsive heap on the floor. She held her breath when he came at her and just waited for it to end.

CHAPTER SIXTEEN

Utzi the Iceman hadn't called Maxine all week and was nowhere to be found at either Rosh Hashanah service. During the morning service, she was sitting two rows behind his daughter Joan's family, and as the opening prayers wound up, she found herself half expecting to catch him sliding in next to them, especially because she knew it would take a relatively major demon to keep him from observing the holidays. Once the rabbi started calling people up to the bema, however, she could no longer delude herself: the man would most certainly be here by now if he was even half lucid.

She mindlessly rose with the rest of the congregation at the rabbi's request and stared uncomprehendingly into her prayer book. She tried to dredge up a clue from the last time she had seen him, a week ago Friday, at dinner. At first she could think of nothing beyond the glimmer that something wasn't right with his research. In fact, he had been unusually jovial that night, even encouraging, nodding appreciatively and holding her gaze as she lectured him about racism in America and later told him about Shelley's transformation into a stunning, if still somewhat bruised and bloated, blonde. He had even agreed to stop by to have a look for himself later in the week. Like so many others, this promise had turned out to be rubbish. Upon reflection, of course, it was obvious: whenever Utzi the Iceman let her ramble without interjecting his own tales, there was trouble brewing.

Joan walked right by her en route to the bathroom with a child. Maxine saw that she was obviously averting her eyes. Ah well, what was there to say, anyway? Both of them knew that her father was insufferable and would eventually resurface, presumably after finding some personal way to repent of his sins while hiding from the world, and from them specifically. Maxine closed her eyes and sank into the soft padded bench. She relished the calm of the room and the utter freedom from any responsibility save the rabbi's frequent requests to rise to chant a prayer, a ritual she suspected had been implanted in prayer books to keep congregants awake. She let the responsive reading wash over her, only occasionally jarred, and amused, by the new prayer book's politically correct transformations of "Lord" and "Father" into the "Eternal One," however awkward, forced, and dissonant it made the once familiar phrases. Otherwise, she allowed herself to drift into a wordless mental fog, inured to the meaning of the familiar, sedating passages and commanding the unaccustomed role of *Yiddishe* Grandmama by doling out occasional tissues or mints to squirming grandchildren.

Dodie, in contrast, appeared engrossed in the service. This baffled Maxine. Dodie sat on the other side of the boys, next to Margaret, reading responsively and singing along with the prayers. Maxine wondered if her daughter's newborn devotion reflected a genuine surge of faith or if it was merely an effort to impress or imprint the children, or perhaps just to pass the time. It was startling enough to witness her rebellious daughter sitting docilely at a service, much less conforming to its ritual. For years Maxine had despaired of Dodie's outright rejections of her religious origins as primitive, hypocritical, and meaningless, and she had partly blamed herself for this attitude: after all, she herself had married out. If truth be told, she herself had rejected the religion in all but name. What she wanted to explain to Dodie, but never could, however, was that while she was not observant, and never had been, she had always felt "Jewish" and carried a certain pride in knowing that she was associated with the heritage of suffering, integrity, and devotion to learning and bettering the world. This did not mean she had to drivel out "mumbo jumbo" in *shul* every week or deprive herself of *traif* lobster dinners, nor did it mean she had to marry a "member of the tribe." However, it did mean that disclaiming her membership or affiliation filled her with a deep sense of betrayal to the ancestors who had literally given their lives so that she could live as she pleased and who, misguided or not, had believed for her. Her mother's own sister and cousins had been torched at Auschwitz. How then could she not acknowledge being a Jew, or the value of being one? And yet, until this recent turn in Dodie, she had always wondered why this sense of loyalty and pride had not been passed on to her children, either Dennis with his blond Laurie and their Christmas tree or Dodie with her agnostic Randall and what, until now, had always been her blatant disdain for all religion.

Maxine found herself bumped up against Joan in the aisle after services. Caught in the current of congregants bursting forth from the sanctuary into the early fall sunshine, they could not help but wish each other a "*L'Shanah Tovah*." Mid-kiss, Joan then asked her point blank if she thought the Iceman was having another episode.

"Presumably. Unless you know something I don't. I haven't heard from him in a week now."

"Me either." Joan stood on tiptoe, trying to spot Chelsea and Alexander, who were hightailing it out of the sanctuary by climbing over benches and sidling past the clogged adults. "I certainly can't think of any other explanation—except, of course, the unthinkable. I mean, honestly, who can tell if the man's dead? He could sit in that pig sty of his for a month before anyone would notice."

"That's a lovely image. Sadly true, however."

"I thought for sure he'd show up today. I spent half my childhood listening to him ranting about services, like I'd end up in hell or something for missing the holidays—or some Jewish version of hell."

"Well, I wouldn't be too concerned, lambie. It's not like your father hasn't done this before....Still, you make a good point. I think I'll call one of the donut boys, just to see if it's only us he's avoiding."

Indeed, she did call Nelson that very afternoon, but he turned out to be very little help, other than confirming that Utzi the Iceman had been absent from their morning sessions that week as well. He added that he had known the fellow far longer than Maxine and assured her that there was no reason to suspect anything other than the usual neurotic hibernation. "Leave the man be," he advised. "It's been what—a week or two? Give him a month. Then we'll break down the doors."

By this time, however, Maxine had convinced herself that Joan might have been right. Periodic disappearances on the part of a senior citizen who lived alone were unacceptable. If he was lying on the floor with a concussion or a broken hip, no one would know for weeks. What if she herself had an accident at home? Dodie, bless her, would undoubtedly worry, and within a day or two come to the condo to check on her. But there was no one to do that for

Utzi the Iceman. He had never offered her a key to his place, self-sufficient old warthog that he was, and from what she could surmise Joan didn't have a key either. That was a situation she needed to correct. She respected the man's right to sulk by himself now and then, but it was downright dangerous to continue this way.

She left a message on his answering machine, asking him to call her, or Joan, anyone he wanted to call, simply to assure the outside world that he was alive. She promised not to bother him until he was ready, but she needed to know he wasn't rotting or dying on the floor. By the time she saw Joan again at *Kol Nidre*, however, neither of them had had a response from him all week. "Ah well," Joan said. "So be it."

"You don't think perhaps the two of us should go pound on his door, do you? Or call the police?"

Joan motioned her children toward their seats. "I learned long ago to mind my own business about this. I know he's putting himself at risk, but he's a grown man."

"Arguably."

"I've had too many doors slammed in my face over the years to care anymore—isn't that an awful thing to say, especially on Yom Kippur? But I can't help it. It's his life."

By the morning service, Maxine had decided that Joan was probably right and that she would leave the man alone until he felt like rejoining the world. In fact, perhaps this interlude was all for the best, particularly in light of all the extra work she had just undertaken training Shelley and working on her after hours. She also reminded herself, as she had had to do repeatedly over the years, that Utzi the Iceman had disappeared for a month or so several times before and then popped up bright and cheerful as though nothing at all had happened. By far the most likely explanation was that this was more of the same, and it was weak and silly of her to let wild speculation and irrational cowardice override probability. There was also no point in being angry about it, or trying to reform him. This was a pattern with him, and given all the other revolting, annoying, demeaning, and demanding patterns of behavior she had been forced to accept in other human relationships, this one really wasn't so bad. At least the Iceman left her to herself during these times, and asked nothing of her. As she grew older, she found herself more and more of a mind with Joan—it was not her role to remedy or reform other people's bad habits, wayward opinions, or existential crises. Dealing with her own was more than enough for a lifetime.

Sunlight streamed through the tall windows several stories above the bema, diagonally radiating translucent, steamy beams like a shower spray into the sanctuary. From her bench farther back in the room, Maxine watched the rabbi and cantor through this luminous curtain, which warmed the heads of the congregants in the front rows and suggested a connection to God as direct as that from God's extended finger in Michaelangelo's *Creation of Adam*. What a contrast this was, she reflected, to the temple's services in years past, many of which had been about as spiritual as a Kiwanis Club supper. The first few years after she'd arrived, services had been held alternately in a Catholic Church, country club, or hotel banquet room. This was the congregation's only choice after a calamity one bitter February night when the roof of the make-shift temple, pieced together on a piddling budget by the temple "pioneers" several decades earlier, had sunk under the weight of unexpectedly zealous Maryland snow. For several years thereafter the congregation had held services in a rented trailer, set out in what would eventually become its parking lot. Every gathering was marked by efforts to raise money for a new sanctuary, the dream of the new, ambitious rabbi imported from Montclair, who dreamed of one day presiding over a serious, grown-up sanctuary.

Now the rabbi had clearly had his dreams fulfilled. The new temple in which they sat that morning was imposing and substantial with its open, lofty spaces, clean white, track lighting, and brash, incongruent angles, a monument, Maxine decided, to simplicity, functionality, and unconventionality like so many things American. It was also the antithesis of the gold-bedecked, chandeliered Sephardic palace of her girlhood. There, when she had attended at all, she had been herded upstairs with the other females and forced to survey the spectacle from the benches in the cramped balcony space, peaking through curtains at the golden doings of the costumed and consumed men below. Along with the other females relegated to the second floor, she had observed with awe, bewilderment, and, in her case anyway, often vexation, the incoherent wailing and moaning, the babbling and sighing in a language she did not understand, the beard-pulling and tallis-tuggings that often made her feel more like a spectator at a royal insane asylum than an uplifted spirit. Oddly enough, though, even now, in this clean, stark new space, surrounded by her stone-faced daughter and squirmy grandsons who kept shedding their *kipahs* (purposely, she thought, so they could drop down, and drop out, to retrieve them), she still felt somehow that nothing had changed. In spite of the modernized setting, she had the distinct feeling that she had been at this service, essentially, many times before, in fact, for her entire life. She felt herself simultaneously here and back at that childhood *shul* and at all the other services in between, not in memory, but literally, as if all the Yom Kippurs of her life had come together into this single, still moment.

It is always Yom Kippur, it occurred to her, and I am always at a Yom Kippur service. It didn't matter that she had never physically sat in this sanctuary on any other Yom Kippur. She had simply always been there, at that service. She felt herself sitting in the trailer last year, hearing the same service, and thinking the same thoughts about the eternal inability of herself, and all human beings, to live the kind of lives they vowed to lead during the High Holy days, vows to push aside the pettiness, jealousy, hatred, cruelty, selfishness, vanity, and perversity that they so earnestly vowed to push aside every single year. She thought about the many times and places she had sat with these or equivalent people, all vowing to rekindle the still dim light in their hearts by listening to these simple words and melodies, all dressed in stiff and uncomfortable clothes, and all daydreaming about the kugel and smoked fish and challah waiting for them at sunset as a reward for their fast. She hadn't sat on these soft padded benches last year, she hadn't smelled this exhilarating new construction aroma of sawdust, paint, and carpet fiber, but, even so, she distinctly felt herself at last year's service in the trailer, just as she simultaneously felt herself at the service the year before that, and the one ten years ago, and the other twenty, and thirty years back. The very sitting and hearing these prayers and chants, ones she had heard in one form or another, with different words and melodies, but essentially saying the same thing, year after year, knowing always that the vows would inevitably be broken, that she would be as petty and nasty a person as she had always been and then still return to vow to live her life more meaningfully, gave her the sense that time had come to an absolute standstill.

The sensation that time slowed, or even dropped away,

as one reached the end of life surprised her. Was this what they meant when they said a person's life passed before him before he died? Her life passed before her increasingly, and, with the images, came the mounting sense that time was coming to a halt, or, at least, was irrelevant. When she had been a younger adult, she had reflected often on the way time persistently seemed to accelerate, meandering during childhood, picking up pace during adolescence, and then, once the babies were born, racing so fast that it slipped out from under you, gone before you noticed it was there. Time flies, and flies faster, the cliché proclaimed, and until recently she, too, would have agreed that each year seemed to pass quicker and quicker, the older you got. But lately she couldn't help feeling that the years had seemed to slow, or at least that they spun from one to the next so incredibly quickly that all time came together and ceased to move, much like the colors on a spinning plate that eventually blurred together into a single, eternal white.

And, thus, it wasn't that last Yom Kippur felt like yesterday, as she had commented so often in the past. This morning's Yom Kippur felt like it literally was last year's Yom Kippur, and all the Yom Kippurs of her life, all wrapped up into this single moment. She felt the same way about Rosh Hashanah. And Pesach. Her birthday. New Year's Eve. The first day of spring, in fact. Any ritual or distinct event that repeated annually became a notch on a spinning wheel, a wheel that had once seemed to roll around faster and faster but now came back around to the notch before it had quite left the previous one. In fact, these notches now seemed to coexist. There were no longer any interstices of time between them. Only one, eternal now.

She had been wrong to think that time passes quickly. Rather, for those brief seconds, she came to understand that time itself was an illusion. The illusory nature of time, in fact, may have been why human beings even bothered to mark it: marking time let people grasp, eventually, that they do not vanish, but that all that ever was always is. It was the elevation of the "now" over all other moments in time that caused the bulk of human misery. Yes, much pain and distress came from the tortures that occurred in the moment, but the bulk of true soul-searing misery came from the longing for times that have passed or times yet to come. Somehow we have a sense that only the moment that "is" counts, and that all other moments are not as real. Thus, we mourn the past and crave the future. If we could only develop a sense that these non-coincident moments are just as real, we would no longer suffer for not "having" them. It is the need to "possess," and the feeling that we only possess the present, that leads to this oppressive yearning. That morning, though, she understood that the moments we call the past, present, and future coexist, so that everything that had ever happened or would ever happen was always present, and of equal consequence. For that reason, she supposed, it didn't matter that you died; it mattered that you lived.

Perhaps that is my glimpse of eternity, Maxine mused, perhaps even my glimpse of God. Because there was no time, she was no longer terrified by its barreling passage and her inability to see it, much less stop it. She was simply here—until she was not. Furthermore, as long as she had memory, these accumulated moments, of which she now had a vast collection, she had nothing to fear from time, or her delusions of time. These moments, in fact, could come together to stop time. The girl who sat in that gold-laden *shul* at age 14 contemplating whether chewing a stick of gum would "count" as breaking the fast turned out to be the same person who sat in this streamlined temple today. Her age, her clothing, the softness of her seat or the smells and closeness of her companions, were irrelevant. Nothing at all had changed.

CHAPTER SEVENTEEN

"Who is it, Michelle?" Hearing the door chimes mid-client often worried Maxine because every so often some liquor-crazed *tsotsi* would wander in, an occupational hazard of having a freestanding office with direct access to the street. There was no one due for another half hour at least, and it was far too early for the mail or the UPS chap. "Did someone just come in?"

"It's me, Zeenie." Dodie appeared in the threshold of the makeup room. "Let me hang my coat, and I'll pop right back. If you can spare a moment, I mean."

"We're just finishing up here. Is something wrong?"

"She's looking lubly," said Tracey, a longstanding client whose lower lip was temporarily doubled in size.

"I hope everything's all right. I can't imagine what she's doing here at this hour. She already stopped by earlier to go over the books with Shel...er Michelle, as it is....Is there some trouble, sugar plum?" Maxine caught some of the overflow from Tracey's lip with gauze. "Hold this here a moment, will you? I have to see what this is about. Just keep gentle pressure on, that's a good girl."

Maxine took Dodie by the arm and led her into the hall. "All right. What's wrong?"

"Nothing, worrywart. Go back to your client. I'll talk to you when she's done."

Maxine led Dodie into the kitchen and closed the door behind them. "Dodie, you have it written all over you when there's a problem. So speak up. Tracey can wait. She's a patient gal."

"It's not a big deal. Really. We can talk when you're through with her."

"Come now. You came all the way over here in the middle of the day. Open up."

"It happens to be lunch hour. But, yes, we do need to talk a bit. Basically, we need to rethink this situation. You, me, and Shelley, I mean."

"Rethink. What is to rethink? *Michelle* and I are getting along swimmingly."

"No, I'm serious. We need to talk, and she needs to be a part of it. All three of us need to discuss this."

"Fine then." Maxine opened the door. "Michelle, could you come in here, please?"

"Yes?" Shelley's limp was scarcely visible now, and it was clear that every step wasn't a willful triumph over torture. However, as she watched Shelley stand at the table resting her weight on her hands, Maxine could still see the telltale hints of the black eye and puffy, brutalized skin on the lips and cheeks. Shelley stared at Maxine with the open, searching eyes of a shocked, wounded animal, a look that somehow made you want to shove or shake her even as she emanated pain and vulnerability—and one that Maxine was beginning to suspect that Shelley had conveyed for many years, well before the latest round of abuse.

"Sit down, please, Michelle. There we go. Dodie needs to discuss something with us, and you might as well get off your feet."

"It's not that big a deal," said Dodie. "I was telling my mother—she should finish the client up first. But—you know how she is. She'll do what she chooses to do, and that's that."

Maxine poured herself a cup of coffee. "We're here, aren't we? Let's stop dithering....Michelle, do you think you could put a bit of sugar in for me?...Thank you, dearie."

"Anyway," said Dodie. "I just stopped by because, as I said to Zeenie, I think the three of us need to rethink this situation. As I just told her, though, I'm not sure that right this second is the most ideal time."

"Oh my god, you saw Rocco, didn't you?," said Shelley. "Does he know I'm here?"

"No, no, nothing like that. I saw his Jaguar drive around the block the other day. Several times. He still thinks you're at the shelter."

Maxine worked off her gloves. "Michelle, go ask Tracey if she has any questions and, if not, see if she wants to book that electrolysis for next week. Then have her wait for you in the reception area."

Dodie waited until Shelley had left. "I made the mistake of being honest with Florence. About Shelley, I mean."

"That's always a big mistake. Honesty."

"Well, Zeenie, it shouldn't be. But I'm too much of an idealist, as you're always so fond of reminding me....However, what's done is done."

"I haven't a clue what you're talking about. As I said, things are just ducky here. I plan to start the micropigmentation work on Shelley as soon as her face heals fully. We already have everything mapped out." Shelley came back into the room, this time with a trace more of her limp. "Shut the door behind you, won't you dear? And, please, take a chair for yourself."

"She's just getting her things together. I'll have to go back to get payment and make that appointment."

"That's fine," said Maxine. "This won't be long—will it, Dodie?"

"Longer than she should have to wait....Anyway, here's the thing. Florence, you know, at Safe Port, asked me about your situation, Shelley. I mean, Michelle. I guess she was updating the files. And so I told her. I mean, I told her before that you had checked out voluntarily, and that was fine. But this time I told her more details, you know, about how you were here with Zeenie and all, and about the permanent makeup thing. I thought she'd be pleased at our ingenuity, but, of course, I should have known better. She's steamed. Big time steamed. She wants you back at the shelter pronto or else signed out of the system permanently. She's terrified they're going to be held liable if something happens to you."

"Held liable?" Shelley at last sat down at the table. "By whom? There's no one who cares what happens to me— and they're not responsible for me anyway."

"No, they're not. But I'm linked to you, you see, and I work for them. So this whole plan of ours is not entirely Shelley on her own—I could be tied into this, Florence thinks, and, through extension, so could Safe Port."

"I wouldn't be surprised if Rocco's behind this," said Shelley. "He probably put some pressure on Safe Port from above. To get me out of there, since he can't come in for me. That's the kind of thing he'd do."

"It's none of their bloody business, now, is it?" Maxine stirred the sugar Shelley had added to the coffee. "Did you happen to bring any of that cream you like, Dodie? This is bitter today."

"It's just not procedure. That's what she said." Dodie went to the refrigerator and took out the pint of half-and-half she had just placed into it. She opened the spout and poured a dash of it into Maxine's cup. "We get funding, you know, from various grant agencies, and we work together with the legal system, and, as a result, we have to follow their rules."

"Even when the rules make no sense whatsoever," said Maxine.

"Well, they make sense, Zeenie, in most cases. They just don't have foresight to accommodate cases like these. The bottom line is that I'm the link between Shelley and Safe Port, and, as a result, I have to remove myself from this whole thing to protect my employer. You see?"

"No. I do not see. It's absurd."

"Well, absurd or not, it is what it is. It was idiotic of me to tell Florence, cockeyed idealist that I am. Don't know what I was thinking. But, anyway, as I said, it doesn't have to be that big a deal if we don't turn it into one. We just need to do what needs to be done to protect Safe Port....So, Michelle, I was sent here to bring you back or get you to sign these release from liability papers. Then you're free to do what you wish. Or, as I said, I can take you back with me to Safe Port now, and we can work on getting you a court date. It's entirely up to you."

"Well, I'll sign the papers, of course. I'm not going back there." She sighed, and finally sat herself down in the chair next to Maxine's. "That would be suicidal, with him lurking out front."

"Okay. But that also means that every contact I have with you puts my job at risk."

"My dear—can't you do whatever you like on your own time? They have no right to dictate to you."

"Not officially, no. But if Florence knew I was 'aiding and abetting' this activity, as she put it, she would have reason enough to fire me. Just because of the appearance of questionable activity, I mean."

"She would not have reason. That would be entirely unreasonable—and unlawful."

"That's your opinion. Solely your opinion."

"Pish tosh."

"I'm sorry I put you in this situation," said Shelley. "Both of you. You are only trying to help. Not just trying."

"Clearly it's a situation of no good deed going unpunished," said Maxine.

"I do have to say that it seems a bit extreme," said Dodie at last. "I mean, I understand it, from a legal perspective, but it does seem ridiculous when their rules never let them do anyone any good."

Maxine put her coffee cup down with a distinct thud. "What do you mean by 'never,' Dodie? You do plenty of good, I'd say."

"Not really. Temporary good. We save some poor woman from a raging man for a week or two or three, but, ultimately, most end up going back for more, and worse. We can't keep them forever. We can't solve the underlying problems that lead them into these situations, or keep them from leaving them. If you look at the long-term picture, all we're doing, most of the time, is delaying the inevitable."

"Well, that's a cheery view now, isn't it?"

"Cheery or not, Zeenie, it's the truth. The shelter system simply does not work. Something else has to happen for these women, who are hidden for a few days or weeks but eventually slip right back into the same miserable cycle. Longer term counseling is all well and good, but most end up where they started. Or worse."

Shelley shrugged. "Well, whether or not that's true—it's too late for Shelley. Michelle is here now, and she's in it for the long haul. Right, Maxine?"

"Absolutely, right. And I shall be in for something myself, too, if you don't get back to Tracey Jones and get a nice fat check from her. As for you, Dodie my dear, you may go back and tell Safe Port that they are free and clear of their Shelley. She is ours."

CHAPTER EIGHTEEN

"All right. Shall we begin then?"

Maxine set a box of cotton swabs on her cart and finished fastening the buttons on her baby-pink lab coat. Her name, inscribed in slightly brighter pink thread above the breast pocket, and for which she had paid a pretty penny, was beginning to fade. Carole should have ordered her a new coat at least a year ago—yet another task left undone. She made a mental note to ask "Michelle" to do that, perhaps first thing tomorrow even before she got back to the inventory work. She would also have her check to see if they made coats with snaps these days, or at least larger buttons; these delicate disks increasingly tyrannized her uncooperative fingers. Michelle could probably manage the task. She was infuriatingly slow and uncertain, asking so many questions you wanted to stop your ears up with cotton, not to mention an utter pig when it came to tidying up her own belongings. But so far she was light years ahead of Carole when it came to conscientiousness.

Maxine settled herself on the stool and began rummaging through the eye pencils. "My dear, you look like you're about to have a gynecological examination or a tooth extraction. Relax. I'm just making up your face. As the ladies do at the department store counters."

"I thought it was permanent."

"Hold still a moment now while I draw on your new eyes." Maxine took an eyebrow pencil and began filling in the brows. "It will be permanent. Of course. But we're not yet ready. I always start by showing clients what they'll look like when we're done. This gives us an opportunity to double check the plan. And, of course, to make changes before everything's set."

"But you said...I thought we were doing the eyes today. All the swelling and bruises are gone, or as much as they're ever going to go."

Maxine put down the eyebrow pencil. She knew from long experience that when clients needed to talk, or hear her talk, it was best (and often profitable) to let them do so. "Seriously, Michelle. Do you understand what you're asking? Be glad we're getting this in at all today. What do we have—forty-five minutes or so before Mrs. Bemis comes in? An hour?"

"I think so. I'd have to recheck the book."

"And that's only because what's-her-name, that dreadful Arlene woman, ducked out on us. That's the third time she's pulled that on me. I've got to tell her it's over. I can't afford it, not these days. When she calls again, you tell her that, you hear me?"

"All right....Anyway, do what you can. I just thought, maybe, we were finally going to do the permanent thing."

"Forty-five minutes, Michelle. I can't possibly do you justice in that time. And we absolutely must begin with a mock-up."

"I understand. But tonight maybe? After work?"

"My dear, please. I don't have that kind of stamina any more. I'm worried sick over Utzi, and now this is a very full day. We'll wait until we can do things right."

"I guess, but...I thought you said he just needed some

time."

"He does. But we can't help ourselves from worrying, now can we?"

"I guess not. But I'm worried too, you know. I feel like Anne Frank, hidden away here. Like I've run away from my life. Forever. Maybe this is all a mistake."

Maxine knew full well that it had to be hard for Shelley never to see the light of day except when a client opened the door, but there was nothing to be done about that, at least right now. She suspected that Shelley occasionally peeked outside when left there alone all night and breathed in the night air, and you could actually see her lighten up when the door opened and the mailman or a client walked in, as though she were trapped in an underground cave like one of those people in circadian rhythm experiments. However, that was the extent of her ventures outside in these early days. Dodie had cautioned them both about daring anything so much as a walk around the block. Perhaps later, when things calmed down, and more work had been done, they might dare take her out in the dark of night and at least have her over for a meal or to watch a video with other human beings. For now, though, it was imperative that Shelley stay safely tucked away in the salon.

"We're doing this at rocket speed as it is." Maxine picked up the pencil and slowly drew it back and forth across Shelley's brows. "Normally I give my clients a week or two to sleep on a plan—to ponder whether the mock-up is actually what they want. You must realize, too—the more time we give your face and spirit to heal, the better you'll do in the long run....Yes, you see?" Maxine picked up the mirror from Shelley's lap and held it out in front of her face. "Two beautiful, even brows. Full, shaping the face....Do you want to watch while I work on the eyeliner? You're welcome to do so."

"It's okay. I'll wait until you've finished."

Maxine placed the mirror back onto her cart and began lining Shelley's eyes with a charcoal stick. "This dark is a lovely contrast if we go with the blue contact lenses. Simply stunning....Of course, if you prefer green or hazel lenses, we might want to go with a dark ash, or, perhaps, chestnut brown. Have you any thoughts on that?"

"Blue is great. If I'm really going to be blonde, I might as well go all the way."

"My dear, you are a blonde. Accept it."

"I'm trying."

"Hush now. You must hold very still for this part. Honestly now. You must be perfectly still if I'm to get the line on straight with these sticks. Eyelining is precision work—yet another reason why you're going to adore having this done once and for all. You'll never have to struggle with a pencil again."

"Not that I try very often."

"Please. You must be absolutely still for just another moment....Here. You should hold the mirror, and watch."

Shelley reluctantly accepted the mirror. Maxine carefully drew lines under her eyelids, praying Shelley would be able to keep her mouth closed long enough to keep the lines straight. Shelley was turning out to be a wiggle-worm as well as a rambler. Although it didn't matter much now, since all this makeup would be removed within the hour, she was going to have to control Shelley better once they started working with the pigments.

"Please....There is nothing more frustrating than trying to get these lines right. But, as I said, you'll soon have beautiful lines forever. You'll simply wake up every morning and—*voilà!*"

"I feel that way already."

"I told you this, too, already—the hair is nothing. Compared to where we're going, nothing."

Maxine fished around the cart looking for the terracotta. If she worked on the lips, Shelley would have to keep quiet, at least for a few minutes. This week might be an excellent time to have her organize the lipsticks once and for all. The girl was a natural organizer, and had already redone the file drawers, unasked, even sorted through the old magazines in the waiting area and laid out the more salvageable ones by name and subject matter. Maxine couldn't bear to think about all the time that Carole's slovenliness had lost her.

Maxine quickly added the lipstick and drew a beauty mark inside a deep pock on Shelley's right cheek. Then she dabbed cover-up over the remaining pits and scars. "There you go. Take a look." She took Shelley's hand and guided the mirror out in front of her face. "Of course, the charcoal liner doesn't contrast as much with your eyes right now as it will when we've turned them blue, but at least you can see the line thickness and so forth. Good?"

"Astounding."

"And, you realize, too, the scars will be camouflaged more expertly once we've gone over them with the RAD machine, and finished the needling, which is going to work so beautifully on those shallow, little lines you've started over your lips. I wouldn't be surprised if we erase them entirely. But here at least you have a good sense of where we are heading....So? Like it? No longer the face of a victim, and more beautiful than ever....Now is the time to speak."

"I can't believe it. It's amazing."

"It will be all that more amazing when it's real. And permanent. Now let's clean all this off and get the day going, shall we? I promise you that we can tackle the eyeliner later

200

this week. It usually takes an hour, maybe two."

"It's really permanent? Forever?"

"As much as anything can be. We're implanting color directly into the dermis, you see?" Maxine pointed to one of the two oversized diagrams taped on the wall, depicting an enlarged color-coded cross-section of skin. The tip of a hugely enlarged needle was inserted through the epidermis and releasing pigments into the reticular layer. "We place the color safely beneath the outer covering, so it's not going to rub off that easily. Now, of course, some will disperse a bit over time, wash away into the body, fade with exposure to UVA radiation, and so forth. The skin is very much alive, connected to blood vessels, exposed to influences that get through the epidermis—'breathing,' I suppose you could say. So you will eventually need a touch-up. But 'eventually' can be as long as five years from now. That's as permanent as things get, you must realize. If you want to look the same way you look today—with or without micropigmentation—you, anyone really, will need a touch-up of one kind or another over the years. That's hardly news now, is it?"

"Will it hurt?"

"Very little. If at all. Maybe a little pricking, sticking here and there. I don't even go as deep as with electrolysis. Have you ever had electrolysis?"

"I'm not a big fan of pain."

"My dear. If you think electrolysis is painful, you don't know from pain. But, of course, you do."

"Yes. There I'm an expert."

"Anyway, micropigmentation is much less painful than the little pricks of electrolysis, because the needle doesn't penetrate as far as the hair follicle. Actually, another term we use for it is dermagraphics, you see, from the Greek *derma*, which means skin, and *graphein*, to write. We are writing on your skin, but only by placing the pigment as deep as the dermal layer. Look at the charts again. You see? This one shows electrolysis, and you see how the needle must reach the hair follicle, all the way down there. We're not going in that far...."

"It's still a needle. I've always hated needles."

"You'll be fine. The pain, if you call it that, is nothing after what you've been through....You needn't worry about allergic reactions either. They recently published a study, you know, in a medical journal—I can't remember which one—that said there was less than a one in a thousand chance of developing a reaction to these hypoallergenic, iron-oxide pigments. It's safer than crossing the street!"

"I just don't want to hurt anymore."

Maxine nodded. "I understand that, my dear, I truly do. To be honest, that's why I wouldn't dream of doing anything more right now. Not because it is going to hurt. No. But you would be better served if you were more relaxed, you see? You'll need to be very still, and very quiet through the procedure. This is delicate work, as I keep telling you, the liner more than anything. You will have to sit very calmly. For an hour or so. Without too much talking and wiggling around."

Shelley scrutinized herself in the mirror again. "This looks great. Unbelievably great....But—here's the thing: why can't I do what you just did with the makeup every morning? Why the permanent thing? I mean, I could also change my wardrobe, couldn't I? And then paint on a new face—that seems a lot easier, and faster, than a year of needles in my face."

"You're going to artfully camouflage your scars with makeup every single day? I wish you luck, darling girl. We just spent nearly an hour here, and I'm a professional.

Within an hour, half of this will run off, blur together, won't it now? You'd have to scoot back into the bathroom every hour on the hour for the rest of your life. You could not swim or run or perspire without losing it all either. I hardly think that's a way to live, do you?"

"I don't know....The more I think about it, the crazier this all seems. Not crazy. I'm sorry. Just unnecessary."

"You're under no obligation. Believe me. I was under the impression that you were in dire straits."

"I was. I mean, I am. But...I'm sorry I'm so dense. It just seems like, I don't know, maybe it's too much."

"Listen for a moment, now, all right? I'm not going to force you into anything you don't want to do. Let's get that straight up front."

"Thank you."

"Well, of course. My goodness, I'm offering thousands of dollars' worth of my services to you for nothing. I've already given you—I can't even calculate what I've already given you, when you count the room and board. Do you think I have nothing else to do? If you don't want this— well, go on now. You may leave. No one is stopping you."

"I'm sorry. You know I can't do that."

"You can do it. You just may not choose to do it. It's your decision entirely. I have better things to do with my time, don't I now? Of course, I'm willing to help Dodie out, that goes without saying, and I realize that you'll be helping me out as well, but, believe me, you aren't the easiest of assistants living on the premises and such." She removed the mirror from Shelley's hands and placed it back on the cart. "I can find better things to do with my time than provide countless hours of unbillable services, my dear. Plenty of better things....Do you understand that?"

"I do. But I still don't see...I'm just dense, that's all.

Sorry."

"What I'm proposing to you is permanent, Michelle. That's the part that makes a difference. I'm not sure you fully understand me."

"No. I understand it's permanent. I do. But I just keep thinking I could get the same result much more quickly with regular makeup."

"Please. Once again, you clearly you do not understand what permanent means, or you would not say that. Permanent. There every day when you wake up, there all day every day whatever you do, wherever you go. Do you understand how that frees you, gives you a safety valve? Regular makeup cannot do that for you. It is going to fail at some point, some day. You of all people cannot risk that. For most of my clients, the permanence is a convenience. A luxury, perhaps. But for you it is a necessity. It is absurd to rely on temporary base and lipstick, not when you're in a situation like yours. You'll see. You will forget one day—no one is perfect. Just one day. That is all it will take. One morning you won't feel like dressing yourself up, one day you won't feel like refreshing the makeup every hour after you sweat it off or you forget just once—well, you know what I'm saying. You will need to run out for milk or medicine in the middle of the night, an emergency....Let me explain something to you, Michelle, in case you have forgotten. You are in a life-threatening situation. This is not a game, and you need to be deadly serious about this. Deadly serious. Do you understand? You can't take chances."

"That's another thing. This micro...what is the name again?"

"Micropigmentation. Or permanent makeup. It's all the same thing."

"The way you describe it—it sounds pretty much like a tattoo. I mean, really, when you think about it...."

"Well, yes. Essentially."

"I mean, I know it's different than back alley stuff. But I just can't help thinking about anchors and roses and 'I love Mamie.'"

"Well, dear, a tattoo, by definition, is merely a procedure in which needles are used to implant permanent color under the skin. So, yes, quite honestly, this is a form of tattooing, although most clients seem to have a prejudice about that particular term."

"Who ever would have thought that Shelley, the JAP from Bloomfield Hills, would get tattooed!"

"JAP?"

"Jewish American Princess."

"Ah, I see....I believe you mean the gals we called kugels. You are hardly a kugel, my dear. Not after what you've been through. Although, I will tell you, plenty of kugels have tattoos. As well as famous beauty queens, real queens, rock stars, and movie stars like Cher and Angelina Jolie, not to mention federal judges, lady athletes, anchor women, politicians and so on."

"Well, maybe. But not me. I mean, beauty salons are one thing we JAPS do pretty well. Tattoo parlors—quite another!"

"Tattooing is an ancient art, my dear. We humans have been tattooing our bodies since the ice age. In many cultures. For many reasons. If I could get my Iceman friend to unfreeze himself right now, I'd have him tell you all about it—more than you ever want to hear, believe me. And by no means just the lowlifes were getting tattooed. No, the aristocrats got into the game as well. Why, the European royalty used to decorate themselves with tattoos back in

Queen Victoria's time."

"Seriously?"

"Of course! It's a pity that body art has come to have such a tatty image...."

"I suppose. But back in the '80s, growing up in Bloomfield Hills, I would have been a marked woman. Literally....Besides, isn't tattooing dangerous?"

"If done in a filthy pit by an untrained technician using unsterilized equipment, yes ma'am. But, as I told you, I do permanent makeup with the standards of a surgeon.... Believe me, sweetpea, under proper conditions there is no opportunity for disease transmission. I don't care if you call it tattooing or micropigmentation or dermagraphics or what-have-you. If you've a properly trained technician who cleans all the instruments with an autoclave, never reuses needles, and has a sanitary environment, there is virtually no chance of spreading any communicable disease. Your Centers for Disease Control tracks these things, you know. They haven't had a single incidence of the AIDS virus attributable to tattooing at all, and in the past ten years, maybe longer, no increase in hepatitis B. So those are your worries, right?"

"I suppose so."

"The biggest mistake women make is not choosing the right technician. They worry about cost or la-dee-dah location or whatever coupon they've clipped out or whatnot when what they really need to be thinking about is finding someone who follows proper sterilization procedures and works in a clean environment. You'd be amazed at the women who let a nose-pierced teenager chomping Juicy Fruit manipulate their skin. They don't look at before and after photos, they think a two-day course is equivalent to real certification or decades of experience, they never even ask about sanitary precautions—or they see for themselves that they're having a procedure done in a room with no ventilation, acrylic nail fumes, cigarette smoke, no running water—you wouldn't believe what goes on out there. That's why tattooing gets a bad reputation, you see? That's why even my business does. But you are in the right hands, my dear, don't you worry a bit."

Maxine pointed to the framed certificates on the wall. "I'm a member, longstanding member, of the Society of Permanent Cosmetic Professionals, Academy of Micropigmentation, and the American Electrology Assocation. I have all my proper certifications as well. That means something, you see. *Ag shame*, so few women know to ask before they let some dumb hadeda run riot over their faces."

Shelley ran her fingers through her hair. "You obviously know what you're doing."

"Close your eyes again." Maxine began scrubbing the makeup off Shelley's face, stroking quickly enough to keep her relatively quiet. "There you go. This is the easy part, eh?"

"Yes. Returning me to my normal, hideous state. Absolutely."

"Enough of that now. When we've done your eyes once and for all, you'll be done with the negativity....As for me, I need a nap....Could you please go check the book and see when the Bemis woman is due?"

"You seem to have more energy than most teenagers."

"Pish tosh. You should have seen me back when. I could work from dawn through the wee hours without a break, except perhaps a few coffees."

Shelley began to unhook the cape from around her neck, but Maxine stopped her hands. "Never mind. I've missed a spot. Stay put, will you please?" She winched herself from the stool and headed for the waiting room, calling back at Shelley. "I used to be a whirlwind once I set my mind to something. You wouldn't know me then. These days...I need my breaks as regularly as my meals." She returned, flipping through the appointment book and then handing it to Shelley. "Can you read this for me, dear?" I seem to have misplaced my reading glasses again."

"Angela Bemis has a half hour at 11. No one until then."

"Is that a touch-up?"

"Um...not clear."

"Well, no matter. I can't remember where she is, but half an hour...it must be a touch-up. So. I do think I'll have a coffee at least." She took a fresh cotton ball and dabbed Shelley's lower lids. "You can tidy up the front room in the meantime, eh? And then you can call to reconfirm tomorrow's bookings. Later, if we have a lull, you can get back to inventory. And the organizing here as well. If you can pull yourself away from those books Dodie keeps bringing you, that is. You have plenty of time for that sort of business in the evenings, I expect."

"That's fine. Thank you."

"There. Spic and span. Honestly, I must rest now. Do we have something made?"

"I'll make a fresh pot. It's been sitting there since 6 a.m."

"Yes, please, we'll be done in just a few seconds now....My God, I need a break, and the day's only begun. It's a dreadful thing, this fatigue, for a person like me who believes that the greatest sin, maybe the only sin, is wasting time. That's what my father used to tell me, anyway, and I suppose I took it to heart. Stupid isn't it?"

"Not stupid."

"At my age? *Ag*, I should learn to smell the roses, eh?"

"I don't know. Look at all you've done with your life."

"Done? What have I done?" Maxine balled up the dirty cotton balls and tossed them into the rubbish basket. "Mind you, I pride myself on my work, I love helping my clients look and feel better. I know I'm helping them, their sense of well-being, their health even. I know that, and I'm proud of it. But you must face reality. It's not like curing cancer now, is it? Or sending a man to Mars?"

"It's pretty great to have the skills to help other people—and to be able to do it for so many of them."

"Hmm. I'm not so sure my father would have said that, although I know he would have been proud of me for taking care of myself." She lightly swabbed moisturizing gel over Shelley's forehead, cheeks, and chin. "That was something he always thought was important for a woman. 'Can't count on a man, my dear,' he'd say, 'and I tell you that as a man.'"

"Sounds like your father was a very unusual person. And smart."

"As clever as they come." Maxine unhooked the cape from around Shelley's neck and folded it into a compact square. "Well, there you go. Let's have that coffee now, shall we?"

CHAPTER NINETEEN

Shelley sometimes suspected—though she did her best to push this thought out of her mind—that a major part of her attraction to Rocco stemmed from his unavailability. Even before he had married Cyndi, he had kept himself aloof. He had made it very clear that he needed his space and always maintained his own house or apartment, no matter how inconvenient or how bleak their finances were at the time. Sometimes she knew he even had other women on the side. This enraged, and yet, at the same time, comforted her. Nothing could send her running faster than a sweet, loyal man.

J.J., the man she had dated right before she met Rocco, and, really, her only other long-term boyfriend, was a case in point. She had met him, a law student, at a college friend's party, and he had pursued her impeccably from that moment on: wining and dining her, sending her flowers, writing her tender notes about her eyes and her sense of humor. He was smart, funny, attractive enough, and kind—but the minute he started talking marriage, she started shutting down. J.J. envisioned a perfect suburban life, and there was nothing she dreaded more. She told him firmly that she wasn't ready for marriage, and, eventually, he stopped trying to persuade her. Then she met the elusive Rocco, who would never commit, who disappeared for weeks or months at a time (often, he claimed, to punish her), who cheated on her, and who, until Cyndi, seemed immune to marriage. As with a Chinese finger trap, the more he pulled away, the more stuck she found herself.

During the funeral home trial, Shelley had been sent to a psychiatrist, who had diagnosed her with borderline personality disorder. He had told her that her history of unstable and intense personal relationships, frantic efforts to avoid abandonment, recurrent threats of suicide, chronic feelings of emptiness, and unrelenting anger toward her mother and stepfather were all classic signs of this mental illness—as was her pattern of attention-seeking, manipulative behavior and histrionic, impulsive outbursts. Rocco made it a point to get a full copy of her psychiatric diagnosis, but after he read it, he tore it into pieces. Sure, she had some issues, and he was "all for" labeling them as a serious mental disorder if that helped attenuate her sentence—and his. But he had no intention of paying for more psychiatrist visits once the trial ended. Psychiatrists were hucksters, he proclaimed, just fast-talking showmen bilking vulnerable people out of hard-earned money. If you had a problem, it was up to you to solve it for yourself, not stick a fancy label on it and expect that paying thousands and spilling your guts to a shrink was going to help you. "Stop whining" was probably the solution to 99% of so-called psychiatric problems, in his opinion. Shelley may well have been "a mixed-up, moody broad"—who wouldn't have been, given her "wacko" family history?—but she merely needed someone to take care of her and show her how to handle things.

Fortunately, she had him, and, indeed, after they moved to western Maryland, he made it one of his personal projects to improve her. Here things would be different. She no longer had any friends or network to speak of, so this was a good time for a fresh start. He started by making her keep a log book to record how she spent each day, whom she saw or talked with on the phone, what she ate, and what she spent and where she spent it, even how many hours she slept each night and how often she moved her bowels. He was still living in his own place—he told her he was not yet ready to move in together—but most nights would stop by after the bars closed (never having trouble making new friends, Rocco quickly found a group of drinking buddies) and inspect her daily entries. If something seemed out of line, he interrogated her. If he noticed a new cat toy, or remembered she had lunch with a neighbor and didn't see it recorded, he would berate her, ridiculing her stupidity or accusing her of hiding something. If she whimsically decided to have a drink with a new friend after work (she had found a job, no questions asked, in the corner coffee shop), or stopped off to browse at the mall when he was expecting her home, he would harangue her until she fell to her knees, sobbing for forgiveness, or "punish" her by disappearing for the next week. As these oversights accumulated, he'd also throw things at her, even shove or whack her, if she didn't immediately respond by begging him for forgiveness, and, sometimes, even if she did.

He kept particularly careful track of food—what went into the house, what went into each of their bodies, and what impact it had on their weights. He'd sleep over most weekends, and every Saturday morning he'd "weigh her in." If she stayed "in range," he'd praise her, reminding her that he was a pushover for such a "hot bod." If she gained more than a pound, he'd go over her food intake and start throwing out all the chips and nuts on her shelves (his shelf, on the other hand, had to be perennially stocked with abundant granola bars, Oreos, and, most importantly, Chex Mix). He required her to record everything she ate and how many calories she consumed each day, and he inevitably commented if she surpassed his limits or added something new to her diet.

She rather enjoyed this kind of attention, not only because it helped keep her in shape but also because the discipline and oversight by someone other than herself came as a relief. She had always been conscious, obsessed even, with what went into her body and what impact it had on her weight, and although he was a taskmaster, being asked to do what she had been doing her whole life anyway came naturally to her. In fact, it felt good that someone else cared, and it was a relief not to carry this burden alone. Rocco weighed himself every week and held himself to a tight discipline, moreover, so she could hardly accuse him of hypocrisy.

She was also grateful to Rocco for helping to reform her "inner slob." She had been a self-proclaimed mess in childhood and in college, oblivious to where things went or to her personal role in getting them there. The number of objects and potential places they could be located and ways they could be handled had seemed infinite, completely beyond her understanding, and so she had pushed the idea out of her mind that she had any control over such matters. Rocco made it easy for her. He had made her a laminated list of "house rules," a page for every room, and by following it, she had immediate mastery. The living room, for example, could be kept tidy, quickly and almost effortlessly, merely by going down his list item by item, daily. In fact, there were only ten things to do:

1. Dust and vacuum daily (make sure lines are

visible).

2. Remove all photos from bookshelf except college graduation, Rocco, and Mrs. Simpson.
3. Keep TV cabinet doors closed after use.
4. Keep plug-in freshener (Island Paradise scent) in outlet next to sofa (replace 1st of every month); keep dry potpourri (hibiscus or floral garden) on media center.
5. Alphabetize all books, DVDs, and CDs on designated shelves.
6. Keep large green pillow against each armrest of sofa, with two brown pillows stacked at 45 degree angle in center with large green/brown pillow between them.
7. Put round green pillow on each armchair.
8. Always leave recliner in upright position.
9. Never leave more than 3 magazines on left end table, neatly stacked and fanned.
10. Replace all books on shelves before bed.

There were similar rule sheets, all laminated, for the dining room, bedroom, bathroom, and kitchen. Now she always vacuumed north to south so you could see the lines in the nap of the carpet, labeled every drawer and book shelf, sorted dresses and skirts by color and length, and even alphabetized the food in the pantry. Although Rocco was obviously a bit obsessive, and although she would never have mentioned the details to her friends (the whole thing would sound pretty "kooky" if she described how seriously he took all this), she had to admit that he helped her and that, without him, she would probably never have managed to make it out of bed.

Most of the time, too, she found following the rules no

more difficult than following a recipe. They were easier, in fact, because the tasks required no special skill, just determination to follow. When she was angry at Rocco, she found herself skimping here and there, perhaps not vacuuming the far corner of the bedroom, or not dusting the top bookshelf, and she couldn't deny a palpable thrill when she failed to record a specific purchase or phone call. However, in general, she followed the rules happily and genuinely felt she was a better person for it—cleaner, more efficient, more in control. Most of the time the rules were no big deal, and following them made her life easier, both because Rocco was calmer and kinder, but also because they made her feel more relaxed.

The rules also vanquished many of the piddling but oppressive questions that had once consumed far too much of her mental energy, questions about what to do and when to do it. She now knew where the cat slept and exactly when to change the kitty litter, the correct way to sort her slacks in the closet (by color—ROYGBIV!), how to arrange her nail polish on her dresser, what to do with mismatched dishtowels (discard immediately), which specific plate to display at the top of her china cabinet, which liqueur to keep in the brandy decanter, and how to display hand towels (folded in thirds with the trim showing). She knew that the toilet seat always had to be kept down, the shower door squeegeed and the tiles sprayed with Tilex after every use, and the nightstand bedecked with two cinnamon candles, its drawer containing the matches to light them. She never had to rummage for the spare ketchup because it was inevitably on the third shelf of the pantry between the hot sauce and the lentil soup, and she never had to puzzle over choices in the supermarket because he had already told her to buy Irish Spring soap and Crest tartar control liquid gel toothpaste with whitener in the stand-up bottle (4.6 oz. size, minty fresh).

What she liked less, however, were Rocco's more general "house rules," which seemed a bit over the top, even to her. He had these rules on a separate laminated sheet, which he kept posted on the refrigerator (it was the only item he allowed to be posted on the refrigerator, in fact). These house rules read, in boldface capital letters:

EVERYTHING NEAT AS A PIN, CLEAN AS A WHISTLE

NO MALE DOCTORS, DENTISTS, HAIR STYLISTS, OR VETS

NO PICTURES OF MEN EXCEPT ROCCO

NO MEN ON PHONE OR IN APARTMENT UNLESS ROCCO IS THERE

GOODNESS IS AS GOODNESS DOES

Yet even while these rules infuriated her, and no matter how many times she had torn them off the refrigerator in a fit of pique, she also knew that they were a vital component of what kept her and Rocco together. However autocratic and domineering the demands appeared, however arbitrary and even absurd, they also signaled to Shelley that Rocco needed her, even if he didn't admit it. And as much as his lack of commitment drew her to him, what kept her in place was the dependency on her that she felt these rules reflected. It was like being sucked between two oppositely charged magnets, her own will depolarized by Rocco's desperation to have, and his determination never to have, her. Either force by itself she could have escaped, and would, in fact, have longed to escape. Coupled, these forces were irresistible.

CHAPTER TWENTY

"Where on God's good earth are my glasses? Maxine had been trying repeatedly to fit the surgical mask over her face without dislodging the puffy, plastic cap she used to keep her hair from her face. After a bit more struggle, she gave up and let the mask hang from her neck by its elastic band.

"Did you check the sink?" asked Shelley.

"Ah—good call! I must have taken them off when I was washing up....Blasted spigot splatters everywhere except into the basin....You'd think it would have been simple enough for that Carole to phone up a plumber now, wouldn't you?"

"I'll take care of that. Later, I mean."

Shelley settled herself back into the high-backed, reclining makeup chair. Between her thumb and index finger she massaged the nylon of her makeup cape, a novelty item imprinted with oversized lush, red-bow lips that Maxine had purchased at a convention in Las Vegas several years back. Shelley had worn this same cape for the mock-up session the other day, and had been seated in this very same chair. This evening, however, Maxine could see that she was distinctly uncomfortable, even edgy. Almost as soon as Maxine had clicked the cape's hook behind her neck, in fact, Shelley had visibly flinched. She claimed to feel "vulnerable, kind of." She said she needed a break.

Maxine shrugged. Many clients carried on this way when it dawned on them that they were embarking on a surgery of sorts, not just a haircut or a facial in a day spa. Rather than feeling excited and pampered the way they did when they hoisted themselves onto those springy, hydraulic styling chairs, or laid themselves back for a shampoo, they were confronted with her streamlined and metallic recliner, which, in the context of the cramped space, white walls, and framed certificates, was reminiscent of the chairs in a dentist's office, or even, perhaps, a dialysis lab.

"Relax, dear. Nervousness is a common reaction to anything new." Maxine pushed the wheeled cart that had been set against a wall toward Shelley's chair and rolled her stool to sit in front of it. The cart was covered with a clean paper sheet and topped with flasks of cotton balls, paper-covered trays, metal canisters, surgical markers, and wrapped needles and syringes, as well as an oversized magnifying glass, eye loupe, two-tiered pigment organizer, and compact plastic tray containing tubes and squeeze bottles of solutions, powders, ointments, and astringents—a set-up that could, Maxine supposed, appear menacing to the uninitiated. On the other hand, that possibility was precisely why she was so fussy about touches like the comfy foyer, elegant ladies room, and soothing music; these details were meant to put clients at ease, and, in most cases, they did. However, some folks, Shelley apparently one of them, were jumpy by nature.

Shelley stared at the cart. "I feel like I'm in an operating room."

"Well, you are, really, when you think of it. Micropigmentation is a paramedical procedure, as I've said. We use it to cover scars—burn scars, like yours, other facial deformities, acquired or birthmarks, as well as scarring from surgical procedures. Mastectomies, for example. We use it to blend and reform areolas and so forth. I've had many of those women here, of course. Very common indeed. And we must certainly follow scrupulous hygienic practices even when we're working for purely cosmetic purposes, no different than any good surgeon would follow. Beautiful does not mean sloppy...."

Shelley lifted her head toward the loudspeaker attached to a corner of the ceiling. "I haven't heard this in decades—Rocco despises the oldies station."

"Could it be magic at last, eh? An oldie but a goodie."

"I always liked Barry Manilow. Even though it wasn't cool to admit."

"They play him all the time, this Lite FM station. The ladies seem to like it. Although I've been thinking about getting one of those loops. So many damn commercials....Perhaps you could look into that for me as well, sweetpea dear?"

Maxine adjusted herself onto the stool and worked her reading glasses, which hung on a neck chain, over the surgical cap. Once again she tried fitting the mask over her mouth and nose, but this time it kept getting entangled in the chain. "Bugger this arthritis...." She tucked a loose strand of hair under the cap, which left the glasses cockeyed and, when she tried to right them, they got caught up once again in the mask's elastic. "I'm afraid it's not the most flattering get-up, particularly the headgear. However, it does keep everything nicely out of the way without destroying the 'coiffure,' eh? Plus these things are disposable—no better assurance of hygiene. And recyclable. Makes our Dodie happy."

"If I weren't the patient, I'd help."

"'The client,' dear, 'the client.' You are not a 'patient.'"

"Sorry."

"Micropigmentation is paramedical, mind you, but 'patient' is not the proper term....Close your eyes now." Maxine, having at last adjusted the cap, mask, and glasses to her satisfaction, poured facial cleanser on a cotton ball and carefully wiped it across Shelley's lids from the inside to the outside corner as she would a baby's. She used another moistened ball on the other eye, ran a third over the extensive acne scars on Shelley's cheeks and forehead, and, although she had no intention of doing any work in that area today, finished by swiping the chin and neck several times. "Keep closed now.... All we need is to apply the anesthetic, and we can get started."

Maxine slowly unscrewed the lid off a tube with her gloved fingers and worked a dab of cream onto a cotton ball. "Lean your head back. That's it." She adjusted Shelley back into the seat.

"I feel like a patient, whatever you say."

Maxine massaged the cream into Shelley's forehead, eyelids, and upper cheeks.

"Though that's not a bad thing," Shelley continued. "I feel like this is going to make me well. Ooo, that stings!"

"Just for a second. This is new, brought out just last year. It was the talk of this summer's conference. Very close to 7.5 pH—the same as human tears. It's quite mild compared to what we had been using, much more tolerable with merely that first zing, and then—nothing. You won't feel a thing in a second....You see? No pain....But we give it 15 or 20 more minutes for full effect....You can open up now." Maxine handed Shelley the mirror so she could watch the procedure. "The worst is over!"

"Except looking at that scar." She handed the mirror back to Maxine. "I still can't stand looking at myself."

"Do yourself a favor, and don't look for a while if it bothers you. When I put on the liner today, you may also find things look a bit harsh as well. That's why some women prefer to wait before scrutinizing themselves."

"Harsh?"

"Not to worry. Colors often appear quite intense at first. This may last for the first week or so, and then everything fades to a more natural look. You may have a little reddening, too, like you see after a good cry. But, again—not to worry."

"If you say so."

"I often advise my clients to avoid peeking into the oven until the roast is cooked. You understand? Give it time...." Maxine began pushing numbers on the timer, setting off an annoying series of beeps. "I'm not charging you, of course, but I like to keep track of time. Keeps me on my toes."

"I see."

Maxine kept pushing buttons. "Drives me bonkers this contraption does. Half the time the blasted thing doesn't work at all. I still long for my old, wind-up. Worked on a simple spring. That's it. Now you have to pay for these digital thingamajibs. They're useless. As far as I'm concerned. Or maybe this one is just worn, I don't know....I asked Carole to pick up a new one for me. They're charging twenty-five dollars for them! Obscene, *isit?* You must pay for the digital these days, although honestly they're cheap as anything to make, and then they work no better—if you ask me, they work worse. I think my last wind-up cost me three, if that, and lasted ten, maybe twenty, years. But you can't find the wind-ups anywhere anymore."

"Maybe I can cover it up with something until you're done with me."

"What? The scar? Please don't give it another thought...."

Maxine removed her reading glasses and strapped a magnifying visor over her head.

"That's easier said than done."

"Just a moment dear. It's one bloody contraption after another with these eyes. Don't get old, sweetpea, you hear me?"

"Can I help you with that?"

"No, no, just give me a moment. There we go. Now, please, sit back, and close your eyes. There we go." She began lining Shelley's eyes with a makeup pencil. "If you like, luv, we can do the scar next—right after we try out this liner. This is the simplest procedure and will tell us if we should expect any problems."

"Great. When's next?"

"I would say we dig into it in a couple of months. Maybe sooner if you heal very quickly. And respond to the RAD machine as we hope."

Shelley jerked up and opened her eyes. "A couple of months! I have to look at that thing for two more months?"

"My dear, I told you before, if I am to work on you, you must have patience. You're not a patient, but you must be 'patient,' you see?" Maxine surveyed her work. The left lid needed a slightly wider wedge at the outer corner to give the eye more lift. "I don't do sloppy work ever, for anyone or anything. And, mind you, change takes time—especially safe change....Now, please, sit back or I'll never get these lines right."

Satisfied at last with the mock-up lines, Maxine set the collyrium and Duration Gel within easy reach, and placed the charcoal pigment and cotton balls beside them. She unwrapped a sanitized paper dish. "Now where is that bloody assembly?...Just when we're ready to go."

"I hope this works." Shelley began gently chewing her

upper lip.

Maxine disengaged herself from the stool and returned to the supply cabinet behind Shelley's chair. She began rummaging through it, noting that it, too, was in dire need of reorganization. "Of course it will work. But you must be patient. You must follow instructions about aftercare and so forth. That shouldn't be a problem, given that you're here, with me minding you."

Maxine resettled herself and turned her attention to unwrapping and inspecting the new pen. "Come along then. I think once we've done these eyes, you'll understand how much farther we can go." She dipped the needle end of her tool into the pigment.

"Still—it can't be reversed. It's permanent....I don't know if I'm ready."

"Ready? Hmph. When will you be ready?"

"I don't know. Maybe tomorrow. Next week. What's the difference? I'm here for a year or more anyway. Just not right now."

"If not now, when? Another one of my father's favorite sayings."

"Funny—Roger used to say that, too. When it served his purposes."

"Roger?"

"My mother's last husband. He was a poet—or so he claimed. Mainly he seemed to watch old movies, pick the skin off the bottom of his feet, and drink vodka."

Maxine withdrew her pen from Shelley's left lower lid and started rearranging the inks on the cart. "Charming."

"He was beyond disgusting, but brilliant according to my mother. An overlooked genius."

"Her last husband, eh? How many did she go through?"

"I can't remember....No, seriously, there were four, not

counting my father. He took off when I was three. And counting the one who lasted about two weeks—I don't even remember his name since I was only six or something. No one could stand being around my mother too long."

"Oh my....Here, sit back and let me finish the lowers."

"Not that those guys were such great specimens themselves. Roger in particular. What a scumbag....Yeeks. It's kind of scary to have needles so close to my eye."

"You need to close your eyes now anyway. So there will be nothing to see. That's a good girl." She began implanting the pigment into Shelley's right upper lid. "You should be glad I don't use rotary or coil. That's like having a power drill come at you. Manual is so gentle by comparison. I just tap in the pigment, like this...gentle, very gentle, you see?"

"It's still my eye."

"Well, of course. But be grateful that I use the safest, gentlest method there is—even though it takes more time. Most clients appreciate the care manual needling requires, particularly in the eye area. But, the truth of it is, the whole face is precious—and, relatively delicate as well."

"I appreciate it. I'll appreciate it even more when we finish though."

"Those other tools, they work well, I suppose, but it's pure laziness on the part of the operators. Plus, the things are so damn noisy. It sounds like a construction site, honest to God. You'll recover more quickly and won't see any clogging of pigments with the manual either—and far less pain and swelling. Far less fading, as well, because those machines push the pigment too deeply into the dermal layer, where much of it gets encapsulated or absorbed by the blood cells, the immune system. You see? I place the pigment gently on the epidermal layer where the immune system cannot break it down and absorb it. You must be highly skilled, of course, and meticulous."

Shelley reopened her eyes and stared down into one of the giant lips covering her bosom as Maxine withdrew the pen.

"So this Roger fellow was a poet you say?"

"He claimed to be a poet. Had an MFA, or so he told us. Personally, I think it was just an excuse for sponging off my mother and leaching off our bodies."

"*Our* bodies."

"He abused me. Sexually I mean."

Maxine set down the pen and flipped up the lenses on the magnifying visor. "Oh, lambie. You poor, poor dear."

"It's okay."

"But you were a child. A baby. Appalling."

"I didn't even have the words for it until Oprah starting talking about things like that. I just thought it was normal."

"Did your mother know?"

"Maybe. Yes. No. I don't know. She was too busy, I think, to notice, or care, what was going on, with me or with anyone. Except herself, of course."

"Heavens! What on earth could she be busy with, not to see that this husband of hers was molesting her little daughter?...Surely she couldn't have known."

"She knew. Vaguely. She didn't care. Roger was a catch. He had an MFA from Cornell and published poems. He lived with us from the time I was nine until I left home. And he got two for the price of one, all that time. Three, actually, because there was my sister Annabel, too. But she left home at 15—smart girl."

"It's inconceivable to me that a mother would tolerate this."

"Denial. It's is a wondrous thing."

"Apparently."

"You had to know my mother to understand. It was just easier for her to think I was crazy. I got moved from one school to the next, or plopped into public school when they got tired of pampering me. I had plenty of psychiatrists, too. They said I had low self-esteem and a personality disorder. Due to my Dad's running out on us."

"And when your sister left? That didn't concern her?"

"I don't think she had time to notice. She was always running out to performances and up late at night writing. Then she'd sleep in until noon every day, school days. Roger got up with me in the morning, and when he was getting up from my bed—which he did, by the way, pretty often from the time I was a teenager—she didn't even notice."

"You talk so calmly about all this."

"Years of psychotherapy. Rocco made me go again, when we were out in Hagerstown. It seems like a story now. Someone else's story."

"You poor lambie."

"It's a lot more common than you think."

"That doesn't make it right. Or easy."

Shelley shrugged. "I grew up and went to college and haven't been back since. You go on."

"Hmmm. And your mother?"

"She sends me birthday cards, most years. She's a wreck. She moved out to Los Angeles last I heard, tried to break into the big time. My sister told me she's in and out of rehab."

"Ah, your sister. Were you able to turn to her, all this time growing up with this Roger fellow around?"

"She's a lot older than me. She cut out before I had much to say....Anyway, we don't communicate much. She's doing the suburban housewife thing down in Boca Raton. Birthday cards with her, too."

Maxine dabbed off a swirl of dye from under Shelley's eye with a cotton swab.

"I'm so sorry, Shelley. Things haven't been easy for you, have they? Quiet now while I get this corner. It's a bit tricky...."

"Ouch! I keep trying to imagine those beautiful waves on your poster, to keep my mind off the poking. But all I keep picturing is a swarm of bees going after my eyes."

"Only a few moments more...."

"Don't get me wrong. My mother was, is, an amazing woman. A force."

"Close your eyes again, please, dear....There we go."

"She ran her own talk show for a while. On cable, when it was new and anyone who breathed could start a show. She interviewed local talent, reviewed shows, stuff like that. I watched sometimes, with Mrs. Simpson. That was pretty much the extent of my relationship with my mother."

"Mrs. Simpson?"

"Our neighbor. Next-door. She was my salvation. Her kids were grown, and she used to talk to me a lot. She'd sit on her porch and see me when I came home from school, listened to me go on and on about saving the manatees, which was my obsession for years, geek-queen that I was, pretty much single-handedly convinced me that I could go off to Goucher if that's what I really wanted to do, whatever my mother and Roger had to say about it. We spent so much time together—I guess today she'd be booked for child abduction. Back then no one cared....Ow!"

"Just relax. And keep closed. That's right....She didn't abduct you. She offered you kindness....Here, take a rest a moment. I'll dab a little more numbing agent there, so you won't feel a thing."

Shelley opened her eyes. "Anyway, Mrs. Simpson used

to be the only reason I regretted never going back to Michigan. She used to call me when I was in college, and she worried a lot when I left. She died ten years ago, though. So now there's no reason to go back. Ever."

"Didn't you feel comfortable telling this Mrs. Simpson about the abuse? She sounds like she would have helped you if she had known....Close again. That's right, stay still, just like that." Maxine gently wiped off the excess color, and blotted the blood oozing down Shelley's cheek.

"I didn't think of it as abuse. Or maybe I did. I don't know. It's hard to explain, but it was kind of a mix of 'this is normal' and 'this is embarrassing' and 'this can't be real.' Like if I just didn't put what was happening into words, it was all my imagination."

"But over time—I would have thought you would have talked enough, and she would have picked up that something wasn't right. Just the fact that no one was ever home for you." Maxine tugged the skin around Shelley's lids gently downward. More blood oozed from the tiny puncture wounds.

"Oh, she definitely thought my mother was a witch. That's for certain. She called her 'Doris,' which my mother found highly insulting. My mother's actual name was Doris, of course, or, rather, Doris was her original name, but when she started that talk show she insisted that everyone call her 'Jaclyn.' Mrs. Simpson wouldn't though. She would watch 'Jaclyn's The Artist Within' with me and go on about 'Doris Ignore-us.'"

"*Ag*, well now things will be better, won't they? Onward and upward!"

"I can't tell you the number of times I still lie awake at night, pretending that I'm only twelve and still have my whole life ahead of me. I tell myself that all the stuff with my mother and Roger was just a dream. There's no father who ran off with the neighbor and no utterly self-absorbed mother. None of that ever happened. And none of the later stuff either—no loneliness, no Lean Cuisines, no anorexia. No lying in bed for days just because there wasn't anyone or anything worth getting up for. That stuff's all vanquished, too. Not to mention Rocco. I just lie there blissfully, feeling the pillow envelope my head and the mattress cradle my body and imagining what I think normal 12-year-old girls imagine."

"Which is?"

"Nothing much. Just your standard middle class fare: dabbing my ears with Jontue and trying on different sweaters while various charming suitors walk up to my front steps with bouquets for me. And then thinking that I'll have memories of all that someday when I'm married with children...."

"All right now. Let me finish you up now by enhancing the lashes. Eh? Hold still. That's it....You have more than twice as many eyelashes on the top lid as the lower—did you know that? We'll get every one of them. There we go."

"But then I suddenly get this pang. This isn't me. This isn't my life. And I don't even want these things, even though I want to want them."

"Well, you may surprise yourself. Who knows what you really want? Or any of us?...All right then, my dear, I think we've accomplished our mission. Just hush a moment while I clean you up." Maxine dabbed Shelley's cheeks and then handed her a small plastic sack. "Here's your care package. Aftercare items....Take a look. Ointment, ice pack, eye drops. I'll be at you to use them all properly. Especially the ointment—don't skimp on that. You hear me? For three days. Always keep the treated area moist, up until you go to sleep. That way you won't get the tightness a few days later. Moist, that's the ticket. You'll soon see a light crust, which will fall off on its own. Whatever you do, please keep your hands off the face—no picking or rubbing the crust."

"I'm so red. Like a clown."

"The color will fade. In some cases, even too much. We'll probably want to reapply more in a month if need be."

"But so red."

"It will go down in a day or so. If you want, use that ice pack—just bend it up and it gets cool. And it goes without saying that you won't be outdoors, but you must keep your face out of the sun as well. No soaps or cleansing creams either until I tell you, even hot water in the shower. Just let the eyes be....And for shame, please don't pick or rub the skin."

CHAPTER TWENTY-ONE

In June 1976 when 15,000 students marched through the streets of Soweto to protest the forced use of the Afrikaans language in schools, Maxine marched through the doors of her Capetown bungalow and left Toad gaping on the front steps. Before he had a chance to follow her back inside, she bolted the upper lock and had young Dennis and Dodie help shove the loveseat, armchair, and ottoman against the door to make sure no one could break it down. She unplugged the telephone and led the children, who thought they were playing Cowboys and Indians, into the kitchen, where they angled the butcher block table against the back door. The three of them stayed holed up in the house for three solid days, eating marmite sandwiches and watching the Minister of Bantu Education on Toad's beloved telly decry the disrespectful youth in the townships. She never heard from Toad again once he had stopped pounding on the door, but two years later an officer came to inform her that her husband, conscripted into the military, had been killed in the line of duty while attempting to put down a trade union revolt.

Years later, Dodie would grill Maxine about those tumultuous times, many of which made the pages of her history books, frequently berating her for removing wrinkles and drawing pink lips onto the faces of self-satisfied matrons when the world around them was imploding. She was appalled by her mother's oblivion, her absorption in superficialities and petty personal problems when there was injustice to fight all around them, injustice so large and oppressive that only a blind rhinoceros could fail to see it.

Maxine's stance, which she made no bones about sharing, was that Dodie, a person who had always had room and board laid at her feet, couldn't possibly understand how for many years of her life, particularly those years, fighting for survival had required all Maxine's time and energy. Not that Toad had ever been much help when it came to income, but at least he had been another adult, someone with whom she could leave the children when she worked even if he was only peripherally present, or send out for milk and medicine when a baby was sick. Once he was out of their lives, she became a single working mother with two small tots to support, and a new and precarious business into which she had as yet to turn a profit or even entice more than a handful of clients. Yes, she acknowledged to Dodie years later, all around her the country had been disintegrating into lawlessness and vigilante justice, with riots in the townships, spiraling inflation, collapsing currency, arson attacks, checkpoints, detainments and intimidations, states of emergency, boycotts, car bombings, mysterious kidnappings, political murders, and guerilla warfare that could come at you in the midst of a shopping trip or a leisurely stroll. Everywhere people she knew were joining illegal organizations or making plans to emigrate, depending on their dispositions. She was well aware of all that, but she couldn't allow it to be more than background noise, nor to see it as something over which she had any power. Instead, she did what she could in her own little world, to pick winnable battles. "Back then my younger self thought it was easier to fight wrinkles," she acknowledged to Dodie many years later. "My younger self was wrong."

Where Dodie was wrong, in contrast, was in estimating the degree to which Maxine devoted herself to "petty" vanities. Certainly Maxine was a crusader when it came to her business, and she unquestionably devoted the bulk of her waking hours and mental machinations to keeping herself up-to-speed and her clients gratified. But all the while her private needs receded. This had not been the plan, of course. When she had decided to give Toad the boot, she had assumed that Rufus Alvarez would move in to fill the void. Instead, she found that the more freedom she had, the less time she had for a lover. In the first weeks and months Dr. Ruf would sometimes stop by her bungalow when the children were sleeping, but everything between them that had previously flowed so naturally now felt shockingly awkward and forced. The problem was the constant and unquenchable constriction she felt as she imagined one of the kiddos overhearing, or walking in on, them. Eventually he started springing for babysitters, which allowed him to take her to dinner or theatre every few weeks or so, after which they'd luxuriate in a deserted wing of the clinic or, on several memorable occasions in the first few years, a hotel room. Even so, within months of Toad's departure something shifted in their relationship, and she realized that, as much as he still brought a lump to her throat, this situation would never improve.

The other surprise was that from the moment Toad left their lives, it was Dodie, and not Dr. Ruf, who became her near constant companion. On her own in Capetown, Maxine could keep Dennis in nursery while she worked, but Dodie at two was still too young: without Toad lounging on the couch in his perfunctory version of childcare, she had no choice but to keep Dodie with her at the salon. In the early years Dodie had napped in a cot Maxine set up for her in the storeroom or spread out with toys Maxine kept for her in a cordoned-off section of the waiting room. Although occasional moods and sulks disrupted a session, and tested her temper, Maxine generally found that the baby relaxed and delighted the clients, who often brought their own little ones, either to play with or oversee Dodie. Some clients even volunteered to stay on an hour or so after their appointments just to amuse her. Before long Maxine had enough business to hire several of them sequentially as her very first receptionists who, among other duties, tended to Dodie's needs if Maxine was caught up with a procedure. Years later, Maxine often marveled that it had been much maligned two-year-olds who had been her salvation during the two most difficult parts of her life—Dodie in those early days after Maxine went on her own, and, many years later, Dodie's own baby Margaret, with whom she spent much of her time when she first moved to the States.

It was the feeling of absolute need and adoration from another human being she got from Dodie that had made Maxine realize just how superfluous Rufus Alvarez was to her life. Maxine had never doubted, ever, that the needs of her children were far and above the needs of any man, whether that man was as vile as Toad or as beguiling as Dr. Ruf. What she hadn't been prepared for, however, was the realization of just how shallow and unspecific these needs of the men really were. Every time she had held little Dodie on her lap, combed the hair that was finally sprouting from the boyish little scalp, or simply gazed on the girl at play, she felt a cord between them. She understood that this cord would never yield no matter how Dodie grew, whoever she turned out to be, and however they temporally felt about each other. She adored Dennis, too, and always would, but she had never been tangled up in him like his sister. She felt tied to him, naturally, certainly felt a love for him that surpassed who he was or what he did, but even as an infant Dennis had been in his own world, devoted to her and appreciative of her, but his own man, always. He would do right by his mother, and she would give her life for him, but even when he was small she knew he was answering to someone other than herself. What she felt for Dodie, in contrast, was as perfect and complete as it was terrifying and inescapable, and nothing she felt for Rufus Alvarez could ever come close to making her feel as distinctive, indispensable, or alive.

The closer Maxine grew to Dodie, the more she came to understand that her initial bond to Dr. Ruf grew largely from her blindness to the limitations of his need for her. As the months on her own went by, she could no longer pretend that she, an aging mother of two, uneducated by his standards, poor, untraveled, implacably sensible, and altogether lacking in sophistication, would be the love of this man's life. Yes, he adored her, genuinely adored her, when he was with her, but he was also a man who lived for the moment. She was old enough and savvy enough to see how believing herself to be the only woman in his life was inconsistent with their twice or thrice monthly encounters. Was she so silly as to think that he sat home knitting with his mother on all those other nights? Of course not. Rufus Alvarez was a man of incredible passion and energy, and although she knew he worked like a dog, she also knew he loved that way as well. She soon came to understand, and accept, that this was a man incapable of attaching himself to anything outside of the moment, whether that moment involved work or flesh. He was a fabulous lover precisely because he focused entirely on the adored object at hand and, when they were together, that object was her. So, yes, when he said she was indeed perfection she took him at his word and thrilled to it, but she simultaneously realized that the words were ephemeral, true for that one beautiful moment but carrying no meaning or weight beyond it. She didn't quite grasp what he meant when he said she was the Platonic incarnation of beauty, but still she relished the rush his words gave her. She also saw that, within a few years, things between them became increasing "platonic" in the lower case sense that she did understand, with the trysts cooling into more of a business, even a father-daughter, partnership.

With Dodie, in contrast, her connection became increasingly complex and inexorable. Dodie, and, to a lesser extent, Dennis had spent a good deal of time with her at work, coloring and counting change in the backroom before they started grade school, and later, becoming integral parts of the business, stocking shelves, scrubbing counters, and, eventually, booking clients. Maxine had always felt that involving the children in the business made them self-sufficient and capable, and, at the very least, kept both out of mischief. As early as age ten, however, Dennis, a vigorous mix of his father's impertinence and his grandmother's numerical wizardry, got caught up with the rugby pools of his political chums and sundry other investments and schemes, which Maxine had always regarded as both inscrutable and questionable but through which he had pocketed enough money to cover a ticket to the United States and business school by the age of 20. He considered himself a newly made American who wanted nothing more to do with his vile country of origin, except, perhaps, to condemn it. That was just as well, Maxine often remarked, given her longstanding conviction that some officer was bound to arrive on her doorstep once again someday, this time to inform her that her son had been tossed into a jail cell or shot down by another bonehead. Dennis shrugged off her dire predictions. It was beyond him why anyone would want to live past the decrepit age of 30 anyway, and if his quest for justice meant sacrificing a few years off that goal, so be it. Like his sister, he had nothing but disdain for her ostrich-like behavior. They'd often have heated battles in which she'd hiss cryptic warnings at him, intimating that, right as he may have been, their family history meant they had to be careful. She reminded him of the Holocaust, in which his own relatives, his great grandparents and great aunt Bella, had perished.

"They've been good to us here, Dennis, very good—which is more than you can say for the Europeans."

"All the more reason to be out there fighting. A person who lived with that injustice ought to be on the front lines."

"It's not a matter of justice, Dennis. It's a matter of survival. As Jews we are always next on the list. We can never forget that."

"What I can't forget is Mr. Mandela standing on that porch talking about our tireless and heroic sacrifices. I can't—and I won't."

How could she explain to him how she felt stuck being who she was, and where she was? How could she convey to him that sometimes it was a matter of choosing the less vile of two vile choices? Her father had always said that a Jew who fought the system was a dead Jew. And he was a good man, a brilliant one as well, who hated what was happening here to the bottom of his soul and would have been proud of Dennis's heart, if not his choices. She had vivid memories of her father in his armchair ranting about how wrong it was to remove the Africans from Sophiatown. She remembered him waving the paper around his red face and going on and on about the criminality of banning ostensible communists—communists being defined by the National Party as anyone who wanted to effect political, social, or economic change—and the hunting down of innocent men. He had been appalled watching the influx of pass laws, curfews, and separate facilities contaminate life in his adopted country, a country that had been good to him and allowed him to build a life from nothing. Both of her parents had been appalled, having seen this happening to Jews in their own lifetimes, and knowing exactly where it led. But, appalled as they were, they were, above all, survivors.

"Dennis, luv, you have to take care of yourself first," was what she usually ended up saying. "If you don't—well, what good can you do anyone else anyway?"

Dennis eventually grasped this on his own. The very next year he met Laurie, an American girl several years his senior, and, with his characteristic sharps, left for the States with her. Maxine immediately recognized this decision as the lesser of two evils, for many reasons, not the least of which was the money into which he married. Meanwhile, Dodie, who continued to help out at the salon even into her teens, became increasingly critical and cantankerous, egged on by her brother's antics, no doubt. Even so, Maxine had been entirely unprepared when, several weeks before Dodie's eighteenth birthday, one of her clients had returned to the makeup room after a session to ask how she could pay her bill: Dodie, who normally came in after school to cover the desk, wasn't there. Maxine found a note on the receptionists' desk, written in Dodie's slanting schoolgirl scrawl on wide-lined notebook paper: "Zeenie, I know if I tell you not to worry you will, but please don't. I am fine, but I can't stay here anymore. Don't call the police—they won't be able to find me. Jenny says she'll work for you for nothing if you write her a recommendation after the summer, so you'll have someone in the front room until autumn. So call her. And buck up. I will be fine, and you must be, too.–Your Dodie."

Maxine closed up the salon right away and spent the rest of the afternoon and most of the evening crying her eyes out in front of Dodie's best friend, Jenny, and her parents, but she couldn't get a clue out of any of them. Over the next few days she phoned up every one of Dodie's friends, the school principal, and several teachers, and grilled each and every one of her clients. No one admitted knowing anything. She called Dennis and Laurie overseas, repeatedly, but all they could say was that Dodie was a big girl, a woman, really, and if she had left a note saying she would be okay, she surely would be. Sometimes kids had to leave home and figure things out for themselves, they reminded her. But where could she be, Maxine asked? She imagined her running off with a man—in fact, she was convinced of it—but the police told her there was nothing that she could do about it, not with a girl that age who had left a note. Didn't they know how dangerous the streets could be, how Dodie wouldn't know where to go, or how to keep herself safe? They merely patted Maxine's hand and gave her cups of tea, observing that teenagers left home all the time, and most of them came back, usually after a few days, or, if not that, weeks or months. Sometimes, years, yes, if things were bad, but they almost always came around eventually. Meanwhile—no news was good news.

Dodie never came around, or back. Just a week after she left, however, Maxine got a telephone call from Dennis, who told her to stop worrying: Dodie was fine, and she was with him, in the States. She would be living with them until the fall, when she was enrolling in college. She would be happier there, where things were more stable, less violent. She could concentrate on her education. He and Laurie would see to that. They had already found a spot for her at the small college in Maryland that Laurie had attended, and Dennis would foot the bill for tuition, room, and board.

Maxine, speechless for the first time in her life, rolled ideas around in her head about buying a ticket or hiring a headhunter, neither of which she could possibly afford or manage, but, in the end, she settled for not speaking to Dodie until she could figure out what to do, and what to think. That took all of two weeks. After that they spoke civilly on the phone, usually once or twice a month, and the assurance that Dodie was, indeed, fine and getting on with her education kept Maxine reasonably sane for the next few years.

Occasionally the calls would lapse into Maxine's pleas for Dodie to return, or at least to visit. But Maxine knew that once Dodie, who already considered herself an American and vowed never to set foot in South Africa again, had made up her mind there was no turning around. Life was real and life was earnest for Dodie, just as it was for Maxine's mother who would undoubtedly have made the history books had she the means and education to do so. "Instead the old brogan frittered away her drive and talent by focusing them on bookkeeping and bake sales," Maxine often told her children. Dodie, Maxine believed, would undoubtedly, with a university education, turn her energies to some grander project. Even when two years later Maxine learned in the course of a single phone call that she now had a granddaughter and son-in-law, she never questioned

Dodie's mulish drive not only to finish her degree and get her U.S. citizenship but to accomplish whatever she set her mind to accomplish.

However distant Dodie might have been, or how many years had passed, Maxine also felt her constant presence in the salon. Dodie had been gestated together with the cosmeceutical business—Maxine had even mailed out the same card to announce the arrival of both daughter and business—and almost literally grown up there. For the rest of her life Maxine was never able to think back to the Capetown shop without seeing Dodie, sometimes as a pale, glassy-eyed adolescent scribbling essays and erasing equations at the front desk, occasionally as an earnest eight-year-old sorting packages or wiping countertops, but, most often, as a preschooler in ruffled gingham scooting across the floor, stacking blocks, somersaulting, and chattering away earnestly with the customers. Even as their phone calls grew terser and rarer, this image of a sweet, engaging two-year-old with whom she had once shared her daily world and who was now buried within this self-righteous, unapproachable woman, never failed to assuage all wounds and melt all rancor.

CHAPTER TWENTY-TWO

Thanksgiving and the holidays slowed Shelley's progress. Maxine insisted that this was to be expected: impending Christmas parties always brought even her stingiest clients back to life, and even after the emergency electrolysis work and touch-up sessions that characterized December, New Year's resolutions routinely brought on a whole new slew of hopefuls throughout January. Maxine simply didn't have the time, not to mention the energy, to squeeze in extra unpaid sessions on Shelley's behalf. Even so, as the winter progressed, Maxine at last got to work on the worst of Shelley's facial scars. She camouflaged the burn on Shelley's forehead so that it would only have been visible to a forensic detective and expertly redrew the singed eyebrow to match its twin. She also began needling some of the lesser lines around Shelley's lips, and planned to address the remaining disfigurements before spring.

By February even Dodie had begun to feel that, although it was taking far longer than she had ever imagined, their scheme might actually succeed. She often stopped by the salon after work, and tonight she had stayed much longer than usual to assess not only Shelley's immediate needs, but also her general state of mind. Throughout their conversation, Dodie kept thinking that Shelley now not only looked different—the changes in her hair alone had jumpstarted that process last fall—but that she looked distinctly better. Besides making substantial inroads into the scars, the permanent makeup had, as promised, essentially reshaped Shelley's eyes and lip line, certainly not as much as risky, not to mention pricey, plastic surgery would have done, but enough, together with the new hair color and style, and blemish-free skin, to suggest a different woman. Even more importantly, Shelley was a different woman. She held herself less rigidly, spoke less guardedly, and, although she still tended to be mordantly self-mocking, she occasionally made a capricious pun or laughed dispassionately at her situation. Shelley even seemed to enjoy the challenges of pleasing Maxine and occasionally enthused about the adventure of living in the salon. At these moments it felt like the three of them were a team, co-conspirators, or even, sometimes, friends. There were increasingly times when the grimness that pervaded the enterprise lifted entirely, perhaps only momentarily, but long enough to sustain a sense of hopefulness in all three of them. Dodie began to imagine that one day in the foreseeable future—assuming Maxine would ever let her go—Shelley might reemerge into normal society with a set of skills and newfound integrity that would free her from dependence on men like Rocco Herkimer. In fact, Dodie increasingly thought that Shelley's chances of doing so were far higher than those of the vast majority of women she saw at the shelter.

What a shame, however, that she could convey none of this progress or her pride in creating it to Florence. Even more shameful were the lies, primarily covert, that she was forced to tell Florence, not to mention the entirely unjustifiable hatred she felt for Florence as her boss because she had to tell her these lies. Dodie could almost feel her skin radiating contempt whenever they spoke. She knew all the time that this was because she was living a lie, and that this mode of existence was something she couldn't continue. She hated not only the complexities inevitably imposed by untruths, the constant pressure to compound them and the fear of being found out, but also the feeling she had that Florence no longer trusted her. Dodie had always prided herself on being straightforward, and, although her recent past as a relatively settled adult had made her forget it, leaving had always come more easily to her than lying.

This new life of constant pretense not only oppressed her spirit, but gave her physical pains. Just hearing Florence's footsteps made her head and neck ache, and speaking to her made Dodie's voice croak and crackle, the edges of every word dragging like dull knives across her larynx. Sometimes when they had an impersonal conversation about readjusting donation procedures or rethinking energy consumption she found herself so hoarse she could barely get a word out of her mouth. Ever since that first conversation about Shelley, nothing had been the same. Every conversation and confrontation between them since then had been tainted because, while polite forms were still being followed, the implicit bond of complicity and admiration between them was dead. This bond had always made her work at the shelter tolerable even at its most frustrating. Now she saw it was true—once you had violated someone's trust, it was almost impossible to restore it, at least completely. She and Florence had never been intimate friends, but until that confrontation last fall they had followed the social conventions associated with them and had always shared an implicit mutual respect. Now, with a single betrayal, all that was gone.

Even worse, Dodie was beginning to think that this was

as it should be. She didn't deserve to be trusted. However much she despised the lying, and despised herself for doing it, she also had no intention of telling Florence about the continuing deal between Shelley and Maxine. The easiest solution was therefore to avoid seeing Florence as much as possible. Although she still served her function at Safe Port, she increasingly came into work late and left early, justifying her behavior to herself by saying she had to shop for Shelley or stop in to check on her.

When she couldn't see all the women in her shortened hours, she'd come back to Safe Port after six, knowing that Florence would be gone by then, and worked for a couple of hours in peace. Her work was more than perfunctory, but certainly neither exemplary nor gratifying. She no longer stopped to chat with Linda or lingered as she often had before to play cards or compare school notes with the clients. Instead, she spent increasing amounts of time with Shelley at the salon, sharing dinner, playing backgammon, or watching movies on the old television/DVD player she had brought from home after Randall had upgraded to a flat-screen.

About once a week, when she could steal time away from the family, Dodie brought Shelley sufficient scarves and hats for camouflage and took her on drives outside the city, or, once, even a chilly walk at Sandy Point Beach, just to keep her from going stir crazy. She took her to a dentist in northern Baltimore for a cleaning and drove her up to Delaware to put together what amounted to a trousseau, including several ensembles for the new Shelley to wear in the salon. On one desolate Thursday afternoon when they knew Rocco had to be busy at a legislative hearing, they even drove to the Smithsonian to see an IMAX documentary on manatees that Shelley, who apparently had been obsessed by these "forgotten mermaids" as a child, had found online. Randall and the children grew used to late dinners, and, on many occasions, to fending for themselves. No one seemed to mind. Randall, although often working late now that the state was sitting on them about mandatory physical education and health classes, was usually home by 4:30 or 5, unless there was an evening Board meeting, and now that Margaret was in high school Dodie could count on her to handle the boys until then. When Randall wasn't willing to spring for pizza or Chinese, the lot of them were usually game for microwaving something out of the freezer before they went back to their respective pursuits, Randall to his orchids and the children to what she liked to think was their homework and practicing. They usually left a load of dishes for her in the sink, and a table and countertops to wipe down, but such tasks seemed to her a fitting penance for her neglect of the family. In fact, she often thought that her ability to attack the nightly chaos and put the kitchen to rights was her only solid accomplishment most days, and, at the very least, a nearly fail-safe means to a deep and instantaneous sleep once she made it to bed.

Tonight two new admits had forced her to stay at Safe Port until eight, and her extended visit with Shelley meant that she didn't leave for home until close to 10 p.m. When she pulled into the driveway, most of the lights in the house were out, which she took as a good sign. The kids might actually be asleep. If she was even luckier, it might even mean that Randall was still preoccupied in the greenhouse, which would allow her to slip into bed unnoticed. Instead, however, she walked in to find Margaret sitting bright-eyed at the kitchen table with none other than Rocco Herkimer. The two appeared to be having a tea party.

"Margaret! What on earth...?"

"Well, greetings, Mrs. Wicklund." Rocco rose and extended his hand to her. "Your charming daughter and I have been having a lovely chat. I have to tell you—she has impressive social instincts for such a young lady. Very impressive indeed."

Dodie ignored his hand and peered into the cups. "Cocoa? You made cocoa for him, Margaret?"

"I couldn't figure out how to use the coffee maker...."

"Where's your father?"

"He's not here. The boys are in bed though."

"Not here? Where on earth is he?...Margaret, what have I told you about letting in strangers when we aren't home?"

"Mom! Relax. Delegate Herkimer isn't a stranger. He's a member of the House of Delegates."

"I'm sorry if I caused Margaret to disobey family rules— or if I caused you any concern. I only stopped by to get your thoughts on the new violence against women bill. Obviously when this came across my desk I thought of you, and wanted your input....I was under the impression that your husband was home." He glanced at his watch. "I had no idea I was here so long. I truly apologize. Naturally it's quite late for a young lady to be up."

"Why didn't you tell me about this, Mom? This bill is awesome. You guys are going to be rich, I think, at Safe Port I mean, if the funding goes through. I mean, if the bill passes. Right, Delegate Herkimer?"

Dodie glared at Rocco. "You need to leave now."

"Mom," whined Margaret. "You don't have to be so rude." She thumped her cup onto the table. "You're being ridiculous."

"No, no, Margaret, your mother is absolutely right. Again, I apologize. The time just flew." He rose, and smiled beatifically down on Dodie. "As I said, your daughter is a

247

terrific hostess—and makes a mean cup of hot chocolate, by the way. But I was wrong to come in here when there wasn't a parent in the home. I fully apologize."

"What they're doing to protect women is cool, Mom. You could at least listen to Delegate Herkimer. Geez, what is it with you?"

"Margaret, go to your room right now. If your homework isn't finished, finish it. Otherwise, bed. Now!"

Margaret began trilling the rim of her cup with her second and third fingers.

"Go ahead, listen to your mother, Margaret. And, please, Mrs. Wicklund, don't be angry at her. I'm sure she wouldn't let just anyone in the door. I can be pretty persuasive, I'm afraid....Anyway, I'll be off now, then, and I apologize if I caused any concern. As I said, I just thought you'd want to know about the bill. Firsthand, I mean."

"I have to help Margaret finish her homework and get her to bed. Immediately. And, listen, I don't think I can make myself any clearer on this, but I'd appreciate it if you'd just go now, all right?"

"I understand. I'll simply plan to stop by the shelter then, later in the week. We can chat then."

"I'm going to ask you to leave one more time. Otherwise, I'm going to have to call the police."

"Mom! You are so friggin' rude. I can't believe you!"

"Don't worry, Margaret. Your mother is right. It's late, and you've got school tomorrow." Rocco picked up his teacup and brought it to the sink. "I'll be in touch, Mrs. Wicklund. I'll plan to stop by your place of work later in the week, as I mentioned. That will give me much more time to fill you in on the details of the bill. And to touch base on the other matter, of course."

"I'm afraid that isn't going to work, Mr. Herkimer. I no

longer work there."

"Ah, well, I'm sure we'll find some other way to communicate then. I'm sure wherever you're now employed, or not, you'll be interested in this. Don't be concerned." He turned to Dodie with the slightest of smiles that could only be detected if you looked in his eyes and saw them narrow. "I'll be following up, one way or another, yes indeed."

After Rocco left, Dodie turned to Margaret who was now standing at the sink, repeatedly filling and refilling her cup with water. For the first time, she felt disconnected from her daughter, as though the long intimate thread that connected their lives for 15 years had suddenly snapped. She wondered if this sense was temporary, or whether it would become one of those moments that became a fixed mental image, one she would keep coming back to with pain and regret. Most moments, of course, were lost, but any, even the most trivial, could remain, with stunning poignancy, far more than the actual, fleeting experience. And that fixed image would not be what she felt originally. When she looked at pictures of her babies today, her heart ached with yearning to hold them again, and yet at the time they had actually been young she had just wanted to get through the day. The image, the feeling, that she had of those three babies now, however, was there for her forever, haunting and tormenting her, even if she had been too busy to notice it, if it ever even existed, in the moment.

"I thought I told you to go to bed."

Margaret turned off the water and turned to face her mother. "I can't believe how rude you were! To a state delegate!"

"I can't believe you let a man into the house when your father wasn't around....Don't you know how stupid that is?"

"Don't you know how 'stupid' it is to be rude to a state

delegate? Shoot, Mom, if I acted like that you would have grounded me or something. Talk about hypocritical!" Margaret loaded the cups into the dishwasher and then turned back to face Dodie. "And what did you mean about not being at Safe Port? They didn't fire you, did they?"

"I resigned."

"You resigned! Since when?"

"Since this minute....Now get yourself upstairs immediately, or you really are going to be grounded. And please mark your calendar. Because the two of us are going to have a discussion tomorrow about Mr. Herkimer, and about letting people into the house when Dad and I aren't home. Really, Margaret, one would think you missed the 'Mr. Stranger Danger' talks in kindergarten."

"Mom, you're insane, okay? I told you, he's not a stranger, he's...."

"I said we'll talk tomorrow. Now get to bed. Now. Before I explode."

"Okay, okay....And, oh yeah. I forgot." She handed Dodie an envelope that had been left lying next to the coffee maker. "Dad left this for you. When he went out."

CHAPTER TWENTY-THREE

"Dodie, dear, you can't let threats from this lunatic dominate your life." Florence placed her hand on top of the phone. "We're going to get a peace order, and...."

"It's not that, Florence. I don't give a flying you-know-what about Rocco Herkimer. I mean, he's one scary guy, but I now think he's just sane enough to keep himself under control if there's any chance he's going to be uncovered. He's a sociopath, but he's not self-destructive. No, I mean, the timing is pretty good here, given that the last thing I want is to have him continue to haunt me. But I'm not leaving because of him. I'm leaving because of me."

"Dodie, I don't know what to say. Except that I think you're making a huge mistake."

"Wait. I didn't finish. After Rocco left, Margaret landed the crowning blow. She handed me a note. From Randall."

Florence sniffed. "A note?"

"Yes. She handed me a ta-ta note from him. He moved out. Last night."

"Did Margaret know what was in the note?"

"I don't think so. I opened it after she went up to bed. But she knew something was up. How could she not? Handing off sealed envelopes from one family member to the next is not the way we usually do business in our family"

"Or any family. But, Dodie, he'll be back. It was

probably a moment of passion. You know. A desperate attention-getting device. He'll be back when he cools down."

"No. He's been thinking about this for quite some time, it seems. Cool headed thinking. He's coming back to cart out all his precious orchids later in the week, as soon as he finds a safe place for them. Where the orchids go, Randall goes."

"Oh, my darling." Florence rose and walked around her desk so that she stood beside Dodie's chair.

"He gave me his attorney's name in the note, too."

"I'm so, so sorry. I can't believe it. Let me give you a hug."

"Thanks, Florence. It's okay. Really....I guess it was a long time coming."

"You said he had been under a lot of stress. At work."

"Well, yes. Not that that's anything new—working for the central office is the definition of stress. Of course, lately, with this physical education and health thing....Everything's about the assessments, of course, on top of the bazillion other requirements. He's being asked to do the impossible."

"Nothing new there."

"Yes, but normally they all get by with passive resistance. Now the state's breathing down their necks."

"Well, there you go. He'll come to his senses when things calm down. I'm sure."

"Things will never calm down. When this crisis ends, they'll find something else. And it'll be on his head until he has the sense to retire....Besides, it's not about work. It's about us."

Florence hugged Dodie with genuine concern, long and tenderly enough to make Dodie realize that the spell between them was broken, at least temporarily. Admitting her fear and vulnerability, particularly with regard to a mutual enemy, a perpetrator of violence against women, was already working its magic. The more she spoke honestly about what had happened over the past week, the better she felt, and the more attentive Florence became. For the first time in months Dodie enjoyed being able to breathe in Florence's presence. Still, she remained keenly aware that Florence's newfound warmth was kneejerk and that this latest saga had merely set off Florence's alarm, an alarm exquisitely primed to sound at the slightest hint of violence against women or the maddening cluelessness and self-absorption of men. Although Dodie let herself melt briefly in the warmth of Florence's arms around her, she never doubted for a moment that any of this would ever be enough. A price had to be paid, and that price was her job.

"This is about you? You really believe that? You've got to be kidding me!" Florence positioned a second straight-backed chair so that she could sit in it and face Dodie. She took Dodie's hands in hers. "You and Randall! Honestly, if a couple like you two can't make it, I don't know who can...."

"Apparently he thinks he's a nonentity. In other words, the world doesn't revolve around him—what a surprise, with three demanding kids around!—and so he's cutting out...."

"Dodie, I'm so, so sorry. I don't even know where to start."

"You'd think the coward would say it to my face, wouldn't you? And certainly have the maturity not to drag the children into it."

"One would hope so. But, then again, there are many things one would hope."

Dodie withdrew her hands from Florence's and walked to the window behind the desk. Listening to Florence's chair creak behind her, she stared silently at the yard's lone tree, a barren dogwood that always looked bedraggled and moribund this time of year but that would soon be resplendent with fresh and abundant white blosssoms. Although she would never admit it to Florence, or to anyone, she actually viewed Randall's leaving as a sort of liberation. Shamed as she was by the implicit failure, saddened by the children's sadness, and angry about the financial and social complications now forced upon her, her head felt clearer than it had felt in years, even euphoric, as if a little air were freed when the arm she had accepted around her neck as an embrace for so many years had been removed. Now that she had been released, she felt, possibly out of self pity, but possibly not, that she had been no less controlled, victimized even, than the women in this shelter, and, worse, she had been a willing partner. Perhaps this was inevitable, she considered, given the inherent power differences between the sexes. These differences meant that women would be victimized, or at least controlled, by men even when they weren't hit or blatantly abused. Even in the best of relationships, a man and woman are always in implicit collusion—she follows or he strikes. Everyone understands that, even if it's never spoken. Even if she goes along willingly, even if she keeps going home, she keeps things on an even keel, or else, because of implicit power differences, there will be an explosion.

"The whole thing is one, big, fat dog's breakfast," Dodie said, without turning from the window.

"I'm so, so sorry, dear...." Florence came to stand beside her, but, getting no response, resumed her seat behind the desk. "Look. Take some time off. Don't think twice about it. You have so much to figure out, reconfigure....And, of course, the children."

"All I want right now is sleep."

"Naturally. You can go lie down, you know. No one's in the front room."

Dodie shook her head despite an almost irresistible urge to curl up on Florence's floor. She craved sleep, partly out of despair and partly out of pure, physical exhaustion. Last night had kept her awake until dawn, each interminable minute filled with an unsettling mix of euphoria, fear, guilt, anger, and relief. She had been shocked when she heard Margaret's alarm go off at 6, having had a vaguely familiar sense, one she hadn't had since early childhood, that time had almost stopped. For the first time since she was eight or nine, she felt time's oppressive infinity, the same sense, so foreign to her adult existence, that had once led her to feel a gaping chasm between 5 and 6 p.m. She remembered this chasm as so vast that it seemed unclosable. As an adult she had been known to say that time rushed through her fingers like a massive waterfall, and even as a grade schooler had generally regarded life as a finite collection of obligations and goals racing through an hourglass. But the sense she had last night was like what she remembered feeling as a very young child, when time was as slow-moving as a dying star, oppressively and inconceivably abundant and leaving her with the impression, largely unconsciousness, that this excruciatingly slow movement would drive her to screaming and wailing unless she willfully distracted herself.

"Do you know what I used to do as a little girl?" she asked Florence. "Zeenie must have thought me loony tunes. Believe it or not, I used to play with crayons, like they were people. Dolls, basically. For hours at a time."

"Children can make toys out of anything. Wrapping paper. Plumbing tubes. Cardboard boxes."

"But this was beyond a momentary thing. I loved those

crayons, probably more than my Barbies. Those families of crayons."

Dodie smiled, and then shivered, trying to understand how there had ever been a time when she had been able to regard inanimate objects as her beloved companions. Told to "go play" by Zeenie, she would spend what had felt like hours at a time blissfully ordering one world or another to her liking with the a sense of godlike omnipotence. Sometimes she would sit cross-legged in front of her dollhouse, arranging Barbie and Skipper into shoebox beds, wrapping and lacing them into wedding dresses and flamenco costumes, wedging their impliable feet into pink plastic shoes, or combing their matted hair, and then braiding or uplifting and spraying it. But, most often, she had gone to the crayons. Cast off by Dennis, who early on had turned to the stock exchange as pretty much his only hobby, these crayons, and crayon bits, were stocked in a chipped Lyle's Golden Syrup tin that Dodie kept stowed under her bed. She often pulled them out when the door was closed, and sprawled across the pink area rug that separated her bed from her dresser, flat on her stomach, knees kicking in the air.

"I didn't draw. Ever. I'd do things like try to balance the crayons vertically, arrange them into families by color. The lighter, more pastel shades—pink, yellow, green, tan—were female. The bolder, stronger shades—red, purple, blue, brown, black—male. I have no idea where I came up with the conviction that certain colors were male or female, but I just knew. It just seemed natural."

"Perhaps the fact that you were living under apartheid had something to do with it, no?"

"Maybe. Huh. I never thought of that, believe it or not. But I'm not sure. I didn't think in terms of races. But maybe you're right. I did have color-based rules: reds could only marry yellows, blues could only marry greens, and so forth. The few unmarred, whole, wrapped Crayolas were the parents, the worn-down one the teens and older kids. And those unwrapped nubs of wax were the infants. I ordered all these crayons by age according to length."

"You simply sound like you were a very creative little girl, Dodie. And one who had to learn how to occupy herself for long periods of time while her mother worked."

This was true, certainly. Whatever the explanation, she had relied on that tin of crayons to get her through many otherwise interminable afternoons. The arranging sometimes occupied Dodie for hours, but she could spend just as much time devising stories and conflicts, loves and rivalries, adventures and competitions for the crayons the way other girls played with dolls. She had a school for the juvenile crayons, a one-room sort of place, where students were arranged by size into rows, a teacher in front. They sometimes recited lessons, sometimes came to the front of the room to give a report about levers, porcupines, the pass laws, or whether the world was being fair to South Africa, all silently rehearsed in Dodie's head.

Some days she would even carry the entire community in the syrup tin to the bathroom. She plugged the drain and filled the sink with cool water, creating a swimming hole where families (even parents, with their wraps left on if she couldn't get them loose—some required taping afterwards), could bathe and romp freely. It turned out only some of the colors rose to the surface immediately, expert swimmers, while others swirled morbidly around the plug. Yellows, for example, were usually buoyant, and they were frequently annoyed at their red kindred for sinking immediately to the bottom. Swimming lessons ensued, and it turned out that if you held the reds a certain way with a certain patience, they managed to stay on top of the water for a respectable length of time. Occasionally one or two colors, thinner ones from a cheaper manufacturer, would float in spite of their color. When her mother was working, she also sometimes let the children have rolling races off a wooden block onto the kitchen linoleum. Dodie would prop one end of the flat, rectangular block against a couch cushion she had brought in from the living room, and then sequentially held each child crayon horizontally across its top, freeing it to roll at will and then measuring its final resting point and logging the distance on a chart the way she had seen a judge once do at a frog jumping contest. The crayon that rolled the farthest got to spend the next 24 hours in her pocket, or, if she didn't have clothes with pockets, which was often the case, in the little string bag she carried with her everywhere.

Dodie turned around, propping herself against the window ledge so that she could face Florence's chair. "I don't want to take time off, Florence. I want to resign."

"Sweetie, you know as well as I do that you should never make major lifestyle decisions in times of trauma. I'm preaching to the choir here. Take a few weeks, a month. I'll see if we can swing paid leave."

"I'm not making this decision in a moment of passion, Florence. I was going to talk to you about this long before the Randall thing. And, as I was explaining, it's not so much that I want to leave as that, I don't know, I just want to change my role. Or have time to think about how to change it. It's gotten to that point where it's beyond demoralizing....I'm frustrated all the time here, Florence."

"Dodie, we're all frustrated. We all got into this field because we want to heal the world. And then we find out that the world resists being healed. Of course, that's frustrating. Infuriating. Depressing. Believe me, I know how you feel. I feel it every day....But sit back and think about what you're doing to yourself."

"I know what I'm doing to myself. I really don't have a choice."

"Dodie, slow down. Listen. You're upset, with good reason. You've been physically and psychologically threatened by a man known to inflict life-threatening violence. Threatened on the job—appalling and unacceptable. And now, of course, at home. Not to mention Randall. You have every right not to be thinking clearly....But I'm going to think clearly for you. Dodie, this is a time when you can't afford to add yet another traumatic transition into your life. Let things alone. Do your job—you're great at your job. And then, when things with Randall have settled, whichever way they're going to settle, we can talk again."

Dodie knew Florence was right. Her timing couldn't possibly have been worse. With Randall playing these games, she couldn't afford to give up her steady paycheck; in fact, it was likely she was going to have to find funds for an attorney, or she might end up in a homeless shelter herself. Resigning at this point was self-indulgent, self-destructive, and, as far as the children were concerned, patently negligent. Or so she would have emphasized if she had been counseling herself. And yet she knew somehow that she had to do it, and that by doing it an answer would come to her. Something rock solid at her core impelled her onward, driving her to move her life into a direction that she recognized as irrational and impetuous, and yet at the same time irresistible and essential. She supposed this was what it meant to "dig your own grave." She had a talent for that sort of thing.

In fact, nothing she heard from Florence or from her own rational brain shook her belief that resigning from Safe Port, at least for a while, would improve life for her entire family. It had to. The path they were on right now was a downward spiral, with or without Randall. Resigning from Safe Port was the first step toward making her life right, and, therefore, the lives of her children. In fact, she finally realized, it would all work out, even if she never found another way to bring in one bloody cent. Randall had been the one who had left her, after all. That was the key. Randall may have been a coward, but that meant he was also too cowardly to thumb his nose at the system. He had worked for the county schools so long that he was at the top of the pay scale and had excellent benefits and an impressive pension coming his way. If she didn't have a steady income, it wasn't a problem. He would pay the mortgage, and the childcare, and put money into the college funds. He wouldn't have the courage to fight these requests, or to fight the societal expectation that he would do so. She knew this as firmly as she knew it was time for a change.

"I just can't be here anymore, Florence," she said at last. "I'm sorry."

CHAPTER TWENTY~FOUR

For Utzi the Iceman this had been the depression to end all depressions. His despair had been deeper and his withdrawal from the world longer lasting than any he could remember, and, despite repeated and conniving phone calls from Maxine and several members of the donut brigade, he didn't fully revive himself until March. The problem had started with the reference librarian who had introduced him to search engines, Google in particular. For decades he had dismissed computers as a passing fad, but having watched the books and magazines disappear from the shelves year by year, and even the microfiche becoming increasingly inaccessible, he had eventually admitted defeat and offered himself up to this earnest, obliging young woman for lessons. She had patiently explained to him what each key did, how to move the infuriatingly uncooperative mouse, and how to locate resources that vastly surpassed anything the county library system could possibly have on hand, even in the days before budget cuts. Most of her words flew by him. He could barely see the damnably small text and elusive cursor and would certainly have given up the whole business had he not so much enjoyed (Maxine was sure of this) the librarian's pleasing smell of maple syrup and soap and the fact that her young breasts, prominently reshaping her pliant cashmere shell, burst pleasantly close to his face whenever she leaned over to help him with the mouse or activate a key.

What she led him to see on the screen, once he got the hang of things, wasn't pleasant however. When he typed the words "Ötzi the Iceman" into the little box, nearly 54,000 entries appeared. And they were hardly all works of amateurs and crackpots. There were news reports (ABC, NBC, BBC, National Geographic even), museum updates from the South Tyrol Museum of Archeology, encyclopedia entries, laboratory reports, speculative discussions, even jokes and video spoofs. When he clicked on any of the several professional-looking sites devoted to the Iceman exclusively, matters got even worse: the links were extensive and thorough, containing all the news clippings he had labored for years to procure, and considerably more— interviews with scientists, explorations of both prominent and arcane theories, background information on glaciers and archeology and the scientists involved—far more than any single individual could collate and process in a lifetime. When he thought about the amount of time and effort it took him to identify, much less locate and scrutinize, a single news article, and then realized how everyone else had just been clicking away like this and capturing all this drek— drek he had thought was his own personal gold until an hour earlier—he wanted to crawl into the glacier himself and pray that he, too, would be frozen and alone for millenia.

Maxine had started calling him regularly last fall after her encounter with Joan in the synagogue, leaving strict messages about the importance of regular communications, even if they were just to confirm that he was alive. After a week of phone calls she was on the verge of storming his condo, when she returned home to a phone message from him. He assured her that he was fine, but he needed some time to "sort things through." He promised to leave her a similar message once a week, and he honored that promise. However, these weeks had extended to months, a hiatus from primping and placating that Maxine found herself somewhat grateful for, given the amount of time she found herself training and tending to Shelley, though as the months passed, she longed for the tenderness and touch that seemed all the more compelling in their absence. It wasn't until spring, a full five months after his initial retreat, that he at last came out of hibernation. He did so in classic Utzi the Iceman fashion, sending Maxine a stunning arrangement of protea (where he had managed to procure these she hadn't a clue) and a formal invitation to Friday night seafood on the Eastern Shore. Although Maxine hated herself for it, she had phoned him up immediately and as gushingly as a school girl agreed to the dinner. However, she did manage to insist that the price for her company would be an explanation. "Half a year is far too long to sulk," she had said. "So either you put a stop to this kind of indulgence immediately—through sheer willpower, if you have it—or you must allow me to set you up with a therapist."

He had taken this lashing with aplomb, and he picked her up Friday evening brushed, combed, and polished. At the same time, she couldn't help noticing as he bored through the bridge traffic that he was less exuberant than he tended to be after his withdrawals. Normally when they drove he turned his boiling red face to her incessantly, his frothy white mustache bobbing up and down as he theorized or recited to her excitedly. That evening, however, his skin was sallow and his eyes dead set on the horizon. He looked thinner to her, which was something she supposed was good, given his girth, but it made him look wan and deflated, as if someone had let the air out of him.

At dinner, he almost seemed himself, however. His appetite was hearty as ever—he nearly inhaled the shrimp cocktail and downed the entire basket of bread before the soup arrived. He was willing to look her in the eye, too, even if the twinkling exuberance was most definitely gone. She began to sense that more than anything he must be ashamed of his behavior, and that perhaps talking to her was slowly allowing him to climb out of the hole. As she listened and nodded, she found that he was more than willing to explain the source of his troubles to her, something he had never done before, at least not in so much depth. Then again, this time around his behavior had far exceeded the bounds of social acceptability. Thus, she decided, he had no choice but to explain himself, at least if he expected to continue any semblance of a normal social relationship with her, or with anyone else.

"But, certainly, all isn't lost," she said to him, turning her gaze back from the porthole-shaped window that looked out onto a ghostly, light-dappled harbor. The tethered boats, bobbing up and down beside the dock as they tried to break free, gave her the illusion of being at sea. "Honestly, even with the Internet—there are still people writing books all the time about all sorts of things, even the same things. You need to stop creating problems for yourself out of thin air, Utzi. Surely no one out there has done what you have done for the Iceman."

"You'd be astounded what people have done."

"I can't imagine anyone giving the same blood, sweat, and tears to the old bugger as you have given. You must have something original to say for all that."

"That's pretty much what Nelson told me, too."

"Nelson."

"Back in October. He came pounding on the door. Blamed it on you."

"He what?"

"He showed up one afternoon with a six-pack and a dozen donuts, actually, thought that would get me to open the door to him. It did."

"He blamed it on me? Really now."

"Said you were hysterical and needed him to check on me. It turned out to be an excellent idea, if you must know."

"I called him last fall, when I was so worried about you. But he told me to lay off you. Grow up....Then he comes to your place? Astounding."

"He's a good guy. He wasn't going to pry. But he did give me some counsel, as he often does, using the old professorial wiles, and he talked exactly like you. About how I should forget about what others had done or were doing. He reminded me I could put my own personal spin on a topic. He's told me that before, of course. I just need endless reminding. That's what the entire academic enterprise is about, he insists—slow, incremental revisions. That's how a 21st century guy gets around studying Shakespeare's sonnets, right? The things have been mauled and pawed and dissected and spun for centuries. But so what? They have yet to be touched by me. That's what he said. Chances were good, perhaps inevitable, that all these folks missed something here or there, or that there's a new or different way of seeing what's already been seen based on new information, a new time period, a new person doing the seeing. It's the same with my pal, the Iceman....Anyway, Nelson pretty much had me sold on this idea that it didn't matter what the computer turned up. I could have my own twist, and, eventually, it came to me that I did have a twist of my own. The Ötzi curse! Isn't that brilliant?"

"The curse?"

"I've told you about it, Zeenie, surely I have. You know, all those people involved in The Iceman story, seven at this point, have met with these bizarre, premature deaths?...The first one was Dr. Henn, who headed up the forensic team, killed in a head-on collision while on his way to give a talk on Ötzi. Remember?"

"Vaguely. You've told me so much. I've never had a mind for details."

"Baloney. You have a mind like a steel trap...However, I will refresh your steely mind for you. I'm sure it will sound familiar. Dr. Henn was victim number one. Then came Kurt Fritz, the mountaineer who led Henn and his team to the body originally, killed in an avalanche. Don't you remember me telling you this? He was a mountaineer, and I suppose you could say that avalanches come with the territory, but this was in a place he knew like the back of his hand. Then the journalist fellow, Holz, an Austrian, who made a documentary about Ötzi the Iceman? He came down with some brain tumor, or something—dead within months. That's three victims, you see?"

"I see. People do die, though, Utzi. Every day."

"And then we hear about Helmut Simon, the German tourist who stumbled upon the body in the first place—he won a big court battle over rights to the mummy, went back to the original spot to celebrate, and got caught up in a freak blizzard and fell off a cliff."

"Gracious."

"Victim five was Dieter Warnecke, who headed up the rescue teaming searching for Simon. Heart attack killed him less than an hour after Helmut Simon was buried, okay? Sound like a curse?"

"To dunderheads. As I've said already, many people die. Particularly those who enjoy hiking in remote mountains."

For a split second, she regretted saying this to the convalescent he still seemed to be. The fact that he had not yet asked her one question about her own life over the past few months—though she was bursting to tell him how well his Shelley plan had been working out—suggested that he remained inwardly focused and fragile, ready to run back to his groundhog hole and the slightest provocation. To her joy and relief, however, he took her up on her goading in old Utzi fashion.

"That's exactly what the skeptics said! That's what Spindler, said, in fact. Remember him? The archeologist? Leading expert on the Iceman, or media hound, depending on your point of view? Whatever he was, he thought the whole thing was hooey, media hype, yada yada yada. Then, just a few years ago, he dies of complications from Lou Gehrig's disease, or maybe it was M.S., I've read both. So we skeptics need to watch what we say!"

"I'm terrified, Utzi, truly."

"Fine. Be skeptical. But it's a gripping story, I'm telling you. So, anyway, Konrad Spindler, dies, right? And then, around the same time—I have to check the dates—another Austrian professor on Spindler's team croaks during open-heart surgery. It didn't stop. The next guy to go was Dr. Loy, a fellow who was doing some genetic research on the body and was just about to finish a book about it. That was back in 2005. These guys weren't old, Zeenie, mid-sixties, I think. Warnecke and Holz were in their forties. So, you see, I'm entering dangerous waters myself."

"But Utzi. Surely this curse rubbish is all over the Internet."

"Of course it is. But, you see, you need to think like a

scholar. Just because someone knows about something doesn't mean they 'know' about it. Yes, the thing's there for all to see. But, just like Nelson said, no one has yet documented the details, explored them in depth."

"I see."

"No one knows the stories I do, or has bothered to feature them. That's the key. I was thinking I would tell stories of other legendary curses, too, like the cursed incursions into ancient tombs. Like King Tut. There was an inscription outside his tomb: 'Death shall come on swift wings to him who disturbs the peace of the King.' Was it crazy? Maybe, but one of the first fellows to inspect the discovery back in the 1920s was bitten by a mosquito, developed a high fever, and—this is the kicker—while he was dying the entire city of Cairo went dark. No power. Then, of course, there's the whole Hope Diamond legend. Remember the guide telling us about it at the Museum of Natural History? The gem was stolen out of the eye of a Hindu statue, and the thief, some French merchant, was then torn apart by wild Russian dogs. When the diamond got in the hands of Marie Antoinette—well, you know what happened to her."

"Really, Utzi, surely you're not attributing the entire French Revolution to some kind of mystic curse, are you? That's absurd."

"No, no. I'm just telling you these curse tales are rich. People love them. The whole Hope family, you know, after whom the diamond was named, went bankrupt, and the subsequent owner had her troubles as well—a son killed in a car accident, a daughter who committed suicide, and a loony tunes husband. And then there's the Rubaiyat of Omar Khayyam—mysterious book, certainly, but especially the famous Sangorski edition, a gorgeous, ornate book that everyone wanted. After the book went down with the Titanic, its creator drowned. There was a replica, but it was bombed to pieces in World War II, in the London Blitz, actually....So, you see, these stories of curses are fascinating. I have no idea if there's anything to them, but I was thinking, a book about the Ötzi curse, along with stories like these—people would really go for that."

"Superstitious people."

"That's most people, I'm afraid....Think about it, Zeenie. That kind of stuff is big. It has true bestseller, even feature film, potential." He nodded at the waitress as she set down their plates.

"Utzi, I don't mean to burst your bubble, but...you really think you could write a bestseller?"

"I'm just as good as anyone else. Once you realize that no one knows anything, you have license."

Maxine rolled her eyes but patted his hand. "Well, I'm glad to have my old rooster back, crowing away."

"I'm serious, Zeenie. Crowing is half the battle." He explained how, all hype aside, even the brilliant archeologists and pathologists, journalists and historians, were as clueless as anyone else when it came to Ötzi. They acted like they knew things, but when you got into the details, you realized that "a good portion of it was show, even, in many cases, pure hand waving." That was why he knew there was a place for him here. He saw things differently, maybe even more clearly, because he wasn't all wrapped up in their world and their assumptions, and in their utterly misplaced self-confidence. That was why, although he was not a trained historian or journalist, he believed that he could have something original to say about the curse and, indeed, do precisely what he set out to do.

"Believing you can do something often makes you

capable of doing it," he told Maxine after the waitress had finished offering condiments and departed. He had recited this maxim to her many times before and explained that he had learned it long ago (and remembered, even believed, it, when he wasn't depressed), mainly from the Mids, who he repeatedly saw do all kinds of things they didn't know how to do, or thought they didn't know how to do, either, whether it was jumping hurdles, writing term papers, or putting their lives on the line when someone told them to do it. More than anything, whenever he doubted his abilities, he thought about a long, lanky Mid he had met half a century ago, an unusually slim-hipped wispy boy he had walked past one very hot, very humid Maryland August day during his ice deliveries. He remembered it as being at least 85 degrees outside, classic Maryland midsummer swelter, but the boy had nonetheless been running furiously in circles through heavy, waterlogged air that oppressed and stilled everything around him—the blades of grass, the branches of the tulip poplars, even, apparently, the waves of the Bay, which normally broke quietly along the shoreline. The boy was huffing and puffing his way around a field at the Academy, pausing every few laps to look at a stopwatch. At one point the Mid had stopped near him, and stood close enough to reveal his beet red face and his copious sweat, which had saturated his gym shorts to the point that they clung in folds to his thighs. He could hear the boy's wheezy breaths, the unmistakable sounds of asthma, presumably undiagnosed or the poor fellow would never have been admitted to the Academy.

Utzi the Iceman combed through his rockfish and pushed aside a tiny, translucent bone. "This kid was clearly not a natural runner. Sure, he had that sprinter build—ectomorph I think it is. But other than that, he wasn't made to run." What he meant by that was that the Mid's length was in his torso rather than his legs, his chest slightly caved, and his limbs rubbery rather than muscled. Had the Navy not insisted that he buzz off his baby blond curls, still evidenced by the wilted, translucent whirls on his forearms, he would have suggested a Romantic poet rather than an Olympic athlete. "Anyway, I put down my bags and offered to get him some water—the kid looked like he was on the verge of fainting—but he responded almost violently. He said he had already cut five seconds off his time but had ten more to go if he wasn't going to be cut from the track team. And sure enough, when I returned from my deliveries a half hour later, the guy was still at it, huffing, puffing, stopping, timing, staring at that Bay, that placid Bay, for inspiration, it seemed to me, and then hurling himself around the field once again. I still can hear him every time I walk through that part of the campus. 'I've got three seconds left to go,' he called to me from across the field. 'If you bring me that water now, I'll bet you I'll be on target.' 'If you don't die first,' I thought."

Despite his skepticism, though, Utzi the Iceman had been inspired by the Mid's determination. Ignoring his mother's repeated warnings not to exert himself in this kind of weather, he had sprinted the three blocks back into town to get water from the shop and then back to the Academy grounds. He found the Mid lying flat on his back, one leg extended into the air, rubbing out the thigh muscle. The Mid sat up, proud that he had, indeed, made his target, and the two boys celebrated together, the Mid sipping the water gingerly—dangerous to drink cold water when overheated, he explained, or to succumb to one's impulses, ever—while the young Iceman guzzled the root beer he had stashed in his pants for himself. For the next four years, he had gone to all the track meets, and watched this Mid, who never won a medal for short-track, but often came close, and who always waved to him as he crossed the finish line.

"I forgot that kid's name years ago, sad to say," Utzi told Maxine. "But I assure you that he had not been recruited into the Academy for his running ability, or even potential, He became a perfectly respectable runner through sheer force of will." Utzi the Iceman had remained convinced for the rest of his life that determination was more important than anything. Admittedly, most of the time his belief in determination was considerably stronger than his ability to maintain it. However, his underlying conviction kept him from ever dismissing any undertaking simply because he had no discernible talent, or training, in the area.

"You give up when you think you don't know what you're doing," he explained to Maxine, folding up his napkin and placing it on the table. "But when you realize that no one else knows either, you're off and running."

CHAPTER TWENTY-FIVE

"I'd take you back here in a flash," Florence told Dodie, who had appeared unexpectedly in her doorway that morning to catch Florence just after she had poured herself a first cup of coffee and before she had a chance to become distracted checking the *New York Times* online. Now Dodie was sitting in front of her desk, looking in some ways as though she had never left and radiating a confidence and calm that Florence hadn't seen in her since the whole Rocco Herkimer business had begun. She sat with her shoulders back and chin up, her face fixed into an almost otherworldly stare, as though ready to deflect anything Florence could throw at her. "I would love to have you working for us again, Dodie. But you're asking the impossible of me."

Dodie scooted forward. With her hands raised as if in prayer, she locked her cheeks between her thumbs and massaged the bridge of her nose with her index fingers. A part of her hated herself for bursting in on Florence without calling, but when she got excited about ideas she liked to act on them right away. She had been unable to sleep all night, entangled in the burgeoning idea that Maxine had planted in her head the evening before. What had set Maxine off was watching Dodie and Shelley chat over their microwaved Lean Cuisines, particularly the way that Dodie listened to Shelley without a hint of mistrust or cynicism no matter how much Shelley whined or rambled. Dodie had even reached out guilelessly to stroke Shelley's hand at the slightest hint of agitation. All of this made something obvious to Maxine that she had never fully grasped: her daughter came into her own in working with a woman like Shelley, and even exuded a seasoned competence that made Maxine beam with motherly pride. Maxine couldn't remember feeling this way about Dodie with purity since she had watched her put together a jigsaw or conquer roller skates. What a shame that Dodie had cut this part out of her life, she thought. What a shame, too, that she herself had so few opportunities to see her daughter in this role. For this feeling, this *"nachas"* she supposed it was, she might even consider doing more work of this sort, if only there were money in it. "Wouldn't it be wonderful," she had said to Dodie, as they later walked to their cars, "if we had a few more of her here for you to counsel? You have a knack for it, dearie lamb, truly you do."

That was all Dodie needed to hear. After getting home, making a batch of spaghetti for the kids, unloading and reloading the dishwasher, wiping down the kitchen counters, spouting a few platitudes to Margaret about homework coming before lacrosse practice, and satisfying herself that even though the children were sprawled in front of the television, they were still doing their (mainly busywork) homework, she went into the greenhouse and let her mind loose. As she spritzed and primped the few remaining orchids (which she found herself unable to neglect, despite her occasional fantasies of throwing them all out on the lawn to freeze), she realized that there could actually be a living in ministering to women like Shelley. She would have to reshape her former role at Safe Port to make it happen, but that could be done simply enough. Later, as she read the boys a story and tucked them into bed, she couldn't free her mind of the idea. She could easily see herself working as an independent operator, contracting with the shelter to ferry women to Maxine for work that would allow them to return to normal life repaired and, in many cases, less recognizable. The more she thought about this idea, the more viable it seemed, in terms of her independence from Safe Port, as well as her freedom to tend to her family's needs. She was so excited that she considered calling Florence at home, immediately, but given the time, sat down at the computer instead and typed up a formal proposal. She didn't get into bed until well after two, and for what remained of the night she bounced in and out of sleep, reviving every fifteen or twenty minutes to see if it was early enough to get up and drive to the shelter.

Florence, however, had been adamant. "You are proposing a plan that puts you in grave physical danger on a regular basis," she told Dodie, handing the typed proposal back to her. "To make something like this work, I'd have to send women out in the dead of night to some undisclosed location—what, a back alley? a private beach?—and then let you whisk them off in your getaway car to your mother's salon for haircuts, dye jobs, and so forth?...My dear, I agree that our clients would often do well to change their looks. For safety's sake. No question either—many of them are marked in ways that will, to put it mildly, preclude them from decent jobs, and decent lives. But think of the risk you'd be putting yourself at, not to mention the risk you'd be asking of our staff."

"I don't see the risks as being any different than now. What I do see are the benefits—way beyond what we can do now, just shoving these women into corners until they can sneak back into their crappy lives. Right now we take a 'watch and wait' approach—fine, I suppose, if there's nothing else that can be done. But I'm proposing something entirely new, proactive...I see it as a positive step toward recovery, and totally complementary to what goes on here."

"I hardly think cosmetic alteration is our clients' deepest need, Dodie. Sorry, but I just don't buy it."

Dodie folded the proposal neatly into quarters and tucked it into the outside pocket of her purse. "I wish you could see Shelley. She's a new person. When she walks out of there—she's going to be able to start her life over. Almost literally. It shouldn't just be her, Florence. I could take so many of the women we've seen to a whole new level. So much more than we can do here."

"I'm not questioning the value of your mother's services. Or yours. But you have already put Shelley, yourself, and Safe Port in serious danger with this business. Now you want to magnify that danger by a hundred-fold."

Dodie sat back in her chair and tried to explain that not every situation was identical to Shelley's. She had also thought about offering services to women in recovery, including scar cover-ups and free transformation work, redoing their looks entirely so they could start new lives. That part wouldn't have to be so undercover. Plus, of course, she'd continue to counsel them.

"Dodie, please, certainly some part of you must understand what I'm saying. Safe Port can't just send people out to places outside the shelter system, or authorize work by outside vendors. If something goes wrong, we're liable. Even if we could do this, legally, we don't have the resources. You know how precarious our funding is already....If you could only step back a bit from your emotions, I'm sure you'd agree. You'd also agree that getting yourself and your mother tangled up in something like this is only going to drag you down further. Taking all this onto yourself—that's going to mean even more personal threats, more risks, more stress. It's also going to mean more panicked calls and pick-ups in the wee hours, more than now, and it's all going to be on your head. Driving victims through town, all the time—do you really think this isn't going to be risky and stressful? Or that you'll be home more to work things through with Randall—or spend time with your kids?"

"There's nothing to work through with Randall. We're done. Or, rather, he's done. He's found himself a townhouse, apparently, and he's counting down the days until the state considers us divorced."

"All the more reason for you to be good to yourself, Dodie. Step back a minute—you'll laugh at how good you are at not following all of the sage advice I've so often heard come from your mouth! No, if I were you, I'd go home, take a hot bubble bath, read a good book, and consider coming back to work here in a month or two when you feel good and rested. Your job and salary will be waiting for you—that I can promise."

"So will Rocco."

"Don't worry about Delegate Herkimer," said Florence. "I don't expect we'll have any more problems from him, now that Shelley is gone and there isn't any baby on the way."

"What do you mean? The man in unhinged. How can you say that?"

"The domestic violence networks bill, Dodie. Who do you think pushed it through the legislature?"

"What are you saying? That I'm supposed to support that insane sociopath because he put his name on this ridiculous piece of legislation that makes him smell good and throws everyone off his trail? You can't be serious."

"Dodie, that ridiculous piece of legislation, as you call it, is what is going to let us restore all those salaries we had to cut last year, and also, frankly, even let me consider getting you a paid leave of absence." Florence rolled her chair forward, propped her elbows on the desk, and leaned toward Dodie. "We're fully funded again—a minor miracle in this economy, really. I'm not fooling around with that, even if it is what you might call 'dirty money.'"

"Dirty money? Florence, that man is shining up his name so that he doesn't end up behind bars. Meanwhile, a woman he abused is living on a cot in a skin care salon, her whole life in shambles. I don't see how on earth you can talk like that."

"Dodie, you actually have no evidence that Rocco Herkimer is the one responsible for Shelley Slavin's injuries. There has never been a court case. And we've seen plenty of women here who pinned the charges on the wrong guy, or made up half the guys in the first place."

"It astounds me that you could talk like this when you're talking to me—I know Shelley like a sister at this point. She is not making this up, Florence. Not to mention the threats that Rocco Herkimer made to me personally. How can you think for one second that all this legislation isn't just a typical slick willy trick of his?"

"He never threatened you, Dodie. He may be a little unconventional in his approaches, but he's a public figure, not a typical guy. You always have to expect people in public office to be a little strange—who else would put themselves in that position, I always say. Think about it. He never touched you, or threatened you directly. He stopped you on the street, asked you to clear charges against him—perfectly reasonable, when you think about it, since he's a public figure and doesn't want his name smeared, especially given his history. Then he called to make sure you followed through. Next, and, again, I know it might have felt scary, he showed up at your house, yes, talked to your teenage daughter. That was unconventional, understandably upsetting. Even so, he didn't do anything illegal, not by a long shot. He never hurt you, left when you asked him to leave, and was unfailingly polite. And, of course, by now it's too late for a peace order, even if you did have evidence."

"Forget about me. What he did to Shelley was as cut-and-dried as it gets."

"Well, naturally, that concerned me," said Florence. "And when he called me to tell me about the legislation, I most certainly expressed my concerns to him, since, of course, by then Shelley had been here. I assumed he'd give us the usual Neanderthal song and dance about freedom of association, due process, and so forth. But, no, he couldn't have been more supportive, nor more concerned about the funding cuts."

"He called you? Herkimer called you?" Dodie slapped her thigh. "I think I'm going to go put water on my face."

"I'm going to tell you something that I never said. You understand me, Dodie? If you tie me up and hold a flame to my feet, I'm going to deny this. But here's the reality. Delegate Herkimer called me last fall and asked me what we needed here. Before all this happened with you, of course. I told him—and, now, well, you saw the news."

"I must be dreaming."

"He called me later, too, a couple of times, like many of the public officials call me, Dodie. That's part of my job, making sure we have support. Naturally I expressed my concerns at the point about how a man with a woman accusing him of such things could be bringing attention to the matter publicly. He pishtoshed the whole thing. Said Shelley is crazy, a lonely woman with fantasies about him who he's tried to help over the years."

"That's what he told me, that night on the street, actually."

"Well, that's what he said to me. Unless Shelley can prove that her injuries came from Rocco Herkimer in court, he's just a victim of his celebrity, like so many other stalked and slandered movie stars and politicians."

"But they were lovers." Dodie suddenly felt overcome with sadness, and she could feel it on her face. She caught Florence's gaze and slowly shook her head, but Florence didn't flinch. "I know Shelley too well, too many details. She couldn't have made that up. What she's been through, there are protections for that."

"The domestic violence protections apply to physical violence by an intimate partner, parent, or guardian. She's none of those."

"What on earth are you talking about? She's not his intimate partner?"

"Not by law. By law an intimate partner is a spouse, a former spouse, a person who shares a child in common with the victim, or a person who cohabits or has cohabited with the victim. You know that. None of those is true of Shelley Slavin and Rocco Herkimer. Never was. Well, the child, almost, but, of course, that's no longer an issue...."

"But she had a protective order, Florence. Back when she was here."

"She had a peace order, which is now expired. And, now, of course, it's too late to get another one, now that you've harbored her all this time—well, I'm not saying that isn't a good thing. Obviously it's wonderful that she's been safe. But she is also ineligible for protection."

CHAPTER TWENTY~SIX

"I don't think she even considers how these women would pay. Or that some of us, me in particular, would need to be paid," Maxine told Utzi the Iceman later that week. They were sitting on Dodie's couch, watching the boys while Dodie took, or, more precisely, dragged, Margaret to Advanced Placement Night at the high school. "She's fed up with Safe Port, and fed up with having her hands tied, which I can understand. But I believe she expects me to give my services away as charity. It boggles the mind that she can still think this way—with no means of support except some theoretical alimony she hopes to get. I tell you, Utzi, I sometimes wonder if that girl is from another planet. Then, again, that's my Dodie for you. A flower child—born a few years too late. It always took a bit longer for worldly trends to catch us down there at the bottom of the world is all....Shame, I suppose."

"Her heart's in the right place."

"And mine isn't? I suppose you think this Shelley business is easy on me?" Maxine had just last week started needling Shelley's acne scars, which were so extensive that they would require at least 12 good hours of work over the next few months. They had already done considerable work on her eyes, lips, and most glaring scars, and quite successfully, but there were still many long evenings ahead of them. And with each passing month, Maxine found that these extra hours after her already full days were taking their toll. She had upped her coffee intake to five cups a day, and found herself dozing during breaks nonetheless. She was also losing or misplacing equipment on a regular basis, or finding herself out of items she was sure she had ordered a month before, although sometimes she wondered if this was due more to Shelley's erratic approach to inventory. "*Ag*, I'm hemorrhaging money, Utzi. Hemorrhaging."

"Shelley is paying her way. She's working for you, at least as I understand it. And you've told me before that she's an organizational wizard, at least when she puts her mind to it."

"She's underfoot round the clock is what she is. Not to mention the time I must spend instructing her, correcting her, picking up after her. She runs hot and cold that way, you see, on top of things one minute, on some outer planet the next. Sometimes I believe I ought to scrap the receptionist idea entirely, for all the good these chickadees do me....Running a small business, it's making less and less sense. In this economy, too....*Ag*, so much of what I do is seen as luxury when people are struggling."

"You'll continue thriving, I'm sure, for centuries to come. Vanity isn't going anywhere."

"Hmph. Even the regulars are not paying on time, or not showing. I can't tell you the number of last-minute cancellations we've had this month! Those dermatologists and their bloody lasers keep leaching off the customers as well....I'll tell you a secret—but you must promise not to tell a soul. Especially not Dodie. I've been thinking of hiring myself out to Chesapeake Dermatology or that outfit near Parole, as an adjunct of sorts. I hate to do it, but, frankly, I'm beginning to think there's no other choice."

"Really? I won't say a word, dear, but—you can't be serious. I can't see you working for others."

"You can't see me living in the streets either. But I will be, soon enough, if business doesn't pick up....Anyway, let that rest. It's Dodie that worries me most. The girl has no sense of reality. This plan of hers makes no sense....Look at this room! She can't even get those boys to put their toys away, or sort through her own mail, much less run her own business!"

"Sometimes the world needs things that don't make sense."

"Well, there you and Dodie are two peas in a pod. And she's just the kind of person who has to do those sorts of things, the ones that make no sense whatsoever....Where are you going?"

"I'm going to put some of those game pieces away. It's the least I can do."

"That's absurd. The boys need to learn. William? Lawrence? Where are you two?"

"Leave them be."

"Utzi, you can't even touch your toes, much less get down into that cesspool. Sit yourself back down, you lummox." She guided him back onto the couch. The boys stood in the doorway. "You two boys get these games cleaned up right now. I want your mother to come home to a clean house."

"She wouldn't know her way around a clean house," said Lawrence.

"Don't be cheeky. Get to it."

"But Zeenie…," whined William. "We were building a fort...."

Lawrence nudged his little brother into the wall. "We were doing our homework, Zeenie. Like you told us to."

"Whatever you were doing, you're now putting those games away. Skedaddle. It should take the two of you precisely two minutes, tops, if you put your minds to it."

Maxine stood over the boys as they worked. Utzi was right in a way, she supposed. She couldn't imagine her life without the salon, or without the control of her own destiny that having her own place gave her. There had been a brief period in her adult life, the six months after she had first moved to the States, when she hadn't worked and instead moved in with Dodie, Randall, and two-year-old Margaret. Throughout these six months she had felt even more miserable and demoralized than she had felt in those last days with Toad, weighed down by an unrelenting sense of worthlessness. She had been running her own place since her late teens; leaving Capetown, and her country, had been hard enough, but it was sobering to realize how easily she could cut out everything that made her feel like she was a distinct and distinguishable human being. Everything that had made her who she was—her house, her friends, her job, what she ate and where she walked, when she slept and how she organized her days, had been wiped away, except, of course, for Dodie and her family.

Within weeks of arriving she remembered getting the itch, the need to make her own life once again. Of course, it hadn't helped that from the moment she'd arrived she'd been victim to Dodie's carping, not to mention Randall's surface resentment of her presence, and possibly her existence, and both of their assumptions that she had nothing better to do with her time than provide on-demand childcare, cooking, and cleaning services. She loved Dodie to death, but they grated on each other's nerves living on top of each other like that—Maxine's theory was two or more adults couldn't live together happily unless they were romantically attached. Then, too, she fell comatose into bed as soon as Randall or Dodie returned from work each day, drained by the sheer physical stamina required to watch over an active toddler, a fatigue she didn't remember from her younger days but that she supposed explained why people generally had children when they were young. More than anything, though, she missed her clients, and she missed running her shop.

It had been easy for her to put down the first month's rent on a new salon in Annapolis the very first day she received the final check from Capetown. That same day she began hunting for a nearby apartment as well. Maxine was no "kugel," something her father had been determined for her not to be. He had held up her mother as an example, bragging about his wife's gift for numbers and the way she had, despite barely completing grade school, turned it to keeping his books pristine. Maxine had always said her mother went through life like Henry Stanley through the jungle with a machete, at least while she still had her health. The woman was in her husband's office daily, even turning up, Maxine recalled, the morning after he died to hire a new manager and negotiate with the lawyer for the sale of the factory. Maxine's father had always been encouraging and proud of his wife, and considered her a full partner in the business, not caring one iota that their little house looked like a gypsy tent and smelled like bread mold and old cheese. Maxine sometimes wondered if her mother even bothered to bathe before bolting out of the house in the morning to open the doors and greet the staff. She certainly never bothered washing a dish after throwing supper at them and heading out to one of her weeknight meetings. She never bought a new dress after the two of them left Poland either, or thought to put a brush to her hair. However, her father loved the woman to death, and held her up as a model for Maxine. He often observed that women with too much time on their hands were the curse of civilization. "Find something useful to do with yourself," he often told her, "and all those things you thought were problems will disappear."

Dodie claimed to be surprised and upset by Maxine's exodus from her home, but Maxine insisted that it had to be a relief for her. It couldn't have been any fun for either Dodie or Randall to have her suddenly tangled in their lives, always there complicating plans and schedules and reminding them, like the grating beeps from a failing smoke alarm battery, that something was unfinished whenever things started to feel normal. Nor could Dodie have possibly enjoyed it when Maxine insisted on stopping everything for afternoon sweets, rearranged the living room furniture, swept the dried oatmeal and peas that Dodie had never even noticed from the kitchen floor, or laid out the table for breakfast the night before to save time in the morning. Dodie never said a word, but Dodie was also the type of person who lived in the ideal and felt compelled to act as though she wanted anything that she was supposed to want. If Dodie had been honest with herself she would have realized that, other than the loss of the free childcare, the only reason she even slightly tolerated Maxine in this domesticated role was that it gave her the illusion that her renegade mother was finally under control. In fact, the reality was that both Randall and Dodie readily helped Maxine put up shelves and signs in the new salon, carry in boxes, set up furniture, and arrange for advertisements, undoubtedly relieved to see her getting on with her life.

The only truly difficult part about moving into her own place had been leaving Margaret, who, despite the physical demands, had burrowed into Maxine's heart. For those first six months, the two of them had learned the world together, walking the orange sand and avoiding the jellyfish at Sandy Point Beach, snarfing jam-filled donuts and sausage biscuits from seedy fast food huts, and exploring the children's museum or trawling the mall during the spring rains for kiddie jewelry, wind-up toy displays, and escalators. Tired as the childcare had made her, Maxine found herself missing little Margaret's sweet dependence, worship almost, that not only reminded her of her time with Dodie so many years ago but also gave her the only sense during those first six months, however fleeting, that her personal existence mattered at all.

Utzi the Iceman came back from the kitchen with a large Tupperware container of pretzels. "Here you go, sirs. Make the workload a bit lighter."

"No eating in the living room," said Maxine.

"We always eat in the living room," said Lawrence.

"Not when you're on my watch, you don't. You finish your cleaning, and then you can go sit at the kitchen table and have your snack. Get snapping now."

Utzi brought the pretzels over to the couch and placed the bowl on his lap. "I don't think you should worry so much about Dodie. Just look how she's handling these kids on her own."

"I'm not worried about her child rearing skills. I'm worried that she lives in a dream world."

"You have to give the girl some credit," he said, popping a pretzel in his mouth while she glared at him. "She wants to do good in the world."

"She's so good at what she does, Utzi, and she isn't doing it. You should see her with Shelley—pity she can't do this all the time. That's where I do see the merit in her plan.

She shines, you know, always knows just the right thing to say."

"You need a hundred Shelleys. Paying Shelleys, that is."

"Ah, well, that would be ideal, wouldn't it? The need for work on these abused women would be endless. The problem, sadly, is that they're the very ones who can't possibly pay me for doing that."

"You and Dodie, though—you make a good team. That's saying something."

"I suppose."

Lawrence looked up from the mounds of tiddlywinks and plastic catapults surrounding him, which he seemed more interested in stacking and shooting than packing into boxes. "No fair. How come he gets to eat in here if we don't?"

"Mr. Utzi is a grown-up, Lawrence. It's hard to be a grownup. So you get certain privileges."

"Can I have pretzels now?" said William.

"You have put precisely two cards away in that box, young man. When I don't see any cards or markers on the floor, and when all the boxes are neatly stacked back in that cabinet, you may have your pretzels. That's a good boy. All right now, Lawrence, here, take this bowl away from Mr. Utzi. The last thing he needs is more pretzels. Take them carefully to the kitchen, and eat them at the table. That a boy."

"I'll be there in a second to get you boys some sodas," said Utzi, reserving a few pretzels for himself and stuffing them between his thighs where he thought Maxine couldn't see them. "Just sit at the table, and we'll be right in." He turned to Maxine. "You know what she needs? She needs a backer—a trust fund...or a grant. Quite seriously, that's actually not a ridiculous idea. She could probably get a grant, from some government agency or maybe some non-profit, women's rights kind of outfit. Think about it—she's proposing doing a public service of sorts, one that no one else is doing."

"There I won't argue with you."

"Seriously, Zeenie. She needs to look into this, find out how it's done, write up a proposal. She doesn't need to ask for much. She just needs enough support to live on while she does it."

"She needs some common sense is what she needs."

"She should throw in something about compensation for your services as well. I'm not kidding. You two, what you two could do together, are naturals for grant support."

It was good to see Utzi the Iceman running at the mouth again, even if he was spewing out complete nonsense. The man was so volatile, as impulsive and flighty as a child, or even a brainless puppy. One minute he'd be rolling on his back, with a squeaky toy. The next he'd be under a chair, whimpering and licking his privates. Until this moment, he had been low this entire evening, not to the point of monosyllables (or, hibernation), but far more focused on her problems than his plans—always a warning sign with him, and a stunning contrast to his nonstop gushing about his research over the past month. He had been seeing her regularly again for nearly a month now, but tonight from the start it was obvious that something had snapped. He hadn't even mentioned the book, and instead let her moan at him, even encouraged her moaning. She was happy enough to exploit this lull after a whole winter without anyone to listen to her moaning, but, under her surface chatter, she took it as an ominous sign.

"Zeenie, are you coming? We're thirsty!"

"You two be patient. We'll be there in good time."

Maxine put her hand on Utzi's knee and shook her head. "This is why you—and Dodie—will drive me into an early grave. The both of you create problems for yourselves out of thin air."

"I don't understand."

"The last thing Dodie needs is to spend the next month researching grant agencies and writing grant proposals. She already has enough on her head. No business, husband, no job—those are real problems. Life brings those to you. You don't need to create more headaches for yourself....You, sir, are exactly the same way. You hunt high and low for something to bring you down, as if that something isn't going to find you very well on its own."

"I beg to differ. I was gung-ho about the curse idea. I can't help it if it's turning out to be less feasible than I originally thought."

"Ah. So that's what it is."

"That's what 'what' is?"

"I knew something was bothering you, Utzi. I can read you like a book. So tell me. What exactly is the problem?"

"It's not a problem. I'm just having a bit of a block, that's all. It happens to all writers."

"Oh dear. That was what I was afraid you were going to say."

"Usually when I can't write, I just keep researching. That generally assuages my guilt and ultimately wakes the muse. But now—it's looking like the curse angle may be another blind alley. The more I look into it, the less is there."

"Well, maybe you haven't looked enough. I'm sure it will come to you, in time."

"Maybe."

"You know, Utzi, sometimes I think you give up too easily." She pushed his hand down as he tried to eat the pretzels he had hidden in his fist, and pried them from his fingers. "You cannot disappear like that again, Utzi. I simply cannot allow it to happen. I missed you all those months, in case you weren't aware of that."

"I missed you, too."

"Did you now? But there was nothing to stop you from seeing me, was there?"

"I'm not that bad, honestly I'm not, but I do find myself in a bit of a rut again. I'll keep searching for a niche. Before though—that was different. I wasn't even looking for a niche, didn't even have a plan."

"So you couldn't see me, simply because you were feeling a bit low?"

"I honestly couldn't, Zeenie. I couldn't see anyone, not even you. Not when I was feeling like that. Most of all you...."

"Am I that much of an ogre?"

"Far from it. But I needed to be myself before I could inflict myself on you. You don't need to see me down and out. I like to make you laugh."

"That's not a relationship, Utzi. That's a playdate."

"It's not something I'm proud of. But when I'm feeling like that, like a wounded animal—everything else is too hard. I don't know if you can possibly understand, a practical person like you....Just the getting showered and shaved and dressed, the pleasantries, the social graces. All the things normal people have to do to get through the day and make themselves tolerable. You wouldn't enjoy me in my bear state...."

"I wish you wouldn't tell me what I'd enjoy. You have no idea...."

"I think you're dead wrong. I found myself in a blind alley last fall, Zeenie, not because I'm perverse, but because reality hit me in the face. I wasn't about to write a book that had nothing new to say. Now I'm up against it again, but at least I know what my goal is. Once I've found something new to say about the Iceman, and, eventually I will–well, once I've found it, I can go forward and write it. I *will* go forward and write it."

"Of course you will, if you so choose," she said. "However, I'm not so sure you've set yourself on the right path."

"It's the right path if I want it to be the right path. It's all in the mind."

"Zeenie, can we get a drink ourselves?" Lawrence called from the kitchen. "You guys are taking forever."

"Don't you dare," said Utzi. "No pouring without me overseeing you." He rose, and offered Maxine a hand.

"You can write the book someday, Utzi," she said, rising to join him. "Maybe even on the curse—who knows what you'll devise, once you keep digging and thinking and whatnot. I don't see the rush, since, as you say, you will eventually have your own twist, and no one can steal that out from under you. I'm also sure, as you say, you can write anything you set your mind to write....For now, however, there might be a better use of your time and talent....You wouldn't know how to write a grant proposal, would you?"

CHAPTER TWENTY-SEVEN

Dodie stood at the reception desk with an ash-blond, fiftiesh woman of sedulously studied attractiveness hovering behind her. "Michelle—you're glowing today. Positively glowing. I don't see a trace of the red."

"Your mom was right on the mark. She said it would fade in three or four days, and today is day three." Shelley ran her fingers down the left side of her face from temple to chin. "Feel this. I used to have a ridge here. It's totally smooth now. And you can barely see a scar."

Dodie turned to her companion. "That's exactly the kind of thing I was telling you about. She can do it for you, too, on top of doing the burn....What's that thing she uses, Michelle? MCA, right? Multi—what exactly does it stand for?"

"Multitrepanic collagen actuation." It was Maxine, calling out from the kitchen.

"Right. That's why I can never remember it." Dodie put her finger into Shelley's appointment book and took her companion by the arm, pulling her up to the desk. "This is Phyllis Kates. You've got her down here for a three o'clock—consultation."

"Dodie? Is that you? Who do you have with you?"

"I've brought a friend, a new client."

"Tell her to have a seat. I'll be out for you just now."

Dodie planted Phyllis with one of the photograph albums and went to retrieve Maxine, for whom the term "just now" generally meant "when I jolly well please." Phyllis was the latest of several new clients whom Dodie had brought for work in the past few months. She had originally met them all at the shelter, but each of them also had means to pay Maxine out of their own pockets, at least at discounted rates. Dodie knew dozens of women who had passed through the shelter and were trying to recover, struggling to their feet after having moved from mansions to condos, and golf outings to Victoria's Secret day jobs. These women needed scar work. For now, Dodie could only steer the most fortunate few among them to Maxine, however. Abuse was an equal opportunity misfortune, and even the wealthiest women in these circumstances couldn't necessarily get their hands on the money they had once had, particularly after they had left, or were trying to leave, the relationships that had put them in those circumstances. Maxine, after considerable cajoling, was willing to do a few of these women at a loss. If they got the grant, Dodie reminded her, she would be fully compensated, and compensated by an abundance of new clients. With the grant money, they would be able to get a van, contract or at least communicate with Safe Port, and discreetly transport the sheltered and still recovering women to the spa, including the many other women who couldn't pay at all.

"I worked with Phyllis at the shelter last year," Dodie explained to Maxine, "but then it also turned out that Randall worked with her ex—not the problem guy, but her first husband—at the Central Office. She's an elementary school principal, actually, interesting woman, and we've kept in touch ever since. Fortunately she's free of all that now— left the asshole, second guy she married, Navy—and has managed to keep him out of her life ever since he hooked up with someone younger and blonder. The usual. Wants to get back her life, and her old face. I said I knew a miracle worker."

"Miracle worker I'm not," Maxine said, carrying her coffee into the reception room at last and shaking Phyllis's hand. "But let me tell you—Phyllis, is it?—if you've got wrinkling or minor scar issues, MCA is going to bring you back decades you never knew you lost."

She flipped open the album on Phyllis's lap to several before-and-after shots. "This one had a face full of acne pitting. And now—look! That's without makeup, mind you….And here, you see the wrinkles on this woman's upper lip! She was forty years old, and looked every minute of it. And there, you see! After the needling, she looks a good twenty years younger!"

"Needling?"

"MCA. Same thing."

"That's extraordinary."

"Yes, it is. Especially when you consider that it was done without surgery. Or lasers….It's criminal, to me, anyway, that so many people flock to lasers, which destroy their epidermis, with all we know…."

"I always wondered if lasers could help. You see ads for them everywhere."

"Such a bunch of rot they're putting over on women. MCA is so much more affordable, so much safer. Lasers, I could go on all day—they destroy your epidermis, burn it to bits on their way down under….With MCA, though, all we're doing is making tiny, miniscule pricks in the skin, easily repaired by the body without permanent damage to the epidermis, without removing the epidermis. Honestly, which would you choose if you knew the truth?"

"I'll vouch for it," said Shelley. "I'm three days out of my last treatment, and, as you see, no red at all."

"A little inflammation is perfectly normal whenever you poke at the epidermis, but it makes no sense to provoke severe inflammation when the dermis is what we're after. That's where you'll see the sun damage, and that's the root of wrinkled and saggy skin. The epidermis has nothing to do with it, so why destroy it? Plus, once you bring in lasers, you must contend with ghastly sun sensitivity, and eventually, skin tightening—not a look any of us want. The epidermis is all we've got to protect us from the environment, dears, microorganisms, toxins, ultraviolet radiation, all the chemicals we surround ourselves with. And it's delicate nonetheless—only 0.2 mm thick." She held up her fingers, barely touching thumb to index finger. "Very thin indeed. You want it healthy. You want the keratinocytes that produce melanin healthy, too."

"My mother despises lasers, in case you hadn't noticed," said Dodie, who had at this point brought coffee for Phyllis and herself.

"Would you mind refilling this for me?" Maxine handed her empty cup to Dodie. "I'm falling asleep this afternoon, don't ask me why. There's a dearie lamb....Well, then, enough on lasers. Needling is a more modern, natural approach—with a much happier outcome. There is some minor local injury, of course, and you see inflammation, tissue formation, and tissue remodeling as with any wound healing, but it's no more than some localized bleeding."

"You've sold me, absolutely....But here you show a needle going right into her lip—that has got to hurt!"

Maxine assured Phyllis that she used a topic anesthetic and that the pain would be nothing compared to laser surgery, explaining how the needle would go directly through the epidermis to the papillary dermis, and set off a cascade of chemical responses. "It's very complex, chemically, but the bottom line result is that you get beautiful new collagen and elastin as the wound heals and new collagen laid down just below the epidermis, you see? The tissue is actually 'remodeled.'"

"Seems too good to be true."

"It's quite simple really. And quite safe." Maxine told Phyllis the story she loved telling her clients about the Beverly Hills doctor who had discovered MCA and quickly found it to be superior to lasers. The scientists soon got on board and did some clinical studies on people who had been given tattoos to cover pale, melanin-free facial scars. Over the years the tattoo pigment faded, but, astoundingly, natural melanin had, to some extent, replaced it.

"Do you hear what I'm saying?," Maxine asked Phyllis. "Just puncturing the skin with a needle—a tattoo gun, in this case—without any pigment at all seemed to break down the collagen in the scar and realign it. At the same time, it stimulated melanogenesis, the production of new color pigments in the skin. You see?"

"Impressive."

"And this was clinically proven, mind you, presented at several scientific meetings in the late 1990s. Now it is patently obvious: MCA is far superior to lasers, although you wouldn't know it if you talked to most dermatologists. Most of them still promote lasers, of course, which bring them considerably more money for considerably less work...."

Phyllis ran her index finger along the creases that extended from each nostril. "Could it do something for these? I have to slather the foundation on every morning, or I scare the children half to death."

"That can be arranged, my dear. Absolutely."

"Of course, lines are the least of her worries," said Dodie. "She's mainly here about a burn."

"That's true—with the scar I'm nothing short of Frankenstein's monster." Phyllis smiled, revealing what once must have been a perfect set of teeth, blanched a blinding white by an overzealous bleach job but now marred by cockeyed incisors and a hole where her upper left canine tooth should have been. "When I take off this sea of foundation, you'll see what I mean."

"But, of course—whatever is needed. Come back now, and we'll have a look....Michelle, dear, would you please get Phyllis set up? I'll be in just now."

When Shelley and Phyllis had gone to the make-up room, Maxine sat down beside Dodie and sniffed at her coffee. "How many of these charity cases do you expect me to handle? Do you think I'm made of money?"

"She's paying you, Zeenie. However many times she needs to come in—she has the money."

"'Fifty percent off' she has the money. Every time she comes in, or any of your women, it's a loss for me."

"It's better than dead air."

Maxine licked her lips. Since childhood, Dodie had known this behavior meant that she had pushed her mother a tad too far and that it was time for a dagger.

"Since when are you a businesswoman?" Maxine said at last. "Do you think I'd be twiddling my thumbs if you didn't bring me these ladies? I'd be out pounding the streets, working on my advertisements, and hitting up the ladies luncheons at the *shul*, my pet. I have ways of bringing in business, but I need the time to do it...."

"I thought you were going to approach dermatologist woman. About subcontracting, I mean."

"Now how can I do that when you're bringing me in charity work night and day, Dodie? Think before you speak."

Dodie gathered up the coffee cups and started back toward the kitchen. "Well, anyway, this conversation is pointless. When we get the grant, everything is going to change. You'll be paid in full for your work. And have more of it than you could ever imagine. I can bring you as much as you want—once cost is no object, I mean."

"Dream on, lambie dear. That's where you shine."

"What do you mean—dream on? Do you know something I don't? Last I heard, Utzi had at least five possible funders, one of them specifically for salons fighting domestic violence. What could be more perfect? He's going to submit something next month, maybe even sooner. Why so pessimistic?"

"Have you actually seen anything Utzi's written?"

"Well, no, not exactly. But he's been gangbusters in the research. And he works like a dog."

"Research is where Utzi shines. He's very good on the intake. It's the output that's the problem."

"If that's what you really think, why do you always sound so upbeat about it to him?"

"Once again, Dodie, your ignorance of the male species never ceases to astound me." She followed Dodie into the kitchen and watched her scrub out each cup. "Don't use too much of that soap. You just need a tiny squirt. That's it....Men need encouragement, Dodie. Above all, they need projects. Otherwise they fight like wild animals, brew mindless vandalism, or shrivel up in despair at their utter uselessness. Utzi needs something to keep him busy, and now he's found that something. As far as I'm concerned, the longer he takes researching and writing this thing, the better.

Once he realizes that whatever it is he's writing must be a polished, perfect product, he's going to despair, and then I'm back where I began—with him in a hole, and me without a dinner companion."

"Or a bed companion."

"Watch your mouth, Missy. Wherever it is, I'm missing him. I'd rather have him around, if truth be known."

"So that's what this is all about—keeping Utzi happy? I had no idea you had so little faith."

"There are many things about which you have no idea, Dodie....However, for now, you must get back to your children, and I must give this poor woman whatever help I can give her. And who knows? I could be wrong. It has happened once or twice in the past. Once or twice."

CHAPTER TWENTY-EIGHT

Maxine's cynicism aside, they got word of grant approval from two separate funders in January. By that spring they were up and running not only a busy reconstruction service for recovering women, but also what amounted to their own subsidiary shelter service. One grant covered Maxine directly for permanent makeup and related services and another funded incidental expenses involved in identifying, transporting, and, in some cases, housing, women recovering from domestic violence, as well as compensating Dodie for her time and gas. Both grants were renewable annually, and Utzi the Iceman, who had set himself up as their budget director, was already at work on the mandatory progress reports as well as two additional sources of funding, including one that would provide Dodie, Maxine, and even Shelley with respectable salaries.

They quickly fell into a routine that at first brought Maxine several new clients per week, and soon, at least several grant-supported women per day. Dodie would make weekly runs to Safe Port, ferrying to the salon the regulars who needed immediate work on old scars, or wanted to get started on transformation work that would eventually allow them to reenter society, whether with their original but no longer blemished faces or with reconfigured looks that kept habitual stalkers at bay. The first treatment or two involved as much instantaneous makeover as possible—haircut and color job, eyebrow shaping, lash dying, absolutely, instruction on camouflage makeup and required supplies, needling on the broken capillaries, lash extension, often, and, occasionally, a trip with Dodie to the optometrist for colored contacts. The grant didn't cover the extensive long-term makeover that Shelley was still in the process of receiving, but not everyone needed one. For many women, Maxine and Dodie were providing a welcome transition between those few days or weeks at Safe Port and absolute abandonment.

Even so, certain commonly needed services, such as scar camouflaging, took months to complete, and Safe Port couldn't possibly house any individual woman that long. Although these services were optional, many women jumped at the chance for more extensive restoration. Dodie quickly discovered that she held the solution in her own hands, not only because she could keep working with the various overflow shelters in the state but also because, with Randall gone, she could provide overflow housing for as many as ten displaced women at a time in her own home. She took out the benches in the abandoned greenhouse and put in ten cots, all expenses covered in full with grant money. She left in Randall's microwave and refrigerator and gave the women access to the first floor bathroom. Meanwhile, Shelley, who continued to work for Maxine although her restoration work was nearly complete, moved into the greenhouse as well until she had saved up enough to fund her own place, something Utzi the Iceman assured her would be entirely possible once the other grants came through. Shelley continued working for Maxine on weekdays, and, other times, helped Dodie and the clients with cleaning and organizing the greenhouse, as well as the downstairs bathroom, which, given its unprecedented volume, required hard-core servicing.

All was going according to plan, except for Margaret. Once a nearly straight-A student, she had spent an unnerving portion of sophomore year in bed, something Dodie had only discovered when her third quarter report card arrived bearing two D's and several C's. (Why no one from the school had called her to alert her to this situation earlier was beyond her, but, sadly, typical of this bureaucratic countywide school system where as long as someone was "academically eligible" to play sports, all was right with the world). Because Dodie so often left the house before dawn to transport clients incognito to Maxine's, and because she only returned at 8 a.m. to rouse her sons and get them to their respective schools, she had never suspected that an unmovable Margaret lurked behind a closed bedroom door; in the old days Margaret would have been out of the house unnoticed by 6:30 a.m. to catch the high school bus. Margaret had made up her missed and botched coursework over the summer—Dodie had seen to that, trying not to dwell much on her daughter's newly constricted college options—but this new school year Dodie had insisted that Margaret forgo Advanced Placement Calculus and enroll in regular rather than Honors or Advanced Placement English to relieve the pressure. The result of her perceived "lack of faith" in her daughter had been disastrous. Instead of receiving a D in English, Margaret was now out-and-out failing it, and Dodie had just received a letter from the school noting that Margaret was in danger of not graduating.

Dodie knew it was unfair to her, in a way. It wasn't, after all, Margaret, or any of the children's fault, that things hadn't worked out with Randall, or that their mother had to find new ways to make ends meet. It was understandable, too, that a slew of strange women wandering through their kitchen at night or turning the downstairs bathroom into a beauty supply house might leave them feeling inconvenienced, bewildered, or even insecure. Then again, as she repeatedly told Margaret in their accelerating spats about which of the two of them was the most selfish and inconsiderate, children from time immemorial had had to endure the circumstances imposed on them by their parents. "Suck it up," Dodie often found herself saying when Margaret, the only one of her children who complained, glared at her with the soul-searing, withering contempt that only teenage girls know how to inflict on their mothers. In their last conversation, Dodie had let loose her gut, her voice rising with each phrase that failed to move Margaret. "I know you didn't choose to have a mother bringing battered women's into your kitchen, but, then again, I didn't choose my mother either." she said. "It could have been way worse for you, you know. Children don't choose to have crack cocaine addicts as mothers, or live in houses where the walls are peeling lead paint, or choose fathers who beat them or rape them or sell their bodies, now do they? Many children get these parents, or parents who ignore them, or suffocate them with attention, or spoil them or shelter them or do any of any number of things parents do every day to ruin their children."

She hoped Margaret would smile, at least a little, but Margaret merely averted her gaze and returned to wrapping tape around the shaft of her lacrosse stick. "I didn't say my life had to be perfect. All I said was that it would have been nice to have a normal family with two parents at home, maybe some dinners together, and a dog or a fish."

"Normal? What's normal? You could have been born to

a mother in Somalia who had you circumcised. You could have been born to a mother in Imperial China who had your feet bound. You could have been born to a mother in India who made you a child bride to an octogenarian and banished you to a widow's *ashram* when he died....You have it good, Margaret, really, when you think about who you could have had for a mother."

"That's crap." Margaret banged her stick on the floor. "I know what I could have had, okay? We had it once, not all that long ago either. But now you give me a bunch of wackos who run around at all hours cackling and crying, mucking up the bathroom...."

"You have it good, Margaret. From any rational perspective, you really do."

"All I'm asking is to be like everyone else around here. Or like we were. That's all. You act like I'm a spoiled brat just to ask to be normal."

"I'm sorry to disappoint you. But, Margaret, as you get older you'll discover that there's no such thing as normal. The question is just which type of dysfunction you get."

"I know that."

"Well, you don't act like you know it. Parents, the best of them, do the best they can. It's the child's job to make the best of it."

"Is that honestly what you think? That my job—and the boys'—is to make the best of you and Daddy? Two educated, socially-minded parents who 'care about evil and social injustice'? That's all you can give us?" She batted her newly wrapped stick around the floor, continually releasing and recovering an imaginary ball. "That's a lot of crap."

"I do the best I can. Margaret, I think you know that I am trying to do some good in the world. Sorry if that's inconvenient or embarrassing to you. It's time you realized, though, that there are people other than you in need. These women in our home are among them. And, believe it or not, your mother, yes, me, is another....Put that stick down, will you? It belongs in the hall."

If Margaret would have listened instead of rolling her eyes, launching an obscenity, and bolting, stick flying, to her room, Dodie would have told her that if these women weren't living in the greenhouse, the four of them would likely have been living in a shelter themselves. The money she got from Randall each month covered the mortgage, barely, and left a little extra for groceries, utilities, insurance, and gas, but there was certainly no discretionary cash, with discretionary loosely defined as clothing, movies, books, school and sports supplies, Hebrew School, camp, piano lessons, and household help, not to mention the inevitable mundane calamities such as broken arms, broken windows, broken water heaters, and broken carburetors.

Clearly if these children were going to be raised the way she wanted to raise them, she was going to have to earn some money, and, at the same time, have childcare for her youngest and transportation and supervision for all three. Randall had the children on weekends, period, and, other than the boys' soccer games and Margaret's lacrosse matches (which she believed he attended and even coached primarily for professional points and vicarious glory), he so far had shown no interest in carting them to other lessons and appointments or looking after them. All that fell on her head, as always. He was, not surprisingly, still a picture-perfect dad to his orchids, which he had paid a pretty penny to transport unscathed through the February winds to his condo just a week after he had left. (In fact, it wouldn't have surprised her if the reason he had chosen to leave in that particular season was that the cool, cloudy weather had been ideal for transporting orchids.) As always, that left little time for the children, especially now that, from what she had heard, he had taken up with one of the resource teachers at the central office, which would pretty much explain his disinterest in all things family.

Dodie found herself surprised at how little any of this mattered to her, even the girlfriend. Let him be happy, she thought. I suppose I might miss him, if I had the time, but, for good or for bad, I don't. In fact, she found herself feeling exhilarated a good deal of the time, other than, of course, her demoralizing encounters with Margaret. She enjoyed no longer being a servant of the system but instead a leader of her own cause. On the downside, the new service took up even more of her time than her old job, and, of course, involved considerably more responsibility, or even, some might say, risk. Working out the daily arrangements with her mother also meant enduring incessant diatribes about imagined abuses, the latest of which involved the onslaught of battered women that kept Maxine from tending to her regular clientele. It wasn't the upscaled activity itself that bothered Maxine. In fact, unlike her daughter, Maxine was acutely aware of how easy it was to slip from not being able to breathe to having absolutely nothing to do. However, the regular customers paid more than the amount per client the Iceman had estimated in the grant.

"I lose money for every one of these gals you bring me," Maxine told Dodie one mild September evening as they headed toward the Chinese place down the street to grab a quick supper while Shelley finished tidying up the salon. She purposely stepped on and crunched a prematurely brown leaf that had just detached itself from a large tulip poplar and drifted across her path.

"That's absurd. You're the one who's been saying for years that your stream is falling off. It's not like you didn't have a slew of empty time slots before we started this."

"And what about you? You had a well-paying job and now...." Maxine stared expectantly at Dodie as the maitre d' nodded them toward their usual booth and filled their water glasses. "How precisely do you plan to go on living? You can't feed your children on good intentions. Or care for them while you're driving around all night."

"The children are fed and cared for, Zeenie. The rest will come in time....Anyway, don't change the subject. The bottom line is that you are being compensated for your services, just maybe not as much as you'd like. The same is true for me, or just about. You're covering the rent now, right?"

"That remains to be seen."

"Can't you ever admit you're wrong? Or proud? Or pleased?"

"Of course I can. When appropriate....Young man, I'll have a mai tai—not too sweet, remember. And my teetotaling daughter will have a club soda, with lime—that's right, isn't it, Dodie?"

Dodie looked at the waiter and winced. "I get a ringing in my ear when I drink alcohol. I can actually feel my heart racing, all the way up in my head. Sorry." She hated to go on like this to total strangers, but she found that refusing a drink almost always required an explanation, even in polite adult company. She was sure the waiter despised her now, figuring a substantial dip in the tab and tip potential, but he simply nodded, repeated their orders, and walked away.

"Honestly, Zeenie, I sometimes think that you just can't ever be happy. Like an old Jewish grandma worried about the evil eye. Do you think some dybbuk is going to come down and take you by the throat if you admit that things are good?"

"I *am* an old Jewish grandma, sugar plum. In case you never noticed."

"Well, that's a switch. Admitting you're a grandma. You never even liked to be a mum—'*Zeenie*.'"

Maxine slipped a tiny plastic bottle of skin toner from her purse and spritzed some into her palm. "Well, now, you're certainly one to talk. You don't think it's a tad ironic, you here aiding and abetting this whole operation? Given your attitude?" Mindlessly, she rolled up her sleeve and began massaging the gel into her upper arm.

"What do you mean, 'my attitude'? I'm as up as I've been in years."

"Dodie, please, be honest for once, will you? Surely you don't think I don't know how you feel, how you resent all this....As I recall you once saying, there is nothing on earth as 'despicable'—wasn't that the word you used?—than pandering to men's base desires?"

"If I ever said that I must have been all of sixteen. How long do you hold grudges, Zeenie?"

"I haven't a clue. But those words stuck with me, like a serpent's tooth. Everything your child says sticks with you....However, I'm glad you've come to see the light."

"I don't know what you're referring to. I may or may not have said as a child, I certainly don't see what we're doing now as pandering to anything or anyone. It's wonderful we can help so many women in need, making them whole. Men have nothing to do with it. Plus, you know, I do see that for many women makeup is a physical way of fighting back, instead of muscles. As you say yourself—it gives women more control than they know....What is that stuff anyway? It reeks worse than the sesame oil."

"Toning gel. It's new in the line, blocks lipogenesis and accelerates lipolysis. You should see what it can do for cellulite—I thought I'd give it a try on these awful arms....I don't know why you find it so bothersome, Dodie—it's fragrance free, for heaven's sake. But that's precisely what I mean. You're frothing with resentment about what I do. And about what we do."

"Not at all."

"Of course you are. We're making these ladies whole by restoring their physical beauty, which, as you once told me, is a 'social construct perpetuated by women to appease men.' I'm almost certain that's precisely what you said. You despise cosmetology, or you did, anyway. In fact, that's why you took flight for the states, isn't it? When you were an angry teen? Fed up with my lifestyle, the hypocrisy of it all. Do you think I have no memory?"

"That's not true." Dodie took the bottle of Maxine's toning gel and squinted at the ingredients.

"Try a bit of it, dear. What I would have given to have some of this around when I was your age....My goodness, I could have gone sleeveless two decades longer, no question."

"You can still go sleeveless, Zeenie. That's your choice. Look at the menu, already. I've got to get home. Margaret said she'd get the boys dinner, but last time I called she wasn't home yet from practice. And she's not picking up her cell phone—not that that's unusual." She caught the waiter's eye. "I'll just have a cup of hot and sour soup, please. Zeenie?"

"That's all you want, luv? You're skin and bones. She'll share something with me. Let me see here." As Maxine customized the menu offerings to her tastes and sent the befuddled waiter off to the kitchen. Dodie stared down at the colorful paper placement. "This seems very fitting for you, Zeenie, this Chinese Zodiac list. It says you are a Dragon lady, with characteristics including conceit, tactlessness, self-assuredness, and quick temper. They've got you pegged, these Chinese, don't they?"

Maxine put on her reading glasses. "Is that so? So I am a Dragon...Ah. Well, perhaps so, but this says that I am also innovative, enterprising, flexible, passionate, and scrutinizing. You skipped those things."

"I was apparently born in the year of the Tiger, the sign of courage. That means I am brave, vehement, self-reliant, friendly, hopeful, and resilient..."

"...as well as vain and disregardful it says here. You skipped those two as well....To be honest, pet, I don't see all that much difference between the Dragon and the Tiger. All those words describe the lot of us....However, I do like this description: 'Dragons are the free spirits, and conformity is their curse. Rules and regulations are made for other people.'"

"It also says you Dragons are beautiful, colorful, and flamboyant. Whereas we Tigers find no value in power or money. Hmph."

"Well, there you see? You do resent what I stand for, just as I said. And yet, here you are."

Maxine was right, Dodie supposed, that as a teenager she had always hated aspects of the business, particularly the way it encouraged women to dwell on themselves and their petty physical imperfections when there was so much suffering outside themselves that needed tending. She probably had never fully stopped despising Maxine's role in aiding and abetting them, at least in contrast with other choices she might have made about how to use her time.

Even if her mother had been out marching with the Black Sash, however, Dodie at seventeen would still have been angry at her, not because her mother spent her time fixing faces but rather because her mother routinely denied everything about herself. She remembered hating how her mother denied her physicality, just as she denied her Judaism, using an Anglicized name. She had denied her humanity in her history of disregard for the blacks of South Africa, her need to praise them only when they were subservient, and her refusal to see the role of the government in fueling the massacre of innocent people, as they recently had in the Boipatong township. She had denied her personhood in the way she had never been able work things out with her mysterious father, someone Dodie only vaguely remembered from her toddlerhood as the sound of wild beating on the windows and doors and incoherent bleating. Rather than talking with him or finding help for his alcohol problems, she had simply locked the door on him, literally, and gone on in her usual oblivious and self-centered fashion. But none of these feelings explained why Dodie had chosen to leave South Africa.

"I left for the very same reason you left, Zeenie."

"Well, there, I'll agree. We both left for you."

"That's your pretty, self-serving story. But it's utter fantasy. No, Zeenie, you didn't leave for me, and you know it damn well. You left because of Dr. Ruf. And so did I."

When the waiter arrived with the drinks, Maxine recapped the toning gel and slipped it back into her purse. "Please see what's taking the food so long, will you? We must get back to the office, so please try to speed things up....I did not leave because of Rufus Alvarez. Where on earth did you get that idea? I left to be with you and your baby."

"There's no point in lying to me, Zeenie, Mummy—whoever you are." Dodie removed the pink and orange umbrella from her drink and twirled it between her fingers. "All right. Listen. I need to tell you a story. I don't want to. But I have to."

"I'm afraid I must visit the ladies' room, if you don't mind. I need to clean this gook off my fingers."

"Hurry up then. I need to say something."

When Maxine returned, she found the table laden with food and Dodie staring blankly at a piece of tofu that she had speared from her soup with a chopstick. "Well, that's the trick, isn't it?," said Maxine. "It's just like the umbrella business—all you need to do to stave off the rain is carry an umbrella. So then, let's tuck in—our Michelle must almost be finished up by now."

Dodie shook the tofu back into the soup. "Did you not hear me, Zeenie? I said I needed to tell you something about why I left South Africa. It involves Dr. Ruf."

"Dr. Ruf? Really? Well, go on then. But do let me give you some of this chicken. Just push over that little plate to me. There you go....That soup is not a meal, and you know it....Now, go ahead, tell me whatever it is you want to tell me."

"All right. Fine. But, brace yourself because this isn't going to be easy."

"At my age, I'm always braced, Dodie. Please speak up already."

"Okay. Before I left home, well you remember, I used to work in the salon. And one night I was working late doing the filing, and he came in with some boxes. Lotions and such that he said you ordered from him. I think you were running errands. Or with your mum. Anyway you weren't there."

313

"Who came in? Rufus Alvarez?"

"Yes. Dr. Ruf. You know exactly who I mean. He came in, and, you know, I should have thought it odd that such an eminent man made his own deliveries, but I was a stupid little girl back then. Whatever. People brought in deliveries all the time, and, of course, he was your friend. I helped him bring the boxes into the supply room, and he started chatting me up. You know how he was. He was charming and amusing, as you well know, but it got uncomfortable after a while. Silences, long ones, and him just staring at me, moving close."

"What do you mean—moving close?"

"I was putting the boxes into the shelves, and he was, you know, right next to me, helping and all. But then he didn't move away. I so wanted him to leave, but I was, you know, official, a receptionist, and, of course, I was only a kid, supposedly respectful to my elders and such. Anyway, he started telling me how much I looked like you and touching my hair, rubbing it in his fingers, pulling it to his face, weird stuff. And then he…."

"Don't you malign him, Dodie. You don't know what you're saying."

Dodie set down her spoon, put both hands on the table, and leaned forward. "I never wanted to tell you this, Zeenie. I knew it would break your heart. But now that I'm older, it seems—well, I've come to think differently. Sometimes we have to have our hearts broken to move on. And we need to move on."

"Really, you should shut your mouth now."

"He pulled me to him and kissed me hard, Zeenie. Not a friendly kiss. A 'let's make no mistake about it' kiss."

Every time Dodie thought about this incident—and she thought about it just about every time she saw one of Dr.

314

Ruf's products on her mother's shelves—she felt a cold wind run through her, and a sense that the person she had been at the time had somehow not been herself. This sense did not come from any kind of violated innocence. Although she had only been 17 at the time, she had hardly been unseasoned when it came to men. Having been raised by a busy, working mother, essentially without a father, she had grown up quickly, and by her early teens had already had several serious boyfriends, including a couple at least a decade older than she was. Dodie had considered herself a "feminist" since grade school and believed entirely in a woman's freedom, even right, to share her body with whomever she so chose, whenever she so chose, as long as all actions were mutually desired and responsible.

For all her experience, however, Dodie had never had a lover whose affections she had actively sought. Several times she had come to enjoy, even cherish, the tender, tentative, consensual caresses of her young boyfriends, but this had inevitably occurred after some tortuous, half-conscious mental machinations in which she persuaded herself that the earnest and eager boy offering himself to her would also be a socially acceptable and fitting match. She had never set out to attract and reel in anyone who had not first set his eyes on her. Although she secretly envied her girlfriends the drama—and power—of their complex strategies to captivate, and capture, the boys of their dreams, she also dismissed such stratagems as demeaning to women and, at the same time, assumed she'd inevitably bungle similar efforts with her unflagging directness. The fundamental problem, though, was that her fantasies had always involved people she could never have, either because she saw them as unobtainable or socially unconscionable. Recently she had had several vivid dreams about one particular classmate, both a brilliant student and star tennis player, whose thick, wavy hair, deep blue eyes, and capable shoulders left her pathetically weak-kneed and dizzy whenever she stood within five feet of him. But she never imagined for a second that he or the few others who had made her feel this way would ever feel the same about her, nor did she have the slightest clue about how she would go about making them feel it. Whether a touch from these unapproachables would have left her woozy she didn't know, since every one of her relationships so far had not been a matter of pursuing the desideratum but of choosing not to reject the tolerable. The only times a touch had sent her spinning and soaring had been when they had come from a friend's cheating boyfriend, a stranger on the city bus running his hand up her thigh, the ample woman teaching lifesaving who hauled her across the pool in a chest hold, or, in this case, a grizzly old man who also happened to be her business associate, as well as her mother's beloved. So it was not so much Dr. Ruf's insult to her innocence that disturbed her, or even repulsion toward the bristly brush of an old man's skin against her cheek or the sour stench of his breath in her mouth. Rather, what terrified her was the way his insistence had infused her with a euphoria infinitely more intense than warm milk or a hot bath, even as she pushed him away.

Maxine stared at Dodie, her expression unreadable. Dodie breathed audibly and waited for the lips to be licked, the tongue to lash out in some vicious dismissal, but Maxine merely continued to stare. A couple followed the maitre d' past their table, the rhythmic clicks of the women's stilettos reverberating from the parquet floor to the ceiling tiles until she slid into the booth behind them. Then Dodie noticed it—a large tear welling at the bottom of her mother's right eye, enlarging and finally oozing down her cheek.

"He was your father."

Maxine pulled a tissue from her bag and blew her nose, but Dodie—who in her initial numbness was fighting the inevitable need to re-process her entire pool of memories—could see that her mother was crying full force, so much so that the tears were blacked with mascara. Maxine pressed both tear-ducts with her middle fingers and sniffed in noisily, but the tears continued to flow.

"I'm not crying because he was your father, you know," Maxine said, as Dodie used her napkin to wipe mascara streaks from Maxine's cheeks. "I'm crying because he knew it."

CHAPTER TWENTY-NINE

None of them voted that year, except Dodie, who went to the polls specifically to vote against Rocco Herkimer. Maxine still wasn't a citizen, and Shelley, though she now felt increasingly anonymous outside the salon and the greenhouse, was concerned that the election judges might question the discrepancy between her new appearance and the one on her driver's license. Dodie felt obliged to cast a vote on their behalf as well as her own, although the last thing on earth she had time or inclination to do that early November morning was wait in line at the elementary school and sip coffee with neighbors she hadn't seen since the last election. Rocco would be reelected, of course— there was virtually no contest, even with the story about the old funeral home scandal that had broken in the middle of his term and that hadn't been mentioned since. Americans didn't care much about history, and there was always some new scandal to distract them from yesterday's. Politicians were scumbags, everyone knew that, but someone had to do the job, and Rocco Herkimer, who had already served four years in office, was putting himself up to do it. He espoused the right values, showed up at the right ceremonies, and now had family money for paid television advertisements and more star-studded yard signs than the county had lawns. Still, Dodie was determined to vote. In fact, ever since she had become an American citizen, she had never missed an election. How could she have, given the world she had been born into? Every voice seemed insignificant, even helpless, but not speaking up when you had a chance to do so was criminal. She felt that she was doing her little part to vote against the Rocco Herkimers of the world. It saddened her, however, that in this country she almost inevitably viewed voting as a means to protest horrors rather than encourage heroes.

On election night Utzi the Iceman brought his weather radio/television to the greenhouse so that Shelley and the other women staying there at the time could watch the returns without disturbing the children's routines in the rest of the house. He spent close to an hour just trying to pick up a signal from a local station, and, once he did, the focus was almost exclusively on Baltimore and Montgomery counties. It took them until well after 9 p.m. to realize they might have better luck with local elections on the Internet. Dodie had the best computer skills among them, which wasn't saying much, and eventually she and the Iceman were able to find a website reporting returns precinct by precinct. This only depressed them more. Rocco Herkimer was taking virtually every one of them by storm, although they took some mild encouragement from the claim that only a small percentage of the precincts had yet filed. By eleven, however, they could no longer cling to any hope. Rocco Herkimer reclaimed his seat handily, beating his quixotic Democratic opponent with well over 60% of the vote.

Two weeks had passed since the elections, and already the hoopla and implicit upheaval that had roused the county like movie music seemed like ancient history. Almost all the red-white-and-blue lawn signs had come down, and only a few soggy, weather-beaten strips in the road and the gullies were left to remind anyone that there had ever been a whisper that lives might someday change. The leaves had largely fallen, the skies had largely grayed, and it was no longer possible to pretend that summer and its promise might sneak back for another glorious day or two. At best they could hope for one of the milder Maryland winters ahead, one in which no one needed to unpack the snow boots and which would be graced by forty-degree sunlit days that brought impetuous blossoms by February.

Tonight, however, the rains came down with as little humor as any late summer storm, as though a late-blooming hurricane was hurrying up the coast in a final revelry before frost and cold winds could overtake it. Dodie sat alone at the kitchen table, watching the intransigent atomic clock and listening to the rain pound the roof of the greenhouse. The atonal ringing, plinking, and plunking of the raindrops against the glass made her clench her teeth, although they didn't seem to bother Shelley or the two other women sleeping in the greenhouse. One of these women, a petite and conciliatory housewife seeking refuge after two decades of marriage, was snoring and sputtering like a gas-starved motor, her jagged gasps occasionally breaking through the symphony of raindrops. Otherwise all three of the women seemed dead to the world. Although Dodie recognized that each one of them had suffered far more than she could ever imagine, she envied their blissful innocence and the fact that they would wake to the sun without ever experiencing this night of agony, or, she hoped, even knowing that such a night had ever existed.

It was only midnight. By rational standards, that should have been little cause for concern, even with a teenager involved. However, midnight was curfew for anyone with a provisional driver's license, which pretty much included anyone likely to be driving Margaret home. She supposed a parent might be in charge, and, in theory at least, understood that the terror she felt, and the obsessive clock watching, were entirely unjustified by the hour. If it were 3 a.m., perhaps 2 or even 1, she could call the police without feeling idiotic. She could cry and scream and shake, and no one would blame her. But it was only midnight. Why wouldn't the clock change?

Margaret was 16, a perfectly reasonable age to be out at the movies with friends on a Friday night, and then, perhaps, to stop for ice cream or merely chat at someone's house before calling for a ride home. But the movie Margaret said they were seeing had ended at 8 p.m.—Dodie had called the theatre to ask— and Margaret had not answered her cell phone any of the three times Dodie had dialed it since then. Normally she wouldn't have been so obsessive, but normally wasn't the operative word with Margaret these days. In fact, for over a year now, their relationship had been denaturing, particularly in terms of the unquestioned sense of trust and respect she had always instinctively had for her oldest child, even as far back as kindergarten. She kept trying to tell herself that it was normal for relationships between parents and teenagers to deteriorate—that was part of the separation process—and that all that mattered was that Margaret managed out there in the world, however bad things might have been at home. The fiasco with Margaret's report cards starting last spring made it abundantly clear that she was deluding herself. Her daughter was no longer managing, and whatever Dodie had been doing up till now was no longer working.

When Margaret's grades had started slipping, Maxine had begged Dodie to take time off, at least for a year or two until Margaret had safely settled in college, but obviously this was delusional. Who, precisely, would shuttle, house, or counsel the disfigured and scarred women who now represented the bulk of Maxine's business, not to mention her own income ever since those two other grants had materialized? That had turned out to be a wise decision, too, given the most recent turn of events: Last month Maxine had gone cold turkey on lotions and potions, formerly a major income source for her. It had taken an entire Sunday afternoon, but she had thoroughly rid her shelves and cupboards of every trace of Rufus Alvarez product, as vigilantly and self-righteously as a *frum* woman rids her cabinets of *chametz* before Pesach. She had tossed each bottle and tube into one of several plastic lawn bags, which turned out to be so heavy that she had to have the Iceman haul them out to Dodie's car. Dodie then drove the lot over to Safe Port. All of this had cost Maxine a pretty penny, given the investment she had made in back stock, but Safe Port happily gave her a blank slip of paper on which she wrote herself a hefty tax deduction.

An unexpected consequence of this purge had been several empty display shelves in the waiting room, but these had been easy enough to fill with the family photos and grandchildren's clay pots that she had kept stored in cardboard boxes at home. More significant were the dwindling number of regular clients, many of whom relied on these products. Maxine had directed them to mail-order outlets or dermatologists' offices for future purchases, although this by itself wasn't the concern. The real problem was that the number of these clients was palpably shrinking week by week. By cutting the cosmetic line, she had also cut the supplemental advertising budget that came with it, and, as a result, no longer advertised at all. This all but assured the demise of her former business. She still had a few regulars, but, one by one, they finished their makeup or electrolysis work with her and disappeared from the salon, requiring the creams and lotions more regularly than touch-ups with Maxine's needles.

At five minutes past midnight, and, again, at seven minutes past, Dodie redialed Margaret's cell, still to no avail. She even tried sending a text message, something she had just figured out how to do, but, again, there was no response. Perhaps she had sent it wrong. She wasn't actually sure if she had ever sent a text message successfully, in fact, although once or twice she had managed to read an incoming one from Margaret. How many times could she dial without Margaret thinking she was a nut case? She did not want to be obnoxious, but the deal had always been that Margaret could go wherever she wanted, provided she kept Dodie abreast of her whereabouts. Now, for the first time, this pact had been violated. How could she help but worry?

She was being reasonable, when you considered the facts. Margaret, after all, had said she'd be back "early." Didn't midnight exceed early? For someone still in high school? Well, perhaps from Margaret's perspective it was still early, and perhaps she had just been distracted— teenagers got distracted quite often, of course. Could Margaret have lost, dropped, or forgotten the phone? She was only a kid, but these cell phones were lifeblood to girls her age. Dodie went to Margaret's room, scoured the floor, the bedclothes, the nightstand, even the bathroom sink, but, of course, there was no phone. She dialed the number again from the portable she had carried with her into the bedroom, but heard no ring. Margaret had to have the phone on her. Could she have forgotten to turn it back on after silencing it in the movie? Very likely. But certainly by now she would have thought to call her mother, if only to update her on the plans. Wouldn't she have? No, no, perhaps the phone had just dropped out of a pocket, or fallen into a toilet (that happened frequently with these kids, the other mothers had told her), or just run out of power because Margaret had forgotten to charge it. That calmed her some, until she realized that by now Margaret, even phoneless, could have borrowed a friends' phone. She shouldn't be on her own at this point.

Dodie knew she needed to stop this, to read a book or watch the news or simply go to bed. But she couldn't help herself. It was a combination of maternal instincts, anxious nature, and, of course, line of work. Perhaps, very likely, Margaret was not with Lindsay and Jessica at all, but, rather, with a boy. Why not? She herself had done the same thing at that age, gone out without explanation, and had various geeky admirers wait for her on the corner so Zeenie wouldn't ask questions and then drop her off several doors down so that she could return home alone, without explanation, ever. She remembered coming home after a night making out with Justin in the parking lot of his parents' club, an officer shining a light in the car to break them up, and then tiptoeing in at 2 so as not to wake Zeenie. She had hoped that her relationship with Margaret would have been closer, she had always tried to convey her openness and acceptance of inadequacies and exude non-judgmentalism and unconditional respect—all deficits in Maxine's relationship to her teenage self that still rankled her—but Margaret had progressively become colder and more withdrawn.

Perhaps that was inevitable. As a mother, Dodie found herself wanting to know all the details, just as she had wanted so desperately to plant herself behind a two-way mirror when she had dropped the kids off at preschool, aching to absorb their every word and witness the way they stacked blocks, held crayons, tugged and tossed the other children, hitched up a waistband. It didn't matter what it was: she had simply *kvelled* in watching them move through the world. And when they went to school, too, or practiced soccer or took a ballet class, she wanted to watch every moment as well, just because.

She had given life to them, had carried them inside her own body from the moment of conception, had known and felt absolutely every aspect of their being for the first nine months, and then, for the next year or two, had been a part of the most intimate of moments, shared the first smile and the first rolling over, sitting up, pulling up, tasting, crawling, babbling, talking, and walking, and she had agonized and outraged with them over that first blemish, injury, pain, and imperfection. She had shared with each child, too, the intimacies of suckling, burping, pooping, peeing, bleeding, projectile vomiting, whole-body diarrhea. And then, slowly, each little person had pulled away, but still, she watched, and largely controlled, the story. She knew the books they read, the shows they watched, the foods they ate. She picked out the bedroom décor, purchased the clothing and oversaw the wearing of it, supervised the haircuts, the shoe buying, the piano practicing. She received lengthy write-ups on report cards, called teachers for details, rehashed concerns with other mothers who shared their own observations, overheard conversations about friends and fights and fears while carpooling. So it only seemed right that she continue to follow how the story came out.

She so wanted Margaret to know that she did not want to change the story, judge it, or interfere with it. She only wanted to know what happened. That seemed perfectly reasonable, at least emotionally, given their history. And yet

Margaret was shutting her out, closing the book, letting it be known that she, Margaret's own mother, was no longer welcome to read on.

She imagined Margaret confronted in the ladies room of the theatre. She saw her fainting in the parking lot, perhaps overcome by menstrual cramps or some sudden fever or flu. But, no, if that were so, surely one of her girlfriends would have noticed by now, and called. Perhaps all three of them had herded at gunpoint into a back corridor of the mall by a drug-crazed gang, or perhaps they had been accosted on the way to the car. She had read several reports about shoppers confronted on their way to their cars at that mall, some of them in broad daylight. Then she started envisioning an auto accident, not much of a stretch when you considered three loud, laughing, inexperienced drivers whipping down a highway on a weekend night, particularly on a damp, moonless night like this one. Perhaps there had been a drunk driver, like the one who had bashed into those three teenage boys who were merely stopped at a red light several years back—killing two of them instantly. Those kids had just been out getting fast food, never dreaming that this would be their last night on earth. Dodie shivered, visualizing the girls flung around the backseat, no way to identify the bodies of the non-drivers, who, most likely, had forgotten to carry their learner's permits and could not be identified. None of their parents could be called.

She went to the computer and checked the Internet for local news. No sign of a traffic accident, but perhaps it wouldn't be reported yet. The rain slowed to a sigh and then shifted into an even stronger but equally tenacious rhythm. She felt a cold wind on her neck and went to shut the window, which must have inadvertently been left open since the freakish string of hot days earlier that week. One would think at least one of the other parents would have called her by now, though, if, in fact, all three had not come home. Could it just be Margaret? The more she thought about it, the more she believed that Margaret had, indeed, lied to her. Maybe there had been no movie in the first place. Maybe there had not even been girlfriends. Or even a mere boy. Perhaps she had hooked up with some creepy twenty- or thirty-something man, who was now driving with her to New Jersey. Really, anything was possible when you considered the irreverence, gullibility, and *chutzpah* of teenage girls.

Dodie went into the living room and pulled back the draperies. The rain was falling as if a dam had broken in the sky. A dark car whizzed past the house, blurred by the rain, its lights briefly illuminating her front lawn to reveal dark patches of puddles and a dogwood held hostage by the wind. For several minutes no more cars came, and through the darkness she watched the raindrops, blown sideways by the quickening wind, glance off the window and ricochet toward the Japanese maples. She heard a vague hum, the way she sometimes intuited a neighbor's lawnmower when her windows were closed, looked expectantly to the left, but saw nothing. Then, a few minutes later, she heard the same vague hum grow into a distinct roar, and soon a squished, two-person sports car, navy or black, raced passed her driveway, tailed by an equally relentless SUV. Then there was nothing, again, except the carping rain and wind.

Dodie, still holding the draperies open, played a game. She would count to 100, and not until then would she expect to see, or let herself worry about expecting to see, the Adams' car pull into her driveway to deliver Margaret. If another car passed before then, she would restart the count. Some kind of antique sedan chugged by as she reached a count of 75, but then, a sheet of water as opaque as molten lead streamed down the windowpane and obscured it. Two minutes went by. She decided to wait until she had seen five more cars pass, and then she would try phoning Margaret again before restarting her counts. For several minutes, there was nothing. Then she heard vague rumblings from around the corner, and as the rumblings crescendoed to roars, a minivan, and then a pick-up truck, hurtled past her driveway. After another minute a two-seater whizzed down the street, followed in what felt like several counts to 100 later, by a lumbering white sedan that seemed to slow just before her driveway. Her heartbeat sped, she went to peek out the front door, but, by the time she got there, the car was gone. She went back to the window to wait for the fifth car, which came a full five minutes later in the form of an impudent pick-up truck, which, like all the others, had somewhere else to go.

Dodie returned to the kitchen table and picked up the phone. Only ten minutes had passed since her last call, but still, she dialed. Now, alone in the kitchen, with the boys asleep, and Margaret somewhere out there in the void, she found herself wishing time onward, wishing it speed. She focused on the numbers on the clock as if she could control them with her eyes, and wondered how they could possibly take so long to flip. Inexplicably, excruciatingly, the clock eventually flipped to 12:30. Still, no word, no change. Far too early to call the police, but a full half hour past driving curfew. She decided to try the Adams family after all, no longer caring that they would think her a lunatic. After four rings, the machine picked up. They were undoubtedly, blissfully, asleep. "So sorry to disturb you at this late hour," she said into the machine. "And sorry to sound hysterical, but it's nearly 1 a.m., and Margaret hasn't come back from the movies. If she's there—or if Lindsay knows where she might be—I would really appreciate a call." Now on a roll, she called the Schwartz's, Jessica's family, and left an almost identical message.

Just a few minutes later the phone rang. Dodie answered it before the first ring, only whispering a hello as she began tiptoeing upstairs. She brought the phone into Margaret's bedroom and quietly shut the door as Ned Adams apologized for not picking up before. He had just been going to bed, but, please, no worries about calling so late. Any parent would do the same. But, no, unfortunately, he didn't know where Margaret might be. Lindsay had come home quite a while ago, or so he thought (his wife kept track of these things, and she was asleep). He checked Lindsay's room, and she seemed to be in the shower. He told Dodie not to worry though; she was sure to be home soon: "You know how these kids are...Although I think they were with another girl. Jessica was it? She might be sleeping there, in fact. We've found Lindsay there more times than I can say."

Dodie fell backwards onto Margaret's bed and let the phone bounce onto the pillow. Her foot grazed Margaret's once-beloved Samantha doll, which had fallen head-first off the bed and was now wedged upside down between the bed and the nightstand. This doll, for which Dodie could still vividly remember Margaret begging tearfully at age six and which had been presented to her at great expense on her 8th birthday, had become a harridan, her once glossy long hair a frightening mass of straw and her once rosy baby-round cheeks gashed and mottled. Samantha rested on her head as though she had taken a swan dive onto the floor, which itself had come to resemble an estuary of both clean and contaminated laundry, rippling with balled-up snotty Kleenexes, stray sneakers and sandals, belts, barrettes, hair elastics, school papers, programs, masticated mouth guards, and dust-bunnied lacrosse balls. Around the edges, and masking the pine floorboards that Randall had installed to avert Margaret's dust-mite allergies, were puddles of spilled nail polish that had congealed into miniature Jackson Pollacks and a crumpled pair of blood-stained panties. Dodie remembered immediately why she tried not to come in here except in passing to deliver a basket of laundry, change sheets, extract Margaret for dinner, or, as earlier this evening, hunt down an errant phone.

Dodie crawled under the tangle of unmade sheets and curled into a fetal position, cradling the phone to her chest and reminding herself that a call to fumigation services would be in order as soon as Margaret left for college—or for wherever it was she would leave. She shut her eyes and let her head sink into the down pillow. For a moment, she felt her anxiety lift. She felt free, unshackled from herself and her history, even cared for. This feeling came as close, she realized, as she could ever come again to that longed-for, lost feeling she imagined you have as a newborn in your mother's arms, aware of nothing but the moment, and lulled by the sense that someone else, eternally wise, powerful, and present, would take care of everything for you, forever.

She wondered if Margaret felt this way when she lay down here to sleep. She hoped so. However, she didn't remember feeling this kind of peace and comfort as a teenager, and she supposed it was probably just a byproduct of the unfamiliar. Margaret, more likely, closed her eyes in this bed and counted the days she had to endure before she could bolt into her own life. Dodie herself had certainly felt that way as a teenager. She could see that Margaret had already put this room, and the life it represented, behind her.

She could also see that, fumigation issues aside, the

room was in dire need of updating. Under the debris was the room of a little girl, with a ruffled pink ponies bedspread lovingly chosen for a preschooler who no longer existed. It must have been years since anyone had noticed, much less dusted, the ten or fifteen soccer and lacrosse trophies on Margaret's top bookshelf, or the collection of scented candles in the form of brightly colored mushrooms, flowers, and forest animals jumbled between them. She doubted that Margaret even realized that sitting among the trophies and candles was a lone plastic-wrapped toy torah from preschool, or, if she had noticed, whether she'd remember what it was or why it had been placed up there.

Dodie scanned the familiar and long-neglected books on the shelf below the trophies, the beloved Unfortunate Series, Babysitters Club, and Gossip Girl paperbacks, volumes of Shel Silverstein poetry, Roald Dahl, Douglas Adams, and every Harry Potter, plus the books she herself had urged upon Margaret and remembered reading to her: Enid Blyton stories, fairy tales by Anderson and Grimm, *The Little Lame Prince*, *All of a Kind Family*, even Babar and Curious George books, which rightfully should have been transferred years ago to the boys' room, and by now, to the grandchildren bin. Covering every free surface on the lower two shelves, and precluding any possibility of a good dusting, was a seemingly random array of collectibles—snow domes, swim medallions, decorative miniature picture frames, glass animals, school photos, Polly Pocket cases, plastic jumping beans, matryoshka dolls, music boxes, and two Beatrix Potter china cups bestowed upon newborn Margaret by one of Randall's relatives, not to mention items better served by the trash can including sales tags, candy wrappers, dried-up bottles of nail polish, half-used packs of chewing gum, ragged rolls of tape, aging Easter candy, uncapped lip glosses, crumpled papers, expired nose spray, and goo-encrusted coins.

Dodie pulled herself up and sat cross-legged at the head of the bed the way Margaret often did, repeatedly flipping the phone across her lap as if she was cradling a ball. Flexibility was her physical gift, one that had always put Randall, the ox-man who somehow couldn't touch his toes, to shame. She glanced at Margaret's alarm clock and then dialed Margaret's phone once again. No answer. She hung up before the message machine could finish and immediately dialed another number.

"Zeenie? Mother? I'm scared."

"Dodie?....What is it? What time is it?" Maxine fumbled about the nightstand for her glasses, vaguely amazed and grateful that the extra glass of Amontillado before bed had worked for once, but vexed that her chances of falling back asleep were now virtually nil. She rolled Utzi the Iceman onto his side, which softened his snoring to a simmer. The man would have slept through an air raid, even on nights without several glasses of sherry.

"It's Margaret, Mother. It's almost 1 a.m., and she hasn't come home. She was at a movie, with friends, I think, but it ended hours ago, at 8. Five hours ago that was. I haven't heard a word from her since."

"Oh, thank goodness. Listen, dearie lamb, I'm sure she's fine...." The gurgling, snorting, and whooping from the Iceman's side of the bed picked up again, and Maxine stood up, pulling the telephone cord as far from the bed as she could. She cupped her hand around the mouthpiece. "She's a teenager, you know. Teenagers go off like this. Take my advice, and boil yourself a cup of tea. I'd say pour yourself a schnapps if you were me, but tea will have to do for my tee-totaller, eh? Why do they call it 'teetotaling,' do you think? I suppose you folks tote tea, and nothing else. Do you suppose that's it?"

"I can't believe you're going on like this."

"Relax, will you? I'll get right back to you. Just calm yourself, and I'll find her."

"You'll find her? I only wish."

"Get that kettle boiling, lambie. You hear me? I'm certain everything is fine."

Dodie set the phone on the nightstand and crawled back under the covers. She picked Samantha off the floor, somewhat rattled when the doll's hinged eyelids bounced open to expose two huge, bituminous balls that caught the light and gleamed beneath the lashes like twin flashlights. Multifaceted and eerily lifelike, these oversized eyes gave the doll an expectant and animated stare that left Dodie feeling guilty for leaving the poor thing on its head all this time, a feeling only reinforced by the tips of the two tiny front teeth exposed by an artlessly parted and suggestively upturned mouth. Dodie hugged the doll to her chest, but the stiff, plastic limbs poked into her ribs uncomfortably, providing none of the blissful feeling of wholeness she associated with cuddling her baby dolls, not to mention her real babies. Clearly, despite her soft torso, this doll had been designed for dressing and displaying, not for loving. She rolled Samantha onto her back, picked several flicks of lint and hard candy from her hair, and then began extracting strands one at a time from the matted clumps by pulling gently up toward the scalp until the ends freed themselves. Little by little she began to restore the glorious dark brown waves, just as she remembered her mother doing for her when she had brilliantly wadded her hair with bubble gum or simply gone days without a brush.

When the phone rang, Dodie's heart pounded so hard

she thought it might wake the boys in the next room.

"Mum? Is that you?"

"It is me indeed. And I'm happy to report she's fine. Margaret's just fine."

"You found her? How on earth....?"

"As I suspected—she's with him."

Dodie sat upright and laid Samantha's head on the pillow. "Him? What him? I'll kill the little shit."

"Him being Randall. Her father. Apparently she's moved in with him."

This was too much for Dodie to process. How and when did she get so out of the loop? She and Margaret weren't the sorts to have heart-to-hearts, but the very fact of their frequent screaming matches had always secretly given Dodie confidence. At least Margaret wore her heart on her sleeve, she'd tell herself. She wasn't the type who buried her resentments, calm and pleasant on the surface but secretly skulking around, plotting and brooding. Margaret let her unhappiness be known, or so Dodie had always assumed. Clearly, though, there had been more lurking than she had ever suspected. She had never been the kind of mother to burrow through her daughter's room to sneak peeks at diary entries, never been one to scroll through the computer memory for remnants of online chats or visits to verboten websites. Such intrusive behavior had always seemed vile to her, ugly indulgences of self-destructive women yielding to their maternal need-to-know. The women who had succumbed—some of them her friends, even co-workers, who had confessed to her—had no lives of their own and no clue about the nature of trust, not to mention respect for the integrity and sovereignty of their children. More to the point, though, was her conviction that she had respectful, open relationships with her children and that they therefore didn't keep secrets from her. So what was to be gained by snooping around for evidence to the contrary? Perhaps she had been wrong though. Perhaps she had been naïve. Perhaps she had even been negligent.

"Dodie? Are you there? Please answer me so I know you're all right."

"I'm here. I'm just stunned, that's all. Stunned. Why didn't she call me? Why doesn't she call?"

"She is at her father's, Dodie. She wants to stay with him for a while. She should have told you, of course, but we can't help that now, can we? She will be fine, trust me. I'm quite serious. Now, please go have that cup of tea, which I'm sure you haven't made for yourself yet, have you now? And Dodie, you must stop fretting. It will all come out in the end.

ABOUT THE AUTHOR

The author of the novels *Time's Fool*, *The Bliss of Solitude*, and *Do Not Go* Gentle, Terra Ziporyn is a an award-winning medical writer and historian whose publications include *The New Harvard Guide to Women's* Health, *Nameless Diseases*, and *Alternative Medicine for Dummies*. She and her political scientist husband, J.H. Snider, live near Annapolis, MD and are the parents of three grown children. Visit her website at terraziporyn.com.